DANCING AT THE RASCAL FAIR

Scotchmen and coyotes was the only ones
that could live in the Basin,
and pretty damn soon the coyotes starved out.
—CHARLES CAMPBELL DOIG (1901–71)

DANCING AT THE RASCAL FAIR

Ivan Doig

Atheneum Publishers
New York   *1987*

Atheneum
Macmillan Publishing Company
866 Third Avenue, New York, N.Y. 10022
Collier Macmillan Canada, Inc.

Library of Congress Cataloging-in-Publication Data

Doig, Ivan.
Dancing at the Rascal Fair.
I. Title.
PS3554.0415D36   1987   813'.54   87-18672
ISBN 0-689-11764-7

10   9   8   7   6   5   4   3   2   1

Printed in the United States of America

SCOTLAND AND HELENA

Harbour Mishap at Greenock. Yesterday morning, while a horse and cart were conveying a thousand-weight of sugar on the quay at Albert Harbour, one of the cartwheels caught a mooring stanchion, which caused the laden conveyance and its draft animal to fall over into the water. The poor creature made desperate efforts to free itself and was successful in casting off all the harness except the collar, which, being attached to the shafts of the sunken cart, held its head under water until it was drowned. The dead animal and the cart were raised during the forenoon by the Greenock harbour diver.
　　—GLASGOW CALEDONIAN, OCTOBER 23, 1889

To SAY the truth, it was not how I expected—stepping off toward America past a drowned horse.

You would remember too well, Rob, that I already was of more than one mind about the Atlantic Ocean. And here we were, not even within eyeshot of the big water, not even out onto the slow-flowing River Clyde yet, and here this heap of creature that would make, what, four times the sum total of Rob Barclay and Angus McCaskill, here on the Greenock dock it lay gawping up at us with a wild dead eye. Strider of the earth not an hour ago, wet rack of carcass now. An affidavit such as that says a lot to a man who cannot swim. Or at least who never has.

But depend on you, Rob. In those times you could make light of whatever. There was that red shine on you, your cheeks and jawline always as ruddy and smooth as if you had just put down the shaving razor, and on this largest day of our young lives you were aglow like a hot coal. *A stance like a lord and a hue like a lady.* You cocked your head in that way of yours and came right out with:

1

"See now, McAngus. So long as we don't let them hitch a cart to us we'll be safe as saints."

"A good enough theory," I had to agree, "as far as it goes."

Then came commotion, the grieved sugar carter bursting out, "Oh Ginger dear, why did ye have to tumble?" and dockmen shouting around him and a blinkered team of horses being driven up at full clatter to drag their dead ilk away. Hastily some whiskered geezer from the Cumbrae Steamship Line was waving the rest of us along: "Dead's dead, people, and standing looking at it has never been known to help. Now then, whoever of you are for the *James Watt*, straight on to the queue there, New York at its other end, step to it please, thank you." And so we let ourselves be shooed from the sight of poor old horsemeat Ginger and went and stepped onto line with our fellow steerage ticketholders beside the bulk of the steamship. Our fellow Scotland-leavers, half a thousand at once, each and every of us now staring sidelong at this black iron island that was to carry us to America. One of the creels which had held the sugar was bobbing against the ship's side, while over our heads deckhands were going through the motions of some groaning chore I couldn't begin to figure.

"Now if this was fresh water, like," sang out one above the dirge of their task, "I'd wager ye a guinea this harbor'd right now taste sweet as treacle."

"But it's not, ye bleedin' daftie. The bleedin' Clyde is tide salt from the Tail of the Bank the full way up to bleedin' Glasgow, now en't it? And what to hell kind of concoction are ye going to get when ye mix sugar and salt?"

"Ask our bedamned cook," put in a third. "All the time he must be doing it, else why's our mess taste like what the China dog walked away from?" As emphasis he spat a throat gob over the side into the harbor water, and my stomach joined my other constituent parts in trepidation about this world-crossing journey of ours. A week and a half of the Atlantic and dubious food besides?

That steerage queue seemed eternal. Seagulls mocked the line of us with sharp cries. A mist verging on rain dimmed out the Renfrewshire hills beyond Greenock's uncountable roofs. Even you appeared a least little bit ill at ease with this wait, Rob, squinting now and again at the steamship as if calculating how it was that so much metal was able to float. And then the cocked head once more, as if pleased with your result. I started to say aloud that if Noah had taken this much time to load the ark, only the giraffes would have lasted through the deluge, but that was remindful of the waiting water and its fate for cart horses and others not amphibious.

Awful, what a person lets himself do to himself. There I stood on that Greenock dock, wanting more than anything else in this life not to put foot aboard that iron ship; and wanting just as desperately to do so and do it that instant. Oh, I knew what was wrestling in me. We had a book—*Crofutt's Trans-Atlantic Emigrants' Guide*— and my malady was right there in it, page one. Crofutt performed as our tutor that a shilling was worth 24 American cents, and how much postal stamps cost there in the big country, and that when it came midnight in old Scotland the clocks of Montana were striking just five of the afternoon. Crofutt told this, too, I can recite it yet today: *Do not emigrate in a fever, but consider the question in each and every aspect. The mother country must be left behind, the family ties, all old associations, broken. Be sure that you look at the dark side of the picture: the broad Atlantic, the dusty ride to the great West of America, the scorching sun, the cold winter—coldest ever you experienced!— and the hard work of the homestead. But if you finally, with your eyes open, decide to emigrate, do it nobly. Do it with no divided heart.*

Right advice, to keep your heart in one pure piece. But easier seen than followed.

I knew I oughtn't, but I turned and looked up the river, east up the great broad trough of the Clyde. East into yesterday. For it had been only the day before when the pair of us were hurled almost all the way across Scotland by train from Nethermuir into clamorsome Glasgow. A further train across the Clyde bridge and westward alongside mile upon brown mile of the river's tideflats and their smell. Then here came Greenock to us, Watt's city of steam, all its shipyards and docks, the chimney stalks of its sugar refineries, its sharp church spires and high, high above all its municipal tower of crisp new stone the color of pie crust. A more going town than our old Nethermuir could be in ten centuries, it took just that first look to tell us of Greenock. For night we bedded where the emigration agent had advised, the Model Lodging House, which may have been a model of something but lodging wasn't it; when morning at last came, off we set to ask our way to the Cumbrae Line's moorage, to the *James Watt*, and to be told in a Clydeside gabble it took the both of us to understand:

"The *Jemmy*, lads? Ye wan' tae gi doon tae the fit of Pa'rick."

And there at the foot of Patrick Street was the Albert Harbor, there was the green-funneled steam swimmer to America, there were the two of us.

For I can't but think of you then, Rob. The Rob you were. In all that we said to each other, before and thereafter, this step from our old land to our new was flat fact with you. The Atlantic Ocean and the continent America all the way across to Montana stood as but the width of a cottage threshold, so far as you ever let on. No second guess, never a might-have-done-instead out of you, none. A silence too total, I realize at last. You had family and a trade to scan back at and I had none of either, yet I was the one tossing puppy looks up the Clyde to yesterday. Man, man, what I would give to know. Under the stream of words by which you talked the two of us into our long step to America, what were your deep reasons? I am late about asking, yes. Years and years and years late. But when was such asking ever not? And by the time I learned there was so much within you that I did not know and you were learning the same of me, we had greater questions for each other.

A soft push on my shoulder. When I turned to your touch you were smiling hard, that Barclay special mix of entertainment and estimation. We had reached the head of the queue, another whiskery geezer in Cumbrae green uniform was trumpeting at us to find Steerage Number One, go forward toward the bow, descend those stairs the full way down, mind our footing and our heads . . .

You stayed where you stood, though, facing me instead of the steamship. You still had the smile on, but your voice was as serious as I ever had heard it.

"Truth now, Angus. Are we both for it?"

Standing looking at it has never been known to help. I filled myself with breath, the last I intended to draw of the air of the pinched old earth called Scotland. *With no divided heart.*

"Both," I made myself say. And up the *Jemmy*'s gangplank we started.

Robert Burns Barclay, single man, apprentice wheelwright, of Nethermuir, Forfarshire. That was Rob on the passenger list of the *James Watt*, 22nd of October of the year 1889. Angus Alexander McCaskill, single man, wheelworks clerk, of Nethermuir, Forfarshire, myself. Both of us nineteen and green as the cheese of the moon and trying our double damnedest not to show it.

Not that we were alone in tint. Our steerage compartment within the *Jemmy* proved to be the forward one for single men—immediately the report went around that the single women were quartered farthest aft, and between them and us stood the married couples and a terrific populace of children—and while not everyone was young, our shipmates were all as new as we to voyaging. Berths loomed in unfamiliar tiers with a passageway not a yard wide between them, and the twenty of us bumped and backed and swirled like a herd of colts trying to establish ourselves.

I am tall, and the inside of the ship was not. Twice in those first minutes of steerage life I cracked myself.

"You'll be hammered down to my size by the time we reach the other shore," Rob came out with, and those around us hoohawed. I grinned the matter away but I did not like it, either the prospect of a hunched journey to America or the public comment about my altitude. But that was Rob for you.

Less did I like the location of Steerage Number One. So far below the open deck, down steep stair after stair into the iron gut of the ship. When you thought about it, and I did, this was like being a kitten in the bottom of a rainbarrel.

"Here I am, mates," recited a fresh voice, that of the steward. "Your shepherd while at sea. First business is three shillings from you each. That's for mattress to keep you company and tin to eat with and the finest saltwater soap you've ever scraped yourself with." Ocean soap and straw bed Rob and I had to buy along with everyone else, but on Crofutt's advice we'd brought our own trustworthy tinware. "Meals are served at midship next deck up, toilets you'll find in the deckhouses, and that's the circle of life at sea, mates," the steward rattled at us, and then he was gone.

As to our compartment companions, a bit of listening told that some were of a fifty embarking to settle in Manitoba, others of a fifty fixed upon Alberta for a future. The two heavenly climes were argued back and forth by their factions, with recitations of rainfall and crop yields and salubrious health effects and imminence of railroads, but no minds were changed, these being Scottish minds.

Eventually someone deigned to ask us neutral pair what our destination might be.

"Montana," Rob enlightened them as if it was Eden's best neighborhood. "I've an uncle there these seven years."

"What does the man do there," sang out an Alberta adherent, "besides boast of you as a nephew? Montana is nothing but mountains, like the name of it."

"He's the owner of a mine," Rob reported with casual grandness, and this drew us new looks from the compartment citizenry. Rob, though, was not one to quit just because he was ahead. "A silver mine at Helena, called the Great Maybe."

All of steerage except the two of us thought that deserved the biggest laugh there was, and for the next days we were known as the Maybe Miners. Well, they could laugh like parrots at a bagpiper. It was worth that and more, to have Lucas Barclay there in Montana ahead of us.

"Up?" offered Rob to me now, with a sympathetic toss of his head. Back to deck we climbed, to see how the *Jemmy*'s departure was done.

As I look on it from now, I suppose the others aboard cannot but have wondered about the larky companion beside me at the deck rail, dispensing his presiding smile around the ship as if he had invented oceangoing. The bearing of a bank heir, but in a flat cap and rough clothes? A mien of careless independence, but with those workworn wheelwright's hands at the ends of his young arms? And ever, ever, that unmatchable even-toothed smile, as though he was about to say something bright even when he wasn't; Rob could hold that smile effortlessly the way a horse holds the bit between his teeth. You could be fooled in a hurry about Rob, though. It maybe can be said my mind lacks clench. Rob had a fist there in his head. The smile gave way to it here when he spotted a full family, tykes to grandfolks, among us America-goers.

"They all ought've come, Angus. By damn, but they ought've. Am I right?" He meant all the rest of his own family, his father and mother and three older brothers and young sister; and he meant it hotly. Rob had argued for America until the air of the Barclay household was blue with it, but there are times when not even a Barclay can budge Barclays. Just thinking about it still made him tense as a harp. "They ought've let the damned 'wright shop go, let old Nethermuir doze itself to death. They can never say I didn't tell them. You heard."

"I heard."

"Lucas is the only one of the bunch who's ever looked ahead beyond his nose. See now, Angus, I almost wish we'd been in America as long as Lucas. Think of all he must've seen and done, these years."

"You'd have toddled off there when you were the age of Adair, would you?" Adair was Rob's sister, just twelve or so, and a little replica of Rob or at least close enough; tease her as I did by greeting her in gruff hard-man style *Hello you, Dair Barclay,* and she always gave me right back, snappy as beans, *Hello yourself, old Angus McCaskill.*

"Adair's the one in the bunch who most ought've come," Rob persisted. "Just look around you, this ship is thick with children not a minute older than Adair." He had a point there. "She'd positively be thriving here. And she'd be on her way to the kind of life she deserves instead of that"—Rob pointed his chin up the Clyde, to the horizon we had come from—"back there. I tried for her."

"Your parents would be the first to say so."

"Parents are the world's strangest commodity, haven't you ever noticed—Angus, forgive that. My tongue got ahead of itself."

"It went right past my ears. What about a walk around deck, shall we?"

At high tide on the Clyde, when the steam tug arrived to tow this behemoth ship of ours to deep water at the Tail of the Bank, Rob turned to me and lifted his cap in mock congratulation.

"We're halfway there," he assured me.

"Only the wet part left, you're telling me."

He gave my shoulder a push. "McAngus, about this old water. You'll grow used to it, man. Half of Scotland has made this voyage by now."

I started to retort that I seemed to belong to the half without webfeet, but I was touched by this, Rob's concern for me, even though I'd hoped I was keeping my Atlantic apprehensions within me. The way they resounded around in there—*Are we both for it? Both*—I suppose it was a wonder the entire ship wasn't hearing them like the thump of a drum.

We watched Greenock vanish behind the turn of the Firth. "Poor old River Carrou," from Rob now. "This Clyde makes it look like a piddle, doesn't it?"

Littler than that, actually. We from an inland eastern town such as Nethermuir with its sea-seeking stream Carrou were born thinking that the fishing ports of our counties of Fife and Forfar and Kincardine and Aberdeen must be the rightful entrances to the ocean, so Rob and I came with the natural attitude that these emigration steamships of Greenock and Glasgow pittered out the back door of Scotland. The Firth of Clyde was showing us otherwise. Everywhere around us the water was wider than wide, arms of it delving constantly between the hills of the shore, abundant islands were stood here and there on the great gray breadth as casually as haycocks. Out and out the *Jemmy* steamed, past the last of the beetle-busy packet boats, and still the Clyde went on carving hilly shores. Ayr. Argyll. Arran. This west of Scotland perhaps all sounded like gargle, but it was as handsome a coast as could be fashioned. Moor and cliff and one entire ragged horizon of the Highlands mountains for emphasis, shore-tucked villages and the green exactness of fields for trim.

And each last inch of it everlastingly owned by those higher than Angus McCaskill and Rob Barclay, I reminded myself. Those whose names began with Lord. Those who had the banks and mills. Those whitehanded men of money. Those who watched from their fat fields as the emigrant ships steamed past with us.

Daylight lingered along with the shore. Rain came and went at edges of the Firth. You saw a far summit, its rock brows, and then didn't.

"Just damp underfoot, try to think of the old ocean as," Rob put in on me.

"I *am* trying, man. And I'd still just as soon walk to America."

"Or we could ride on each other's shoulders, what if?" Rob swept on. "No, McAngus, this steam yacht is the way to travel." Like the duke of dukes, he patted the deck rail of the *Jemmy* and proclaimed: "See now, this is proper style for going to America and Montana."

America. Montana. Those words with their ends open. Those words that were ever in the four corners of my mind, and I am sure Rob's, too, all the minutes since we had left Nethermuir. I hear that set of words yet, through all the time since, the pronouncement Rob gave them that day. America and Montana echoed and echoed in us, right through my mistrust of journeying on water, past Rob's breeze of manner, into the tunnels of our bones. For with the *Jemmy* underway out the Firth of Clyde we were threading our lives into the open beckon of those words. Like Lucas Barclay before us, now we were on our way to be Americans. To be—what did people call themselves in that far place Montana? Montanese? Montanians? Montaniards? Whatever that denomination was, now the two of us were going to be its next members, with full feathers on.

My first night in steerage I learned that I was not born to sleep on water. The berth was both too short and too narrow for me, so that I had to kink myself radically; curl up and wedge in at the same time. Try that if you ever want to be cruel to yourself. Too, steerage air was thick and unpleasant, like breathing through dirty flannel. Meanwhile Rob, who could snooze through the thunders of Judgment Day, was composing a nose song below me. But discomfort and bad air and snores were the least of my wakefulness, for in that first grief of a night—oh yes, and the *Jemmy* letting forth an iron groan whenever its bow met the waves some certain way—my mind rang with everything I did not want to think of. Casting myself from Nethermuir. The drowned horse Ginger. Walls of this moaning ship, so close. The coffin confines of my bedamned berth. The ocean, the ocean on all sides, including abovehead. *Dark Neptune's labyrinthine lanes/'Neath these savage liquid plains.* I rose in heart-rattling startlement once when I accidentally touched one hand against the other and felt wetness there. My own sweat.

I still maintain that if the Atlantic hadn't been made of water I could have gone to America at a steady trot. But it seems to be the case that fear can sniff the bothering places in us. Mine had been in McCaskills for some eighty years now. The bones of the story are this. With me on this voyage, into this unquiet night, came the fact that I was the first McCaskill since my father's grandfather to go upon the sea. That voyage of Alexander McCaskill was only a dozen miles, but the most famous dozen miles in Great Britain of the time, and he voyaged them over and over and over again. He was one of the stonemasons of Arbroath who worked with the great engineer Robert Stevenson to build the Bell Rock lighthouse. On the clearest of days I have seen that lighthouse from the Arbroath harbor and have heard the story of the years of workships and cranes and winches and giant blocks of granite and sandstone, and to this moment I don't know how they could do what was done out there, build a hundred-foot tower of stone on a reef that vanished deep beneath every high tide. But there it winks at the world even today, impossible Bell Rock, standing in the North Sea announcing the Firth of Forth and Edinburgh beyond, and my great-grandfather's toolmarks are on its stones. The generations of us, we who are not a sea people, dangle from that one man who went to perform stonework in the worst of the waters around Scotland. Ever since him, Alexander has been the first or second name of a McCaskill in each of those generations. Ever since him, we have possessed a saga to measure ourselves against. I lay there in the sea-plowing *Jemmy* trying to think myself back into that other manhood, to leave myself, damp sackful of apprehension that I was, and to feel from the skin inward what it would have been like to be Alexander McCaskill of the Bell Rock those eighty years ago. *A boat is a hole in the water*, began my family's one scrap of our historic man, the solitary story from our McCaskill past that my father would ever tell. In some rare furlough from his brooding, perhaps Christmas or Hogmanay and enough drinks of lubrication, that silence-locked man my father would suddenly unloose the words. *But there was a time your great-grandfather was more glad than anything to see a boat, I'm here to tell you. Out there on the Bell Rock they were cutting down into the reef for the lighthouse's foundation, the other stonemen and your great-grandfather, that day. When the tide began to come in they took up their tools and went across the reef to meet their boat. Stevenson was there ahead of them, as high as he could climb on the reef and standing looking out into the fog on the water. Your great-grandfather knew there was wrong as soon as he saw Stevenson. Stevenson the famous engineer of the Northern Lights, pale as the cat's milk. As he ought have been, for there was no boat on the reef and none in sight anywhere. The tide was coming fast, coming to cover all of the Bell Rock with water higher than this roof. Your great-grandfather saw Stevenson turn to speak to the men.* "This I'll swear to, Alexander the Second," *your great-grandfather always told me it just this way.* "Mister Stevenson's mouth moved as if he was saying, but no words came out. The fear had dried his mouth so." *Your great-grandfather and the men watched Stevenson go down on his knees and drink water like a dog from a pool in the rock. When he stood up to try to speak this time, somebody shouted out,* "A boat! There, a boat!" *The pilot boat, it was, bringing the week's mail to the workship. Your great-grandfather always ended saying,* "I almost ran out onto the water to hail that boat, you can believe."

"You ask was I afraid, Alexander the Second?" My father's voice became a strange, sad thunder when he told of my great-grandfather's reply to him. "Every hour of those three Bell Rock years, and

most of the minutes, drowning was on my mind. I was afraid enough,
yes. But the job was there at the Bell Rock. It was to be done, afraid or
no afraid."

The past. The past past, so to speak, back there beyond myself.
What can we ever truly know of it, how can we account for what it
passes to us, what it withholds? Employ my imagination to its
utmost, I could not see myself doing what Alexander McCaskill did
in his Bell Rock years, travel an extent of untrustable water each
day to set Abroath stone onto reef stone. Feed me first to the flam-
ing hounds of hell. Yet for all I knew, my ocean-defying great-
grandfather was afraid of the dark or whimpered at the sight of a
spider but any such perturbances were whited out by time. Only his
brave Bell Rock accomplishment was left to sight. And here I lay,
sweating steerage sweat, with a dread of water that had no logic
newer than eighty years, no personal beginning, and evidently no
end. It simply was in me, like life's underground river of blood.
Ahead there, I hoped *far* ahead, when I myself became the past—
would the weak places in me become hidden, too? Say I ever did
become husband, father, eventual great-grandfather of Montana
McCaskills. What were they going to comprehend of me as their
firstcomer? Not this sweated night here in my midnight cage of
steerage, not my mental staggers. No, for what solace it was, eventually all that could be known of Angus Alexander McCaskill was
that I did manage to cross the Atlantic Ocean.

If I managed to cross it.

Through the night and most of the next day, the *Jemmy* steamed
its way along the coast of Ireland to Queenstown, where our Irish
came aboard. To say the truth, I was monumentally aware of
Queenstown as the final chance to me to be *not* aboard; the outmost
limb-end where I could still turn to Rob and utter, *no, I am sorry, I*
have tried but water and I do not go together. So far I had managed not
to let my tongue say that. It bolstered me that Rob and I had been
up from Steerage Number One for hours, on deck to see whatever
there was, blinking now against the sun and its sparkle on the blue
Queenstown harbor. And so we saw the boats come. A fleet of small
ones, each catching the wind with a gray old lugsail. They were
steering direct to us and as the fleet neared we could make out that
there was one man in each boat. No. One woman in each boat.

"Who are these, then?" I called to a deckhand sashaying past.

"Bumboats," he flung over his shoulder. "The Irish navy. Ye'll learn some words now."

Two dozen of the boats nudged against the steamship like piglets against a sow, and the deckhand and others began tossing down ropes. The women came climbing up like sailors—when you think of it, that is what they were—and with them arrived baskets, boxes, creels, buckets, shawls. In three winks the invaders had the shawls spread and their wares displayed on them. Tobacco, apples, soap. Pickled meat. Pinafores. Butter, hardbread, cheese. Pots of shamrock. Small mirrors. Legs of mutton. Then began the chants of these Irishwomen singing their wares, the slander back and forth between our deckhands and the women hawkers, the eruptions of haggling as passengers swarmed around the deck market. The great deck of the steamship all but bubbled over with people.

As we gaped at the stir of business Rob broke out in delight, "Do you see what this is like, Angus?" And answered himself by whistling the tune of it. I laughed along with every note, for the old verse thrummed as clear to me as an anthem.

> *Dancing at the rascal fair,*
> *devils and angels all were there,*
> *heel and toe, pair by pair,*
> *dancing at the rascal fair.*

From the time we could walk Rob and I had never missed a rascal fair together—that day of fest when Nethermuir farmers and farm workers met to bargain out each season's wages and terms and put themselves around a drink or so in the process. The broad cobbled market square of our twisty town, as abrupt as a field in a stone forest, on that one day of magic filled and took on color and laughter. Peddlers, traveling musicians, the Highland dancer known as Fergus the Dervish, whose cry of *hiiyuhh!* could be heard a mile, onlooking townfolk, hubbub and gossip and banter, and the two of us like minnows in that sea of faircomers, aswim in the sounds of the ritual of hard bargaining versus hard-to-bargain.

I see you wear the green sprig in your hat. Are you looking for the right work, laddie?

Aye, I am.

And would you like to come to me? I've a place not a mile from here, as fine a field as ever you'll see to harvest.

12

Maybe so, maybe no. I'll be paid for home-going day, will I?

Maybe so, maybe no. That locution of the rascal fair, up there with Shakespeare's best. I have wondered, trying to think back on how Rob and I grew up side by side, how the McCaskills and the Barclays began to be braided together in the generation before us, how all has happened between us since, whether those bargaining words are always in the air around us, just beyond our hearing and our saying, beyond our knowing how to come to terms with them. But that is a thought of now, not then. Then I knew of no maybes, for Rob was right as right could be when he whistled of the rascal fair there on the *Jemmy*'s deck; with these knots of dickering and spontaneous commotion and general air of mischief-about-to-be, this shipboard bazaar did seem more than anything like that mix of holiday and sharp practice we'd rambled through in old Nethermuir.

Remembered joy is twice sweet. Rob's face definitely said so, for he had that bright unbeatable look on him. In a mood like this he'd have called out "fire!" in a gunshop just to see what might happen. The two of us surged along the deck with everybody else of the *Jemmy*, soaking in as much of the surprise jubilee as we could.

"Have your coins grown to your pockets there in Scotland?" demanded the stout woman selling pinafores and drew laughing hoots from us all.

"But mother," Rob gave her back, "would any of those fit me?"

"I'd mother you, my milktooth boy. I'd mother you, you'd not forget it."

"Apples and more apples and more apples than that!" boasted the next vendor.

"Madam, you're asking twice the price of apples ashore!" expostulated a father with his wife and eager-eyed children in a covey around him.

"But more cheap, mister man, than the ocean's price of them."

"I tell ye," a deckhand ajudged to another, "I still fancy the lass there with the big cheeses—"

The other deckhand guffawed. "Cheese, do ye call those?"

"—and ye know I en't one that fancies just anyoldbody."

"No, just anybody born of woman."

"Muuuht'n, muuuht'n," bleated the sheep-leg seller as we jostled past.

"Green of the sod of Ireland!" the shamrock merchant advertised to us.

So this was what the world was like. I'd had no idea.

Then we were by a woman who was calling out nothing. She simply stood silent, both hands in front of her, a green ball displayed in each.

Rob passed on with the others of our throng, I suppose assuming as I first did that she was offering the balls as playthings. But children were rampant among this deck crowd and neither they nor their parents were stopping by the silent woman either.

Curiosity is never out of season with me. I turned and went back for a close look. Her green offerings were not balls, they were limes.

Even with me there in front of her, the woman said nothing. I had to ask. "Your produce doesn't need words, missus?"

"I'm not to name the ill they're for, young mister, else I can't come onto your fine ship."

Any schoolboy knew the old tale of why Royal Navy sailors came to be called limies, and so I grinned, but I had to let Madam Irish know I was not so easily gulled. "It takes a somewhat longer voyage than this to come down with scurvy, missus."

"Tisn't the scurvy."

"What, then?"

"Your mouth can ask your stomach when the two of them meet, out there on the herring pond."

Seasickness. Among my Atlantic thoughts was whether the crossing would turn me as green as the rind of these limes. "How can this fruit of yours ward off that, then?"

"Not ward it off, no. There's no warding to that. You only get it, like death. These fruit are for after. They clean your mouth, young mister. Scour the sick away."

"Truth?"

She nodded. But then, what marketeer wouldn't.

It must have been the Irish sun. I fished for my coins. "How much for a pocketful?"

Doubtful transaction done, I made my way along the deck to where Rob was. He and the majority of the other single men from our compartment had ended up here around the two youngest Irishwomen, plainly sisters, who were selling ribbons and small mirrors. The flirting seemed to be for free.

The sight of the saucy sisters elevated my mood some more, too, and so I stepped close behind Rob and caroled appropriately in his ear:

DANCING AT THE RASCAL FAIR

"Dancing at the rascal fair,
show an ankle, show a pair,
show what'll make the lasses stare,
dancing at the rascal fair."

"Shush, you'll be heard," he chided, and glanced around to
see whether I had been. Rob had that prim side, and I felt it my
duty every so often to tweak him on it.

"Confess," I urged him. "You'd give your ears for a smile
from either of these lovelies."

Before he could answer me on that, the boatswain's whistle
shrilled. The deck market dissolved, over the side the women
went like cats. In a minute their lugsails were fanned against the
sparkling water of Queenstown harbor, and the *Jemmy* was underway once more.

After Queenstown and with only ocean ahead for a week and a
day, my second seagoing night had even less sleep in it than my
first. Resolutely telling myself there was no back door to this ship
now, I lay crammed into that stifling berth trying to put my mind
anywhere—multiplication, verse, Irish sisters—other than Steerage
Number One.

What I found I could spend longest thoughts on, between
periodic groans from the *Jemmy* that required me to worry whether
its iron was holding, was Nethermuir. Rascal fair town Nethermuir.
Old grayrock town Nethermuir, with its High Street wandering
down the hill the way a drowsy cow would, to come to the River
Carrou. Be what it may, a fence, a house, a street, the accusing
spire of a church, Nethermuir fashioned it of stone, and from below
along River Street the town looked as though it had been chiseled
out complete rather than erected. Each of the thousand mornings
that I did my route to open the wheelwright shop, Nethermuir was
as asleep as its stones. In the dark—out went the streetlights at
midnight; a Scottish town sees no need to illumine its empty
hours—in the dark before each dawn I walked up River Street from
our narrow-windowed tenements past the clock tower of the linen
mill and the silent frontages of the dye works and the paper mill and
other shrines of toil. Was that the same me back there, trudging on
stone past stone beneath stone until my hand at last found the
oaken door of the 'wright shop? Climbing the stair to the office in

15

the nail loft and coaxing a fire in the small stove and opening the ledger, pen between my teeth to have both hands free, to begin on the accounts? Hearing the workmen say their day-starting greetings, those with farthest to come arriving first, for wasn't that always the way? Was that truly me, identical with this steerage creature listening to a steamship moan out greetings to disaster? The same set of bones called Angus McCaskill, anyway. The same McCaskill species that the Barclays and their wheelwright shop were accustomed to harboring.

To see you here is to lay eyes on your father again, Angus, Rob's father Vare Barclay told me at least once a week. A natural pleasantry, but Vare Barclay and I equally knew it was nowhere near true. When you saw my father there over his forge in an earlier time, you were viewing the keenest of wheelsmiths; the master in that part of Scotland at making ninety pounds of tire-iron snugly band itself onto a wagon wheel and become its invincible rim. Skill will ask its price, though. The years of anvil din took nearly all of my father's hearing, and to attract his attention as he stood there working a piece of iron you would have had to toss a wood chip against his shirt. Do that and up he would glance from his iron, little less distant when he was aware of you than when he wasn't. Never did I make that toss of contact with him, when sent by my mother on errand to the 'wright shop, without wondering what it would take to mend his life. For my father had gone deaf deeper than his ears.

I am from a house of storm. My parents Alex and Kate McCaskill by the middle of their marriage had become baffled and wounded combatants. I was their child who lived. Of four. Christie, Jack and Frank, who was already apprenticing with my father at the Barclay 'wright shop—in a single week the three of them died of cholera. I only barely remember them, for I was several years the youngest— like Rob's sister Adair in the Barclay family, an "afterthought" child; I have contemplated since whether parents in those times instinctively would have a late last child as a kind of insurance—but I recall in all clarity my mother taking me to the farm cottage of a widow friend of hers when the killing illness began to find Nethermuir. When my mother came for me six weeks later she had aged twice that many years, and our family had become a husk the epidemic left behind. From then on my father lived—how best to say this?—he lived alongside my mother and me rather than with us. Sealed into himself, like someone of another country who happened

to be traveling beside us. Sealed into his notion, as I grew, that the
one thing for me was to follow into his smithy trade. *I'm here to tell
you, it's what life there is for us and ours. A McCaskill at least can have
an honest pair of hands.* Oh, there was war in the house about that.
My father could not see why I ought to do anything but apprentice
myself into hammer work in the Barclay wheelshop as he had, as
my brother Frank had; my mother was equally as set that I should
do anything but. His deafness made their arguments over me a
roaring time. The teacups rattled when they went at it. The school-
leaving age was thirteen, so I don't know how things would have
gone had not my father died when I was twelve. My mother at once
took work as a spinner in the linen mill and enrolled me with the
'venture schoolteacher Adam Willox. Then when I was sixteen, my
mother followed my father into death. She was surprised by it,
going the same way he had; a stroke that toppled her in the evening
and took her in the early morning. With both of them gone, work
was all the family I had. Rob's father put me on as clerk in the
'wright shop in the mornings, Adam Willox made me his pupil-
teacher in the afternoons. Two half-occupations, two slim wages,
and I was glad enough to have them, anything. Vare Barclay promised me full clerkwork whenever the times found their way from
bad to good again, Adam Willox promised I could come in with him
as a schoolkeeper whenever pupils grew ample enough again. But
promises never filled the oatmeal bowl. So when Rob caught America fever, I saw all too readily the truth in what he said about every
tomorrow of our Nethermuir lives looking the same. About the
great American land pantry in such places as his uncle's Montana,
where homesteads were given—given!—in exchange for only a few
years of earnful effort. The power of that notion of homesteading in
America, of land and lives that would be all our own. We never had
known anything like it in our young selves. *America. Montana.* This
ship to them. This black iron groaner of a ship that—

I was noticing something I devoutly did not want to. The *Jemmy*
seemed to be groaning more often.

I held myself dead still to be sure.

Yes, oh sweet Christ and every dimpled disciple, yes: my berth
was starting to sway and dive.

A boat is a hole in the water. And a ship is a bigger boat.

I heard Rob wake with a sleepy "What?" just before full tumult
set in. The *Jemmy* stumbled now against every wave, conked its

iron beak onto the ocean, rose to tumble again. The least minute of this behavior was more than enough storm for a soul in steerage, but the ruckus kept on and on. Oftener and oftener the ship's entire iron carcass shuddered as the propellor chewed air. Sick creatures shudder before they die, don't they. I felt each and every of these shakings as a private earthquake, fear finding a way to tremble not merely me but every particle of existence. Nineteen did not seem many years to have lived. *What if the old Bell Rock had drowned me?* my father remembered being asked in boyhood by Alexander Mc-Caskill at the end of that floodtide tale. *Where would you be then, Alexander the Second?* What if, still the question.

Even yet this is a shame on me to have to say, but fear brought a more immediate question, too, insistent in the gut of me and below. I had to lay there concentrating desperately not to soil myself.

Amid it all a Highlands voice bleated out from a distant bunk, "Who'd ever think she could jig like this without a piper?" Oh, yes, you major fool, the ranting music of bagpipes was the only trouble we lacked just now. The Atlantic had its own tune, wild and endless. I tried to wipe away my sweat but couldn't keep up with it. I desperately wanted to be up out of Steerage Number One and onto deck, to see for myself the white knuckles of the storm ocean. Or did I. Again the ship shook; rather, was shaken. What was out there? My blood sped as I tried to imagine the boiling oceanic weather which could turn a steamship into an iron cask. Cloudcaps darker than night itself. High lumpy waves, foaming as they came. Wind straining to lift the sea into the air with it, and rain a downward flood determined to drown the wind.

The storm stayed ardent. Barrels, trunks, tins, whatever was movable flew from side to side, and we poor human things clung in our berths to keep from flying, too. No bright remarks about jigs and pipes now. The steerage bunks were stacked boxes of silence now. Alberta, Manitoba, Montana were more distant than the moon. I knew Rob was clamped solidly below me, those broad wheelwright hands of his holding to whatever they had met. The worst was to keep myself steady there in the bunk while all else roved and reeled. Yet in an awful way the storm came to my help; its violence tranced a person. From stem to stern the *Jemmy* was 113 of my strides; I spent time on the impossibility of anything that length not being broken across canyons of waves. The ship weighed more than two thousand tons; I occupied myself with the knowledge that nothing weighing a ton of tons could remain afloat. I thought of the Greenock dock where I ought to have turned back, saw in my closed eyes the drowned cart horse Ginger I was trying every way I knew not to see, retraced in my mind every stairstep from deck down into Steerage Number One; which was to say down into the basement of the titanic Atlantic, down into the country where horses and humans are hash for fish.

Now the *Jemmy* dropped into a pause where we did not teeter-totter so violently. We were havened between crags of the sea. I took the opportunity to gasp air into myself, on the off chance that I'd ever need any again. Rob's face swung up into view and he began, "See now, McAngus, that all could have been worse. A ship's like a wagon, as long as it creaks it holds, and—" The steam-ship shuddered sideways and tipped ponderously at the same time, and Rob's face snapped back into his berth.

Now the ship was grunting and creaking constantly, new and worse noises—you could positively feel the *Jemmy* exerting to drag itself through this maelstrom—and these grindstone sounds of its effort drew screams from women and children in the midship compartments, and yes, from more than a few men as well, whenever the vessel rolled far over. Someone among the officers had a voice the size of a cannon shot and even all the way down where we were could be heard his blasts of "BOS'N!" and "ALL HANDS!" Those did not improve a nonswimmer's frame of mind, either.

The *Jemmy* drove on. Shuddering. Groaning. Both. Its tremors ran through my body. Every pore of me wanted to be out of that berth, free from water. But nothing to do but hold onto the side of the berth, hold myself as level as possible on a crooked ocean.

Nothing, that is, until somebody made the first retching sound.

Instantly that alarm reached all our gullets. I knew by heart what Crofutt advised. *Any internal discomfort whilst aboard ship is best ameliorated by the fresh air of deck. Face the world of air; you will be new again.* If I'd had the strength I'd have hurled Crofutt up onto that crashing deck. As it was, I lay as still as possible and strove not think of what was en route from my stomach to mouth.

Steerage Number One's vomiting was phenomenal. I heaved up, Rob heaved up, every steerage soul heaved up. Meals from a month ago were trying to come out of us.

Our pitiful gut emptyings chorused with the steamship's groans.

Our poor storm-bounced guts strained, strained, strained some more. Awful, the spew we have in us at our worst. The stench of it all and the foulness of my mouth kept making me sicker yet. Until I managed to remember the limes.

I fumbled them out and took desperate sucks of one. Another I thrust down to the bunk below. "Rob, here. Try this."

His hand found mine and the round rind in it.

"Eat at a time like now? Angus, you're—"

"Suck it. For the taste." I could see white faces in the two bunks across from us and tossed a lime apiece over there as well. The *Jemmy* rose and fell, rose and fell, and stomachs began to be heard from again in all precincts of the compartment. Except ours.

Bless you, Madam Irish. Maybe it was that the limes put their stern taste in place of the putrid. Maybe that they puckered our mouths as if with drawstrings. Maybe only that any remedy seemed better than none. Whatever effect it may have been, Rob and I and the other lime-juiced pair managed to abstain from the rest of the general gagging and spewing. I knew something new now. That simply being afraid was nowhere near so bad as being afraid and retching your socks up at the same time.

Toward dawn the Atlantic got the last of the commotion out of its system. The *Jemmy* ploughed calmly along as if it had never been out for an evening gallop at all. Even I conceded that we possibly were going to live, now.

"Mates, what's all this muss?" The steward put in his appearance and chivied us into sluicing and scrubbing the compartment and sprinkling chloride of lime against the smell, not that the air of Steerage Number One could ever be remedied much. For breakfast Rob and I put shaky cups of tea into ourselves and I had another lime, just for luck. Then Rob returned to his berth, claiming there was lost sleep to be found there, and I headed up for deck, any-where not to be in that ship bottom.

I knew I still was giddy from the night of storm. But as I began to walk my first lap of the deck, the scene that gathered into my eyes made me all the more woolheaded.

By now the weather was clement, so that was no longer the fore-most matter in me. And I knew, the drybrain way you know a map fact, that the night's steaming progress must have carried us out of

sight of land on all sides. But the ocean. The ocean I was not prepared for nor ever could be.

Anywhere my eyes went, water bent away over the curve of the
world. Yet at the same time the *Jemmy* and I were in a vast washbasin, the rims of the Atlantic perfectly evident out there over us.
Slow calm waves wherever I faced, only an occasional far one bothering to flash into foam like a white swimmer appearing and disap-
pearing. No savage liquid plains these. This was the lyric sea,
absently humming in the sameness of the gray and green play of its
waves, in its pattern of water always wrinkling, moving, yet other
water instantly filling the place. All this, and a week of water extending yet ahead.

I felt like a child who had only been around things small, suddenly seeing there is such a thing as big. Suddenly feeling the
crawling fear I had known the past two nights in my berth change
itself into a standing fact: if the *Jemmy* wrecked, I would sink like a
statue, but nobody could outswim the old Atlantic anyway, so why
nettle myself over it? Suddenly knowing that for this, the spectacle
of the water planet around me, I could put up with sleepless nights
and all else; when you are nineteen and going to America, I learned
from myself in that moment, you can plunder yourself as much as is
needed. Maybe I was going to see the Atlantic each dawn through
scared red eyes. But by the holy, see it I would.

I made my start that very morning. Ocean cadence seemed to be
more deliberate, calmer, than time elsewhere, and I felt the draw of
it. Hour by slow hour I walked that deck and watched and watched
for the secret of how this ocean called Atlantic could endlessly go
on. Always more wrinkling water, fresh motion, were all that made
themselves discernible to me, but I kept walking and kept watching.

"How many voyages do you suppose this tea has made?"

"Definitely enough for pension."

"Mahogany horse at dinner, Aberdeen cutlet at supper." Which
was to say, dried beef and smoked haddock. "You wouldn't get
such food just any old where."

"You're not wrong about that."

"The potatoes aren't so bad, though."

"Man, potatoes are never so bad. That's the principle of potatoes."

"These ocean nights are dark as the inside of a cow, aren't they."
"At least, at least."
"We can navigate by the sparks." The *Jemmy*'s funnel threw constant specks of fire against the night. "A few more times around the deck will do us good. Are we both for it?"
"All right, all right, both. Angus, you're getting your wish, back there on the Clyde."
"What's that, now."
"You're walking us to America."

"Listen to old Crofutt here, will you. *We find, from our experience, that the midpoint of the journey is its lowest mark, mentally speaking. If doubt should afflict you thereabout, remonstrate with yourself that of the halves of your great voyage, the emigration part has been passed through, the immigration portion has now begun. Somewhere there on the Atlantic rests a line, invisible but valid, like Greenwich's meridian or the equator. East of there, you were a leaver of a place, on your way FROM a life. West across that division, older by maybe a minute, know yourself to be heading TO a life.*"

"Suppose we're Papists yet?" Sunday, and the priest's words were carrying to us from the Irish congregation thick as bees on the deck's promenade.
"I maybe am. There's no hope whatsoever for you."

"This Continental Divide in Montana that old Crofutt goes on about, Angus. What is that exactly?"
"It's like, say, the roof peak of America. The rivers on this side of it flow here to the Atlantic, on the other they go to the Pacific."
"Are you telling me we're already on water from Montana, out here?"
"So to say."
"Angus, Angus. Learning teaches a man some impossible things, is what I say."

"Too bad they're not bumboats. I could eat up one side of a leg of mutton and down the other about now." Autumn it may have been back in Scotland, but there off Newfoundland the wind was hinting winter, and Rob and I put on most of the clothes we possessed to stay up and watch the fishing fleets of the Newfoundland coastal banks.

"And an Irish smile, Rob, what about. Those sisters you were eyeing at Queenstown, they'd be one apiece for us if my arithmetic is near right."

"Angus, I don't know what I'm going to do with you. I only hope for your sake that they have women in America, too."

"There's a chance, do you think?"

"Shore can't be all so far now."

"No, but you'll see a change in the color of the ocean first. New York harbor will be cider instead of water, do you know, and it'll start to show up out here."

Then came the day.

"Mates," the steward pronounced, "we're about to pass old Sandy Hook. New York will step right out and meet us now. I know you've grown attached to them, but the time is come to part with your mattresses. If you'll kindly all make a chain here, like, and pass them along one to the next to the stairway . . ." Up to deck and overboard our straw beds proceeded, to float off behind us like a flotilla of rafts. A person would think that mine ought to have stood out freshest among them, so little of the sleep in it had been used.

New York was the portal to confusion, and Castle Garden was its keyhole. The entire world of us seemed to be trying to squeeze into America through there. Volleys of questions were asked of us, our health and morals were appraised, our pounds and shillings slid through the money exchange wicket to come back out as dollars and cents. I suppose our experience of New York's hustle and bustle was every America-comer's: thrilling, and we never wanted to do it again. Yet in its way, that first hectic experience of America was simply like one of the hotting-up days back in the 'wrightshop, when the bands of tire iron were furnaced to a red heat and then made to encircle the newly crafted wagon wheels. Ultimately after the sweating and straining and hammering, after every kind of commotion, there was the moment as the big iron circle was cooling and clasping itself ever tighter around the wheel when you would hear a click, like a sharp snap of fingers. Then another, and another—the sound of the wheelspokes going the last fraction of distance into their holes in the hub and the rim, fitting themselves home. And if you listened with a bit of care, the last click of all came when the done wheel first touched the ground, as if the result was making a little cluck of surprise at its new self. Had you been somewhere in the throng around Rob and me as we stepped out of Castle Garden's workshop of immigration into our first American day, to begin finding our way through a city that was twenty of Glasgow, you might have heard similar sounds of readiness.

Then the railroad and the westward journey, oceanic again in its own way, with islands of towns and farms across the American prairie. Colors on a map in no way convey the distances of this earth. What would the place Montana be like? Alp after alp after alp, as the Alberta adherent aboard ship assured us? *The Territory of Montana,* Crofutt defined, *stands as a tremendous land as yet virtually untapped. Already planetarily famous for its wealth of ores, Montana proffers further potentialities as a savannah for graziers and their herds, and where the hoofed kingdom does not obtain, the land may well become the last great grain garden of the world. Elbow room for all aspirants will never be a problem, for Montana is fully five times the size of all of Scotland.* How was it going to be to live within such distances? To become pioneers in filling such emptiness? At least we can be our own men there, Rob and I had told each other repeatedly. And now we would find out what kind of men that meant.

America seemed to go on and on outside the train windows, and our keenness for Montana and Lucas Barclay gained with every mile.

"He'll see himself in you," I said out of nowhere to Rob. I meant his uncle; and I meant what I was saying, too. For I was remembering that Lucas Barclay had that same burnish that glowed on Rob. The face and force to go with it, for that matter. These Barclays were a family ensemble, they all had a memorable glimmer. Years and years back, some afterschool hour Rob and I were playing fox-chase in the woodyard of the wheelwright shop, and in search of him I popped around a stack of planks into my father and Lucas and Rob's father Vare, eyeing out oak for spokes. I startled both myself and them by whirling into the midst of their deliberation that

24

way, and I remember as clear as now the pair of bright Barclay faces and my father's pale one, and then Lucas swooping on me with a laugh to tickle his thick thumb into my ribs, *I met a man from Kingdom Come, he had daggers and I had none, but I fell on him with my thumb, and daggered and daggered 'um!* Was that the final time I'd seen Lucas before his leaving of Scotland, that instant of rosy smile at a flummoxed boy and then the tickling recital? The lasting one, at least.

"I hope Lucas doesn't inspect too close, then," Rob tossed off. "Else we may get the door of the Great Maybe slammed in our faces."

"Man," I decided to tease, "who could ever slam a door to you? Shut with firmness and barricade it to keep you from their wives, daughters and maiden aunts, maybe, but—"

Rob gave my shoulder a push. "I can't wait to see the surprise on Lucas," he said, laughing. "Seven years. I can't wait."

"I wonder just what his life is like, there."

"Wonder away, until sometime tomorrow. Then you can see the man himself and know."

In truth, we knew little more than the least about Lucas Barclay in these Montana years of his. Rob said there had been only a brief letter from Lucas to Nethermuir the first few Christmases after he emigrated, telling that he had made his way to the city of Helena and of his mining endeavor there; and not incidentally enclosing as his token of the holiday a fine fresh green American banknote of one hundred dollars. You can be sure as Rob's family was that more than a greeting was being said there, that Lucas was showing the stay-at-homes the fruit of his adventure; Lucas's decision against the wheelwright shop and for America had been the early version of Rob's: too many Barclays and not enough wagon wheels any more. Even after his letters quit—nobody who knew Lucas expected him to spend time over paper and pen—that hundred dollars arrived alone in an envelope, Christmas after Christmas. *The Montana money*, Rob's family took to calling it. *Lucas is still Lucas*, they said with affection and rue for this strayed one of the clan; *as freehanded a man as God ever set loose.*

I won't bother to deny that in making our minds up for America Rob and I found it persuasive that money was sent as Christmas cards from there. But the true trove over across in Montana, we considered, was Lucas himself. Can I make you know what it meant to us to have this uncle of his as our forerunner? As our American edition of *Crofutt*, waiting and willing to instruct? Put yourself where we were, young and stepping off to a new world in search of its glorious packets of land called homesteads, and now tell me whether or not you want to have a Lucas Barclay ahead, with a generous side that made us know we could walk in on him and be instantly welcome; a Lucas who would know where the best land for homesteading beckoned, what a fair price was for anything, whether they did so-and-so in Montana just as we were accustomed to in Scotland, whether they ever did thus-and-such at all. Bold is one thing and reckless is another, yes? I thought at the time and I'll defend it yet, the steamship ticket could only take us to America and the railroad ticket could only deliver us across it—Rob and I held our true ticket to the Montana life we sought, to freedom and all else, in Lucas Barclay.

Helena had three times the people of Nethermuir in forty times the area. Helena looked as if it had been plopped into place last week and might be moved around again next week. Helena was not Hellenic.

A newcomer had to stand and goggle. The castellated edge of the city, high new mansions with sharp-towered roofs, processioned right up onto the start of the mountains around. Earth-old grit side by side with fresh posh. Then grew down a shambles of every kind of structure, daft blurts of shack and manor, with gaping spots between which evidently would be filled when new fashions of habitation had been thought up. Lastly, down the middle of it all was slashed a raw earthquakelike gash of gulch, in which nested block after block of aspiring red-brick storefronts.

"Quite the place," I said.

"So it is," said Rob.

Say for Helena, gangly capital city of the Territory of Montana and peculiar presbytery of our future with Lucas, it started us off with luck. After the Model Lodging House of Greenock, we knew well not to take the first roost we saw, and weary as we were, Rob and I trudged the hilly streets until we found a comparatively clean room at Mrs. Billington's, a few blocks away from Last Chance Gulch. Mrs. Billington observed to us at once, "You'll be wanting to wash the travel off, won't you," which was more than true.

Those tubbings in glorious hot water were the first time since Nethermuir that we had a chance to shed our clothes.

"Old Barclay? Oh hell yeah," the most veteran boarder at Mrs. Billington's table aided us. "He works down at the depot. Watch sharp or you'll trip right over him there."

Here was news, Lucas in a railroad career, and our jauntiness was tinged with speculation as to how that could have come about. Down the steep streets of Helena Rob wore the success of our journey as if it was a helmet. And when we came into sight of the depot, his triumphant face could not have announced us more if he'd had a trumpet in front of it. I was proud enough myself.

Until we stepped into the depot, asked a white-haired shrimp of a fellow in spectacles where we might find the railway clerk named Barclay, and got: "I'm him. Elmer W. Barclay. Who might you be?"

Elmer W. was nothing at all like Lucas, but he definitely was the Barclay everyone in Helena seemed to know about, in our next few hours of asking and asking. We found as well the owner of the Great Maybe mine, but he was not Lucas either. Nor were any of the three previous disgusted owners we managed to track down. In fact, Lucas's name was six back in the record of ownership the Second Deputy Clerk and Recorder of Lewis and Clark County grudgingly dug out for us, and there had been that many before Lucas. It grew clear to Rob and me that had the Great Maybe been a silver coin instead of a silver mine, by now it would be worn smooth from being passed around.

By that first night, Rob was thoughtful. "What do you suppose, Lucas made as much money from the Great Maybe as he thought was there and moved on to another mine? Or didn't make money and just gave the mine up?"

"Either way, he did move on," I pointed out.

"Funny, though," Rob deliberated, "that none of these other miners can bring Lucas to mind."

That point had suggested itself to me too, but I decided to chide it on its way. "Rob, how to hell could they all remember each other? Miners in Montana are like hair on a dog."

"Still," he persisted, "if Lucas these days is anything like the Lucas he was back in Nethermuir, somebody is bound to remember him. Am I right?"

"Right enough. We just need to find that somebody."

"Or Lucas. Whichever happens first."

"Whichever. Tomorrow we scour this Helena and make Lucas happen, one way or the other."

But the next day Helena provided us not Lucas, but history. Rob and I met our first Montana frost that November morning when we set out, and saw our breath all the way to the post office, where we asked without luck about Lucas. We had just stepped from there, into sunshine now, to go and try at the assay office when I saw the fellow and his flag on a rooftop across the street.

"Stay"-something, he shouted down into the street to us, "stay"-something, "stay"-something, and ran the American flag with 41 stars on it up a tall pole.

Cheers whooped from others in the street gaping up with us, and that in turn brought people to windows and out from stores. Abruptly civilization seemed to be tearing loose in Helena as the crowd flocked in a tizzy to the flag-flying edifice, the *Herald* newspaper building.

"What is this, war with somebody?" Rob asked, as flabbergasted as I.

"Statehood!" called out a red-bearded man scurrying past. "The president just signed it! It took goddamn near forever, but Montana's a state at last! Follow me, I'm buying!"

And so that eighth day of November arose off the calendar and grabbed Rob and me and every other Helena Montanian by the elbow, the one that can lever liquid up to the lips. Innocents us, statehood was a mysterious notion. However, we took it to mean that Montana had advanced out of being governed from afar, as Scotland was by the parliament in London, into running its own affairs. Look around Helena and you could wonder if this indeed constituted an improvement. But the principle was there, and Rob and I had to drink to it along with everyone else, repeatedly.

"Angus, we must've seen half the faces in Helena today," Rob estimated after we made our woozy way back to the lodging house. "And Lucas's wasn't among them."

"Then we know just where he is," I found to say. "The other half."

The day after that and the next several, we did try the assay office. The land office. The register of voters. The offices of the newspapers. The Caledonian Club. The Association of Pioneers. The jail. Stores. Hotels.

Saloons, endless saloons. The Grand Central or the Arcade or the Iroquois or the Cricket, the IXL or the Exchange or the Atlantic, it all ran the same:

"Do you know a man Lucas Barclay? He owned the Gre—a mine."

"Sometimes names change, son. What does he look like?"

"More than a bit like me. He's my uncle."

"Is he now. Didn't know miners had relatives." Wipe, wipe, wipe of the bartender's towel on the bar while he thought. "You do look kind of familiar. But huh-uh. If I ever did see your face on somebody else it was a time ago. Sorry."

Boarding houses.

"Good day, missus. We're trying to find the uncle of my friend here. Lucas Barclay is his name. Do you happen to know of him?"

"Barkler? No, never heard of him."

"Barclay, missus. B-A-R-C-L-A-Y."

"Never heard of him, either."

Finally, the Greenwood cemetery.

"You boys are good and sure, are you?" asked the caretaker from beside the year-old gravestone he had led us to.

We stood facing the stark chiseled name. "We're sure," said Rob.

The caretaker eyed us regretfully.

"Well, then," he declared, abandoning hope for this stone that read LEWIS BERKELEY PASSED FROM LIFE 1888, "that's about as close as I can come to it for you. Sorry."

"See now, we can't but think it would need to be a this year's burial," Rob specified to the caretaker, "because there's every evidence he was alive at last Christmas." He meant by this that the Montana money from Lucas had arrived as always to Nethermuir.

"B-A-R-C-L-A-Y, eh?" the caretaker spelled for the sixth time. "You're sure that's the way of it?" Rob assured him for the sixth time he was. The caretaker shook his head. "Nobody by that name among the fresh ones. Unless he'd be there." He nodded to the low edge of the graveyard, down near where the railroad right-of-way crossed the Fort Benton road. The grave mounds there had no markers.

Realization arrived to Rob and me at the same instant. The paupers' field.

Past a section of lofty monuments where chiseled folds of drape and tassels were in style, we followed the caretaker down to the poorfield.

"Who are these, then?" asked Rob.

"Some are loners, drifters, hoboes. Others we just don't know who the hell they are. Find them dead of booze some cold morning up there in the Gulch. Or a mine timber falls on them and nobody knows any name for them except Dutchy or Frenchy or Scotty." I saw Rob swallow at that. The caretaker studied among a dozen bare graves. "Say, last month I buried a teamster who'd got crushed when his wagon went over on him. His partner said the gent called himself Brown, but a lot of folks color theirselves different when they come west. Maybe he'd be yours?"

It did not seem likely to either Rob or me that Lucas would spurn a life of wagons in Nethermuir and adopt one here. Indeed, the more we thought, the less likely it seemed that Lucas could be down among the nameless dead. People always noticed a Barclay.

Discouragement. Perplexity. Worry. All those we found abundantly that first week in Helena but no Lucas.

Not one least little bit did Rob let go of the notion of finding him, though. By week's end he was this minute angry at the pair of us for not being bright enough to think where Lucas might be, the next at Lucas for not being anywhere. Then along came consternation— "Tell me truth, Angus, do you think he can be alive?"—and then around again to bafflement and irk: "Why to hell is that man so hard to find?"

"We'll find him," I said steadily to all this. "I can be stubborn and you're greatly worse than that. If the man exists in this Montana, we'll find him."

Yet we still did not.

We had to tell ourselves that we'd worn out all investigation for a Helena version of Lucas, so we had better think instead of other possible whereabouts. The start of our second week of search, we went by train to try Butte. That mining city seemed to be a factory for turning the planet inside out. Slag was making new mountains, while the mountains around stood with dying timber on their slopes.

The very air was raw with smelter fumes and smoke. No further Butte, thank you, for either Rob or me, and we came away somehow convinced it was not the place Lucas Barclay would choose either.

Back at Helena we questioned stagecoach drivers, asking if they had heard of Lucas at their destination towns, White Sulphur Springs and Boulder and Elkhorn and Diamond City. No and no and no and no. Meanwhile, we were hearing almost daily of some new silver El Dorado where a miner might have been drawn to. Castle. Glendale. Granite. Philipsburg. Neihart. We began to see that tracking Lucas to a Montana mine, if indeed he was still in that business of Great Maybes, would be like trying to find out where a Gypsy had taken up residence.

That week of search ended as empty as our first.

Sunday morning, our second Sabbath as dwellers of Helena, I woke before the day did, and my getting out of bed roused Rob. "Where're you off to?" he asked as I dressed.

"A walk. Up to see how the day looks."

He yawned mightily. "McAngus, the wheelwright shop is all the way back in Scotland and you're still getting out of bed to open it." More yawn. "Wait. I'll come along. Just let me figure which end my shoes fit on."

We walked up by the firebell tower above Last Chance Gulch. Except for the steady swimming flight of an occasional magpie, we were up before the birds. Mountains stretched high everywhere around, up in the morning light which had not yet found Helena. The business streets below were in sleeping gray. Over us and to the rim of the eastern horizon stretched long, long feathers of cloud, half a skyful streaked extravagantly with colors between gold and pink, and with purple dabs of heavier cloud down on the tops of the Big Belt Mountains. A vast sky tree of glow and its royal harvest beneath.

"So this is the way they bring morning into Montana," observed Rob. "They know their business."

"Now that I've got you up, you may as well be thoroughly up, what about." I indicated the firebell tower, a small open observation cabin like the top of a lighthouse but perched atop an open spraddle of supports.

Rob paused as we climbed past the big firebell and declared, "I'd like to ring the old thing and bring them all out into the streets. Maybe we would find Lucas then.''

Atop the tower, we met more of dawn. The land was drawing color out of the sky. Shadows of trees came out up near the summit of Mt. Helena, and in another minute there were shawls of shadow off the backs of knolls. Below us the raw sides of Last Chance Gulch now stood forth, as if shoveled out during the night for the next batch of Helena's downtown to be sown in.

Rob pondered into the hundred streets below, out to the wide grassy valley beyond. Nineteen thousand people down there and so far not a one of them Lucas Barclay. A breeze lazed down the gulch and up the back of our necks. "Where to hell can he be, Angus? A man can't vanish like smoke, can he?''

Not unless he wants to, I thought to myself. But aloud: "Rob, we've looked all we can. There's no knowing until Christmas if Lucas is even alive. If your family gets the Montana money from him again, there'll be proof. But if that doesn't happen, we have to figure he's—'' Rob knew the rest of that. Neither of us had been able to banish that Lewis Berkeley tombstone entirely from mind. I went on to what I had been mulling. "It's not all that far to Christmas now. But until then, we'd better get on with ourselves a bit. Keep asking after Lucas, yes. But get on with ourselves at the same time.''

Rob stirred. He had that cocked look of his from when we stepped past the drowned horse on the Greenock dock, the look that said out to the world *surely you're fooling?* But face it, this lack of trace of Lucas had us fooled, fully. "Get on with ourselves, is it. You sound like Crofutt.''

"And who better?'' I swept an arm out over the tower railing to take in Helena and the rest of Montana. As full sunrise neared, the low clouds on the Big Belts were turning into gold coals. On such a morning it could be believed there was a paunch of ore on every Montana mountain. By the holy, this was a country to be up and around in. "Look at you here, five thousand miles from Scotland and your feet are dry, your color is bright, and you have no divided heart. Crofutt and McCaskill, we've seen you through and will again, lad. But the time has arrived to think of income instead of outgo. Are we both for that?''

He had to smile. "All right, all right, both. But tell me this, early riser. Where is it you'd see us to next, if you had your way?''

We talked there on the bell hill until past breakfast and received the scolding of our lives from Mrs. Billington. Which was far short of fair, for she gained profit for some time to come from that fire tower discussion of ours. What Rob and I chose that early morning, in large part because we did not see what else to decide, was to stay on in Helena until Christmas sent its verdict from Nethermuir.

Of course we needed to earn while we tried to learn Montana, and if we didn't have the guidance of Lucas Barclay we at least had an honest pair of hands apiece. I took myself down to a storefront noticed during our trekking around town, Cariston's Mercantile. An Aberdeen man and thus a bit of a conniver, Hugh Cariston; but just then it made no matter to me whether he was the devil's half-brother. He fixed a hard look on me and in that Aberdonian drone demanded:

"Can ye handle sums?"

"Aye." I could, too.

I am sure as anything that old Cariston then and there hired me on as a clerk and bookkeeper just so he could have a decent Scots burr to hear. There are worse qualifications.

In just as ready a fashion, Rob found work at Weisenhorn's wagon shop. "Thin stuff," he shook his head about American wheels, but at least they made a job.

So there is the sum we were, Rob, as our Scotland-leaving year of 1889 drew to a cold close in new Montana. Emigrants changed by the penstrokes of the Cumbrae Steamship Line and Castle Garden into immigrants. Survivors of the Atlantic's rites of water, pilgrims to Helena. Persons we had been all our lives and persons becoming new to ourselves. How are past and present able to live in the same instant, and together pass into the future?

You were the one who hatched the fortunate notion of commemorating ourselves by having our likenesses taken on that Hogmanay, New Year's Eve, as they tamely say it here in America. "Angus, man, it'll be a Hogmanay gift such as they've never had in Nethermuir," you proclaimed, which was certainly so. "Let them in old Scotland see what Montanians are." We had to hustle to get to Ball's Photographic Studio before it closed.

That picture is here on my wall, I have never taken it down. Lord of mercy, Rob. Whatever made us believe our new muttonchop sidewhiskers became us? Particularly when I think how red mine were then, and the way yours bristled. We sit there in the photograph looking as if the stuffing is coming out of our heads. Once past those sidewhiskers, the faces on us were not that bad, I will say. Maybe an opera house couldn't be filled on the basis of them, but still. Your wide smile to match the wide Barclay chin, your confident eyes. Your hair black as it was and more than bountiful, the part in it going far back on the right side, almost back even with your ear. It always gave you that look of being unveiled before a crowd, a curtain tugged aside and the pronouncement: *Here, people, is Robert Burns Barclay*. Then, odd—I know this is only tintype history, catching a moment with the head-rod in place on the back of the neck—but there is a face-width gap between us as we pose, Rob, as if the absence of Lucas fit there. And then myself, young as you. As for my own front of the head, there beside you I show more expanse of upper lip than I wish was so, but there is not much to be done about that except what I later did, the mustache. The mouth could be worse, the nose could be better, but they are what I was given from the bin. The jaw pushes forward a little, as if I was inspecting into the camera's lens tunnel. My eyes—my eyes in our photograph are watching, not proclaiming as yours are. Even then, that far ago, watching to see what will become of us.

GROS VENTRE

*We dislike to speak ill of any civic neighbor, yet it
must be said that the community of Gros Ventre is
gaining a reputation as Hell with a roof on it.
Their notion of endeavor up there is to dream of
the day when whiskey will flow in the plumbing. It
is unsurprising that every cardsharp and hardcase
in northern Montana looks fondly upon Gros Ventre as a second home. We urge the town fathers, if
indeed the parentage of that singular municipality
can be ascertained, to invite Gros Ventre's rough
element to take up residence elsewhere.*
—CHOTEAU QUILL, APRIL 30, 1890

W ORD FROM Scotland reached us in early February, and it
was yes and then some. As regular as Christmas itself, the Montana money from Lucas had again wafted to Nethermuir; and together with it this:

Gros Ventre, Mont., 23 Dec. 1889

My dear brother Vare and family,
    *You may wonder at not hearing from me this long while. Some day
it will be explained. I am in health and have purchased a business.
This place Gros Ventre is a coming town. I remain your loving
brother,*

Lucas Barclay

"The man himself, Angus! See now, here at the bottom! Written
by our Lucas himself, and he's—"

35

"Rob, man, did I ever give up on a Barclay? It takes you people some time to find the ink, but—"

We whooped and crowed in this fashion until Mrs. Billington announced in through our door that she would put us out into the winter streets if we didn't sober up. That quelled our eruption, but our spirits went right on playing trumpets and tambourines. Weeks of wondering and hesitation were waved away by the sheet of paper flying in Rob's hand: Lucas Barclay definitely alive, unmistakably here in Montana, irrevocably broken out in penmanship—I managed to reach the magical letter from Rob for another look.

When Lucas finally put his mind to it, he wrote a bold hand. Bold scarcely says it, in fact. Each and every word was a fat coil of loops and flourishes, so outsize that the few sentences commanded the entire face of the paper. I thought I had seen among Adam Willox's pupils of the 'venture school all possible performances of pen, but here stood script that looked meant to post on a palace wall.

I said as much to Rob, but he only averred, "That would be like Lucas," and proceeded to read us the letter's contents aloud for the third time. "This place Graws Ventree. Ever hear of it, did you?"

Neither of us had word one of French, and the town name had never passed my ears before. "We can ask them at the post office where it is," I suggested. "A letter got from the place all the way to Scotland, after all."

He already was putting on his coat and cap and I mine. To see our haste, you'd have thought we had only to rush across the snowy street to be in Gros Ventre.

"Grove On," the postal clerk pronounced Lucas's town, which was instructive. So, in its way, was what he told us next. "It's quite a ways toward Canada, up in that Two Medicine country. Not a whole hell of a lot up there but Indians and coyotes. Here, see for yourselves."

What we saw on the map of post routes of Montana was that our first leg of travel needed to be by train north along the Missouri River to Craig, easy as pie. Then from Craig to Augusta by stagecoach, nothing daunting either. But from Augusta to the map dot Gros Ventre, no indication of railroad or stage route. No postal road. No anything.

The clerk did not wait for us to ask how the blank space was to be found across. "You'll need to hitch a ride on a spine pounder."

Rob and I were blanker than the map gap.

"A freight wagon," the clerk elaborated. "They start freighting into that country whenever spring comes."

And so we waited for spring to have its say. In Montana, that is most likely to be a stutter. By the time snow and mud departed and then abruptly came back, went off a second time and decided to recur again, I thought I might have to bridle Rob. He maybe thought the same about me. But the day at last did happen when we stepped off the train at Craig, wandered along the banks of the Missouri River flowing swift and high with first runoff, and presented ourselves at the stagecoach station. There we were looked over with substantial curiosity by the agent. Rob and I were topped off with Stetson hats now, but I suppose their newness, and ours, could be seen from a mile off.

At five minutes before scheduled departure and no sign of anyone but us and the spectating agent, Rob asked restlessly: "How late will the stage be?"

"Who said anything about late?" the agent responded. "Here's the fellow now who handles the ribbons." In strode a rangy young man, tall as myself, who nodded briskly to the agent and reached behind the counter to hoist out a mail sack. Likely the newcomer wasn't much older than Rob or I, but he seemed to have been through a lot more of life.

"Yessir, Ben," the agent greeted him. "Some distinguished passengers for you today, all both of them."

The stage driver gave us his brisk nod. "Let's get your warbags on board."

We followed him outside to the stagecoach. "Step a little wide of those wheelers," he gestured toward the rear team of the four stagecoach horses. "They're a green pair. I'm running them in there to take the rough spots off of them."

Rob and I looked at each other. *And how did you journey from Craig to Augusta, Mr. McCaskill and Mr. Barclay? Oh, we were dragged along behind wild horses.* There was nothing else for it, so we thrust our bedrolls and bags up top to the driver. When he had lashed them down, he pulled out a watch and peered at it. "Augusta where you gents are aiming for?"

"No," I enlightened him, "we're going on to Gros Ventre." Meanwhile Rob was scrutinizing the wheels of the stagecoach and I was devoutly hoping they looked hale.

The driver nodded decisively again. "You'll see some country, up there." He conferred with his pocket watch once more, then put it away. "It's time to let the wheels chase the horses. All aboard, gents."

No two conveyances can be more different, but that stagecoach day was our voyage on the *Jemmy* out the Firth of Clyde over again. It has taken me this long to see so, among all else that I have needed to think through and through. But my meaning here is that just as the Clyde was our exit from cramped Scotland to the Atlantic and America, now Rob and I were leaving one Montana for another. The Montana of steel rails and mineshafts and politics for the Montana of—what? Expanse, definitely. There was enough untouched land between Craig and Augusta to empty Edinburgh into and spread it thin indeed. Flatten the country out and you could butter Glasgow onto it as well. So, the widebrimmed Montana, this was. The Montana of plain arising to foothills ascending to mountains, the continent going through its restless change of mood right exactly here. And the Montana of grass and grass and grass and grass. Not the new grass of spring yet—only the south slopes of coulees showed a green hint—but I swear I looked out on that tawny land and could feel the growth ready to burst up through the earth. The Montana that fledged itself new with the seasons.

The Montana, most of all to us that wheel-voyaging day, of the world's Rob Barclays and Angus McCaskills. We had come for homestead land, had we? For elbow room our ambitions could poke about in? For a 160-acre berth in the future? Here began the Montana that shouted all this and then let the echoes say, come have it. If you dare, come have it.

The stagecoach ride was a continuing session of rattle and bounce, but we had no runaway and no breakdown and pulled into

Augusta punctual to the minute, and so Rob and I climbed down chipper as larks. Even putting up for the night at what Augusta called a hotel didn't dim us, cheered as we were by word that a freight wagon was expected the next day. The freighter had passed with supplies for a sheep ranch west of town and would need to come back through to resume the trail northward. "Better keep your eyes skinned for him," our stage driver advised. "Might be a couple weeks before another one comes through."

Toward noon of the next day, not only were our eyes still skinned but our nerves were starting to peel.

"He must've gone through in the night," Rob declared, not for the first time. "Else where to hell is he?"

"If he's driving a wagon through this country at night, we don't want to be with him anyway," I suggested. "The roads are thin enough in daylight."

"Angus, you're certain sure it was light enough to see when you first stepped out here?"

"Rob. A wagon as long as a house, and four horses, and a man driving them, and you're asking if they got past me? Now maybe they tunneled, but—"

"All right, all right, you don't have to jump on me with tackety boots. I'm only saying, where to hell—"

What sounded like a gunshot interrupted him. Both of us jumped like crickets. Then we caught the distant wagon rumble which defined the first noise as a whipcrack.

Rob clapped me on the shoulder and we stepped out into the road to await our freight wagon.

The freighter proved to be a burly figure with a big low jaw which his neck sloped up into, in a way that reminded me of a pelican. He rubbed that jaw assiduously while hearing Rob, then granted in a croaky voice that he could maybe stand some company, not to mention the commerce. We introduced ourselves to him, and he in turn provided: "Name's Herbert."

Rob gave him the patented Rob smile. "Would that be a first name, now? Or a last?"

The freighter eyed him up and down as if about to disinvite us. Then rasped: "Either way, Herbert's plenty. Hop on if you're coming."

We hopped. But while stowing our bags and bedrolls I took the chance to inventory the wagon freight. You don't work in a store such as Cariston's without hearing tales about wagonloads of blasting powder that went to unintended destinations.

Boxes of axle grease, sacks of beans, bacon, flour, coffee. Some bundles of sheep pelts, fresh enough that they must have come from the ranch where the freighter had just been. Last, a trio of barrels with no marking on them. Herbert saw me perusing these.

"Lightning syrup," he explained.

"Which?"

"Whiskey. Maybe they've heard of it even where you men come from?"

The first hours of that journey, Rob and I said very little. Partly that was because we weren't sure whether Herbert the freighter tolerated conversation except with his horses. Partly it was because nothing really needed speaking. Now that we were on our last lap to Lucas's town, Rob all but glittered with satisfaction. But also, we were simply absorbed in the sights of the land. A geography of motion, of endless ridges and knob hills and swales the wagon track threaded through. And instead of mountains equally all around as in Helena, here tiers of them were stacked colossally on a single horizon, the western. Palisades of rock, constant canyons. Peaks with winter still on them. As far ahead north as we could see, the crags and cliffs formed that vast tumbled wall.

I at last had to ask. "How far do these mountains go on like this?"

"Damn if I know," responded Herbert. "They're in Canada this same way, and that's a hundred fifty miles or so."

On and on the country of swales and small ridges rolled. Here was land that never looked just the same, yet always looked much alike. I knew Rob and I would be as lost out here as if we had been put on a scrap of board in the middle of the sea, and I was thanking our stars that we were in the guidance of someone as veteran to this trail as Herbert Whomever or Whoever Herbert.

Just to put some words into the air to celebrate our good fortune, I leaned around Rob and inquired of our shepherd: "How many times have you traveled this trail by now?"

"This'll make once."

The glance that shot between Rob and me must have had some left over for the freighter, because eventually he went on: "Oh, I've drove this general country a lot. The Whoop-up Trail runs along to the east of here, from Fort Benton on up there into Canada. I've done that more times than you can notch a stick. This trail meets up with that one, somewhere after this Gros Ventre place. All we got to do, men, is follow these here tracks."

Rob and I peered at the wheel marks ahead like two threads on the prairie. This time Rob did the asking.

"What, ah, what if it snows?"

"That," Herbert conceded, "might make them a little harder to follow."

After we stopped for the night and put supper in us, Herbert grew fidgety. Twice he got up from beside the campfire and prowled to the freight wagon and back, and then a third time. Maybe this was only his body trying itself out after the day of sitting lumplike on the wagon seat, but somehow I didn't think so.

Finally he peered across the fire, first at Rob, then at me.

"Men, you look like kind of a trustable pair."

"We like to think we're honest enough," vouched Rob. I thought I had better tack on, "What brings the matter up?"

Herbert cleared his throat, which was a lot to clear. "That whiskey in the wagon there," he confessed. "If you two're interested as I am, we might could evaporate a little of her for ourselves."

I was puzzling on "evaporate" and I don't know what Rob was studying, when Herbert elaborated: "It ain't no difference to the saloonkeeper getting those barrels, if that's what you're stuck on. He's just gonna water them up fuller than they ever was, you can bet your bottom dollar. So if there's gonna end up being more in those barrels than I started out with anyhow, no reason not to borrow ourselves a sip apiece, now is there? That's if you men think about this the way I do."

If Rob and I had formed a philosophy since stepping foot into Montana, it was to try to do as Montanians did, within reason. This seemed within.

Herbert grabbed the lantern and led as we clambered into the freight wagon. Rummaging beneath the seat, he came up with a set of harness awls and a hammer. Carefully, almost tenderly, he began tapping upward on the top hoop of the nearest whiskey barrel. When the barrel hoop unseated itself to an inch or so above its normal latitude, Herbert placed the point of a small awl there in a seam between staves and began zestfully to drill.

"That's a thing I can do," Rob offered as soon as the freighter stopped to rest fingers. Rob had hands quick enough to shoe a unicorn, and now he moved in and had the drilling done almost before he started.

This impressed even Herbert. "This ain't your profession, is it?"

"Not quite yet. Angus, have you found the one with the tune?"

A straw to siphon with was my mission, and from a fistful off the floor of the wagon I'd been busily puffing until I found a sturdy one that blew through nicely. "Here's one you could pipe the Missouri River through." Rob drew his awl from the hole and delicately injected my straw in its place. Herbert had his cup waiting beneath when the first drops of whiskey began dripping out. "She's kind of slow, men. But so's the way to heaven."

When each of our cups was about two inches moist and the barrel hole plugged with a match stick and the hoop tapped back into place to hide it, Herbert was of new manufacture. As we sat at the campfire and sipped, even his voice sounded better when he asked intently: "How's the calico situation in Helena these days?"

I had a moment of wondering what was so vital to him about that specific item of dry goods. Then it dawned on me what he meant. Women. And from there it took no acrobatics of logic to figure out what sort of women.

Rob raised his cup in a mock toast and left the question to me. Well, there was rough justice in that, you could say. I had been the first to investigate the scarlet district of Helena, with promptitude after I'd begun earning wages at the mercantile. Not that Rob was six counties behind me, for it had been the next time I said I was setting off up the gulch that he fidgeted, scratched an ear, cleared something major from his throat, then blurted: "You can stand company, can't you?" That too had been new of America, transit from the allure of the Nethermuir mill girls with the boldest tongues to those Helena brothel excursions of ours winterlong. Without ever saying so to each other—it was the side of life Rob did not like to be noticed in—we both well knew that among the deepest of the Nethermuir traps we were escaping from was one of those accident marriages. A wedding beside the cradle, as was said. It happened to so many we knew and it had been just as likely to happen to either of us sooner or later, by the nature of things probably sooner. So, yes, America, Montana, Helena had been new open terms of possibility in more ways than one.

"Worst thing about being a freighter," Herbert was proclaiming after my tepid report on Helena, "is how far she is between calico. Makes the need rise in a man. Some of these mornings, I swear to gosh I wake up and my blanket looks like a tepee."

From Herbert the rest of that evening, we heard of the calico situation at the Canadian forts he freighted to. (Bad.) The calico situation in New Orleans, where he'd been posted as a soldier in the Union army. (Astounding.) The calico situation at Butte as compared with anywhere else in Montana. (A thousand times better.) The calico situation among the Mormons, the Chinese, the Blackfeet, the Nez Perce, and the Sioux.

When we had to tell him no, we hadn't been to London to find out the English calico situation, he looked regretful, tipped the last of his cup of whiskey into himself, and announced he was turning in for the night. "Men, there's no hotel like a wagon. Warm nights your room is on the wagon, stormy nights it's under it." Herbert sniffed the air and peered upward into the dark. "I believe tonight mine's going to be under."

Herbert's nose knew its business. In the morning, the world was white.

I came out of my bedroll scared and stayed that way despite the freighter's assessment that "this is just a April skift, maybe." From Rob's blinking appearance, he, too, could have done without a fresh white surprise this morn. After Helena's elongated winter of snow flinging down from the Continental Divide, how was a person supposed to look at so much as a white flake without thinking the word *blizzard?* Nor was there any checking on the weathermaking intentions of the Divide mountains now, as they were totally gone from the west, that direction a curtain of whitish mist. Ridges and coulees nearest us still could be picked out, their tan grass tufting up from the thin blanket of freshfall. But our wagon trail, those thin twin wheel tracks—as far as could be told from the blank and silent expanse all around us, Herbert and Rob and I and the freight wagon and four horses had dropped here out of the sky along with the night's storm.

The snow had stopped falling, which was the sole hope I saw anywhere around. But was the sky empty by now? Or was more winter teetering where this plopped from?

Rob put his head back and addressed firmly upward into the murk: "Can't you get the stove going up there?" But he still looked as discomfited as I must have.

"She sure beats everything, Montana weather," Herbert acknowledged. "Men, I got to ask you to do a thing."

Rob and I took turns at it, one walking ahead of the wagon and scuffing aside the snow to find the trail ruts while the other rode the seat beside Herbert and tried to wish the weather into improvement.

"When do you suppose spring comes to this country?" Rob muttered as he passed me during one of our walking-riding swaps.

"Maybe by the end of summer," I muttered back.

Later: "You remember what the old spinster in the story said, when somebody asked her why she'd never wed?"

"Tell me, I'm panting to know."

"'*I wouldn't have the walkers, and the riders went by.*' Out here, she'd have her choice of us."

"She'd need to negotiate past Herbert first."

Later again: "Am I imagining or is Montana snow colder than snow ever was in Scotland?"

"If you're going to imagine, try for some sunshine."

Still later: "Herbert says this could have been worse, there could have been a wind with this snow."

"Herbert is a fund of happy news."

It was morning's end before Herbert informed us, "Men, I'm beginning to think we're going to get the better of this."

He no more than said so when the mist along the west began to wash away and mountains shouldered back into place here and there along that horizon. The light of this ghostly day became like no other I had ever seen, a silver clarity that made the stone spines of ridges and an occasional few cottonwood trees stand out like engravings in book pages. Any outline that showed itself looked strangely singular, as if it existed only right then, never before. I seemed to be existing differently myself. Again as it had happened on that first full Atlantic morning of mine when I watched and watched the ocean, I could feel a slowing of the day; a shadowless truce while light speaks to time.

At last the sun burned through, the snow began melting into patches, the wheel tracks emerged ahead of us like new dark paint. Our baptism by Montana spring apparently over, Rob and I sat in grateful tired silence on the freight wagon.

We were wagoneers for the rest of that day and the next, crossing the Teton River and observing some distant landmark buttes which Herbert said were near a settlement called Choteau. Then at supper on the third night Herbert reported, "Tomorrow ought to about get us there." In celebration, we evaporated the final whiskey barrel to the level of the two previous nights', congratulating ourselves on careful workmanship, and Herbert told us a number of chapters about the calico situation when he was freighting into Deadwood during the Dakota gold rush.

Not an hour after we were underway the next morning, the trail dropped us into a maze of benchlands with steep sides. Here even the tallest mountains hid under the horizon, there was no evidence the world knew such a thing as a tree, and Herbert pointed out to us alkali bogs which he said would sink the wagon faster than we could think about it. A wind so steady it seemed solid made us hang onto our hats. Even the path of wagon tracks lost patience here; the bench hills were too abrupt to be climbed straight up, and rather than circle around endlessly among the congregation of geography, the twin cuts of track attacked up the slopes in gradual sidling patterns.

Herbert halted the wagon at the base of the first long ruts angling up and around a benchland. "I don't think this outfit'll roll herself over, up there. But I thought wrong a time or two before. Men, it's up to you whether you want to ride her out or give your feet some work."

If Herbert regarded these slopes as more treacherous than the cockeyed inclines he had been letting us stay aboard for . . . Down I climbed, Rob prompt behind me.

We let the wagon have some distance ahead of us, to be out of its way in case of tumbling calamity, then began our own slog up the twin tracks. *And how did you journey from Augusta to Gros Ventre, Mr. McCaskill and Mr. Barclay? We went by freight wagon, which is to say we walked.* The tilted wagon crept along the slope while we watched, Herbert standing precariously on the lazyboard, ready to jump.

"Any ideas, if?"

"We're trudging now, I suppose we'd keep on. Our town can't be that far."

"This is Montana, remember. You could put all of Scotland in the watch pocket of this place."

"True enough. Still, Gros Ventre has to be somewhere near by now. Even Herbert thinks so."

"Herbert thinks he won't tip the wagon over and kill himself, too. Let's see how right he is about that, first."

The benchlands set us a routine much as the snow had done: trudge up each slope with the wind in our teeth, hop onto the freight wagon to ride across and down the far side, off to trudge some more. The first hour or so, we told ourselves it was good for the muscles. The rest of the hours, we saved our breath.

"Kind of slaunchwise country, ain't she?" remarked Herbert when we paused for noon. Rob and I didn't dare study each other. If Gros Ventre was amid this boxed-in skewed landscape; if this windblown bleakness was where we had plucked ourselves up across the world to find Lucas Barclay . . .

Mid-afternoon, though, brought a long gradual slope which the wagon could travel straight up in no peril, and we were able to be steady passengers again. By now Rob and I were weary, and wary as well, expecting the top of each new ridgeline to deliver us back into the prairie infantry. But another gradual slope and widened benchland appeared ahead, and a next after that. And then the trail took the wagon up to a shallow pass between two long flat ridges.

There in the gap, Herbert whoaed the horses.

What had halted him, and us, was a change of earth as abrupt as waking into the snow had been.

Ahead was where the planet greatened.

To the west now, the entire horizon was a sky-marching procession of mountains, suddenly much nearer and clearer than they were before we entered our morning's maze of tilted hills. Peaks, cliffs, canyons, cite anything high or mighty and there it was up on that rough west brink of the world. Mountains with snow summits, mountains with jagged blue-gray faces. Mountains that were free-standing and separate as blades from the hundred crags around them; mountains that went among other mountains as flat palisades of stone miles long, like guardian reefs amid wild waves. The Rocky Mountains, simply and rightly named. Their double magnitude here startled and stunned a person, at least this one—how deep into the sky their motionless tumult reached, how far these Rockies columned across the earth.

The hem to the mountains was timbered foothills, dark bands of pine forest. And down from the foothills began prairie broader than any we had met yet, vast flat plateaus of tan grassland north and east as far as we could see. Benchland and tableland countless times larger than the jumbled ridges behind us, elbow room for the spirit.

Finally, last in our looking, about a mile in front of us at the foot of the nearest of these low plateaus, a line of cottonwood trees along a creek made the graceful bottom seam across this tremendous land.

I just sat and let it all dazzle at me. Rob was equally stone-still at my side.

"Oh yeah, I see where we are now," contributed Herbert. "There's old Chief." He pointed out to us Chief Mountain, farthest north on the mountain horizon and a step separate, independent, from the rest of the crags. "She's Canada up beyond that. Between her and here, though, comes the Two Medicine River. Can't see that from where we're at, but this whole jography is called the Two Medicine country."

I so wish Rob and I right then had performed what we ought to: politely request Herbert to close his eyes and cover his ears, step off the wagon together, face ourselves to this Two Medicine country, and then leap high and click our heels in the air loud enough to be heard in Nethermuir. For every soul that has ever followed a notion bigger than itself, we ought to have performed that. To send our echo into the canyons of time: *here is Montana, here is America, here is all yet to come.*

Now Herbert was finding for us the Sweetgrass Hills, a cluster of bumps on the plains far northeast of us. "Men, unless I'm more

wrong than usual, those're about seventy-five miles from where
we're at." Montana distances made your head swim. "Then this
kind of a tit over here, Heart Butte." A dark breastlike cone that
rose northwest near the rougher Rockies. Much closer to us, west
along the line of creek trees, stood a smaller promontory like the
long aft sail of a windship, with a tree-dark top. "Don't know what
that butte is, she's a new one on me," Herbert confessed as our
wagon began to jostle down toward the creek's biggest stand of cottonwood trees. In this landscape of expanse the local butte did not
stand particularly high, it was not monumentally shaped, yet it
managed to speak prominence, separateness, managed somehow to
preside. A territory of landmarks as clear as towers was this Two
Medicine country. Already I felt able to find my way in this clean-
lined land.

Rob and I interrupted our gaping to trade mighty grins. All we
needed now was Lucas Barclay and his coming metropolis.

Herbert cleared his gallon of throat and gestured toward the cottonwood grove ahead. When we didn't comprehend, he said:

"Here she is, I guess."

Gros Ventre took some guessing, right enough.

Ahead of us under the trees waited a thin scatter of buildings, the
way there can be when the edge of town dwindles to countryside.
None of the buildings qualified as much more than an eyesore, and
beyond them on the far bank of the creek were arrayed several
picketed horses and a cook wagon and three or four tents of ancient
gray canvas, as if wooden walls and roofs hadn't quite been figured
out over there yet.

From the wagon seat Rob and I scanned around for more town,
but no. This raggle-taggle fringe of structures was the community
entire.

Rather, this was Gros Ventre thus far in history. Across the far
end of the single street, near the creek and the loftiest of the cottonwoods, stood a two-story framework. Just that, framework, empty
and forlorn. Yellow lumber saying, more like pleading, that it had
the aspiration of sizable enterprise and lacked only hundreds of
boards and thousands of nails to be so.

Trying to brighten the picture for Rob, I observed: "They, ah, at
least they have big plans."

Rob made no answer. But then, what could he have?

"Wonder where it is they keep the calico at," issued from Herbert. He pondered Gros Ventre a moment further. "Wonder if they *got* any calico."

Our wagon rolled to a halt in front of what I took to be a log barn and which proved to be the livery stable. Rob and I climbed down and were handed our luggage by Herbert. As we shook hands with him he croaked out companionably, "Might see you around town. Kind of hard to miss anybody in a burg this size."

Rob drew in a major breath and looked at me. I tried to give him a grin of encouragement, which doubtless fell short of either. He turned and went over to the hostler who had stepped out to welcome this upsurge of traffic. "Good afternoon. We're looking for a man Lucas Barclay."

"Who? Luke? Ain't he over there in the Medicine Lodge? He always is."

Our eyes followed the direction the stableman jerked his head. At the far end of the empty dirt street near the bright skeleton of whatever was being built, stood a building with words painted across the top third of its square front in sky blue, startling as a tattoo on a forehead:

MEdICINE

LOdGE

I saw Rob open his mouth to ask definition of a medicine lodge, think better of it, and instead bid the hostler a civil, "Thank you the utmost."

Gathering ourselves, bedrolls and bags, off we set along the main and only street of this place Gros Ventre. I was wrong about the street being empty; it in fact abounded with cow pies, horse apples, and other animal products.

"Angus," Rob asked low, as we drew nearer to the skelter of tents and picketed horses across the creek, "what, do they have Gypsies in this country?"

"I wish I knew just what it is they have here." The door into the Medicine Lodge whatever-it-was waited before us. "Now we find out."

Like Vikings into Egypt, we stepped in.

And found it to be a saloon. Along the bar were a half dozen partakers, three or four others occupied chairs around a greentop table where they were playing cards.

"Aces chase faces, Deaf Smith," said one of the cardsters as he spread down his hand.

"Goddamn you and the horse you rode in on, Perry," responded his opponent mildly, and gathered the cards to shuffle.

Of course Rob and I had seen cowboys before, in Helena. Or what we thought were. But these of Gros Ventre were a used variety, in soiled crimped hats and thick clothing and worn-down boots.

The first of the Medicine Lodge clientele to be aware of us was a stocky tan-faced man, evidently part Indian. He said something too soft for us to hear to the person beside him, who revolved slowly to examine us over a brownish longhorn mustache. I wish I could say that the mustached one showed any sign we were worth turning around to look at.

Had someone been counting our blinks—the Indian-looking witness maybe was—they'd have determined that Rob and I were simultaneous in spying the saloonkeeper.

He stood alone near one end of the bar, intently leaning down, busy with some task beneath there. When he glanced up and intoned deep, "Step right over, lads, this bunch isn't a fraction as bad as they look," there was the remembered brightness of his Barclay cheeks, there was the brand of voice we had not heard since leaving Nethermuir.

Lucas possessed a black beard now with gray in it like streaks of ash. The beard thickly followed his jaw and chin, with his face carefully shaved above that. Above the face Lucas had gone babe-bald, but the dearth of hair only emphasized the features of power dispersed below in that frame of coaly whiskers: sharp gray eyes under heavy dark eyebrows, substantial nose, wide mouth to match the chin, and that stropped ruddiness identical to Rob's.

Rob let out a breath of relief that must have been heard all the way to Helena. Then he smiled a mile and strode to the bar with his hand out as far as it could go:

"Mister Lucas Barclay, I've come an awful distance to shake your hand."

Did I see it happen? Hear it? Or sheerly feel it? Whichever the sense, I abruptly knew that now the attention of everyone in the saloon weighed on Rob and me. Every head had pivoted to us, every eye gauged us. The half-breed or whatever he was seemed to be memorizing us in case there was a bounty on fools.

The saloonkeeper himself stared up at us thunderous. If faces could kill, Rob and I would have been never born.

The two of us stared stunned as he glowered at Rob. At me. At Rob again. Now the saloonkeeper's back straightened as if an iron rod had been put in his spine, but he kept his forearms deliberately out of sight below the bar. My mind flashed full of Helena tales of bartenders pulling out shotguns to moderate their unruly customers. By the holy, though, could anyone with eyes think Rob and I were anything like unruly right then?

Finally the saloonkeeper emitted low and fierce to Rob what his face was already raging out: "Are you demented? Who to hell are you anyway, to come spouting that?"

"Rob!" from Rob the bewildered. "Lucas, man, I know you like myself in the mirror! I'm Rob, your nephew."

The saloonkeeper still stared at him, but in a new way. Then:

"By Jesus, you are. Chapter and verse. By Jesus, you're Vare's lad Robbie, grown some."

The fury was gone from Lucas Barclay's face, but what passed into its place was no less unsettling. All emotion became unknown there now; right then that face of Lucas Barclay could have taught stoniness to a rock.

Still as baffled as I was, Rob blurted next: "Lucas, what is the matter here? Aren't we welcome?"

At last Lucas let out a breath. As if that had started him living again, he said as calm as cream to Rob: "Of course you're welcome. It's pure wonderful that you're here, lad. You've come late, though, to do any handshaking with me."

Lucas raised his forearms from beneath the bar and laid on the dark polished wood the two stumps of amputation where his hands had been.

I tell you true, I did not know whether to stare or look away, to stay or turn tail, to weep or to wail. There was no known right-

ness of behavior, just as there was no rightness about what had
happened to Lucas. Like the clubs of bone and flesh he was ex-
hibiting to us, any justice in life seemed ripped, lopped off. To
this day the account of Lucas Barclay's mining accident causes
my own hands to open and close, clench their fingernails hard
against their palms, thankful they are whole. It happened after
the Great Maybe and Helena, when Lucas had moved on to a
silver claim called the Fanalulu in the outcropping country between Wolf Creek and Augusta. *My partner on that was an old Colo-
rado miner Johnny Dorgan. This day we were going to blast. I was
doing the tamping in, Johnny was behind me ready with the fuse. What
made this worse was that I had miner's religion, I always made sure to
use a wooden tamp on the powder so there'd be no chance of spark.* But
this once, the blasting powder somehow did go off. Dorgan had
turned to reach for his chewing tobacco in the coat behind him and
was knocked sprawling, with quartz splinters up and down his back.
He scrambled on all fours to where Lucas had been flung, a burned
and bloody mass. The worst was what was left—what was gone—at
the ends of Lucas's arms. Dorgan tied a tourniquet on each, then
took Lucas, a wagonload of pain, to the Army post hospital at Fort
Shaw. *Johnny thought he was delivering a corpse, I suppose. He very
near was.* The surgeon there saved what he could of Lucas, starting
at the wrists. *Did I want to die, at first? By Jesus, I wanted worse than
that. I wanted the world dead. I hated everything above snake-high.* For
months, Lucas was tended by the Fort Shaw surgeon. *I was his pastime, his pet. He made me learn to handle a fork and a glass with these
stubs. He said if a man can do that, he can make himself a life.*

There in the Medicine Lodge, Lucas's maiming on show in front
of him, Rob's case of stupefaction was even worse than mine. He
brought his hand back to his side as if burned and stammered,
"Lucas . . . I . . . we never—"

"Put it past, Robbie," his uncle directed. "Have a look at these
to get used to them. Christ knows, I've had to."

While Rob's eyes still were out like organ stops, Lucas's powerful
face turned toward me. "And who's this long one?"

Would you believe, I stupidly started to put my hand out for a
shake, just as Rob had. Catching myself, I swallowed and got out:
"Lucas, I'm Angus McCaskill. You knew my father, back—"

"You're old Alex's lad? By Jesus, they must have watered you. You've grown and then some." His gaze was locked with mine. "Is your father still the best wheelsmith in the east of Scotland?"

"No. He's, he's dead."

Lucas's head moved in a small wince of regret. "I'm sorry to hear so. Death is as thorough on the good as the bad." His arm stumps vanished briefly beneath the bar again and came up delivering a whiskey bottle clutched between. "Down here among the living we'd better drink to health, ay?"

Lucas turned from us to the line of glasses along the back bar shelf, grasped one between his stumps, set it in place in front of me, turned and did the same with one for Rob, a third time with a glass for himself. Next he clasped the whiskey bottle the same way and poured an exactly even amount in each glass. It was all done as neatly as you or I could.

"Sedge, Toussaint, you others," Lucas addressed the rest of the clientele, "line your glasses up here. You're not to get the wild idea I'm going to make a habit of free drinks. But it's not just any old day when a Barclay arrives to Gros Ventre."

Lucas poured around, lifted a glass of his own as you would if you had to do it only with your wrists, and gave the toast:

"Broth to the ill, stilts to the lame."

Our drink to health became two, then Lucas informed Rob and me he was taking us to home and supper and that he may as well show us the town while we were out and about. The half-breed, Toussaint, assured us, "This Gros Ventre, there never was one like it," and chuckled. The mustached man, called Sedge, stepped behind the bar to preside there, and Lucas led Rob and me out on tour.

Gros Ventre could be taken in with two quick glimpses, one in each direction along the street, yet it registered on me in a slow woozy way, like a dream of being shown somewhere at the far end of the world. Or maybe a dream of myself dreaming this, reality a phase or two away from where I was. At any rate, my mind was stuck on Lucas and his maiming and he was energetically intent only on showing us Montana's Athens-to-be. Rob and I did much nodding and tried to mm-hmm properly as Lucas tramped us past such sights as Fain's blacksmith shop, encircled by odds and ends of scrap iron. Kuuvus's mercantile, a long, low log building which sagged tiredly in the middle of its roofbeam. A sizable boarding house with a sign above its door proclaiming that it was operated by C.E. Sedgwick—which was to say, the mustachioed Sedge—and his wife Lila. Near the creek in a grove of cottonwoods, a tiny Catholic church with the bell on an iron stanchion out front. (A circuit-riding priest circulated through "every month or so," Lucas noted favorably.) Dantley's livery stable where Herbert the freighter had disembarked us. Next to it Gros Ventre's second saloon, Wingo's: a twin to the Medicine Lodge except it was fronted with slabs instead of boards. To our surprise—we now knew why Herbert hadn't materialized at the Medicine Lodge—we were informed in an undervoice by Lucas that the town did have a calico supply, ensconced here in Wingo's. "Two of them," Lucas reported with a disapproving shake of his head. "Wingo calls them his nieces."

We also became enlightened about the tents and picketed horses. "That's the Floweree outfit, from down on the Sun River," Lucas told us. "Trailing a herd of steers north. These cattle outfits all come right through on their way up to borrow grass. I tell you, lads, this town is situated—"

"Borrow?" echoed Rob.

"From the Indians. Blackfeet. Their reservation is north there"—Lucas gestured beyond the creek with one of his stubs; would I ever get used to the sight of them?—"fifteen miles or so, and it goes all the way to Canada. Cattle everywhere on it, every summer."

And how did the municipality of Gros Ventre strike you, Mr. McCaskill and Mr. Barclay? We found the main enterprise to be theft of grass, and our host had no hands.

Be fair, though. The fledgling town was not without graces. It proffered two. First and finest was its trees, cottonwoods like a towering lattice above the little collection of roofs. When their buds became leaf, Gros Ventre would wear a green crown, true enough. And the other distinction stood beside the Sedgwick boarding house: a tall slender flagpole, far and away the most soaring construction in Gros Ventre, with its somewhat faded 41-star American flag energetically flapping at the top. When Rob or I managed to remark on this public-spirited display, Lucas glanced upward and said there was a story to that, all right, but he marched us across to what he plainly considered the centerpiece of Gros Ventre, the building skeleton at the end of the street.

"Sedge's hotel," Lucas identified this assemblage of lumber and air for us. "I've put a bit of money into it too, to help him along. The Northern, he's going to call it."

Rob and I must have looked less comprehending than we already were, for Lucas impatiently pointed out that the hotel site was at the north end of town. "You'll see the difference this hotel will make," he asserted. "Sedge and Lila will have room for dozens here."

Thinking of what it had taken for Rob and me to reach this speck on the map, I did wonder how dozens at once were going to coincide here.

Lucas faced the pair of us as if he'd heard that. He thrust his stubs into his coat pockets and looked whole and hale again, a bearded prophet of civic tomorrows.

"Robbie, Angus. I know Gros Ventre must look like a Gypsy camp to you. But by Jesus, you ought've seen what a skimpy place it was when I came three years ago. You had to look twice to see whether anybody lived here but jackrabbits. The Sedgwicks and Wingo, Kuuvus and his wife and Fain and his, they've all come in since then. And they're just the start. This'll be a true town before you know it."

Evidently we did not manage to appear convinced. Lucas started anew.

"Lads, you have eyes in your heads. If you used them at all on your way here, you saw that there's land and more land and then more of more, just for the taking here in Montana. And by Jesus, people will take it. That's the history of the race, in so many words. They'll flock in here, one day, and that day not long from now. The railroad is being built, do you know, up north of the Two Medicine River. That's what'll bring them, lads. Steam and steel is the next gospel. And when people come, they'll need everything a town can furnish them," concluded the lord of the Medicine Lodge.

There was a brief silence, reverent on Lucas's part, dazed on ours. Then he did some more dream-building for us, in a confiding way:

"My belief is we'll see a railroad of our own here. After all, they talk of building one to that piddle spot beside the road, called

Choteau. A squeak of a place like Choteau gets a railroad, we ought to get a dozen, ay?"

Lucas gazed out the solitary street to the straight-topped benchland south of us, then past the flagpole to the jagged tumble of mountains along the west. Up came an armstub that thoughtfully smoothed the black-and-gray beard as he contemplated. "This is rare country," he murmured. "Just give our Gros Ventre a little time and it'll be a pure grand town."

"*Whom never a town surpasses,*" issued from me, "*for honest men and bonny lasses.*" I suppose I was thinking out loud. For the long moment Lucas contemplated me, I much wished I'd kept the words in me.

"Is that old Burns," he asked at last, "as in the middle of our Robbie's name?"

"The same," I admitted.

"Angus is a lad of parts," Rob roused himself to put in, "he can recite the rhyming stuff by the yard. See now, he was pupil teacher for Adam Willox."

"I knew Adam," recalled Lucas. "He had a head on his shoulders." Lucas eyed me again, as if hoping to see the start of one growing on me, then declared the next of Gros Ventre's matchless attractions was supper.

Past the rear of his saloon and across a wide weedy yard he led us toward a two-story frame house. The house needed paint—this entire town needed that—but it sat comfortably between two fat gray cottonwood trees, like a mantel clock between pewter candlesticks. Lucas related to us that the house had come with the Medicine Lodge, he'd bought both from the founder of Gros Ventre, named DeSalis. It seemed DeSalis had decided the begetting of Gros Ventre was not a sufficient source of support in life, and had gone back to Missouri. But we had the luck, Lucas pointed out, that DeSalis first sired five children here and so provided ample guest space for us.

As we reached the front porch, Lucas stopped as if he had suddenly butted up against a new fact.

"Now you'll meet Nancy," he said.

"Nancy?" I could see that Rob was buoyed by the sight of the considerable house, and now this news that Lucas at least had been fortunate enough to attain a mate in life. "The Mrs.! And doesn't that make her my aunt, I ask you? Lucas, man, why didn't you tell—"

Lucas's face underwent another change to stone. "Did you hear me say one goddamned thing about being married? Nancy is my— housekeeper."

Rob reddened until he looked like he might ignite. "Lead on, Lucas," I inserted in a hurry. "We're anxious to meet Nancy."

He manipulated the doorknob with his stubs and led us into the front parlor. "Nancy! We have people here."

From the kitchen doorway at the far end of the parlor stepped a young woman. Her dress was ordinary, but that made the only thing. Hair black as a crow's back. A figure tidily compact yet liber- ally curvaceous. A squarish face, the nose and cheekbones a bit broad; the upper lip surprisingly rising a bit in the very middle, revealing the first teeth in a way that seemed steadily but calmly questioning. None of this Nancy-the-housekeeper was lovely in any usual way but her each feature was more attractive on second no- tice, and even more so on a third. Remarkable dark, dark eyes, perhaps black, too. And her skin was brown as a chestnut, several shades darker than that of the half-Indian or whatever he was in the Medicine Lodge, Toussaint.

Rob was trying not to be frog-eyed, and failing. I suppose I was similar. Lucas now seemed to be enjoying himself.

Deciding the situation could stand some gallantry, I stepped to- ward the woman of the inquisitive lip and began, "How do you do, Miss—"

Lucas snorted a laugh, then called to me: "Buffalo Calf Speaks."

"Excuse me?"

"Buffalo Calf Speaks," Lucas repeated, more entertained than ever. "She's Blackfeet. Her Indian name is Buffalo Calf Speaks. So if you're going to call her Miss, that's what Miss she is."

"Yes, well." Strange sensation it is, to want to strangle a grinning handless man. I put myself around to the woman again and tried anew: "Nancy, hello. My name is Angus McCaskill." I forced a grin of my own. "I'm from a tribe called Scotchmen."

"Yes," she answered, but her eyes rapidly left me to look at Rob, his shining resemblance to Lucas. Lucas told her, "This is my brother's son. His name is Rob."

"Rob?" Her intonation asked how that word could be a name.

57

"Like Bob Wingo," Lucas instructed, "except Scotchmen say it Rob. They never do anything the way ordinary people do, right, lads?"

"Rob," Nancy repeated. "From Scot Land."

"That's him, Nancy. Rob and Angus are going to be with us for a while. Now we need supper." The woman's dark eyes regarded us a moment more, then Lucas, and she went back through the kitchen doorway.

So that was Nancy. Or at least the start of her.

"Don't stand there like the awkward squad," Lucas chafed us. "Come sit down and tell me news of Nethermuir. If the old place has managed to have any, that is."

That supper, and that evening, were like no other.

I am all too sure that neither Rob nor I managed to learn, at least on the first many tries, how to keep a face under control when a meat platter or a spud dish was passed to it between those bony stubs at the ends of Lucas's sleeves. What we did learn was that a person without hands needed to have his meat cut for him—Nancy sat beside Lucas and did the knifework before ever touching her own plate—but he then could manipulate a fork the way a clever bear might take it between its paws, and he could spoon sugar into his coffee without a spill and stir it efficiently. We learned by Lucas's telling of it that he could dress himself except for the buttoning; "I'd like to have my knee on the throat of the man who invented buttons." That he could wind his pocket watch by holding it against his thigh with one stub and rolling the stem with the other. That, what I had wondered most about, he had taught himself to write again by sitting down night after night, a pen between his stubs, and copying out of an old book of epitaphs. "*Stone Stories,* the title of it was. It fit my mood. I made myself work at a line a night, until I could do it first try. Then two lines a night, and four, on up to a page of them at a time. Not only did I learn writing again, lads, the epitaphs were a bit of entertainment for me. The Lillisleaf steeplejack's one: *Stop, traveler, as you go by/I too once had life and breath/but I fell through life from steeple high/and quickly passed by death.* Angus, what would your man Burns think of that one, ay? Or the favorite of mine. *In the green bed 'tis a long sleep/Alone with your past, mounded deep.* By Jesus, that's entirely what I was, alone, after the accident to my hands. At least"—he indicated Nancy, buttering bread for him—"I'm over that now." We learned by Lucas's ironic telling that he had earned good money from the Fanalulu mine before the accident—"the great secret to silver mining, lads, is to quit in time; otherwise, the saying is that you need a gold mine to keep your silver mine going"—and we inferred from this house and its costly furnishings those were not the last dollars to find their way to Lucas. Where did this man get the sheer strength to wrestle the earth for its silver and then, when that struggle had done its worst to him, to wrestle a pen for the months of learning to write again?

We learned as much as he could bring himself to tell us about that letter that found its way to us in Helena. "Why did I write it, after these years?" Lucas lifted his coffee cup between his stubs and drank strong. "Matters pile up in a person. They can surprise you, how they want out. I must have wanted to say to old nose-in-the-air Nethermuir that I'm still living a life of my own. Even so, I couldn't bring myself yet to tell about the accident, about my—condition. How do you say to people, 'I'm a bit different these days than you remember, my hands are gone'?" Lucas gave us a gaze across the table, and Nancy added her dark one to it. A jury of two, waiting for no answer we could give.

After a moment, Lucas resumed: "And now that you lads are here, I know it'll get told without me. That's a relief. Why I don't know, but someway that's a relief."

Back in the saloon, when Lucas went to close up for the night and decided we needed one more drink to health and that happened to lead to another, we learned about Nancy.

"She came with, when I bought the Medicine Lodge and the house," Lucas imparted. "Lads, you're trying not to look shocked, but that's the fact of it. Nancy was living with the DeSalises—this all goes back a few years, understand—when I bought out old Tom. You met Toussaint Rennie, the half-breed or whatever arithmetic he is, in here when you came. Toussaint is married to Nancy's mother's sister, and that's all the family she has. The others died, up on the reservation in the winter of '83. The Starvation Winter, these Blackfeet call that, and by Jesus they did starve, poor bastards them, by the hundreds. Pure gruesome, what they went through. The last of the buffalo petered out that year, and the

winter rations the Blackfeet were supposed to get went into some
Indian agent's pocket, and on top of it all, smallpox. They say
maybe a third of the whole tribe was dead by spring. Nancy was
just a girl then, twelve or so, and Toussaint and his wife took her to
raise. Then the winter of '86 came, a heavier winter than '83 ever
thought of being, and Toussaint didn't know whether he was going
to keep his own family alive up there on the Two Medicine River,
let alone an extra. So he brought Nancy in here and gave her to the
DeSalises. There's that shocked look again, lads." Himself, Lucas
somehow appeared to be both grim and amused. "They say when
Toussaint rode into town with her, the two of them wrapped in buffalo robes, they had so much snow on them they looked like white
bears. When I came up here and bought the saloon and the house
and DeSalis pulled out with his family for Missouri, Nancy stayed
on with me. She can be a hard one to figure, Nancy can. By now
she's part us and part them"—Lucas's nod north signified the reservation and its Blackfeet—"and you never quite know which side is
to the front, when. But Nancy has always soldiered for me. By
Jesus, she's done that. I need some things done, like these damn
buttons and shaving and all little nuisances like that. She needs
some place to be. So you see, it's an arrangement that fits us both."
Lucas shrugged into his coat, thrust his arm ends into its pockets
and instantly looked like a builder of Jerusalems again. "This isn't
old Scotland, lads. Life goes differently here."

Differently, said the man. In the bedroom that night, I felt as if
the day had turned me upside down and shaken me out. Lucas
without hands. This end-of-nowhere place Gros Ventre. The saga of
Nancy.

Rob looked as if he'd received double of whatever I had. "Christ
of mercy, Angus. What've we gotten ourselves into here?"

It helped nothing to have the wind out of Rob's sails, too. I tried
to put a little back in by pointing out: "We did find Lucas, you have
to say that for us."

"Not anything like the one I expected. Not a—" He didn't finish
that.

"The man didn't lose those hands on purpose, Rob."

"I never meant that. It's a shock to see, is all. How could something like that happen?"

"Lucas told. Tamping the blasting powder and someway—"

"Not that, Angus. What I mean, how could it happen to *him?*" To a Barclay, he really meant. My own weary guess was that fate being what it is, it keeps a special eye for lives the size of Lucas's. A pin doesn't draw down lightning. But how say so to Rob this unearthly night and make any sense. He was rattling at top speed now: "Lucas always was so good with his hands. He was Crack Jack at anything he tried—and now look at him. I tell you, Angus, I just—and Nancy Buffalo-whatever. There's a situation, now. Housekeeper, he calls her. She must even have to help him take a piddle."

"That's as maybe, but look at all Angus does manage to do."

"Yes, if it hadn't been for that damned letter he managed to write—" Rob shook his head and didn't finish that either.

Well, I told myself, here is interesting. A Barclay not knowing what to make of another Barclay. The history of the world is not done yet.

From our bedroom window I could see the rear of the Medicine Lodge and the patch of dirt street between the saloon and the forlorn hotel framework. Another whisper from Burns came to mind: *Your poor narrow footpath of a street/where two wheelbarrows tremble when they meet.* Those lines I had the sense to keep to myself and said instead: "Anyway, here is where we are. Maybe Gros Ventre will look more grand after a night's sleep."

Rob flopped onto his side of the bed but his eyes stayed open wide. All he said more was, "Maybe so, maybe no."

And do you know, Gros Ventre did improve itself overnight, at least in the way that any place has more to it than a first glimpse can gather. In the fresh weather of dawn—Montana's crystal mornings made it seem we'd been living in a bowl of milk all those years in Scotland—I went out and around, and in that opening hour of the day the high cottonwoods seemed to stand even taller over the street and its little scatter of buildings. Grave old nurses for a foundling town. Or at least there in the daybreak a person had hope that nurture was what was happening.

Early as the hour was, the flag already was tossing atop the Sedgwick flagpole. Beyond, the mountains were washed a lovely clean blue and gray in the first sunlight. The peaks and their snow stood so clear I felt I could reach out and run a finger along that chill rough edge. At the cow camp across the creek the cook was at his fire and a few of the cowboys, or riders, as Lucas referred to them, were taking down the tents. I heard one of the picketed horses whinny, then the rush of the creek where the water bumped busily across a bed of rocks.

"Angus, you are early," came a voice behind me. "Are you seeing if the sun knows how to find Gros Ventre?"

I turned around, to Toussaint Rennie. Lucas had said Toussaint was doing carpenter work for Sedge on the famous hotel. *Toussaint does a little of everything and not too much of anything. He's not Blackfeet himself—it is not just entirely clear what he is—but he has a front finger in whatever happens in this country. Has had for years, and it's not even clear how many years. A bit like a coyote, our Toussaint. Here and there but always in on a good chance. He comes down from the Two Medicine, works at a little something for a while, goes home long enough to father another child, comes down to work at whatever presents itself next.* And came once in a blizzard to deposit his wife's niece to the house I had just stepped from.

Was this person everywhere, every time? I managed to respond to Toussaint, "The day goes downhill after dawn, they say."

"I think that, too," he vouched. The strange lilting rhythm in his voice, whatever its origins; as if warming up to sing. "You live good at dawn." Toussaint nodded toward the flagpole and its flapping banner. "You ought to have been here then."

"Then?"

"That statehood. Sedge put up the flagpole in honor. Lila had the idea, fly the flag the first of anyone. We did, do you know. The first flag in Montana the state, it was ours. Here in Gros Ventre."

I thought of the flag unfurling atop the *Herald* building in Helena that November morning, of the other flags breaking out all over the city, of the roaring celebration Rob and I had enlisted in. "How are you so sure this one was the first?"

"We got up early enough," testified Toussaint. "Way before dawn. Sedge woke up me, I woke up Dantley, we woke up everybody. Wingo and his nieces, the Kuuvuses, the Fains, Luke and"— Toussaint glanced around to be sure we were alone—"that Blackfeet of his. Out to the flagpole, everybody. It was still dark as cats, but Dantley had a lantern. Lila says, 'This is the day of statehood. This is Montana's new day.' Sedge puts up the new flag, there it was. Every morning since, he puts it up." Toussaint chuckled. "That flag. The wind has a good time with it. Sedge will need a lot of flags, if he keeps on."

The morning was young yet when Fain of the blacksmith shop came to ask if Rob might help him with a few days of wheelwork. Rob backed and filled a bit but then concluded he supposed he could, and I was glad, knowing he was privately pleased to be sought out and knowing, too, that a chance to use his skill would help his mood. The two of us had decided we'd give our situation a few days and conclude then whether to go or stay. I say decided; the fact that we had to wait anyway for another freight wagon or some other conveyance out of Gros Ventre was the major voice in the vote.

When Rob went off with Fain, I offered to Lucas to lend a hand—just in time I caught myself from putting it that way—in the saloon.

The notion amused Lucas. "Adam Willox taught you how to swamp, did he?"

I said I didn't know about that, but people had been known to learn a thing if they tried.

"I've heard of that myself," Lucas answered dryly. "You at least don't lack attitude. Come along if you want, we'll show you what it's like to operate a thirst parlor."

Swamping was sloshing buckets of water across the floor and then sweeping the flood out the door, I learned promptly, and when the saloon had been broomed out, there were glasses to wash and dry, empty bottles to haul out and dump, beer kegs to be wrestled, poker tables and chairs to be straightened, spittoons to be contended with. Lucas meanwhile polished the bar from end to end, first one foreshortened arm and then the other moving a towel in caressing circles on the wood. I am not happy to have to say this, but as happened the evening before when he was showing off Gros Ventre to us, the person that Lucas was to me depended on whether his stubs were in the open or out of sight as they now were in the towel. Part of the time I could forget entirely that Lucas was maimed as he was. Part of the time there was nothing I was more aware of. I wondered what kind of courage it took to go on with life in public after damage such as Lucas's.

Eventually Lucas called a pause in our mutual neatening tasks. "Do you feel any thirst?" he asked. I did. He nodded and stated: "We can't have people thinking we sit around in here and drink. So we'll take a standing one, ay?"

I watched astounded as Lucas wrestled forth a small crock and poured us each a beerglass of buttermilk.

"Buttermilk until well into the afternoon, Angus," he preached. "The saloonman doesn't live who can toss liquor into himself all day long and still operate the place."

As we sipped the cow stuff and Lucas told me another installment of Gros Ventre's imminent eminence, my gaze kept slipping to his stubs. I needed to know, and since there was no good time to ask this it may as well be now as any.

"Lucas, would you mind much if I ask you a thing?"

He regarded me in the presiding way of Rob aboard the steamship. "About my hands, you mean. The ones I haven't got. It's pure wonderful how interesting they are to people. Everyone asks something eventually. All but Nancy. All the others—'But how do you tie your shoes,'" he mimicked. "'But how do you get your dohickey out to take a piddle.' Well? Bang away, Angus lad."

I gulped, not just on the taste of buttermilk. "Do they—does it ever still hurt, there?"

Lucas looked at me a very long moment, and then around the Medicine Lodge as if to be sure there were no listening ghosts in its corners. "Angus, it does. Sometimes it hurts like two toothaches at once. Those are the times when it feels as if I still have the hands but they're on fire. But I don't have them, do I, so where does that pain come from?" The asking of that was not to me, however, and Lucas went on: "There, then. That's one. Next question?"

"That one was all, Lucas."

After Lucas began to see that I could do saloon tasks almost half as well with two hands as he could with none, he made strong use of me. Indeed, by the second day I was hearing from him: "Angus, I've some matters at the house. You can preside here till I get back, ay?" And there was my promotion into being in charge of the Medicine Lodge during the buttermilk hours of the day.

———

"How do, Red."

The taller of the pair who were bowlegging their way to the bar gave me the greeting, while the short wiry one beside him chirped, "Pour us somethin' that'll cheer us up, professor."

In that order of presentation, Perry Fox and Deaf Smith Mitchell these were. Riders for the Seven Block cattle ranch, out near the Blackfeet reservation. Progeny of Texas who, to hear them tell it, had strayed north from that paradisiacal prairie and hadn't yet found their way back. The one called Deaf Smith was no more hard of hearing than you or I, but simply came from a Texas locality of that name. Not easy to grasp logically, was Texas.

In not much more time than it would have taken Lucas to serve an entire saloonful, I managed to produce a bottle and pour my pair of customers a drink.

They lifted a glass to each other and did honor to the contents, then Perry faced me squarely. "Red, we got somethin' to ask you."

This put me a bit wary, but I said: "I'm here listening."

"It's kind of like this. Luke's been tellin' us there's these Scotch soldiers of yours that put a dress on when they go off to war. Is he pullin' our leg, or is that the God's truth?"

"Well, the Highlanders, yes, they have a history of wearing kilts into battle. But Lucas and Rob and I come from the Lowlands, we're not—"

"Pay me," Perry drawled to Deaf Smith. "Told you I could spot when Luke is funnin' and when he ain't."

Deaf Smith grudgingly slid a silver dollar along the bar to Perry. To me, he aimed: "Just tell us another thing now, how the hell do you guys make that work, fightin' in dresses? What's the other side do, die of laughin'?"

The dilemma of the Lowlander. To venture or not into the Highlands thicket of kilts, bagpipes, the Clearances, clan quarrels, and all else, the while making plain that I myself didn't number among those who feuded for forty generations over a patch of heather. The voice of my schoolmaster Adam Willox despairing over the history of the Highlands clans swam to mind: *If it wasn't for the Irish, the Highlands Scotch would be the most pixied people on earth.* But Lucas's voice floated there in my head, too: *Conversation is the whetstone of thirst, Angus. These Montanians in their big country aren't just dry for the whiskey, they're dry for talk.*

"Gents, let's look at this from another way." Before going on, I nodded inquiringly toward the bottle. Perry and Deaf Smith automatically nodded in turn. Pouring them another and myself a buttermilk, I made change from Perry's fresh dollar and began: "As I hear it, this geezer Custer was more fully dressed than the Indians at the Little Big Horn. Am I right so far?"

"How do you suppose Lucas spends his afternoons?" Rob asked near the end of our arrival week in Gros Ventre, no freight wagon having reappeared nor news of any. We were waiting for Lucas to show himself and take over bar duty from me, so that we could go around to the house for our turn at supper.

"With Nancy on hand, how would you spend yours?" I asked back reasonably.

Rob looked at me with reproach and was about to say further when Lucas materialized, striding through the Medicine Lodge doorway as if entering his favorite castle. "Lads, sorry I'm late. Affairs of business take scrupulous tending, you know how it is. Carry yourselves over to the house now, Nancy has your feast waiting."

"She does put him in a good frame of mind," Rob mused as we went to the house.

"Man, that's not just a frame of mind, there are other compartments involved, too."

"You can spare me that inventory," he retorted with a bit of an edge, and in we went to eat. But I was impressed from then on with Rob's change of attitude about Nancy and her benefit to Lucas. Indeed, at supper he began the kind of shiny talk to her that for the first time since we landed in Gros Ventre sounded to me like the characteristic Rob.

The rumor is being bruited that a hotel, possibly of more than one story, is under construction in Gros Ventre. The notion of anyone actually desiring to stay overnight in that singular community: this, dear readers, is the definition of optimism.

Some such salvo was in each of the past issues of the Choteau newspaper I was reading through to pass time in the Medicine Lodge. But I thought little of them until the slow afternoon I came across the one:

Gros Ventre recently had another instance of the remarkably high mortality rate in that locale. Heart failure was the diagnosis. Lead will do that to a heart.

I blinked and read again. The saloon was empty, and in the street outside nothing was moving except Sedge's and Toussaint's hammers sporadically banging the hotel toward creation. Gros Ventre this day seemed so peaceful you would have to work for hours to start a dogfight. Even so, as soon as Lucas came in I pressed him about the *Quill* item.

"People die everywhere, Angus."

"As far as I know, that's so. But the *Quill* seems to say they have help here in Gros Ventre."

"You know how newspapers are."

"The question still seems to be how Gros Ventre is."

"Angus, you are your father's son, no mistake. Stubborn as strap iron and twice as hard to argue with. All right, then. A man or two died before his time here, the past year or so. But—"

"A man or two?"

"Three, if you must count. But what I'm saying if you'll listen, two of those would have gone to their reward wherever they were. Cattle thieves. Not a race known for living to old age, lad."

"What happened with them?"

Lucas stroked his beard with a forearm. "That is not just entirely clear. Williamson out at the Double W might know, or Thad Wainwright"—owners of big cattle ranches north of town, I had heard. "Or maybe even Ninian Duff." Evidently another lord of cattle, though this one I hadn't heard of before.

"And man three?"

"What would you say to a glass of buttermilk?" Lucas busily began to pour himself one. "It's good for all known ailments, and—"

"Lucas, I'm swimming in the stuff. The particular ailment we're talking about is man number three's."

"That one, now." A major gulp of buttermilk went down him. "That one, I do have to say was ill luck."

When nothing further seemed forthcoming from Lucas except continued attention to his buttermilk, I persisted: "Dying generally is ill luck, we can agree on that. But I still haven't heard the man's ailment."

"He was shot in an argument over cards."

"What, in here?"

"Don't be pure ridiculous, lad. In Wingo's, of course." Lucas looked at me with extreme reproach, but I held gaze with him. After a bit he glanced away. "Well, you may have a point. It would have happened in here if it hadn't been the gambler's week there instead. But after that, Wingo and I talked it over and we've given gamblers the bye. Pleasant games among local folk, now. A coming town like this has its good name to think of, you know."

Was it in spite of Gros Ventre's fresh reputation for excitement that the two of us the very next day let pass the chance to go on a freight wagon retracing our route toward Augusta and Helena? Or in hope of it? Either case, the notion grew on me now that maybe I might as well go ahead and try a bit of land-looking between intervals of helping Lucas in the saloon, just to be sure we weren't missing some undisclosed reason for hope here in Gros Ventre's neighborhood.

This supposition met no objection from Rob. He was staying in demand with Fain for as much wheelwork and other repair as any pair of hands could do, so there was sound sense in him earning while I scouted about. "It could be you'll find a Great Maybe for us," he said, though not within Lucas's hearing. "Have at it, McAngus, why not. I'll keep Gros Ventre in tune while you're out and around."

Lucas of course was several thousand percent in favor of my intention. "By Jesus, Angus, now you're talking. The best part of the world is right out there waiting for you and Robbie. Tell you what, I'll even make a contribution to your exploring. Follow me." I tracked after him to the shed room behind the saloon.

"There now," he plucked the peg from the door hasp with his stubs and grandly pushed the door open, "choose your choice."

Saddles were piled on other saddles, and the walls were hung with bridles as if it was raining leather. Seeing my puzzlement, Lucas spelled the matter out:

"Collateral. These cattle outfits seem to specialize in hiring men who are thirstier than they have money for. I'm not running the Medicine Lodge as a charity, and so my borrowers put up these, ay? Go ahead, have your pick."

Several of the saddles were larger than the others, large enough that they looked as if they would house a horse from his withers to his tail. "What're these big ones?"

"Lad, do you even need to ask? Those are Texas saddles."

Since Nethermuir, the progression had been train, steamship, stagecoach, freight wagon, and shoe leather, and to it I now added the plump little pinto mare named Patch, rented to me by the half-day by Dantley and saddled maximally with my new Texican saddle. The pony's gaily splotched colors made me feel as if I was riding forth into the country around Gros Ventre in warpaint, but I suppose the actuality is that I sallied out looking as purely green as I was.

The earth was mine to joggle over aboard Patch, at least until each midday. (Lucas was strict that he wanted me to continue my saloonkeeping afternoons so he could take care of what he termed "business at the house.") Now the question was the homestead-seeker's eternal one, where best to seek?

Whatever compass is in me said south first. Not south as a general direction of hope, for as Rob and I tramped through those steep treeless benchlands in the wake of Herbert's freight wagon ten days before, we had plenty of time to agree that living there would be like dwelling on top of a table. But south a mile or so from Gros Ventre, to the pass where Herbert had halted the wagon to give us our unforgettable first glimpse into the Two Medicine country, was where I felt I needed to start, up for a deeper look at it all.

Everything was in place. The continent's flange of mountain range along the west. The dark far butte called Heart and the nearer slow-sloping one like an aft sail. The grass plateaus beyond Gros Ventre and its cottonwood creek. The soft rumple of plains toward the Sweetgrass Hills and where the sun came from. Enough country that a century of Robs and Anguses would never fill it. As I sat awhile on Patch, above to my right a hawk hung on the wind, correcting, correcting. I let myself wish that I had that higher view, that skill to soar to wherever I ought to be. Then I reined Patch east, the hawk's direction.

Three mornings in a row I rode different tracts eastward of Gros Ventre, following along the creek and its fringe of willow and cottonwood until the land opened into leveler prairie, flattening and fanning into an even horizon which Lucas's maps showed were incised by the big rivers, the Marias, the Milk, and ultimately the Missouri. This prairie before the rivers, though, had no habitation nor showed much sign it wanted any. In that trio of mornings I met only one other human being, a rider named Andy Cratt who was another of the Seven Block ranch's Texans or Texicans or whatever they called themselves. He was suspiciously interested in the origin of my saddle until I invoked Lucas. When Cratt and I parted, it took the next half hour for his moving horseback figure to entirely dwindle from my over-the-shoulder looks. Noble enough country, this eastward prairie—Toussaint told me it had been thick with buffalo when he first came—but so broad, so open, so exposed, that I felt like a field mouse under the eye of the hawk out there.

North needed only a single morning. North was red cattle on buff hills, north was ranch after ranch already built along a twisty stream called Noon Creek—Thad Wainwright's large Rocking T, Pat Egan's sizable Circle Dot, three or four smaller enterprises upstream toward the mountains, and most of all, Warren Williamson's huge Double W, which held fully half of that Noon Creek country. General opinion I had overheard in the Medicine Lodge was that you could rake hell from corner to corner and not find a nastier item than Warren Williamson. Or, as was supposedly replied to a traveler who innocently wondered what the cattle brand WW stood for, Wampus Cat Williamson. I'd only glimpsed Williamson when he stepped into the Medicine Lodge to summon a couple of his riders, a thickset impatient man several shades paler than his weather-browned cowboys. Evidently those white-handed men of money were here as in Scotland, those whose gilt family crests properly translated would read something like, *Formerly robbers, now thieves*. There where the road ran along the benchland between Gros Ventre and Noon Creek, I gazed down at the fortlike cluster of Double W ranch buildings and wondered whether Rob and I would ever possess a fraction as much roof over us.

"You're becoming a regular jockey," Rob tossed cheerily as he came out from dinner and I rode up to grab a bite before spelling Lucas at the saloon.

"You're missing all the thrill of exploration," I replied as I climbed off Patch and stiffly tottered toward the house.

That evening in the Medicine Lodge I mentioned to Lucas that I thought I might ride west the next day by following the creek up from town toward the area that lay nestled under the mountains.

Lucas had not remarked much on my land-looking, maybe on the basis that he figured I ought to see plenty before making my mind up. But now he said:

"That'll be worth doing. That North Fork is pure handsome prospect. Plan to spend the full day at it, there are a lot of miles in that country up there." To my surprised look, Lucas cleared his throat and allowed: "Business at the house can rest for an afternoon."

"That's more than generous of you," I said with what I hoped was a straight face.

"Angus, here's a pregnant thought for you. While you're about it tomorrow, pay a visit to Ninian Duff. His is the first place up the North Fork, just there after the creek divides."

Here was a name Lucas had mentioned in connection with the vanishment of cattle rustlers. When I reminded him so, Lucas gave me one of his long perusals and instructed, "You'll remember, lad, I only said maybe. But you might do well to stay away from the man's cows."

Lucas paused, then added: "Don't particularly tell Ninian you're working here in the saloon with me. He and I are not each other's favorite, in that regard."

I thought that over. "If I'm to meet the man, I could stand to know something more about that, Lucas."

"Angus, you're one who'd want to know which way the rain falls from. I've nothing against Ninian Duff. It's just that he and his are more churchly folk."

Orthodox, orthodox/who believe in John Knox./Their sighing canting grace-proud faces/their three-mile prayers and half-mile graces. I knew the breed. Maybe I would pay a visit to some old holy howler and maybe I wouldn't, too.

Wind was my guide west, early the next morning. It met me face-first as soon as I rode around the creek bend where the big cotton-woods sheltered Gros Ventre. The stiff breeze required me to clamp my hat down tight and crinkle my eyes, but no cloud showed itself anywhere there in the Rockies where the wind was flowing from, and the first sunshine made a promise of comfort on my back. Who knew, maybe this was simply how a Two Medicine day whistled.

The road today wasn't honestly one, just twin prints of wheel marks such as those Herbert's freight wagon had tracked to Gros Ventre. Yet this was peopled land along the main creek, homesteads inserted into each of the best four or five meadows of wild hay. Here was handsome, with the steady line of grassed benchland backing the creek and the convenient hedge of willows and sturdy trees giving shelter all along the water. The long-sloped promontory butte with its timber top poked companionably just into sight over the far end of this valley of homesteaders, but beyond that butte where the tiers of mountains and forest began to show, it looked like tangled country. This was the best land I'd yet seen: any one of these established homesteads down here I would gladly own. Were Rob and I already latecomers?

The mare Patch of course decided to drink when we came to a crossing of the creek, and as usual in those first days of my horsemanship I of course forgot to climb off and have myself one before she waded in and muddied the water. Today, though, the streambed was thoroughly gravel, several-colored and bright under the swift clean flow as a spill of marbles, so Patch didn't roil the drinking site. I rode her on across before getting down and drinking the fresh brisk water from my hands.

Now that I was on that side of the crossing I could see past the willows to another creekline, coiling its way as if climbing leisurely, between the benchland I had followed all the distance from town and a knobby little pine ridge directly in front of me. Here I was, wherever I was: by Lucas's description that other water had to be the North Fork, this the South. To me the natural thing was to point Patch toward the top of the knob, for a scan around. Patch did not necessarily agree, but plodded us up the slope anyway.

You would imagine, as I did, that this climb to see the new country would bring anticipation, curiosity. And there you'd be as wrong as I was. For what I began to feel was a growing sense of familiarity. Of something known, making itself recognized. The cause of the feeling, though, I kept trying to place but couldn't. The wind, yes, that. Smell of new grass, which I had been among for several days of riding by now. A glimpse of a few grazing cattle below near that north creek branch, like stray red specks from the Double W's cow hundreds. Cold whiff from where a snowbank lay hidden in some north-facing coulee. All those but something more.

At the knob top, I saw. The earth's restless alteration of itself here. The quickening swells of plains into foothills and then the abrupt upward spill of the mountains. While Rob and I were aboard the stagecoach between Craig and Augusta we had watched this, the entire interior of America soaring through its change of mood. That same radical mood of terrain I was feeling here—the climb of the continent to its divide, higher, greater, more sudden than seemed possible; like a running leap of the land.

Here was magnificent. And here, just below me, one single calm green wrinkle amid the surrounding rumpus of surging buttes and tall timbered ridges and stone cliff skyline, lay the valley of the North Fork.

To say the truth, it was the water winding its way through that still valley—its heartstream, so to speak—that captured me then and there. When the summitline up along these mountains, the Continental Divide, halved the moisture of America's sky, the share beyond went west to the Pacific Ocean while that of this slope was destined to the Atlantic. *Are you telling me*, Rob shipboard, *we're already on water from Montana, out here?* Aye, yes and yea, Rob. This supple little creek below me, this North Fork, was the start of that water which eventually touched into the Atlantic. This was the first flowing root of that pattern of waves I watched and watched from the deck of the emigrant ship. But greatly more than that, too, this quiet creek. Here at last was water in its proper dose for me. Plentiful fluid fuel for grass and hay, according to the browsing cows and the green pockets of meadow between the creek's twists. Shelter from the wind and whatever rode it in winter stood in thick evidence, creekbank growth of big willows and frequent groves of quaking ash. The occasional ponds behind beaver dams meant trout, a gospel according to Lucas. And by its thin glitter down there and the glassy shallowness of the main creek back where the mare and I crossed, not any of this North Fork ran deep enough to drown more of me than my knees.

I sat transfixed in the saddle and slowly tutored myself about the join of this tremendous western attic to the rest of the Two Medicine country. No human sign was anywhere around, except for the tiny pair of homesteads just above the mouth of the North Fork,

one of them undoubtedly that of the old Bible-banger Whoo-
jamadinger whom Lucas mentioned to me. Other than those, wherever I looked was pure planet. There from the knob I could see
eastward down the creek to where Gros Ventre was tucked away;
for that matter, I could see all the way to the Sweetgrass Hills,
what, more than eighty miles distant, that Herbert had pointed out
to Rob and me. By the holy, this was as if stepping up onto the hill
above the Greenock dock and being magically able to gaze across
all of Scotland to Edinburgh. My eyes reluctant to leave one direction for the next, nonetheless I twisted to scan each of them over
and over: north, the broad patient benchland and the landmark
butte that lifted itself to meet it; southward, the throng of big dry-
grass ridges shouldering between this creek branch and the South
Fork . . .

West. West, the mountains as steady as a sea wall. The most
eminent of them in fact was one of the gray-rock palisades that lay
like reefs in the surge of the Rockies, a straight up-and-down cliff
perhaps the majority of a mile high and, what, three or more miles
long. A stone partition between ground and sky, even-rimmed as
though it had been built by hand, countless weathers ago. That rimming mountain stood nearest over the valley of the North Fork. A
loftier darkly timbered peak loomed behind the northernmost end
of the cliff rim, and between the pair a smaller mountain topped
with an odd cockscomb rock formation fitted itself in. Close as I was
now to these promontories, which was still far, for the first time
since Rob and I came to Gros Ventre these seemed to me local
mountains. They were my guide now, even the wind fell from mind
in their favor. Seeing them carving their canyons of stone into the
sky edge, scarps and peaks deep up into the blue, a person could
have no doubt where he was. The poor old rest of the earth could
hold to whatever habit of axis it wished, but this Two Medicine
country answered to a West Pole, its own magnetic world top here
along its wildest horizon.

Someway in the midst of all my gawking I began to feel watched
myself. Maybe by someone at either of the homesteads along the
creek, but no one was in view. By the cows then? No, they seemed
all to have their noses down in their daydream fashion of eating.
Nothing else, nobody, anywhere that I could find.

As much as I tried to dismiss the feeling, though, the touch of eyes would not leave me. Who knew, probably these seven-league mountains were capable of gazing back at me. Nonetheless I cast a glance behind me for surety's sake.

On a blood bay horse not much farther away than a strong spit sat a colossally bearded figure.

He was loose-made—tall, thin, mostly legs and elbows, a stick man. And that beard was a dark-brown feedbag of whiskers halfway down his chest. He also had one of those alarming foreheads you sometimes see on the most Scottish of Scots, a kind of sheer stark cliff from the eyes up. As if the skull was making itself known under there.

All of this was regarding me in a blinkless way. I gaped back at the whiskers and forehead, only gradually noticing that the horseman's hands were either side of his saddle horn, holding another lengthy stick of some sort across there and pointing it mostly towards me. Then I realized that stick was a rifle.

"You have business here, do you?" this apparition asked.

"I hope to," I answered, more carefully than I had ever said anything before. From the looks of him, the lightest wrong word and I was a gone geezer. "I'm, I'm looking for homestead land to take up."

"Ay, every man who can walk, crawl or ride is looking for that. But not many of them find here."

"That's their loss, I would say. This country"—I nodded my head cautiously to the North Fork and the butte—"is the picture of what I'd hoped for."

"Pictures are hard to eat," he gave me for that. Maybe I was hoping too much, but I thought his stare had softened a bit as he heard more of my voice. At least the rifle hadn't turned any farther in my direction. Any mercy there was to this situation, I would devoutly accept. He levied his next words: "You are new to here?"

"As the dew," I admitted, and told him in general but quick about Rob and myself and our homesteading intention, and that if we needed any vouching it could be obtained in full at the Medicine Lodge saloon from none other than Lucas Barc—

By the time I caught up with what my tongue was saying, His Whiskerness made up his mind about me. "Lucas Barclay has had a misfortunate life," he announced. "He can answer to God for it. Or knowing Lucas, more likely argue with Him about it until the cows

come home to Canaan. But so far as I can see, you are not Lucas."
He slid the rifle into its scabbard. "My name is Duff."

So. I could well believe that this personage and Lucas came keen
against each other, as iron sharpens iron.

I introduced myself and we had a handshake, more or less. Ninian Duff immediately turned to inquisition:

"You are from?"

"Nethermuir, in Forfar."

"Ay, I know of your town. Flora and I are East Neuk of Fife
folk. As are Donald and Jen Erskine, next along the creek here. We
made the journey together, three years since." People were leaving
even the fat farms of Fife, were they? Old Scotland was becoming a
bare cupboard.

As if he had run through his supply of words for this hour, Ninian
Duff was now gazing the length of the valley to where the far shoulder of the butte angled down to the North Fork. I kept a sideway
eye on him as much as I dared. Ninian Biblical Rifleman Duff,
scarecrow on a glorious horse. Was there no one in this Two Medicine country as normal as me? He sat silently studying the calm
swale of green beneath us as if making certain every blade of grass
was in place, as if tallying the logs in the two lonely homestead
houses. Abruptly:

"You are not afraid of work?"

"None that I've met yet."

The whiskers of Ninian Duff twitched a bit at that. "Homesteading has brands of it the rest of the world never heard of. But that is
a thing you will need to learn for yourself. Were I you"—a hypothesis I wasn't particularly comfortable with—"I'd have a look at the
patch of land there aneath Breed Butte, along the top of the creek.
Then you can dinner with us and we will talk." Ninian Duff started
his powerful red-brown horse down off the knob. "We eat at noon,"
he declared over his shoulder in a way that told me he did not mean
the first minute beyond twelve o'clock.

When I rode back into Gros Ventre it was nearly suppertime. I
was vastly saddle-tired—cowboys must have a spare pair of legs
they put on for riding, I was learning—but could feel the North
Fork, the future, like music under my skin. Could bring back into
my eyes that valley I rode up after encountering Ninian Duff, the

long green pocket of creekside meadow, the immense ridges that were timber where they weren't grass and grass where they weren't timber, the Montana earth's giant sawline of mountains against the sky beyond, the nearer gentler soar of the timber-topped prominence called Breed Butte. Could hear echo all of what Ninian told me at dinner: *I have found that cattle do well enough, but the better animal hereabout may be sheep. A person can graze five or six of them on the same ground it takes for one cow. Ay, these ridges and foothills, the mountains themselves, there is room up here for thousands and thousands of sheep. The Lord was the shepherd of us, so we have His example of extreme patience to go by, too. But nothing born with wool on its back can be as troublesome as we who weave it before wearing, I believe you will agree . . . Don't come thinking a homestead is free land. Its price is serious sweat, and year after year of it . . . But were I you, the one place I'd want to homestead is here along the North Fork while there is still the pick of the land . . .*

Too thrilled yet to settle into a chair, I decided instead I'd relieve Lucas in the saloon, let him have a long supper in preparation for a Medicine Lodge Saturday night. Then Rob and I could go together for our own meal and talk of our homesteads. By the holy, the two of us would be owners of Montana yet.

Stopping by the house to tell Nancy this calendar, I swung off the pinto horse like a boy who has been to the top of the world. The kitchen door was closest for my moment's errand. With my mind full of the day's discovery, in I sailed.

In on Rob and Nancy.

She was at the stove. He was half-perched, arms leisurely crossed, at the woodbox beside the stove. True, there was distance between them. But not quite enough. And they were too still. Too alike in the caught look each cast me.

All this might have been mistakable. It is no long jump to the nearest conclusion, ever. There was something more, though. The air in the room seemed to have been broken by me. I had crashed into the mood here as if it was a door of glass.

Rob recovered first. "McAngus, is there a fire?" he called out swift and smooth. "You're traveling like there's one in your hip pocket."

"The prospect of supper will do that to me." I almost added *You're in here amply early yourself,* but held it. "Nancy, I just came to say I'll go to the saloon for Lucas, then eat after he does, if you please."

Her dark eyes gave away nothing. "Yes," she acknowledged.

I turned to Rob again. "Get your eyes ready for tomorrow, so I can show you heaven."

"The homesteads? You've found a place?"

"I have, if you like the land there an inch as much as I do. Lord of Mercy, Rob, I just wish you'd been with me today to see it all. It's up the North Fork, good grass and water with trout in it and timber to build with and the mountains standing over it and—"

"I'll hope it doesn't blind me, all that glory," Rob broke in. "So tomorrow I need to hoist myself onto a horse, do I?"

"You do. Rob, you'll fall head over heels for this land as quick as you see it."

"I'd bet that I will." He came across the kitchen with a smile and clapped me on the shoulder. "Angus, you've done a rare job of work, finding us land already."

My riding muscles did not feel like already, but I let that pass. "Right now I'd better find Lucas for supper. Come along, can't you? I'll even serve you the first drink and keep the majority of my thumb out of it."

"This North Fork must be a place, it's sending you that giddy," Rob said back, still smiling in his radiating way. "But I'll stay on here to keep Lucas company for supper. You'll owe me that drink later."

Well, I thought as I crossed the space to the saloon, it's time to stir the blood around in our man Rob, and soonest best.

That evening in the Medicine Lodge I managed to put a few extra drinks into myself, and Rob followed without really noticing. As matters progressed, Lucas sent us a couple of looks but evidently decided we deserved to celebrate my discovery of our homesteads-to-be. He moved us down to the quiet end of the bar he called the weaning corner, set a bottle in front of us and went to tend some parched Double W riders who had just stormed in. After a bit, I proposed:

"Let's go see about the calico situation, why don't we. Those calico nieces of Wingo's down the street."

Rob looked surprised, and when he hesitated with an answer, I pressed:

"Man, haven't you noticed, the bedcovers on my side look like a tepee these mornings?"

He laughed loud and long over that. I was sober enough to notice, though, that he didn't make the logical joke in return about our bedding resembling a two-pole tent.

But he went with me, and the bottle came along, too.

On our way back from Wingo's belles, I was feeling exceptionally clever about having invented this mind-clearing evening for Rob, and we were both feeling improved for the other reason, so we halted ourselves in front of the hotel framework for nocturnal contemplation and a further drink or so. Not that we could hold many more without tamping them in.

A quarter moon lent its slight light into the Montana darkness. I commemorated dreamily, "It is the moon, I know her horn."

"This Montana even has its own moon," declared Rob in wonder, lurching against me as he peered upward. "You don't find a place like this Montana just any old where."

I chortled at how wise Rob was. Right then I couldn't see how life could be any better.

Rob tugged at my sleeve and directed my attention down the lonely single street of Gros Ventre. "See now, Angus. This is what a coming town looks like by night."

"Dark," I observed.

"But its day will dawn, am I right?" He made his voice so much like Lucas's it startled me. Now Rob straightened himself with extreme care and peered like a prophet along the dim street. "You'll see the day soon, lad, when the Caledonian Railway"—the line of our journey from Nethermuir to Greenock—"will run through the middle of this town Gros Ventre. By Jesus, I think I can hear it now! *Whoot-toot-toot! Whoot-toot-toot!*"

"The train will stop exactly here"—I made a somewhat crooked X in the dirt with my foot—"and Queen Victoria and the Pope of Rome will climb off and step into the Medicine Lodge for a drink with us."

"And I'll own all the land that way"—Rob pointed dramatically north—"and you'll own all the other"—now pointing south—"and we'll have rivers of red cattle we'll ship to Chicago on our train."

"And we'll have Texas cowboys," I threw in. "Thirteen dozen of them apiece."

Rob was laughing so hard I thought he would topple both of us into the dirt of the street. "Angus, Angus, Angus. I tell you, man, it'll be a life."

"It will," I seconded. And we lurched home to the house of Lucas and Nancy.

As clear as today, I remember how that next morning went. The weather was finer than ever and even had the wind tethered somewhere, the mountains stood great and near, and as Rob and I rode past my knob of yesterday onto Breed Butte to see straight down into the heart of the valley, I thought the North Fork looked even more resplendent than I had seen it the day before. We sat unspeaking for a while, in that supreme silence that makes the ears ring. Where the bevels of the valley met, the creek ran in ripples and rested in beaver ponds. A curlew made deft evasive flight across the slope below us as if revealing curlicues in the air. Everything fit everything else this day.

Rob too said how picture-pretty a patch of the earth this truly was. Then he started in with it.

"I don't just know, though. Maybe we ought to wait, Angus."

"Wait? Isn't that the thing that breaks wagons?" I tossed off, although I was stung. Wait for what, Eden to reopen? "Man, I've seen this country from here to there, these past days, and there's none better than this valley. It decides itself, as far as I'm concerned. This North Fork is head and shoulders over anything else we could choose. But if you want to ride with me around to where I've been and see for yourself, tomorrow we can—"

"Angus, I mean wait with this whole idea of homesteading."

I thought my ears were wrong. Then I hoped they were. But the careful look on Rob told me I'd heard what I'd heard.

"Rob, what's this about? We came half across the world to find this land."

"Homesteading would be a hard go," he maintained. "We'd better do some thinking on it before we rush in. See now, we're too late in the year to buy cattle and have calves to sell this fall. As to sheep, we'd need to bring sheep from Christ knows where and we don't have the money for that. Two houses to build, fences, everything to be done from the ground up—it'd be main sweat, all the way." As if our lives so far have been made of silk, do you mean,

Rob? But I was so dumbstruck that the words didn't find their way out of me. Rob gazed down at the North Fork and shook his head once as if telling it, sorry, but no.

And then he had a matter to tell me. "Angus, I'm thinking strong of going in with Fain. There's plenty of work for two in his shop. Everything in Montana with a wheel on it can stand repair. Fain's offered to me already, and it'd be a steady earn. And a chance to stay on in Gros Ventre, for a time at least." He glanced off at the North Fork again, this time not even bothering to dismiss it with a headshake. "I'd be nearer to Lucas that way."

"Lucas? Man, Lucas is managing in this life at least as well as either of us. He has—" It hit me before her name fell off my tongue. "Nancy." The mood I broke when I walked in on the two of them the evening before. The way Rob outshined himself at every meal. The change from his first night's distaste for Lucas's domestic arrangement. I almost somersaulted off my horse just thinking of how much more there was to this than I'd noticed. This was no routine rise of the male wand, this was a genuine case of Rob and Nancy, and maybe what would be greatly worse, of Nancy and Rob. Whoever the saint of sanity is, where are you when we need you?

"Angus, think it over," Rob was going on. "There's always a job for a schooled man like yourself in a growing town. When we see how things stand after we get some true money together there in Gros Ventre, well, then can be the time to decide about homesteading. Am I right?"

I answered only, "I'll need to think, you're right that far." Then I touched the pinto into motion, down off the butte toward the North Fork and Gros Ventre, and Rob came after.

I thought of nothing else but Rob and Lucas and Nancy the rest of that day and most of the next. I hadn't been so low in mood since those first Atlantic nights in the pit of the *Jemmy*'s stomach. Within my mind I looked again and again and again from one of these alarming people to the other to the third, as you would scan at the corners of a room you were afraid in.

Nancy seeing Rob as a younger Lucas. A Lucas fresh and two-handed. Nancy whose life had been to accept what came.

Lucas in his infatuation with town-building not seeing at all that under his own roof, trouble was about to grow a new meaning.

Rob—Rob unseeing too, not letting himself see the catastrophe he was tipping himself and Lucas and Nancy toward. Rob who could make himself believe water wasn't wet. Of his sudden catalog of excuses against the North Fork, not a one came anywhere close to the deep reason of why he wanted to stay in Gros Ventre. But if I knew that, I also knew better than to try to bend Robert Burns Barclay from something he had newly talked himself into. Take and shake Rob until his teeth rattled and they'd still be castanets of his same tune.

Here the next of life was, then. A situation not only unforeseen from the stone streets of Nethermuir or the steerage berth in the *Jemmy* or the fire tower hill of Helena or the freight wagon seat from which Rob and I first saw Gros Ventre, it couldn't have been dreamed of by me in thousands of nights. Rob coveting—not another's wife in this case, but close enough. There was an entire commandment on that and you didn't have to be John Knox to figure out why. Particularly if the one coveted from was not mere neighbor but of one's own blood.

Dampness in my eyes, the conclusion to the floodtide of all this. Normally I am not one to bathe in tears. But it ought to make the sea weep itself dry, what people can do to people. I had undergone family storm in Nethermuir and that was enough. I had not come to Montana to watch the next persons closest to me, Rob and Lucas, tear each other apart; in the pitting of a Barclay against a Barclay no one could ever win unripped. Even the North Fork, grandeur though it was, wasn't worth taking sides in this. Nothing was. Search myself and the situation in every way, this I could see nothing to do but leave from.

I said as much—just the leaving; I didn't want to be the one to utter more than that—to Lucas as soon as he strode humming into the saloon near the end of that second afternoon.

"Up to the North Fork already? Aren't you getting ahead of yourself? You and Robbie will need to file your homestead claims at the land office in Lewistown first, you know."

"No, leaving is what I mean. Away from here."

Lucas broke a frown and studied me, puzzled. "Not away from this Two Medicine country, you don't mean."

"Lucas, I do mean that. Away."

"Away where?" he erupted. "Angus, are you demented? You know there's no better country in all of Montana. And that's damn close to meaning all of the world. So where does leaving come in, sudden as this? Here, let's have some buttermilk and talk this over."

"Lucas, it's just that I've had—second thoughts."

"Your first ones were damn far better." Lucas had plunked down a glass of buttermilk apiece for us, instantly forgot them and now was violently polishing the bar I had just polished. "Leaving! By Jesus, lad, I don't know what can have gotten into you and Robbie. I have heard strange in my time, but you two take the prize. Now if the pair of you can just get enough of a brain together to think this through, you'll—"

"It's only me leaving. Rob intends to stay on with Fain."

"Robbie says that, after coming all the way from Nethermuir to get away from the wheel shop?" Lucas polished even more furiously. "Put a hammer in a Barclay's—" he stopped, then managed to go on—"a Barclay's hand and he doesn't know when to put it down, ay?"

I let silence answer that, and Lucas was immediately back at me: "Tell me this, now. If you're so set on leaving, what wonderful damn place is it you're going to?"

"I'll maybe go have another look at that Teton River country we came through on the freight wagon. Or around Choteau—"

"The Teton? Choteau?" I might as well have said the Styx and Hades to this man. "Angus, are you entirely sober?"

I assured him I was never more so. Lucas shook his head and tried: "Well, at least you can stay on for a bit, can't you?"

My turn to shake a head.

"Lad, what's your headlong hurry?" Lucas demanded, as peeved as one person could be. "Weary of my hospitality, are you?"

"Lucas"—I sought how to say enough without saying too much— "a welcome ought not be worn out, is all."

Lucas stopped wiping the bar and gazed at me. Abruptly his face had the same look of thunder as when Rob first stepped up to him asking for a handshake. What a thorough fool I was. Why had I said words with my real meaning behind them?

Lucas moved not at all, staring at me. Then with great care to say it soft, he said:

"I don't consider it's been worn out. Do you?"

"No, no, nothing of the sort. I just think I'd better be on my way before—it might."

At last Lucas unlocked his gaze from me. "I ought to have seen. I ought to have, ay."

He stared down at his stubs on the bar towel, grimacing to the roots of his teeth as he did, and I knew I was watching as much pain as I ever would. Hell itself would try to douse such agony. I reached across the bar and gripped Lucas halfway up each forearm, holding him solid while he strained against the invisible fire inside his sleeves.

Gradually Lucas's breath expelled in a slow half-grunt. At last he swallowed deep and managed: "Any sense I ever had must've gone with my hands."

I let go my grasp of the stubbed arms. "Lucas, listen to me. There's nothing happened yet, I swear it. I—"

He shook his head, swallowed trouble one more time, and began randomly swiping the bar with the relentless towel again even though each motion made him wince. "Not with you, no. You I can believe, Angus. You're in here telling me, and that's a truth in itself."

So I had said all, and he had heard all, without the names of Rob and Nancy ever being spoken. More than ever, now, I felt the need to be gone from Gros Ventre. I wished I already was, and far.

Lucas swabbed like a man possessed until he reached the two glasses of buttermilk, glowered at them and tossed their contents into the swill pail. In an instant he had replaced them with glasses of whisky and shunted mine along the bar to me with his forearm.

"Here's to a better time than this," he snapped out, and we drank needfully.

Still abrupt, he queried: "Have you told our Robbie you're leaving?"

"Not yet, but I'm about to, when he comes off work."

"Hold back until tonight, why not." Lucas gazed out across the empty Medicine Lodge as if daring it to tell him why not. "I'll get Sedge to take the saloon for a while and the three of us at least can have a final supper together. We may as well hold peace in the family until then, don't you think?"

I thought, peace is nowhere in the outlook I see among the Barclays. But aloud I agreed.

When Lucas and Rob and I went around to the house that evening, supper already waited on the table, covered with dish towels. Three places were set, with the plates turned down.

"We're on our own for a bit," Lucas announced. "Nancy has gone home with Toussaint, up to the reservation to visit her aunt. So tonight, lads, it's a cold bite but plenty of it." He sat down regally, reached his right stub to the far edge of his plate and nudged the dish toward him until it lipped over the edge of the table; that lip he grasped with both stubs and flipped the plate over exactly in place. *"Turn up your plates and let's begin/Eat the meat and spit the skin,"* he recited tunefully. "Most likely *not* old Burns, ay, Angus?"

Dismay and concern and suspicion had flashed across Rob's face rapidly as a shuffle of cards and now he was back to customary confidence again. I could see him wanting to ask how long an absence "a bit" amounted to, but he held that in and said instead, "Angus and I can be bachelors with the best of them. We've been practicing at it all our lives. Here, I can do the carving," and he reached over to cut Lucas's cold beef for him.

My meal might as well have been still on the cow, I had so little enthusiasm for it. Rob jabbed and chewed with remarkable concentration. Lucas fed himself some bites in his bearlike way. Then he began out of nowhere:

"I've been thinking how to keep you two out of mischief."

My heart climbed up my throat, for I thought he meant what the two on my mind, Rob and Nancy, were heading headlong into. This would teach me to keep my long tongue at home.

But Lucas sailed on: "When you lads take up your land, I mean."

I gave him an idiot's stare. Had he forgotten every word I said in the Medicine Lodge this afternoon?

"It can be a hard go at first, homesteading," Lucas imparted as if from God's mountaintop. I caught a didn't-I-say-so glance from Rob, but we both stayed quiet, to find out whatever this was on Lucas's mind. "Hard," repeated Lucas as if teaching us the notion. "Nobody ever has enough money to start with, and there's work to be done in all directions at once, and then there's the deciding of what to raise. The North Fork there, that's sinfully fine country but it'd be too high to grow much of anything but hay, do you think?"

I recited yes, that was what I thought. Rob offered nothing.

"So the ticket up there will need to be livestock, ay?" Ay and amen, Lucas. "Cattle, though, you're late to start with this year, with calving already done. You'd be paying for both the cows and their calves and that's a pure dear price. And horses, this country is swimming in horses, the Indians have them and Dantley deals in them and there's this new man Reese with them on Noon Creek. No sense in horses. But I'll tell you lads what may be the thing, and that's sheep. This Two Medicine country maybe was made for sheep. As sure as the pair of you are sitting here with your faces hanging out, sheep are worth some thinking about. Say you had some yearling ewes right now. You'd have the wool money this summer, and both lambs and wool next year. Two revenues are better than one," he informed us. "It's more than interesting, Angus, Ninian Duff saying to you that he's thinking of selling his cattle for sheep. Ninian is a man with an eye for a dollar." Tell us too, Lucas, does a fish swim and will a rock sink and can a bird fly? Why be trotting out this parade of homestead wisdom, when Rob wants none and I've already told you I'm leaving?

Sermon done, we finished eating, or in my case gave up on the task. Lucas swung his head to me and requested: "Angus, would you mind? My chimney."

I fetched his clay pipe, tobaccoed it, and held it to him as he took it with his mouth. After I lit it and he puffed sufficiently, he used a forearm to push it to the accustomed corner of his mouth, then quizzed: "What do you lads think of the sheep notion?"

Rob looked at me but I determinedly kept my mouth clamped. He was the one bending the future to awkward angles, let him be the one to describe its design to Lucas.

Instead, Rob bought himself another minute by jesting, "Sheep sound like the exact thing to have. Now if we only had sheep."

Lucas deployed a pipe cloud at us, and with it said:

"I'll go with you on them."

Neither Rob nor I took his meaning.

"The sheep!" Lucas spelled out impatiently. "I'll partner the two of you in getting sheep. A band of yearling ewes, to start you off with."

Rob sat straight up. Probably I rose some myself. Lucas puffed some more and went right on: "I can back you a bit on the homestead expenses, too. Not endlessly, mind you; don't get the wild idea I'm made of money. But to help you get underway. You pair are going to need to dive right to work, Montana winters come before you know it. I'd say tomorrow isn't too soon for starting. But spend the rest of spring and summer up there at it, and the North Fork will have to make room for you two."

"Lucas, man," Rob burst out, "that's beyond generous." Hesitation was gone from him. This again was the Rob I had come from Nethermuir and Helena with.

"You're for it, Robbie, are you?" Lucas made sure.

"Who wouldn't be? A chance like this?" Somewhere in his mind Rob had to adjust about Nancy. But with her absent to Toussaint's household and Lucas's offer laying like money to be picked up, you could all but hear Rob click with adjustment.

I knew Lucas had one more piece to put into place, and it came, it came.

"There's still one constituency to be heard from," he dispatched benignly around his pipe to me. "What do you say to the idea, Angus? Can I count on you both?"

Lucas Barclay, rascal that you knew how to be even without hands. Your bearded face and Rob's bare bright one waited across that supper table. Waited while my mind buzzed like a hive. *This isn't old Scotland, lads.* Waited for the one answer yet to come, the last answer of that evening and of the time that has ensued from it. *Life goes differently here.* The answer, Lucas, that you and I knew I could not now avoid saying, didn't we?

And say it I did.

"Both."

SCOTCH HEAVEN

*Prophetic indeed was the man who uttered, "You
can fight armies or disease or trespass, but the settler never." Word comes of yet another settlement
of homesteaders in this burgeoning province of
ours. Who can ever doubt, with the influx which is
peopling a childless land and planting schools by
the side of sheep sheds and cattle corrals, that
Choteau County is destined to be the most popu-
lous in Montana? Of this latest colony, situated
into the foothills a dozen or so miles west of Gros
Ventre, it is said so many of the arrivees originated in the land of the kilt and the bagpipe that
Gros Ventrians call the elevated new neighborhood
Scotch Heaven.*
                        —CHOTEAU QUILL, JULY 3, 1890

"**H**OTTER'N NOT, said the Hottentot."

"And what else do you expect, man. Montana is up so high it's
next door to the sun."

"Speaking of high, your lifting muscles are ready, are
they?"

"As ready as they'll ever be." We each grasped an end of the
next log.

"Then here it comes, house. Up she goes. Tenderly, now. Up a
bit with your end. Up up up, that's the direction. A hair more.
Almost there. There. Ready to drop?"

"Let's do."

With a sound like a big box lid closing, the log fell into
place, its notched ends clasping into those of the cabin's side
walls.

"Well?" demanded Rob the log hewer. "Does your end fit?"

I squinted dramatically at the wink of space between the log we had just placed and the one below. "Snug enough. You'll barely be able to toss your cat through the crack."

That brought him in a rush. He eyed along the crevice—which would vanish easily enough when chinked—and lamented, "A tolerant tolerance, my father and Lucas would have called that in the wheelshop. See now, these Montana trees have more knots in them than a sailor's fingers."

"Lucky thing we're just practicing on this house of yours," I philosophized for him. "By the time we build mine, now——"

"Lucky thing for you I'm so much a saint I didn't hear that."

God proctored poor dim old Job about how the measures of the earth were laid. Had Job but been a homesteader, he could have readily answered that the government of the United States of America did it.

The vast public domain westward of the Mississippi River, as Crofutt put the matter for us when Rob and I were somewhere back there on his oceanic border from emigration to immigration, *where the stalwart homesteader may obtain legal title to his land-claim by five years of living upon it and improving it with his building and husbandry labors, has been summed in an idea as simple as it is powerful: the land has been made into arithmetic. This is to say, surveyors have established governing lineations across the earth, the ones extending north and south known as principal meridians and those east-to-west as base lines. Having thus cast the main lines of the net of numeration across half a continent, so to speak, they further divided the area into an ever smaller mesh, first of Ranges measured westward from the meridians and then of townships measured from the base lines. Each township is six miles square, thus totaling thirty-six square miles, and—attend closely for just a few moments more—it is these townships, wherein the individual homesteader takes up his landholding, that the American penchant for systemization fully flowers. Each square mile, called a section, is numbered, in identical fashion throughout all townships, thusly:*

6	5	4	3	2	1
7	8	9	10	11	12
18	17	16	15	14	13
19	20	21	22	23	24
30	29	28	27	26	25
31	32	33	34	35	36

As can be seen, the continuousness of the numeration is reminiscent of the boustrophedon pattern a farmer makes as he plows back and forth the furrows of his field—or, indeed, of the alternate directions in which earliest Greek is written! Thus does the originality of the American experiment, the ready granting of land to those industrious enough to seek it, emulate old efficacious patterns!

Rob's remark at the time was that Crofutt himself verged to Greek here. But upon the land itself, there on the great earthen table of the American experiment, the survey system's lines of logic wrote themselves out so clearly they took your breath away. Why wasn't the rest of humankind's ledger this orderly? Filing our homestead claims of 160 acres apiece, the allowable amount one person could choose out of a square-mile section of 640 acres, amounted merely to finding section-line markers—Ninian Duff could stride blindfolded to every one of them in the North Fork valley—and making the journey to the land office at Lewistown and putting a finger on the registrar's map and saying, this quarter-section is the patch of earth that will be mine. The land has been made into arithmetic indeed. On the Declaration of Applicant there in front of me my land's numbers were registered as *SW ¼ Sec. 31, Tp. 28 N, Rge. 8 W,* on Rob's they were *NE ¼ Sec. 32, Tp. 28 N, Rge. 8 W,* and with our grins at each other we agreed that ink had never said anything better.

Here then is land. Just that, land, naked earthskin. And now the due sum: from this minute on, the next five years of your life, please, invested entirely into this chosen square of earth of yours.

Put upon it house, outbuildings, fences, garden, a well, livestock, haystacks, performing every bit of this at once and irrespective of weather and wallet and whether you have ever laid hand to any of these tasks before. Build before you can plan, build in your sleep and through your mealtimes, but build, pilgrim, build, claimant of the earth, build, build, build. You are permitted to begin in the kind delusion that your utensils of homestead-making at least are the straightforward ones—axe, hammer, adze, pick, shovel, pitchfork. But your true tools are other. The nearest names that can be put to them are hope, muscle and time.

"Ay, Robert, you will eat your fill of wind up here," Ninian Duff brought along as a verdict one forenoon when he rode up to inspect our house progress.

Rob's choice of land was lofty. His homestead claim lay high as it could across the south slope of Breed Butte itself, like a saddle blanket down a horse's side. Those early summer days when we were building his house—we bet the matter of whose to build first on which of a pair of magpies would leave their snag perch sooner, and would you not know, Rob's flew at once—those summer-starting days, all of the valley of the North Fork sat sunlit below Rob's site; and if you strolled a few hundred yards to the brow of the butte each dawn, as I did, you even saw the sun emerge out of the eastward expanse of plains all the way beyond the distant dunelike Sweetgrass Hills.

Rob found Ninian's decree worth a laugh. "Is there somewhere in this country that a man wouldn't have wind in his teeth?"

Even while we three stood gazing, the tall grass of the valley bottom was being ruffled. A dance of green down there, and the might of the mountains above, and the aprons of timber and grazing land between; this would always be a view to climb to, you had to give Rob that. Even Ninian looked softened by it all, his prophetic beard gently breeze-blown against his chest. I was struck enough to announce impromptu: "You did some real choosing when you found us the North Fork, Ninian."

The beard moved back and forth across the chest. "None of us has bragging rights to this country yet."

After Ninian had ridden away and Rob and I climbed up to resume with raftering, there still was some peeve in Rob. He aimed his chin down at the Duff and Erskine homesteads, one-two there beside the creek at the mouth of the valley. "By damn, I didn't come all the miles from one River Street to live down there on another."

"You can see almost into tomorrow from up here, I will say that," saying it against my own inclination in the matter. For, unlike me as it was to be in the same pulpit with Ninian, to my way of thinking, too, this scenery of Rob's had high cost. By choosing so far up onto the butte he was forfeiting the meadow of wild hay that meandered beside the North Fork the full length of the valley, hay that seemed to leap from the ground and play racing games with the wind as we went back to hammering together Rob's roof. And more serious than that, to my mind, he was spurning the creek itself, source for watering livestock. True, at the corner of his land nearest to mine a spring lay under a small brow of butte, like a weeping eye, and Rob gave me to know that I would see the day when he built a reservoir there. But we live in the meantime rather than the sometime and to me a nearness to the creek was the way to begin the world at the right end, in a land as dry as this Montana. Which was why my own homestead selection, southwest from Rob's and just out of view behind the dropping shoulder of Breed Butte, was down into the last of the North Fork valley before foothills and mountains took command of the geography. There at my homestead meadows of wild hay stood fat and green along both sides of the creek, and the bottomland was flat enough beside the clear little stream to work on my house-to-be and its outbuildings in level comfort; for all the open glory of Rob's site, you always were trudging up or down slope here.

But try telling any of this, as I had, to Rob, who assured me in that Barclay future-owning style: "In the eventual, a dab of hay or water more or less won't make the difference. What counts, see now, is that no one can build to the west of me here," and the timbered crest and long rocky shoulder of Breed Butte indeed made that an unlikelihood. "Angus, this butte will be the high road into all the pasture there ever was and I'll be right here on it, am I right?"

There he had me. *Crofutt* notwithstanding, anyone with an eye in his head could see that the key to Scotch Heaven was not our homestead acreage, because no piece of land a half mile long and wide is nearly enough to pasture a band of a thousand sheep on. They'll eat their way across that while you're getting your socks on in the morning. No, it was the miles and miles of free range to the west, the infinity of grass in the foothills and on up into the mountains, that was going to be the larder for our flocks of fortune. Ninian Duff had seen so, and Rob and I, not to mention our treasurer Lucas, could at least puff ourselves that we glimpsed Ninian's vision.

"Our woolly darlings," Rob broke these thoughts now, "can you spot them up there?"

"Just barely. They're grazing up over the shoulder of the butte. One of us is going to have to, again. You know I'd gladly tell you it's my turn, except that it isn't."

Rob swore—sheep will cause that in a man, too—and went down the ladder, the fourth time that morning one or the other of us had to leave off roof work to ride around our zestful new band of yearling ewes and bring them back within safe view.

"Angus, I wish we had oakum to do the chinking with. Make nice dark seams against the logs instead of this clay."

"Toussaint told you how to darken it."

"Considering the cure, I'll accept the ill, thank you just the same." The Toussaint Rennie formula for darkening the chinking clay was: *You take horse manure. Mix it in nice with that clay.*

A buckboard was coming. Coming at speed along the road beside the North Fork, past Duffs' without slowing, past Erskines' just short of flying. It looked like a runaway, but at the trail which led up the butte to us, the light wagon turned as precisely as if running on a railroad track. Then Rob and I saw one of the two figures wave an arm. Arm only, no hand to be seen. Lucas. And Nancy was driving.

The rig, one of Dantley's hires, clattered to a stop just short of running over us and the house. The horses were sweat-wet and appeared astounded at what was happening to them. Behind their reins Nancy seemed as impervious as she did in the kitchen. Lucas was as merry as thick jam on thin bread.

"By Jesus, there's nothing like a buggy ride to stir the blood," he announced as the buckboard's fume of dust caught up with the contingent. "Air into the body, that's the ticket. Angus, lad, you're working yourself thin as a willow. Come to town for some buttermilk one of these evenings." Both arms cocked winglike for balance, Lucas bounded down from the wagon. "So this is your castle, Robbie. I've seen worse, somewhere, sometime."

"You're a fund of compliments," Rob said back, but lightly. "This will do me well enough until I have a house with long stairs."

"And a wife and seven sons and a red dog, ay? That reminds me, lads, Gros Ventre has progress to report," announced Lucas. His stubs were in his coat pockets now, he was wearing his proprietor-of-Montana demeanor. "A stagecoach line! Direct from up there where they're building the Great Northern railroad, to us. What do you say to that? I tell you, our town is coming up in the world so fast it'll knock you over."

There was more than a little I didn't know about stagecoaches, but I had a fair estimate of the population of Gros Ventre and its surroundings. Helena had more people on some of its street corners. "What, they're running a stage line just to Gros Ventre? Where's their profit in that?"

"Oh, the stage goes on to Choteau too," Lucas admitted, "but we'll soon have that place out of the picture."

"Up here we have news of our own," Rob confided happily in turn. "Ninian has had word of three families from the East Neuk of Fife on their way to here."

"Grand, grand," exulted Lucas. "The Scotch are wonderful at living anywhere but in Scotland. I suppose they'll all be Bible-swallowers like Ninian, but nobody's perfect." Lucas rotated himself until he stood gazing south, down the slope of Breed Butte to the North Fork and its clump of willows. Beyond, against the sky, stood the long rimrock wall we now knew was named Roman Reef, and then a more blunt contorted cliff called Grizzly Reef, and beyond Grizzly other mountains stood in rugged file into the Teton River region. "By Jesus, this is the country. Lads, we'll see the day when all this is ranches and farms. And Robbie, you're up in the place to watch it all." A whiff of breeze snatched at Lucas's hat and he clamped an arm stub onto the crown of it. "You'll eat some wind here, though."

While we toured our visitors through the attractions of the homestead and Lucas dispensed Gros Ventre gossip—Sedge and Lila were very nearly ready to open the hotel but couldn't agree what sign to paint on it; Wingo had another new niece—I tried to watch Rob without showing that I was. He was an education, this first time he had been around Nancy since Lucas's bargain made homesteaders of us. So far as Rob showed, Nancy now did not exist. His eyes went past her as if she was not there, his every remark was exclusive to Lucas or to me or to the human race with the exception of one. It was like watching the invention of quarantine.

Nancy's reaction to this new Rob, so far as I could see, was perfectly none. She seemed the exact same Nancy she had been at the first moment Rob and I laid eyes on her in the doorway of Lucas's kitchen, distinct but unreadable. That always unexpected flash of front teeth as she turned toward you, and then the steady dark gaze.

Meanwhile Lucas was as bold as the sun, asking questions, commenting. "Lads, you're a whole hell of a lot further along with all this than I expected you'd be. Do you even put your shadows to work?" Nearly so. Never have I seen a man achieve more labor than Rob did in those first homestead months of ours, and my elbow moved in tandem with his.

Rob gave a pleased smile and said only: "You're just seeing us start."

"I know this homesteading is an uphill effort. At least Montana is the prettiest place in the world to work yourself to death, ay?" Lucas paused at a rear corner of the long low house, to study the way Rob's axework made the logs notch together as snug as lovers holding hands. While Lucas examined, I remembered him in the woodyard in Nethermuir, choosing beech worthy for an axle, ash for shafts, heart of oak for the wagon frame. I could not help but wonder what lasts at the boundaries of such loss. At his empty arm ends, did Lucas yet have memory of the feel of each wood? Were the routes of his fingers still there, known paths held in the air like the flyways of birds?

"And the woollies," Lucas inquired as he and Nancy returned to the wagon. "How are the woollies?"

That was the pregnant question, right enough. The saying is that it takes three generations to make a herdsman, but in the considerable meantime between now and the adept grandson of one or the other of us, Rob and I were having to learn that trying to control a thousand sheep on new range was like trying to herd water. How were the woollies? Innocently thriving when last seen an hour ago, but who knew what they might have managed to do to themselves since.

Rob looked at me and I at him.

"There's nothing like sheep," I at last stated to Lucas.

Lucas and Nancy climbed into the buckboard, ready for the reversal of the whirlwind that brought them from Gros Ventre.

"Well, what's the verdict?" Rob asked in a joking way but meaning it. "Are we worth the investment?"

Lucas looked down at him from the wagon seat.

"So far," he answered, "it seems to be paying off. Pound them on the tail, Nancy, and let's go home."

That first Montana summer of ours was determined to show us what heat was, and by an hour after breakfast each day Rob and I were wearing our salt rings of sweat, crusted into our shirts in three-quarter circles where our laboring arms met our laboring shoulders. Ours was not the only sweat dripping into the North Fork earth. In a single day the arrival of the contingent from Fife almost doubled our valley's population—the Findlater family of five, the young widower George Frew and his small daughter, and George's bachelor cousin Allan. Two weeks later, a quiet lone man named Tom Mortensen took up a claim over the ridge south from my place, and a week after that, a tumbleweed family of Missourians, the Speddersons, alit along the creek directly below Rob. As sudden as that, the valley of the North Fork went from almost empty to homesteaded.

"Who do you suppose invented this bramble?" Barbed wire, that was meant. Neither of us liked the stuff, nor for that matter the idea of corseting our homesteads in it. But the gospel according to Ninian Duff rang persuasive: *If you don't fence, you will one morning wake up and find yourself looking into the faces of five hundred Double W cows.*

"Never mind that, why didn't they invent ready-made postholes to go with it?"

Rob and I were at my homestead. We had bedded the sheep on the ridge and come on down to wrestle a few more postholes into my eternal west fenceline before dark. There were occasional consequences from nature for decreeing lines on the earth as if by giant's yardstick, and one of them was that the west boundary of my homestead claim went straight through a patch of rock that was next to impossible to dig in. Small enough price, I will still tell you all these grunted postholes later, to have the measures of the earth plainly laid for you; but at the time—

"Now, you know the answer to that. A homestead is only 160 acres and that's nowhere nearly enough room to pile up all the postholes it needs."

"Dig. Just dig."

Can a person be happy while he's weary in every inch of himself? Right then, I was. I entirely liked my homestead site. Maybe you could see around the world and back again from Rob's place on Breed Butte, but mine was no blinkered location. Ridges, coulees, Roman Reef in the notch at the west end of the valley, the peak called Phantom Woman, the upmost trees on Breed Butte—all could be seen from my yard-to-be. The tops of things have always held interest for me. Rob's house was just out of view behind the shoulder of the ridge. Indeed, no other homesteads could be seen from mine, and for some reason I liked that, too.

"Digging holes into the night this way—back in Nethermuir they'd think we're a pair of prime fools."

"We're the right number for it, you have to admit."

Dusk slowly came, into this country so appropriate for dusk—the tan and gray of grass and ridge looking exactly right, the soft tones a day should end with. This time of evening the gullies blanked themselves into shadow, the ridgelines fired themselves red with the last sunset embers. But we were here to make homesteads, not watch sunsets. And by the holy, we were getting them made. Just as soon as Rob's house was done we began on our sheep shed, at the lower end of my homestead for handiness to the creek. The shed work we interrupted with the shearing crew for our sheep. We finished the wool work just in time to join with Ninian and Donald in putting up hay for the winter. Any moment free from haying, we were devoting to building fencelines. And someway amid it all we were hewing and laying the logs of my house, to abide by the spirit of the homestead law, even though I was going to share the first winter under Rob's roof; we were reasonably sure President Harrison wouldn't come riding over the ridge to check on my residency.

Full dark was not far from being on us but we wanted to finish my fenceline. Between bouts with shovel and crowbar and barbed wire, we began to hear horses' hooves, more than one set.

"Traffic this time of day?" Rob remarked as we listened. "Angus, what are you running here, an owl farm?"

We recognized the beanpole figure of Ninian Duff first among the four who rode out of the deep dusk, long before he called out: "Robert and Angus, good evening there. You're a pair who chases work into the night."

"It's always waiting to be chased," Rob said back. I ran a finger around the inside leather of my hat, wiping the sweat out. Besides

Ninian the squadron proved to be Donald Erskine and the new man Archie Findlater and a settler from the South Fork, Willy Hahn. Every kind of calamity that could put men on saddle leather at the start of night was crossing my thoughts. Say for Ninian, you did not have to stand on one foot and then the other to learn what was on his mind.

"Angus, we've come to elect you."

I blinked at that for a bit, and saw Rob was doing the same. *What was I, or my generation, / that I should get such exaltation?* "Elected, is it," I managed at last. "Do I get to know to what?"

"The school board, of course," Ninian stated. "There are enough families herearound that we need a proper school now, and we're going to build one."

"But—but I'm not a family man."

"Ay, but you were a teacher once, over across, and that will do. We want you for the third member of our school board."

"Together with—?"

"Myself," Ninian pronounced unabashedly, "and Willy here." Willy Hahn nodded and confirmed, "You are chust the man, Anguss."

"The old lad of parts!" Rob exclaimed, and gave my shoulder a congratulatory shove. "He'll see to it that your youngsters recite the rhyming stuff before breakfast, this one."

"That fact of the matter is," Ninian announced further, "what we need done first, Angus, is to advertise for a teacher. Can you do us a letter of that? Do it, say, tomorrow?"

I said I could, yes, and in the gathering dark there at my west fenceline the school was talked into shape. Because of their few years' headstart in settlement, the South Fork families had a margin more children of schoolable age than did Scotch Heaven, and so it was agreed to build the schoolhouse on their branch of the creek.

"You here in Scotch Heafen will haff to try hard to catch up with uss," Willy Hahn joked.

"Some of us already are," came back Ninian Duff, aiming that at the bachelorhood of Rob and me.

"The rest of us are just saving up for when our turn comes," Rob contributed. That drew a long look from Ninian, before he and the other three rode away into the night.

It was morning of the third week of August, still a month of summer ahead on the calendar, when I came in from the outhouse with my shoes and the bottoms of my pantlegs damp.

Yawning, Rob asked: "What, did you miss your aim?"

I almost wished I had, instead of the fact to be reported: "Frost on the grass."

That forehint of North Fork winter concentrated our minds mightily. In the next weeks we labored even harder on Rob's outbuildings and fences, and when not on those, on the schoolhouse or on my house; and when not any of those, we were with the sheep, keeping a weather eye on the cloudmaking horizon of the mountains. Soon enough—too soon—came the morning when the peaks showed new snow like white fur hung atop.

On the day when Donald Erskine's big wagon was to be borrowed for getting our winter's provisions in Gros Ventre, we bet magpies to see which of us would go. Mine flew first from the gate. "Man, you're sneaking out here and training them," Rob accused. But off he went to the sheep and I pointed my grin toward Gros Ventre.

The Medicine Lodge was empty but for Lucas. "Young Lochinvar is come out of the west," he greeted me, and produced an instant glass between his stubs and then a bottle.

"What's doing?" I inquired.

"Not all that much. People are scarce this time of year, busy with themselves. We'll soon have snowflakes on our heads, do you know, Angus."

"We will and I do," I answered, and drank.

"You and Robbie are ready for old winter, are you?"

"Ready as we'll ever be, we think."

"Winter can be thoroughly wicked in this country. I've seen it snow so that you couldn't make out Sedge's flagpole across there. And my winters here haven't been the worst ones by far. Stories they tell of the '86 winter would curl your dohickey."

"I'll try not hear them, then."

"You and Robbie have worked wonders on those homesteads of yours, I have to say. Of course I could tell from the moment the pair of you walked in here that you were going to be a credit to the community."

"Credit. Do you know, Lucas, there's the word I was going to bring up with you."

"Angus, Angus, rascal you." Shaking his head gravely, Lucas poured a drink for himself and another for me. His toast, odd, was the old one of Scottish sailors: "Wives and sweethearts."

After our tipple, Lucas resumed: "What do you and Robbie do, sit up midnights creating ways to spend my money? What's the tariff this time?"

"Pennies for porridge. We need groceries enough to get us through the winter, is all."

"All, you say. You forget I've seen you two eat."

"Well, we just thought if you maybe were to mortgage the Medicine Lodge and your second shirt—"

"I surrender, Angus. Tell Kuuvus to put your groceries on my account. By Jesus, you and Robbie would have to line up with the coyote pups for supper on the hind tit if I didn't watch over you."

"We might yet, if half of what you and Ninian keep saying about winter comes true."

"Put me in the same camp with Ninian, do you. There's a first time. How is old Jehovah Duff? Still preaching and breeding?"

"In point of fact, Flora does have a loaf in the oven. As does Jen Erskine. As does Grace Findlater. If our neighbors are any example to the sheep, we're going to have a famous lamb crop come spring."

"Lambs and lasses and lads," Lucas recited with enthusiasm. "By Jesus, we'll build this country into something before it knows it." I raised an eyebrow at his paternal "we" there. Lucas raised it a good deal higher for me by declaring next: "Angus, I believe you need to think of a woman."

"I do, do I." Truth known, on my mind right then was the visit I was going to make to Wingo's niecery as soon as I was finished with other provisioning. "Along any particular lines, do you recommend?"

"I'm talking now about a wife. All right, all right, you can give me that look saying I'm hardly the one to talk. But the situation of Nancy and myself is—well, not usual." That was certainly so. "You're young and hale and not as ugly as you could be," he swept on, "and so what's against finding a wife for yourself, ay? I tell you, if I were you now—"

"Just half a moment, before you get to being me too strenuously. What brings this on?" It wasn't like Lucas to suddenly speak up for womanhood at large. "Is this what you're prescribing today for all your customers?"

"Just the redheaded ones." My eyebrow found a new direction

to cock itself. Why was I the subject of this sermon instead of Rob? He was the one Lucas had needed to negotiate away from Nancy.

"Oh, I know what you're thinking," and as usual, he did. "But that's another case entirely, our Robbie. The first bright mare who decides to twitch her tail at Robbie, she'll have him. He's my own nephew, but that lad is sufficiently in love with himself that it won't much matter who he marries. Whoever she is, she'll never replace him in his own affections. You though, Angus. You're not so much a world unto yourself. You, I'd say, need the right partner in this old life."

I hoped the Lucas Barclay Matrimonial Bureau was about to close for the day. "I'm already in partnership with a pair of Barclays," I pointed out, "which seems to keep me occupied twenty-five hours a day eight days a week."

"Mend your tongue," Lucas answered lightly, but with a glance that seemed to wonder whether I'd heard any word he'd been saying. "Robbie and I'll have you so prosperous you can take your pick of womanhood. But who's that going to be, ay? It wouldn't hurt you a bit to start thinking in that direction."

"And was Lucas in fettle?" asked Rob as we unloaded the wagon of groceries.

"Lucas was Lucas," I attested, "and then some."

Was it a long winter Rob and I put in together, that first homestead one? Yes, ungodly so. And no, nothing of the sort. How time can be a commodity that lets both of those be equally true, I have never understood.

November and December only snowed often enough to get our attention, but the North Fork had ice as thick as a fist and we were chopping a water hole for the sheep and our workhorses each morning. Of course that was the time of the year the bucks were put with the ewes to breed spring lambs, and so at least there was warm behavior in the pastures, so to speak.

"See now, McAngus, don't you just wish it was spring? To watch those lambs come—man, it'll be like picking up money along the road."

"That's what it had better be like, or we're going to be in debt to Lucas down to our shoe soles."

You might not think it, but with winter we saw more of the other homesteaders than ever. People neighbored back and forth by horse and sled to escape cabin fever, and no more than a few weeks ever passed without Scotch Heaven having a dance that brought out everyone, for even the Duffs and Erskines were not so skintight they could resist waving a foot to a tune. I thought many a time that to watch Ninian on the dance floor was like hearing a giggle out of God.

Not, let me say, that Ninian got all that much of my watching that winter, nor Rob's nor George Frew's nor Allan Frew's nor old Tom Mortensen's either. We of the bachelor brigade were too busy appreciating that Scotch Heaven's balance sheet of men and women was less uneven than it had been, with the teacher Mavis Milgrim and Archie Findlater's sister Judith, newly come from Scotland, now on hand. Miss Milgrim always had a starch to her that she thought a schoolma'am had to have, and Judith Find-later had a startling neck that was not so much swanlike as goose-like, but they helped the situation of the sexes, they helped. Most especially Judith. She was a sweet, quiet woman, of the kind in the old saying *she's better than she's bonny*, and there were moments at those dances when I had to wonder whether she was that prescription of Lucas's for me. Along those lines, the single time I found a decent chance to get Judith aside and coax a kiss out of her, she delivered one that I could feel all the way to my ears.

Something to put away for spring, although whenever I looked in a mirror I still was not seeing anything that resembled marriage.

When the last day of the calendar came—no Hogmanay com-memorative portrait of Rob and myself this year, except the one that memory draws—we were invited down to see out the eve at the Duffs', together with the five Erskines and the six Findlaters, as many people as could breathe in one house that size. The right way to bridge years, in company with those we had come to know best in our homestead effort. Donald Erskine was a fretful man, who changed his mind so often he went around half-dizzy. Yet Donald would leap a mile to your aid, letting his own work stand while he pitched in on yours. Ninian Duff on the other hand would think three times before offering to lend you the sleeves of his vest, but there was no one more sound in advice than God's solemn brother Ninian. Their wives Jen and Flora were equally broad women, grown wide as wagons in childbearing, and each as capable as a mother lion. Archie Findlater was a plump man, like a grouse—I admit, his roundness caused me to wonder what Judith's future shape would be—but sharp in his head, a calculator. Grace Findlater did the talking of their household, but as she was the one person in Scotch Heaven who could quote more verse than I could, I figured she had every right.

As midnight neared, there was acclamation from all these, led by Judith with a bit more enthusiasm than I was comfortable with that I of course had to be one to first-foot the new year in for Ninian and Flora.

"Can't I wait for a year when the weather is better out there?" I protested. But at a minute before 1891, out I went into the cold blustery middle of the night.

I stood alone there in the mountainous dark where weather comes from, where years come from. Then turned myself around to the homestead house.

"Now there's a year's worth of good luck if I ever saw him," announced Rob after I stepped back in across the Duff threshold without a word, strode to the stove and poked the fire into brisker flame. Not that any of us at all believed the superstition about a tall unspeaking man who straightway tended the hearth fire being the year's most propitious first foot, but still.

"He will do," granted Ninian, while Flora handed us steaming cups of coffee with just a tip of whiskey therein. "Warm yourselves, you may need it riding home."

"What do you make of this weather, Ninian?" I wondered. By the sound of it the wind was whooping harder every minute. "A squall, is this?"

"It may be. Or it may be the start of winter."

For the next eight days, all the wind in the world tore at Scotch Heaven. We had wind that took the hay as we struggled to feed the sheep, wind that coated us and the workhorses with snow, wind every breath of the day and wind in our sleep.

And then came cold. Probably Rob and I were lucky not to know until later that from the tenth of January until the twenty-second, Donald Erskine's thermometer never rose above fifteen below zero.

"Angus, you're my favorite man, but there are times when I wish your name was Agnes."

This was ribald from Rob. I gave him back: "What times are

those, I wonder? January can't be one, surely. A month of snow-white purity—"

"You say snow one more time and you'll be out in it."

Winter engines, us now. The pale smoke of Rob's breath as he chopped ice from the waterhole, I could see from the top of the haystack two hundred yards away. As our workhorses Sadie and Brandy pulled the haysled in a great slow circle in the snow while we fed the hay off, they produced regular dragonsnort. Our exertions were not the only ones there in the air; there was the whacking sound of Tom Mortensen at his woodpile over the ridge from my place, and the spaced clouts of George Frew next down the creek breaking out the water hole for his livestock. It was a new way to live, bundled and laborious and slow, oddly calm, and you had to wonder how Eskimos put up with it all the time.

A Saturday of February. The day had been blue and still. Rob's whistling was the liveliest element around. We had not been to Gros Ventre since Christmas, and we were preparing to remedy that. Haircuts had been traded, baths had been taken, boots blacked with stovelid soot. Mustaches were our winter project, which meant meticulous trimming. We were putting on our clean shirts when a white gust was flung past the south windows, as if someone had begun plucking geese.

"Don't be that way," Rob told the weather.

"Probably it's only a flurry."

"It had better be."

It was not. The snow drove and drove, sifting out of the silent sky as if to bury the planet. In minutes the west window to the mountains was caked white.

"That's that, then," Rob admitted at last. "Goodbye, Gros Ventre."

"We'll go twice next time." That was brighter than I felt, for I was as keen as Rob for a meal cooked by Lila Sedge, for a drink poured by Lucas, for talk in the air of the Medicine Lodge, for what waited at Wingo's.

"Next time is the story of homesteading, I'm beginning to think," Rob gloomed.

"You're coming down with winter fever. Elk stew is the only known antidote." Or at least the only supper we had now that Lila Sedge's cuisine was out of the picture.

"Lord of mercy, man. No town, and now Ninian's elk that bends forks?"

"The same famous one." The bull elk shot by Ninian was so elderly he had a set of antlers that would have scaffolded Canterbury Cathedral. "Old Elky, grandfather of beasts."

"And enemy of teeth. Tell me again the price of mutton."

I raised my thumb to him. "One, the cost of a sheep herself." Then extended my first finger. "Two, the cost of the hay she's eaten so far this winter." Next finger. "Three, the loss of her lamb next spring." Next finger. "Four, the loss of her fleece next summer." Final finger. "Five, explaining to Lucas that we've been sitting out here eating an animal he put up good money for."

Rob studied my display. "McAngus, if you had more fingers on that hand, you'd have more reasons too. All right, all right, the sheep are safe again. Elk stew by popular demand."

To cheer him up while I heated the familiar stew, I resorted to: "Surely you've never heard the story about Methuselah and his cook?"

"This weather has me to the point where I'll listen to anything. Tell away."

"Well, Methuselah's cook got tired of cooking for that houseful. All those begattings, more and more mouths at every meal—a couple of hundred years of that and you can see how it would start to get tiresome. So she went to Methuselah and said, 'What about some time off, like?' 'No, no, no,' he tells her, 'we can't possibly spare you, you're too good a cook. In all these years have I ever complained once about your food?' She had to admit he hadn't. 'No, nor will I,' he says. 'If you ever hear me complain, I'll do the cooking myself, for the rest of my life.'

"The cook went away thinking about that. Methuselah was only around four hundred years old at the time, still doing all that begatting, and he looked as if he maybe had another five hundred years or so in him. The cook kept thinking, five hundred years off from all that cooking if she could just get Methuselah to complain. So the next morning for breakfast, the first thing she does is put a handful of salt in Methuselah's coffee and send it out to the table. Methuselah takes a big swallow and spews it right back out. The cook starts to take her apron off. *'By Jehovah!'* he says, and she can hear him coughing and sputtering, *'the coffee is full of salt!'* She's just ready to step out of that kitchen forever when she hears him say: *'Just the way I like it!'*"

After laughter, Rob went quiet during the meal. I was hoping that after the last bite of elk he might put down his fork and proclaim *Just the way I like it*, but no, the evening was not going to be that easy. He pushed back his chair and said instead: "Angus, do you know what I think?"

"When it starts out that way, probably not."

"I think we need more sheep."

"What, so we can eat some? Rob, it won't be elk forever. As soon as we can get to town—"

"I'm serious here," Rob attested. "More sheep would be just the ticket we need, is what I think."

"If I understand right what those bucks were doing to those ewes, we're pretty soon going to have more."

"Not just the lambs, man. We ought to be thinking about buying more ewes. Another five hundred, maybe another thousand. It can't be that much more trouble to run two thousand sheep than it is a thousand."

"It's twice the hay, though." My meadows were just enough to get us through a winter such as this, if we were lucky. "Where's that going to come from?"

"We can buy it. Jesse Spedderson would a lot rather sell us his hay standing in the field than exert himself to put it up, I'll bet you this kitchen table on that."

"Say he does, then. What do we use to buy these famous further sheep with?" Although I thought I knew.

"We'll get Lucas to back us."

"Rob, we're already in debt to Lucas a mile deep."

"Angus, look at it this way: if we're going to be in debt, Lucas is our best choice anywhere around. Naturally there's a bit of risk, taking on more sheep. But if you're going to homestead, you have to take risk, am I right?"

I peered over at him, to be sure this was the same Rob who had been ready to spurn the North Fork for going in with Fain in the blacksmith shop.

"These sheep we have now can be just the start of us, man," he galloped right on. "That's why it was worth coming from Scotland. Worth even finding Lucas—the way he is. His hands maybe are gone but none of his head went with them. No, Lucas has the fact of it. This Two Medicine country will grow. It's bound to. And we're in on the ground floor."

I directed his attention to the white outside the window. "Actually we may be down in the cold cellar."

"Angus, Angus. By damn, I wish it was spring. You'd be in a brighter mood, and you'd see in a minute what I'm talking about here."

If my ears were to be trusted, he was talking about the theory of sheep, which is the world's best. In theory a band of sheep is a garden on legs. Every spring a crop of lambs, every summer a crop of wool. Feed us and clothe us, too; not even potatoes yield so beneficially. But the fleecies are a garden that wanders around looking for its own extinction, and in the Two Medicine country there were many sources willing to oblige their mortal urge. Coyotes, bear, cliffs, blizzards, death camas, lupine. Not least, themselves. I can tell you to this moment the anguish when, the second day after we had trailed our yearlings home to the North Fork from their former owner in the Choteau country, Rob and I found our first dead sheep. A fine fat ewe on her back, four legs in the air like hooved branches. In her clumsy cocoon of wool she had rolled helplessly onto her back when she lay down to scratch a tick itch and couldn't right herself again. Rob was shocked, and I admit I was a bit unsettled myself. And as any sheep owner must, we began thinking the terrifying arithmetic: what if we lose another ewe two days from now . . . Lord of mercy, what if we lose one again *tomorrow* . . . A little of that and in your mind you soon not only have no sheep left, you possess even fewer than that—cavities of potential loss of however many sheep you could ever possibly buy to replace the ones that right now are out there searching for ways to die. Thus you draw breath and try to think instead of the benefits of sheep. Watch them thrive on grass a cow wouldn't even put its head down for. Watch the beautiful fleeces, rich and oily to the touch, unfold off them as they are sheared. Dream ahead to when you can watch your first crop of lambs enlarge themselves week by week. As Rob was doing now in his winter rhapsody about more sheep. But I didn't want that tune, expensive as it promised to be, to get out of hand, and so I responded:

"Rob, I see that we don't even know yet if we're going to get through this winter with *these* sheep alive, let alone twice that many that we don't have."

"With an attitude like that," he retorted a bit quick and sharp, "you're not looking ahead beyond the end of your nose, you know."

And you're looking right past all the precipices there are, I thought but managed not to say. This was new. Usually when Rob and I disagreed it was about some speck of a matter that was gone by the next day. Even during our months here in the white cave of Montana winter, our most spirited argument had been over whose turn it was to bring in the firewood. But I knew too well that if Rob Barclay decided to believe in a thing as if it were fairy gold, words weren't an antidote. I shook my head now, both at Rob and at the silliness of us filling the kitchen with debate about phantom sheep. "You're working hard on the wrong source here," I pointed out to him. "It's Lucas's wallet you're going to have to persuade."

"I can see winter isn't the season to reason with you," he gave me back. "Let's talk this over in the spring, what do you say."

"I say, knowing you, we're sure to talk it over, all right."

That at last drew a smile and a short laugh from him, and he got up and went to the south window. The snow no longer was flailing past, but clouds covered the mountains, and more storm was only minutes away.

"McAngus, who of your old poets called clouds the sacks of heaven?"

"*Undo the silver sacks of heaven,/seed the sky with stars./See every gleam grow to seven,/*something something *Mars.* I can't think now, which."

"He ought to be shot," Rob stated.

Then in March, this.

"There. Hear that?" We were feeding the sheep their hay beside the North Fork, on a morning as icy as any of the winter had been.

"Hear what? The sound of me pitching hay and you standing there with your ears hanging out?"

"There, that rushing sound up in the mountains. That's new."

"Just the wind."

"What wind? There isn't a breath of one."

"Running water, then?"

"That creek is frozen stiffer than I am."

"Creature, maybe?"

"Making a noise that size? We'd better hope not."

The sheep began to raise their heads from the hay, nosing the air.

"They hear it, too."

"Listen. Isn't it getting louder?"

Off came our flap caps, not just for keener listening but because the air strangely no longer seemed chilly. In minutes the great flowing sound was dispensing itself down from the peaks and crags as a sudden stiff breeze, but a breeze warm all through. A day that had been firmly fifteen degrees below zero began to feel tropical. As we finished the pitchfork work we had to shed our scarves, then our coats. Not until Rob and I talked with Ninian a few days later, the snow already gone from every south slope and elsewhere retreating down into its deep coulee drifts, did we learn the word of that miracle wind, which was chinook. But driving the haysled home from the sheep on that chinook day, our gloves next off, the two of us kept flexing our pale winter hands, one and then the other as if shedding old skin, in that astonishing blowing air of springtime.

In the after years, Rob always made the jest that the winter with me was what caused him to marry Judith Findlater.

"Your cooking, of course I mean to say, Angus. Every recipe you knew was elk, do you remember. Judith brought one of her mince pies to a dance and I was a gone gosling."

I laughed ritually each time, but what Lucas had forecast about Rob's route into marriage always tinged the moment. For I did see it come, Judith's quiet sorting of us during her husband-looking winter—me too wary and waitful, George Frew so gawkishly silent, Allan Frew too irresponsible, Tom Mortensen too old and bachelorly, but Rob bright and winnable, Rob always pleased to find himself reflected back in someone's attention. When Archie Findlater came that March to ask Rob for a few days' skilled help in building lambing pens, work which anybody who could fit fingers around a hammer could do, and mentioned "Take your meals with us too, why not, and save yourself the ride back and forth," he may as well have brought Judith and the marriage license with him.

The wedding, in almost-warm-enough weather you could step into blindfolded and know it was May in Montana, was in Rob's front yard. All of Scotch Heaven assembled there under the crest of Breed Butte for the valley's first matrimony, and as best man I had the closest look of anyone except the minister at how Rob and Judith gleamed for each other. He was newly dismustached and his smile seemed all the fresher. Judith already looked wifely, quietly natural beside Rob. He'd teased her beforehand that when the major question came he was going to respond, "Can I toss a coin to decide that?" But when the moment arrived, Rob spoke out "I do" as if telling it to generations before and aft.

Afterward we ate and danced and talked and danced and drank and danced. As evening came on, before heading home I got Rob and Judith aside to congratulate them one last time.

"For people who just got married beyond redemption, you both look happy enough about it," I assessed for their benefit.

"You're the best best man there could be," Judith nicely assured me and rose on tiptoes to kiss my cheek while Rob warned merrily, "Not too much of that, now."

Riding toward home with the bunch from the wedding, I took full notice that the May dusk was telling us the lengthened days of summer were truly on their way, but otherwise I heard with only half an ear the jokes and chat that were being passed around. Until silent George Frew and I swung off together on the trail to our homesteads. Then George, who was sloshing a bit with the amount of wedding drink in him, jerked his head back toward Breed Butte and blurted: "They're at it now."

No doubt Rob and Judith were. I'd have been, in Rob's place. But George's whiskeyed words set off something in me. I rode home thinking over whether I ought to have made the maneuvers—maybe I flattered myself, but I believed it would not have taken any too many—that would have put me in Rob's place. And decided again, no. The same voice in me that said all winter about Judith, *not yet, not this one,* was saying even stronger now, *wait, let time tell.* Oh, I knew that all you can count on in life is your fingers and toes, but I was determined to do marriage as right as I could when I did it at all. Did I have an enlarged sense of carefulness, where weddings were concerned? Maybe, but I felt it had grown naturally in me. My parents' case, a marriage locked in ice whenever it wasn't shaking with thunder, was not anything I intended to repeat. No, there had to be better than that. And the matrimonial exchange I had just witnessed on Breed Butte: Judith bagging a husband, Rob pocketing a wife. I hated even to think it of two people I so prized, but there had to be better than that, too. A high idea, maybe, but the North Fork valley around me and the strong mountains over me seemed the place for such a thought. If better could not be done here, on new land on a new continent, myself a new version of a McCaskill—the American version—where could it ever be done?

Say you are a stone that blinks once a year, when the sun of spring draws the last of winter from you. In the wink that is 1891, you see nine houses in the valley of the North Fork where there had been but those two of the Duff and Erskine homesteads. You note the retreat of timber on Wolf Butte where Rob and myself and Archie Findlater and Jesse Spedderson and old Tom Mortensen and the Frew cousins George and Allan sawed lodgepole pines to build those houses. You notice lines of new fence encasing each of Scotch Heaven's homesteads, straight and taut as mesh. You see Vinia Spedderson's laundry flying from a hayrack, to the disgust of the other wives. You see the Erskine boy Davie riding his pony along the creek as if in a race with the breeze-blown hay.

Your next glimpse, 1892, shows you newborn Ellen, the first of Rob and Judith's girls. You see slow-grazing scatters of gray which are the sheep of one or another of us, maybe mine and Rob's working the grassy foothills west of my homestead, maybe the new band belonging to Rob and Lucas there on the slope of Breed Butte. (Were not stones famously deaf, you would have heard Rob try to the end to persuade me to come in with him and Lucas on that second thousand of sheep, *Angus, you're thinking small instead of tall, I'm disappointed in you, man;* and from me, to whom deeper debt did not look like the kind of prosperity I wanted, *Rob, if this is the first time or the last I disappoint you, you're lucky indeed.*) You see rain booming on the roofs in the rare two-day May downpour that brought the North Fork twice the crop of hay any of us had expected or imagined. You behold Ninian Duff coming home from town with a bucket of calcimine, and you watch as every Scotch Heaven household, mine included, quickly whitens a wall here or there.

And now in your third blink, 1893, you notice an occasional frown as we lords of sheep hear how the prices are beginning to drop in the distant wool and lamb markets. You see my life as it was for the rest of that year, achieveful yet hectic as all homestead years seemed to be, tasks hurrying at each other's heels: turn out the last bunch of ewes and their fresh lambs onto new pasture and the garden needs to be put in; do that, and fence needs mending; mend that, and it is shearing time; shear the beloved woollies, and it is haying time. You see me look up, somewhere amid it all, to a buck-board arriving, drawn by Ninian Duff's team of matched bay horses.

On the seat beside Ninian perched Willy Hahn. School board business, this could only be.

Ninian pulled his bays to a halt and announced down to me: "News, Angus. We've lost our teacher. George Frew is marrying her." With the school year so close on us, Ninian was saying what was in our three minds in the last of his pronouncement: "Maybe she can teach him to speak up sooner."

"So we've a fast advertisement to write, have we?" I responded. "Come down and come in, I'll—"

Ninian interrupted, "In point of fact, Willy and I already have located a replacement teacher. Haven't we now, Willy?" Willy dipped his head yes. "More than that even," Ninian swept on, "we've voted to hire." Willy dipped again.

I was peeved to hear this. By damn, I was more than that. These two old puffed-up whiskerheads. "Well, then. Since the pair of you are running the school board so aptly without me, we haven't any-thing more to talk about, now have we. Don't let me keep you here, busy persons like yourselves."

Ninian winked solemnly to Willy. "The man doesn't see it."

"What's to see?" I blazed. "You two parade in here and—"

"Anguss," Willy put in mildly. "It iss you we voted to hire."

Ordain me here and now as the Lord High Kafoozalum and I would be no more surprised than I was to be made the South Fork schoolteacher. Not that there was ever any supposition I was the pedagogical genius the world had been seeking since Jesus went upstairs; after all, back there in Nethermuir I had only ever been the pupil-teacher assisting Adam Willox, never the actual master of a schoolroom. What designated me now, as Willy and Ninian cheer-fully made plain, was that time was short and I was nearest.

"Temporary, just for the year," Ninian assured me as if school-teaching could be done with my little finger.

"Can't Flora fill the situation as well as I can?" I astutely retorted to him, citing the only other person in the vicinity who had experi-ence at standing at the front of a classroom. Willy tittered, cast a glance toward Ninian on the wagon seat beside him, then looked down at me severely. Which caused me to remember that Flora Duff was currently a prominent six months in the family way.

Ninian and Willy proceeded to argue qualm after qualm out of me. Yes, they would see to it that I had help with my homestead tasks as needed. Yes yes, they would put in a word with Rob about the necessity of adjusting our sheep arrangement if I took the school. Yes yes yes, they would find someone more suitable for the position next year.

"There is of course the matter of the teacher's wage," Ninian at last found around to, and there he met me coming, I do have to admit. That year of 1893 was the sour kind that we hadn't known was in the calendar of America. Prices of wool and lambs both were falling through the floor while I still was trying to climb out of Lucas's wallet. And be it said if it needs to, no homesteader was ever his own best paymaster. Besides, I had come across the bend of the world looking for a different life, had I? The one thing certain about a year as the South Fork teacher was that it would be different.

"All right, then," I acquiesced to my electors. "If you haven't come to your senses in the last minute, I'm your schoolkeeper for this year."

"Anguss, you are chust the man," Willy ratified, and I swear Ninian very nearly smiled at me.

That first South Fork morning. The Hahn brothers were the earliest to trudge down the road toward the waitful school and waitful me, dragging with them the invisible Gibraltar of burden of having a father on the school board. The children from the other families of that branch of the creek as well, the Petersons and Roziers and Van Bebbers, all lived near enough to walk to school and soon they were ricocheting around outside in those double-quick games that erupt before the class day takes everyone captive. I turned from the window for one last inventory of my schoolroom. Desk rows across the room. Blackboard and a roll-down map of the world fastened above. Framed portraits of Washington and Lincoln, men whose lives I knew only the vaguest of, staring stoically at each other on the far wall. I hammered days of nails when this schoolhouse was built, I came here many a time with Ninian and Willy to tend to our teacher, I had danced on this schoolroom's floor, mended its roof. Yet I tell you, it was a place foreign to my eyes as I waited for the minute when it would fill with pupils. My pupils.

For the dozenth time I looked at the alarm clock ticking on my solitary desk at the front of the schoolroom. This time it told me I had to ring the bell to begin school, even though a significant half of my pupil population hadn't yet appeared.

Ring I did.

In trooped the South Fork boys and girls.

I hemmed and hawed and had them take temporary seats until the others arrived.

But still no others.

Accident? Boycott? Jest of the gods? Possibilities trotted around in me until I needed to do what I had been resisting, retreat out onto the porch and peer up the North Fork road. With me went the echo of Lucas's reaction to my new and quite possibly stillborn career: *By Jesus, Angus, you're the first swamper the Medicine Lodge ever had that's turned out to be a schoolmarm.* Maybe I was in over my head, trying to be schoolkeeper as well as homesteader as well as sheep partner with Rob. Maybe . . .

Here they came, the child cavalry of Scotch Heaven. The three Findlaters on a fat white horse named Snowy. Susan Duff regal on one of Ninian's blood bay geldings. Jimmy Spedderson on a beautiful blazeface black worth more than the rest of the Speddersons' homestead combined. George Frew's daughter Betsy on an elderly sorrel. Davie Erskine on his fast-stepping roan with small sister Rachel clinging behind him.

I let out a breath of thanks. But to show them I did not intend for tardiness to become habit, I stood conspicuously waiting while they put their horses on picket ropes. Already there on a length of grazing tether was the Dantley mare Patch that I still rode, and with all our horses picketed around the schoolhouse, the scene suddenly hit me as one of life's instants I had been through before—Rob and I gawking at the Floweree outfit's cow camp the day we arrived green as peas into Gros Ventre. I reminded myself how greatly more veteran in life I was by now, and tried to believe it in the face of what advanced on me here, Susan Duff.

She poised below me as if bearing a message from Caesar. "We cut through our lower field and couldn't get the gate open and the top loop was too tight and barbwire besides," she reported in funereal tones. "My father will need to fix that gate." Unaccountably my spirits rose as I thought of Ninian having to deal with this daughter. "Meg Findlater's nose is running and she doesn't have a hanky, and Davie Erskine forgot to bring his and Rachel's lunch." This seemed to conclude Susan's docket, and up the porch steps and into the schoolhouse she marched with the other Scotch Heaven children in a straggle behind her.

I kick myself yet for not anticipating the next snag of that morning, although I am not sure what I could have done about it. My gender. In Scotland schoolmasters were thick on the ground. But here, having a man teacher proved to be an unexpected thought to pupils accustomed to Miss Milgrim. The larger boys were plainly restless about me, and I was afraid little Meg Findlater's eyes would pop from her head every time I leaned far down to bring my handkerchief to the rescue of her nose.

My predecessor still governessed that schoolroom in another way, too. After I had everyone sorted and seated and the littlest ones were more or less occupied with the new things called desks and books, I started on my upper grades in what I thought was peerless emulation of Socrates, "Tell me, anyone please, the presidents from Washington to Lincoln."

I drew back stares.

There I stood wondering what had taken their tongues, until Susan Duff informed me that it was the practice of Miss Milgrim to tell the pupils such matters as the presidents to Lincoln, while they listened.

"That's as may be, Susan. But I look very little like Miss Milgrim, don't I, and so I need to do things my own way. Now who'll tell the presidents, Washington to Lincoln?"

A silence deep as a corner of eternity. As the silence yawned on, my only immediate hope was Susan again. But a look at her told me she had lent me all the instruction she currently intended to.

This tiny box of school, on the universe's ocean. How could we in here ever hope to know enough to get by on, let alone improve the race at all? I despaired and was starting to reach for the chalk and begin listing presidents, anything to stir this congealed schoolroom, when I heard:

"Hickory Jackson."

I turned, blinking. Davie Erskine was regarding me with a helpfulness that managed to be vague and earnest at the same time. I'd made mental note to share my lunch with him and his little sister Rachel; this opening effort of Davie's resolved me to give them it all. Taking my surprise for encouragement, the boy visibly searched around in his head some more. After a while:

"Quincy Adams."

Yet another Davie spell of thought—Shakespeare could have written a couple of acts during this one—and:

"Some other Adams."

I was desperately debating within myself whether to shut off this random trickle of presidents, try to suggest some order into it, or what, when Davie's thought-seeking gaze lit on the wall portraits.

"Abe Lincoln," he announced to us. "George—"

It was too much for Susan Duff. Up shot her hand. "Washington-johnadamsjefferson," she launched, "Madisonmonroejohnquincy-adams—"

My pupils, my minnow school of new Montana. It was like having tailor's samples, swatches, of Scotch Heaven's families all around you daylong. Susan Duff had bones longer than they knew what to do with themselves, in the manner of Ninian, so that her elbows stuck over the aisle the way his poked wide when he cut his meat. The Findlaters all were marvels at arithmetic. The Hahn boys had cherubic lispy voices like Willy's, you would never suspect that one or more likely both of them had just been in a blazing fistfight during recess. Yet I always needed to watch out not to peg a child according to his parents or older brothers and sisters. Along came small Karen, of the cog-at-a-time Petersons, and she had a mind like a magic needle. It penetrated every book I managed to find for her, and of my bunch in that schoolroom Karen was the one spellbound, as I had been at her age, by those word rainbows called poems.

And so there I stood before these sons and daughters of the homesteads, their newly minted teacher of such topics as the history of the United States of America, with my Scottish schooling which had instructed me thoroughly in the principal events from Robert the Bruce to the Union of the Crowns. My daily margin of American history over my various grades was the pages I'd scurried through the night before. Fortunately, not all the subjects were as lion-sized as history. Even in America lessons in handwriting were lessons in handwriting, and reading was reading. And spelling was spelling except when *harbour* arrived to this side of the ocean as *harbor*, *tyre* as *tire*, and sundry other joggled vowels. But geography. The grief of American geography. When it came to geography, my pupils and I had to be strange pickles together. In that schoolroom of mine were children born in Bavaria and Scotland and Norway and Alsace-Lorraine, and others who never had been farther in the world than ten miles down the creek to Gros Ventre. Our sole veteran traveler of the continent we were on was Jimmy Spedderson, seven years of age, who had lived in Missouri, Kansas, North Dakota, Manitoba, and now Montana—a life like a skipping stone. Whatever the roll-down map of the whole world proclaimed, every one of us there came from a different earth and knew only the haziest about anyone else's. For me, terra incognita was the 99% of Montana where I had never been. I could instruct my pupils perfectly well that Thomas Carlyle—he of *I don't pretend to understand the universe; it's a great deal bigger than I am*—originated at Ecclefechan, pronounced Eckle-FECK'n, county of Dumfries in southmost Scotland, near to Carlisle and the Solway Firth. But I had to learn along with them the sixteen counties of Montana and the mysterious town names of Ekalaka, Ubet, Saco, Missoula, Shawmut, Rimini, Ravalli, Ovando . . .

One geographic inspiration I did have. The piece of the planet that stayed with me as no other, the Atlantic. Vivid as this minute, that time of Rob and myself on the *Jemmy*, down in Steerage Number One, deep there in the hole in the water. The Hahn boys and the three Findlaters and Daniel Rozier and Susan Duff and Davie Erskine also all remembered crossing the ocean to America. I strived to have them make the other pupils understand that feat of crossing, and to hold it in their own minds ever and ever. And got more than I bargained for when Jenny Findlater hesitantly raised her hand and asked if when I was on the ocean, was I scared any?

"Jenny, I was," I said to Daniel's smirk and the careful gazes of all the others. "An ocean is dangerous enough to be afraid of. As are the rear hooves of our horses out there, and blizzards, and just a number of things in life. But we try to use our judgment and be afraid only when it's worth it, don't we, and then only as much as we have to be. Is that how it was with you, Jenny, when you were on the ocean?" Jenny's vigorous nod carried me from that trouble.

Thank heaven arithmetic is a neutral country. At least I could put addition and subtraction and multiplication and division into my pupils like nails into a shingle roof, pound pound pound pound. Here was once when old Scotland came back to help me out, for when I had been pupil-teacher under Adam Willox in Nethermuir he made arithmetic my particular topic. *They can become literate from me, Angus, and learn to be numerate from you.*

So maybe it was numbers alone that kept me, that school year, from ever riding into the Duff homestead and saying "Ninian, start advertising for someone else, this is beyond me." Instead, day upon day I ransacked my brain for how Adam Willox had done things. Then amended nearly all of that, for Adam never had the situation of the Hahns' dog Blitzen following them to school and howling by the hour; of keeping track of whose turn it was among the big boys to go to the creek and fill the water bucket; of Einar Peterson's perpetual tendency toward nosebleed and Jenny Findlater's toward hiccups; of having to watch for ticks on everyone, including myself.

Of having to deal with Daniel Rozier about the issue of the girls' outhouse.

A country school such as South Fork was not an individual receptacle of knowledge, it was an educational trinity. You saw all three as you came to where the streambed of the North Fork met that of the South Fork and made the main creek; just upstream within a willow-thick bend, the white schoolhouse and behind it the white twin toilets, girls' to the left, boys' to the right. Each waiting to do its duty, they sat there like an attentive hen and two pullets. My problem, or more accurately the girls' problem, was Daniel Rozier's fascination with the possibilities of that left-hand outhouse.

It all began with garter snakes. Most of the girls were not normally afraid of them, but go seat yourself appropriately and glance down to find restless green reptiles beside you, and see what you think.

I heard out the girls' lamentations, and made my threats about what would happen to whomever I caught at snakework. But the Rozier homestead was just down the creek from the school, near enough for Daniel to sneak back before or after the rest of us, and try as I did I never could convict Daniel.

Susan Duff, rather than I, ended the snake episode the recess time when she stormed out of the girls' toilet grasping a writhing foot-long serpent by the tail, carried it around to the side of the schoolhouse where Daniel Rozier was in a game of ante-I-over, and whapped him across the bridge of the nose with the thing.

Even if she was the avenging figure of justice, Daniel was livid about being hit by a girl.

"SUSAN-DUFF-YOU'RE-WORSE-THAN-SNOT!" he screeched.

"The next snake I find in there I'll hit you with twice," she vowed in return.

And so only two of the trinity were standing when I rode into sight of the South Fork the morning after that. The casualty naturally was the girls' outhouse, flat on its back as a dead beetle. The bad fact now was that even Daniel Rozier at his most indignant wasn't strong enough to tip over a two-hole outhouse. He'd had help from the other boys. It took Daniel and Davie Erskine and the Hahn brothers, conscript labor all, and me to lift the structure upright.

Two mornings later, the girls' outhouse was horizontal again.

By then I knew Daniel Rozier was the sort you could punish until he was jelly and he'd still behave the same. Instead, I opened school that day with the observation: "A freak of nature seems to have struck the girls' outhouse." Smirk from Daniel to Susan Duff, glower from her to him. "Until it comes along again and puts the toilet back up, chivalry will have to be in force. Who'll tell me the spelling of chivalry? Daniel, crack at it, please."

The smirk went and confusion came. "Unngg, ah, is it s-h-o-v-u-l-r-y?"

"Closer than you might think," I granted. "Susan, enlighten Daniel as to chivalry, please." Which she did as fast as the letters could prance out her mouth.

"Thank you, Susan. Now the definition, at least in this case. The boys will yield their toilet to the girls."

Little Freddie Findlater, a lad with a nervous kidney, had his hand up in an instant. "Where will the boys go, then?"

I directed attention to the willow thicket along the creek. "Like Zeus on Mount Olympus, Freddie, all of outdoors is your throne." Looks were cast toward Daniel Rozier, but the boys sat firm, so to speak, on their outhouse position.

Montana weather being Montana weather, I didn't have to wait long for the day I needed. Squalls were getting up speed in the mountains as I reached into my cupboard that morning, and by noon hard wind and blasts of sleet shot against the schoolhouse windows.

"My eyes must have been big this morning, I brought more than

I can eat," I confessed during lunchtime. "Daniel, pass those around please," handing him the big bag of prunes. In groped his paw for the first haul, then the fruit began its fist-diving circle among the other boys.

When the prunes had time for full effect, and boy after boy trooped back in from the bushes as if dragging icicles behind, I decided here was my moment. "I've been meaning to ask, how many of you can stay after and put the outhouse back up?"

Where it then held.

"A coyote can too run faster than a dog, Fritz Hahn." Jimmy Spedderson's contention wafted in through an open window as I was at my desk cramming that afternoon's American history.

"Can't either. Our dog Blitzen runs after coyotes all the time, see."

"Your dog can't catch coyotes! That's a fat lie. Liar, liar, pants on fire!"

"Didn't say he catches them."

"See, then."

"He'd have to run *faster* to catch them. What he does is he *keeps up* with them. So a dog and coyote run the same, see."

"They don't, either. After recess we'll ask McAsker."

"All right then. McAsker will know."

McAsker, was I now. It could have been worse.

For all the daily tussle of schooling, there were distinct times when I wished the rest of the world were made of children as well. I had wondered what some of the community thought of having me as a teacher, and I found out when the first dance of the year was held in the schoolhouse. Just after I had done a schottische with Rob's Judith, Allan Frew called out to me in a high girly voice: "Angus, aren't you afraid your petticoat will show when you kick up your heels like that?"

I stepped over within arm's reach of Allan, which made him blink and think.

"Ask me that outside," I urged him, "and I'll answer you by hand."

That ended that.

Then there was the matter that fists have never been able to settle. Of course it had to be Ninian to bring me word of this, and I give him full due, he looked nowhere near happy to be performing it.

"Angus, this business about the universe being too big to understand and so on. I'm hearing from a few folks that they would like a bit more orthodox view of things told to their children."

Of anything to be scanned and poked and sniffed in the making of education, this. So far as I could see I was doing the job of teaching as well as I knew how. Probably better. To have it all snag on a sentence from Carlyle, himself a God-wrestler right in there with the most ardent—it put my blood up.

"Ninian, I can't get into that. You can say all day long you just want a bit of orthodoxy, but there's my-doxy, your-doxy, this-doxy, that-doxy. They're all *somebody's* orthodoxy. I don't notice Willy being here with you. Has he been saying I don't trot Martin Luther into the classroom often enough? Then there are the Roziers. I can invite the Pope to visit from Rome to please them, too, of course?"

"Angus, I am troubled myself with this. The matter was simpler when we were over across in Scotland."

"Oh, was it? Then you don't hold with the fellow who said the history of Scotland is one long riot of righteous against righteous."

"Now Angus, don't start."

"Ninian, you and the others can fill your children with funnels of religion at home, as far as I'm concerned. But I won't do it for you here at school. If you want a kirk school, then you'd better sack me and find yourself a preacher."

Ninian by now looked more bleak than I'd ever seen him, which is saying a lot.

"Ay, well. That's your last word, then?"

"It's even the one after that."

"Angus, we will leave this where it was. I have to go and tell them I told you." The long beard moved on Ninian's chest as he shook his head at me. "They don't need to know how hard of hearing you can be."

And then there was Rob.

"You know you're demented to be spending yourself there in the school." He said it smiling, but I could tell he more than half meant it. "Of course," he swept on, "that goes without saying, about anyone as redheaded as you are. But—"

"—you'll be glad to say it for me even so," I finished for him.

"And here I thought you'd be relieved to know there's a solid mind at the school, what with all the Barclays that seem to be on their way to the place," I said, Judith being notably along then toward their second child. You had to wonder, with the wives of Scotch Heaven as fruitful as they were, was there a permanent pregnancy that simply circled around among them?

"Solid is one word for it. Thick is another. Angus, man, you're missing a golden chance by not coming in with Lucas and me on more sheep. With prices down where they are, we can buy enough woollies to cover this country from here to there."

We. *Lucas and thee and his money make three,* I thought to myself. But said: "If you and Lucas want to be up to your necks in sheep, that's your matter. I have all I can handle and still take the school."

"You're a contrary man, McAngus, is what you are. Give you bread and roses and I swear you'd eat the petals and go around with the loaf in your buttonhole." Rob shook his head as if clearing it of vapors caught from me. "You're missing serious opportunity," he reiterated, "passing up Lucas's pocket this way when he has it open. Don't say I never told you."

"Rob, I never would."

"I can only hope you're saving up your brains to contend with this horse dealer," Rob switched to with a laugh, and quick as that, the how-many-sheep-are-enough? debate was behind us one more time and he was the other Rob, the sun-bright one. A Saturday, this, and the pair of us were pointing our horses across the divide of Breed Butte and down, north, to Noon Creek. Our mission was a new horse for me, poor old mare Patch no longer having enough step in her for my miles back and forth to the school and out and around our band of sheep when I took them from Rob each weekend—I seemed to use the saddle for a chair anymore. Patch's plodding pace here beside Rob's strong roan reinforced my conviction that buying another horse from Dantley's stable in Gros Ventre would be like throwing the money in the stove, so we were resorting to elsewhere. I say we; Rob was avidly insistent, when I mentioned to him my rehorsing intention, that Patch's successor be a partnership horse. *Angus, man, you'll be using him on the band of sheep we own together, so it's only logical I put up half the price of him. He can be the horse of us both, why not.* In fine, going in with me on the purchase of the horse was Rob's roundabout way of helping me to juggle the school along with the homestead and the sheep, without having to say out loud that it was something worth juggling. Maybe the right silences are what keep a friendship green?

Isaac Reese's horse ranch was as far up Noon Creek as mine was along the North Fork, comfortably near the mountains without having them squat on you. As we approached the place Rob now asked, "Do you know this geezer Reese at all?"

"Only by hearsay."

Isaac Reese, long-mustached and soft-eyed, had been issued the right face for a horse trader, for he showed no twitch of anticipation when I stepped off the Dantley nag as if I was a plump hen seeking a chopping block. When I told him my purpose, he only asked in some accent my ears were not prepared for: "How much horse?"

I took that to mean how much was I willing to pay for a horse, and began the sad hymn of my finances. But Isaac Reese meant what he said. He studied me, eyeing my long legs, and judged: "You vant about him high," holding his arm out at a height considerably more lofty than the back of old Patch.

Plainly this was a man who knew horses. What else he knew was as unclear to me then as his version of English, which had Rob covering a smile as he witnessed our conversational free-for-all. By common report, this Isaac Reese was a Dane who alit in America as a penniless teamster—likely about the time of Rob and me ourselves, for he looked to be only a few years older than us—and soon had horse crews of his own at work on the railroad that was being built north of the Two Medicine River. My bet is that he learned his English, to call it that, from someone else who didn't speak it as an original language. It was Isaac who made famous a Noon Creek winter day when the temperature rose from twenty below to zero by observing, "Der t'ermometer fall up dis morning."

What Isaac Reese led out for me was a high horse, no question about that. A tall young gelding of a strong brown color odd in a horse, remindful of dark gingerbread. Maybe Rob and I were no great equinists, but at the wheel shop in Nethermuir we had seen enough horses pass through to fill a corner of Asia, and with a quick look at each other we agreed that here was a strikingly handsome animal. Both of us stepped closer to admire the steed and began companionably rubbing his velvet neck while I asked Isaac: "What's his name?"

"Skorp Yun," Isaac informed me. That had a pensive homely Scandinavian ring to it, and I was on the verge of asking what it translated to. When it came clear to me, and Rob at he same instant.

Both of us stepping with great promptness back to where we had begun, I gulped for verification: "His name is Scorpion?"

There ensued from Isaac a scrambled-egg explanation that the horse was titled not for his personality but for the brand on his right hip. Rob and I looked: yes, a spidery long-tailed script M brand— *M* . Isaac's explication of the brand sounded to me as if the horse originated on a ranch which belonged to the Mikado. Later Lucas clarified that the *M* was the mark of the Mankato Cattle Company in North Dakota, and *No, Angus, I wouldn't know either what a Mankato horse is doing six hundred miles from home, nor would I ask into the matter as long as I had a firm bill of sale from Isaac.*

There in the Reese corral I cast a glance at Rob. Studying the big brown horse gravely, he told me: "It's your funeral, McAngus." But I knew from the way his head was cocked that he would be pleased to own half of this lofty creature.

While I was making up my mind about Scorpion, Isaac Reese was eyeing my colossal saddle on the Dantley nag. He inquired dubiously, "Do you came from Texus?"

"No, not quite that bad. How much do you want for this fanciful horse?"

Flow gently, sweet Afton, among thy green braes,
Flow gently, I'll sing thee a song in thy praise;
My Mary's asleep by thy murmuring stream—
Flow gently, sweet Afton, disturb not her dream.

Songtime in the schoolroom each week hinged on whatever Burns was in my mind just then and wherever Susan Duff's fine clear lilt led us. Neither premise was much my choice. But a thousand hymns had built Susan a voice, even I had to admit, and I'd found it was like pulling teeth to draw song suggestions from my other pupils, even though the schoolyard often rang with one chant or another. Children are their own nation and they hold their anthems to themselves. Ritually, though, I tried to pry music out of them:

"You're like a school for the mute today. Now who'll tell, please, what we can sing next?"

"I know one, Mr. McCaskill," piped Davie Erskine, standing and swallowing a number of times. Here was surprise.

"Do you, Davie? Can we hear it now?"

Another salvo of swallows. Then out quavered:

I came down from Cimarron, alooking for a job
riding for the outfit they call the Jinglebob.
The boss told me "Stranger, let's have ourselves some fun.
Come and throw your saddle on our horse called Zebra Dun."
    Oh, that old zebra dun,
    that bucking son of a gun,
    a-pitching his walleyed fit,
    while upon him I did sit.
The punchers came and gathered, laughing up their sleeves
counting on their zebra bronc to do just what he pleased.
And when I hit the saddle, old Dunny quit this earth
went right up to try the sky, for all that he was worth.

Susan Duff was wrinkling her nose at Davy's minstrelsy. But as soon as I gave her a severe look, she joined in the chorus with Davie and me, and the rest of the children followed her. Onward Davie warbled with his verses:

Old Dunny pawed the moon and passed right by the sun
He chased some clouds a while then came down like a ton.
You could see the tops of mountains under our every jump
But I stayed tight upon his back just like the camel's hump.

We bucked across the prairie, scattered gophers as we went
kicked the cook and stewpot right through the boss's tent.
But when the fray was over and Zebra done all he did
No doubt was left in this world: that outlaw I had rid.

The boss whooped hurrah! and threw the hat high off his head.
He shook my hand until it ached and here is what he said:
"If you can toss the lasso like you rode old Zebra Dun
You're the man I have looked for since the year of one."

"Davie Erskine, that was—remarkable." It was more than that. There were days when Davie was so drifty he could scarcely remember how many fingers he had. "And where did you learn that tune?"

"From Mr. Fox and Mr. Mitchell." I had to expend a long moment to translate Mr. Fox and Mr. Mitchell: the riders Perry and Deaf Smith. "They took supper with us, when they were riding for strays. They said it's a song from Texas," Davie reported as if the place was blue heaven. "Texas is where I'm going when I grow up."

"That may be, Davie. But for now you're going to arithmetic. Davie and Susan and Daniel and Einar, your book is page 132. Karen, show the others where they're to read, please."

At the close of school that day, I stepped out as always to watch the children start for home, the walkers up the South Fork, the riders up the North Fork. The white horseload of little Findlaters, Susan Duff aboard her blood bay and Jimmy Spedderson on his black pony with the blaze face and Betsy Frew atop her old sorrel, Davie Erskine urging his roan with Rachel tight behind him. It was Davie I was seeing most of all. Seeing older Davies, although their names were Rob and Angus, hearing their own tunes of a far place.

A late afternoon near the end of the school year, Ninian Duff appeared in the schoolroom as I was readying to go home.

"Angus, I've been by to see Archie and Willy and we have made our decision on next year's schoolteacher."

"Have you, now?" I'd been more and more aware that my time at the South Fork was drawing to a close, but it made me swallow to hear the fact. "I hope you've found a right one."

"Ay, we do too," he delivered right back. "It is you again. Temporary, of course, just for another year."

Three times more in the next three years, Ninian made that same ay-it-is-you-again call on me at the schoolhouse. "Ninian," I at last inquired of him, "did you ever happen to have a look at the word *temporary* in a dictionary?" But he knew as well as I did that the teaching job pleased me, and I was more than glad, too, to have its wage, because in that set of years spawned by the economic crash of 1893 the rewards of raising sheep were more aptly counted in small coins than in major currency. Even our prophet of profit Lucas looked perturbed, as if the sun had begun coming up in the wrong end of the sky. I don't know who among us in Scotch Heaven said in 1894 or 1895 or 1896 that despite the calendar, it still seemed to be 1893. But ever after, we spoke of this hard time as the years of '93.

In truth, though, the years of '93 were most harsh not in their lamb and wool prices—money is only money—but in abrupt occurrences among our people of the North Fork. Events that might have happened anyway took on darker shadow from the weight of the times. We had an unforgettable lesson when Archie Findlater lost half his band of sheep to a May blizzard, ewes and lambs smothered and frozen by the hundred out on the distant foothills where he had put them a week too soon. We had a heartsickening departure when the Spedderson family simply vanished, abandoning their ramshackle homestead and leaving in the night without a word to any of us. My next several days I taught with a lump in my throat, thinking of small Jimmy in that family that slunk from one piece of earth to the next.

And we had our first deaths. Gram Erskine, Donald's mother who had come with the Erskines and the Duffs on the ship to America when she was nearly eighty, died on a first fine green spring day. Odd, how the old so often last through the winter and then let go. Not a week after Ninian said the words over Gram Erskine, Rob and I had to be the ones to find Tom Mortensen. We were moving a bunch of ewes and week-old lambs over onto a slope of new grass just south of my place, and from there we noticed that, chilly day though it was, no smoke was rising from the chimney of the Mortensen cabin. When the two of us went down to see, a magpie was strutting along the ridgepole of the cabin, watching us cagily. Tom we found sprawled beside his chopping block, on his side, curled up as if napping. I knelt beside him, had a look, and threw up. Rob saw over my shoulder and did the same.

"Lord of mercy, if there is one," Rob choked out after we both retched ourselves dry and I managed to go to the house for a blanket to put over Tom. Rob grabbed up a stone and flung it clattering along the cabin roof toward the black and white bird, causing the magpie to swim away silently through the air. "I'll find something here to make a coffin," he said. I said, "And I'll fetch Ninian."

At Ninian's I told him it looked as if Tom's heart had given out. He started to the house for his Bible, saying "I'll come in the wagon with Flora, she can help lay out the body."

"No. Don't bring Flora."

"Ay? Whyever not? Flora has seen a man dead before."

"Not like this one. Ninian, the magpies have been at his eyes."

Death had been to Nethermuir, too. I remember bringing out the letter, small taut handwriting on it I did not recognize, when I came back from a grocery trip into Gros Ventre, and Rob at the wagon ripping it open as quick as he saw that writing. The news was on his face, although he read all the letter before passing it to me with the words, "My father's dead." Vare Barclay in the woodyard of the wheelshop, my father and Lucas beside him; Vare who had given me work as his clerk—the letter was from Rob's sister Adair, telling that her mother could not bring herself to write yet, that the Barclay house on River Street had been sold for what little they could get, that she and her mother would live now with Rob's oldest brother, who was closing down the wheelwrighting but would try to stay in business by making wheelbarrows and suchlike small stuff. As much sadness as paper can absorb was in that letter.

Rob set his jaw to go into the house to tell Judith and then make the ride into town to tell Lucas. But first he put a hand on my shoulder. "We were right to come, Angus. Hard as times ever can get here, we're better off than them over across in Scotland." I thought of Rob's mother and young Adair, being seen to in a household not their own. Being seen to. Not much of a prospect in life, not much at all. I had sheep waiting and school preparation waiting, but I stood and watched the erect American back of Rob as he took the news of his father's death into the house on Breed Butte. And watched again not half a year later, when word came that his mother, too, had passed away, dwindled away really. The strangest news there is, death across a distance; the person as alive as ever in your mind the intervening time until you hear, and then the other and final death, the one a funeral is only preliminary to, confusedly begins.

"By Jesus, the woollies do make a lovely sight," intoned Lucas. "If we could just sell them as scenery, ay?"

The time was September of 1896, a week before shipping the lambs, and Lucas and Rob and I were holding a Saturday war council on the west ridgeline of Breed Butte where we could meanwhile keep an eye on our grazing bands. By now Rob and Lucas's sheep had accumulated into two oversize bands, nearly twenty-five hun-

dred altogether, as Rob kept back the ewe lambs each year since
'93 rather than send them to market at pitiful prices. The band he
and I owned in partnership I always insisted keeping at a regular
thousand, as many as my hay would carry through a winter. So here
they were in splendid gray scatter below us, six years of striving and
effort, three and a half thousand prime ewes and a fat lamb beside
each of them, and currently worth about as much as that many
weeds.

"Next year is going to be a bit tight," Rob affirmed, which was
getting to be an annual echo out of him.

"These tight years are starting to pinch harder than I'm comfortable with," he was informed by Lucas. Lucas's Jerusalem, Gros
Ventre, was not prospering these days. Nowhere was prospering
these days. I noticed how much older Lucas was looking, his beard
gray now with patches of black. The years of '93 had put extra age
on a lot of people in Montana. "So, Robbie lad, we have sheep
galore. Now what in the pure holy hell are we going to do with
them?"

"Prices can't stay down in the well forever," Rob maintained.
"People still have to wear clothes, they still have to eat meat."

Lucas squinted at the neutral September sun. "But how soon can
we count on them getting cold and hungry enough?"

"All right, all right, you've said the big question. But Lucas,
we've got to hang onto as many sheep as we can until prices turn
around. If we don't, we're throwing away these bands we've built
up."

"Robbie," said Lucas levelly, "this year we've got to sell the ewe
lambs along with the wether lambs. Even if we have to all but give
the little buggers away with red bows on them, we've just got to—"

"I'll meet you halfway on that, how about," Rob put in with a
smile.

"Halfway to what, bankruptcy?" retorted Lucas in as sharp a
tone as I had ever heard from him.

I saw Rob swallow, the only sign of how tense a moment this was
for him. Then he brought it out: "Halfway on selling the lambs,
Lucas. I'm all for selling the ewe lambs, just as you say. But this
year let's keep the wether lambs."

"Keep the wethers?" Lucas stared astounded at Rob. "What in
the name of Christ for? Are you going to make history by teaching

the wethers"—which was to say, the castrated male sheep whose sole role was mutton—"how to sprout tits and have lambs?"

"We'd keep them for their wool," Rob uttered as rapidly as he could say it. "Their wool crop next summer. Lucas, man, if we keep the wethers until they're yearlings they'll shear almost ten pounds of wool apiece. And if wool prices come back up to what they were—"

Lucas shook his head to halt Rob and brought up a stub to run vigorously along his beard. "I never listen to a proposition beyond the second *if*."

"Lucas, it's worth a try. It's got to be." If conviction counted, Rob right then would have had the three of us in bullion up to our elbows. "See now, the man McKinley is sure to be president, and that'll be like money in the bank for the sheep business." True, there was talk that McKinley could bring with him a tariff on Australian wool. If he did, prices for our fleeces then could climb right up. Pigs could fly if they had wings, too.

"Angus, what do you say to this new passion of Robbie's for wethers?"

"Maybe it's not entirely farfetched," I conceded, earning myself a mingled look from Rob.

Lucas still looked skeptical. "Here's the next thing you can enlighten me about, Robbie—how in holy hell do you handle that many sheep next summer? Tell me that, ay?" I knew it already was costing dear on them to hire herders for their two bands while Rob and I shared the herding of our one, and for them to add a third herder—

He was ready, our Rob. "I'll herd the wether band myself. Judith will have kittens about my doing it." And well she might, because with Rob herding in the mountains all summer she would need to manage everything else of the homestead, not to mention three daughters. "But she'll just have to have them, she married Breed Butte when she married me."

I regarded Rob for a waitful moment, Lucas glancing uncomfortably back and forth between us. Finally I said what was on my mind and Lucas's, even if it didn't seem to be within a hundred miles of Rob's:

"That leaves just one band of sheep unaccounted for."

"Yours and mine, of course," Rob spoke up brightly. "And

there's where I have a proposition for you, Angus. If you'll take our band by yourself next summer, I'll give you half of my half."

I made sure: "On the wool and the lambs both?"

"Both."

Translated, half of Rob's half meant that I would receive three-fourths of any profit—wool and lambs both, the man had said it—on our band of sheep next year. And if wool went up as Rob was betting on . . . if lamb prices followed . . . Never listen to a proposition beyond the second *if*, ay, Lucas?

"Done." I snapped up Rob's offer, which would make me money while he made money for himself and Lucas on the wethers. "That is, if Lucas agrees to your end of it."

Lucas studied the two of us, and then the three-about-to-be-four bands of sheep below.

"There are so goddamn many ways to be a fool a man can't expect to avoid them all," he at last said, as much to the sheep as to us. "All right, all right, Robbie, keep the wethers. We'll see now if '97 is the year of years, ay?"

Let me give the very day of this. The twentieth of April, 1897. Here in the fourth springtime that I had watched arrive outside the windows of the South Fork school, I perched myself on the water-bucket stand at the rear of the classroom while Karen Peterson, small but great with the occasion, sat at my big desk reading to us from the book of stories.

"One more sun," sighed the king at evening, "and now another darkness. This has to stop. The days fly past us as if they were racing pigeons. We may as well be pebbles, for all the notice life takes of us or we of it. No one holds in mind the blind harper when he is gone. No one commemorates the girl who grains the geese. None of the deeds of our people leave the least tiny mark upon time. Where's the sense in running a kingdom if it all just piffles off into air? Tell me that, whoever can."

"If you will recall, sire—"

In the trance of Karen's reading, even Daniel Rozier squirmed only ritually, and I took quiet pleasure in seeing those still rows of oh so familiar heads in front of me. I swear to heaven Susan Duff could have ruled France with the crown of her head. How such chestnut luster and precise flow of tress had derived from old dust-mop Ninian was far beyond me. But Davie Erskine's crownhair flopped in various directions and no definite one, and that seemed distinctly Erskinian. But then there was the bold round crown of Eddie Van Bebber, so that you'd have thought half the brains of the human race were packed under there, and Eddie Van Bebber was only barely bright enough to sneeze.

"Why is it that the moon keeps better track of itself than we manage to? And the seasons put us to shame, they always know which they are, who's been, whose turn now, who comes next, all that sort of thing. Why can't we have memories as nimble as those? Tell me that, whoever can."

"Sire, you will recall—"

Each of those South Fork and Scotch Heaven heads in front of me, a mind that I as teacher was to make literate and numerate. The impossibly mysterious process of patterning minds, though. How do we come to be the specimens we are? Tell me that, whoever can.

"Oblivion has been the rule too long. What this kingdom needs in the time to come is some, umm, some blivion. There, that's it, we need to become a more blivious people. Enough of this forgettery. But how to do it, it will take some doing. What's to be done? Tell me that, whoever can."

"If you will recall, sire, this morning you named a remembrancer."

"Eh? I did? I mean, I did. And what a good idea it was, too. For a change things are going to be fixed into mind around here. Send me this remembering fellow."

"Bring forth the king's remembrancer!"

In time to come, during what the fable king would call blivion, I always remembered Daniel Rozier more vividly than Karen Peterson, and in no way under heaven was that fair.

In time to come, when Susan Duff had grown and herself become a teacher in Helena—I've always been sure that Helena is the better for it—I could wonder if I truly affected that in any meaningful way.

In time to come, when Davie Erskine—

But that was waiting some hundreds of days to come, Davie's time. Memory still had everything to make between here and there.

This was a full-fledged spring day in the Two Medicine country, breezy along with sunny, melt and mud along with greening grass and first flowers. The afternoon was better than my afterschool chore, which was to call on the replacement teacher newly arrived at Noon Creek. Old Miss Threlkeld, who held forth there since Cain and Abel, toward the end of winter had suffered palpitation of the heart, and about this sudden successor of hers I more than half knew what to expect and fully dreaded it.

"Ramsay is her name," Ninian Duff reported, "they are a new family to here, down from Canada. Man and wife and daughter. The Mrs. seems to be something of an old battle-axe, I do have to say." Coming from Ninian, that was credential for her indeed. "They bought the relinquishment up there to the west of Isaac Reese," he went on, "with a bit of help from Isaac's pocket from what I hear."

Given the basis that Isaac Reese headed the Noon Creek board as Ninian did ours, I couldn't let pass the opportunity to declare: "Now there's the way for a school board to operate."

Ninian broadly ignored that and stated, "When you find a spare moment, Angus, you would do well to stop by the schoolhouse over across there and offer hello. Our schools are neighbors and it would not hurt us to be."

"Maybe not severely," I had to agree, and now Scorpion and I were descending from the divide between our valleys to Noon Creek, a prairie stream twice as twisty as the North Fork ever thought of being. Scorpion was pointed to the country where I bought him—the Noon Creek schoolhouse was within easy eyeshot of Isaac Reese's horse ranch—and I wondered if he held horse memories of this stretch of territory. "Skorp Yun, lad, what about that?" I inquired of him and patted his rich-brown velvet neck. Scorpion's ears twitched up and I suppose that was my answer, as much as the horse clan was willing to tell a man.

A quick how-do here and home was my intention. This schoolhouse was much like mine—for that matter, so was its attendant pair of outhouses—except for standing all but naked to the wind, Noon Creek providing only a thin sieve of willows instead of the South Fork's broadback clumps of cottonwoods. Ask any dozen people passing and thirteen of them would tell you my school site was the obvious superior.

Pleased with that and armored with the thought that, however howlingly formidable Mrs. Battle-Axe Ramsay might try to be, I was the senior teacher hereabout, I tied Scorpion beside the Noon Creek teacher's horse and strode to the schoolhouse.

"Hello, anyone," I called in, and followed my words through the doorway.

A woman did look up from the teacher's desk. A woman whose shoulders drew back nobly and whose breasts came out nobler yet. A woman my age or less. A woman with the blackest of black hair done into a firm glossy braid, and with perfect round cheeks and an exactly proportionate chin and a small neat nose, and with direct blue eyes. A glory of a woman.

She granted me an inquiring half-smile, the rest of her expression as frank as a clock. "Hello," she enunciated, although what was being said was And What Is Your Business Here, If Any?

I told her me. And made about as much impression as a mosquito alighting on a stone fence.

"I am called Anna Ramsay," she stated in return, and I was going to need to ask Ninian what he thought a battle-axe talked like. Hers was a liltful voice which may have paused in Canada but only after fully flowering in Scotland.

"I'm the teacher at the South Fork school, over across, Mrs. Ramsay," I hurried to clarify.

"I am the teacher here," said she, "and it is Miss Ramsay."

Rob, Lucas, my unhearing father, my sorrowful mother, all who have ever known me, and generations yet to come: did you feel any of this catchbreath instant together with me, this abrupt realization in the throat that said here was the end to all my waiting, this surprise swale of time while I traced step by step back to the brain of Ninian the Calvinian? Ninian Duff had told me Mrs. Ramsay was an old battle-axe. He had told me the new Noon Creek teacher could stand a cordial look-in. He had never bothered to tell me those two formulations did not add up to the same person.

"Yes, well. Miss Ramsay, now. I, ah, seem to have been misinformed," I understated. "In any case, I came by to say hello"—her look told me that had been more than amply done by now, and not in ribbon-winning fashion—"and to see if there's any help I can offer."

"That's kind," she decided. "But I know of none."

In that case, Miss-not-Mrs. Ramsay, help me and my dazed tongue. What do you think the price of rice in China will reach? And are you the absolute lovely thing you appear to be under the crust?

"I'm trying to place your voice," I managed, true enough in its way: trying to coax the sound of it into my ears for as long as possible. "Your town in Scotland is—?"

"My town was Brechin." Brechin! Not all that far from my own Nethermuir, in the same county of Forfar. The magic that life is. She and I must have grown up sharing the same days of sun, the same storms from the sea.

I at once told her of my Nethermuir nativity, which did not noticeably set her afire with interest. "This Montana is different from old Scotland, isn't it," I imparted.

She regarded me steadily as ever. "Yes."

"Although," I began, and had no idea where to head from there.

"Mr. McCaskill, you've just reminded me, there is one matter you may be able to help me with." Anything, anything. Wheelbarrowing a mountain from here to there. Putting socks on snakes. "I find I'm in short supply of Montana geography books. Mr. Reese promised me more, but he's away buying horses."

"I have loads extra," I offered as fast as I could say it. Later would be soon enough to calculate whether or not I actually had any. "You're more than welcome to them."

Anna Ramsay shook that matchless head of hers, but in general perturbance at men who would see to horses before geography, rather than at my offer. "I've had to put the pupils to making their own."

I was as flummoxed now as a duck in thunder. "You've—?"

"Yes, they're a bit makeshift but better than nothing," she said, and gestured to the stack of them at the corner of her desk. They were pamphlets of as many colors as a rainbow, bound with yarn, with My Montana Book and each pupil's name bold on the cover. More than just that, the pamphlets were scissored into the unmistakable shape of the state of Montana, twice as wide as high and the entire left side that curious profile of a face looking down its bent nose at Idaho. I opened the pamphlet proclaiming Dill Egan, grade four, to be its author. Intently—not only was I curious but I was not going to forfeit this opportunity to hover in the near vicinity of Miss Anna Ramsay—as I say, intently as I could manage with so much distraction so close, I started through the pamphlet pages. PRODUCTS OF MONTANA, and Dill Egan's confident map of where gold, copper, cattle, sheep and sundry grains each predominated. AREA AND POPULATION OF MONTANA, 147,138 square miles and 132,159 persons respectively, and his enstarred map showing

Helena, Butte, Bozeman, Missoula, Great Falls, Billings, Miles City and the now twenty-four county seats. MOUNTAINS OF MONTANA and another map showing the western throng of ranges, Bitterroot and Cabinet and Garnet and Mission and Flathead and Swan and Tobacco Root and on and on until the Little Rockies and Big Snowys outposted the eastern majority of the state. DRAINAGES OF MONTANA and yet another map of all the rivers and what must have been every respectable creek as well, with the guiding message *The Continental Divide separates the Atlantic and the Pacific slopes of America.* MINERALS OF MONTANA. RAILROADS OF MONTANA. I had a sudden image of this brisk, beautiful woman beside me as the goddess of geography, fixing the boundaries of this careless world as unerringly as Job's prosecutor or even the U.S. General Land Office. Anna Ramsay's ten-year-olds all too evidently knew more about Montana than I did. Every one of them a Crofutt in the bud.

I swallowed hard. I took a look around me. High on the blackboard behind us was chalked the majestically handwritten single word:

chilblain

Other than it, the blackboard was not only freshly cleaned, it shone black. The best I could scrape together to remark was: "Your chalk keeps talking after school, does it?"

"Yes, that's tomorrow's word in the air," she explained. "I write a different one up there for each day. That way, when the pupils' eyes go wandering off into air, they at least are looking at how one word of the language is spelled."

"A sound principle," I vouched sagely, wishing I'd thought of it the first day I stepped into my South Fork classroom. Contemplate the miracle of *chilblain* spelling itself, even approximately, into the mind of Daniel Rozier. My eyes moved on from the blackboard. Her schoolroom gleamed like the Queen's kitchen. This Miss Ramsay seemed to be a stickler about everything.

"You, ah, you were a teacher in Scotland, were you?" I entirely unnecessarily asked.

"In a dame school, back in Brechin." It seemed to me a magnificent beneficence when she tilted her head ever so slightly and decided to add: "As you say, this is different."

I wanted to sing out to her, so are you, so are you. I wanted to hang Ninian Duff from a high tree by his beard. I wanted to go back out that schoolhouse door, turn myself around three times, and start this anew. I wanted—instead I managed to draw in enough breath to clear my head and free up my tongue: "I'll fetch the geographies to you. Tomorrow, I even could. And if there's anything else whatsoever you need—"

"Mr. Reese will be back from his beloved horses any day. It is his job to see that I have what the school needs." Again that first half-smile of hers and the simultaneous clocklike frankness, in which I desperately tried to discern a momentworth more of warmth than when I arrived. "Mr. McCaskill, I do appreciate that you came."

"It's been my pleasure, Miss Ramsay."

Riding home, I was the next thing beyond giddy. Scorpion must have compassed his own route around the west shoulder of Breed Butte and down to my homestead, or he and I would be circling there yet.

Astonishment. That was my word in the air. The coming of dusk was an astonishment, the last of this April day coloring a blue into the gray of the mountains as if sky had entered rock. My homestead was an astonishment, in expectant welcome there beside the North Fork like the front porch to the future. The greening grass, the dabbed yellow of buttercups, the creek rattling mildly over smooth stones, the rhythm of Scorpion's hooves against the earth, the ever-restless air of the Two Medicine country traveling over my skin, the pertinent Burns: *my heart was caught/before I thought,* astonishments all. For that matter, I was an astonishment to myself, how fertile for love I was. Is this life? Just when you have lived long enough to think you know yourself, behavior such as this crops out?

But the braided marvel that touched alive all these others. Anna Ramsay. Where, really, did I stand with her, after an acquaintance that would have barely boiled an egg? I didn't know. I didn't even know how to know. Thunder tumbling out of an absolute clear sky, was the way this had fallen on me. The one certainty I held was that the women I had met in my life so far were no training for this one.

Oh, I tried to tell myself whoa and slow. And by the time I'd cooked supper twice—my first try burned conclusively—I had myself half-believing I was somewhere near to sane again. Steady, Angus, don't rush in brainless. For that matter, Miss Anna Ramsay did not look anything like a person who tolerated rushing.

But I did go to bed with the thought that tomorrow, nothing known on earth could keep me from delivering those geography books to her.

"This was kind of you"—she, even more glorious on second inspection. "To make the ride over here so soon again."

"Not at all"—myself, earnest without even trying. "If one schoolkeeper can't lend a hand to another schoolkeeper, the world is a poor place."

Just over Anna's head as she stood behind her desk was her blackboard word for today, *accommodate,* which for the first time in my life I noticed contains more than one *m.*

"Mr. McCaskill, before you go"—I had no thought of that—"I do have something further I wonder if you might advise me about."

"Miss Ramsay, if I can I will. What?"

"How do you keep the big boys from playing pranks that have to do with"—she never blinked—"the girls' outhouse?"

With teacup delicacy I outlined to her the curative effects of the boys having to go in the brush. Throughout, she regarded me steadily. Then she swung to the schoolroom window and studied the willow supply along the creek. As I watched her at this it came to me that she was very much a practitioner of the Scottish verdict, Not Proven, this Anna Ramsay. Guilty or Innocent could stand on either side of a matter until their tongues hung out, but she was going to do justice firmly from the middle ground of proof and nowhere else. I also stored away forever the fact that her braid gloriously swung almost all the way down her glorious back.

Evidently she judged the Noon Creek willows ample to their duty, sufficient thatch of them to screen a boy but not enough to thwart the chilly seeking nose of the wind, for she turned around to me and nodded with spirit. "Yes, that should do it. Thank you for that advice, Mr. McCaskill. Well. I have grading—"

"As do I," I put in, as accommodating as can be imagined. "But now there's a question I need to put to you. I've visited your school, and I'd much like you to visit mine. We're holding a dance, Saturday next week. Could I see you there?"

She grew as intent as if I'd thrown her a major problem in multiplication. "It's early to say." Seeing my hope plummet, she provided me a half-smile to grapple it back up. "But possibly—"

"I could come for you."

"That won't be necessary."

"Oh, no trouble."

"But it would be." She was looking at me a bit askance, as if wondering how a grown man could not see that an extra stint on horseback equaled an inconvenience for himself. Anna Ramsay plainly could out-teach me in spelling and geography, but there was at least one variety of arithmetic she didn't yet understand.

"I'm sure others from Noon Creek will be attending," she elucidated for me, "and I can come with them."

Come in a congregation, come by your lovely lone self, come dogback or come in a purple carriage with wheels of gold, but just come. Aloud, I granted: "A sensible solution. I'll see you at South Fork then, on the night."

When I went to the lambing shed to relieve Rob that evening, he greeted me with: "And how is life among all you schoolkeepers?"

Already. The way news flew in a country with so few tongues to relay it, I never would comprehend.

Stiff as a poker, I retorted to Rob: "You seem to know at least as much about my doings as I do."

"Angus, Angus. Just because there's a fresh path worn this deep"—he indicated to his knee—"between the South Fork schoolhouse and the Noon Creek schoolhouse, I thought I might inquire."

"Well, you've done." But I couldn't stay miffed where Anna was concerned. "She needed a bit of help on a geography matter."

"Geography," Rob mused. "That's the word for it these days, is it."

"Rob, aren't you on your way home to supper?"

"You're certain sure you know what you're getting into with all this geography business? From what I hear, Miss Noon Creek is a bit of a snooty one."

I was outraged. "Speaking of snoots, you can just keep your own damn one out of—"

"All right, all right. If you're not in a mood to hear wisdom, you're not." The words were light enough, although behind them Rob still seemed peeved. But a day in overshoes in the muck of a lambing shed will do that to a man, and he sounded thoroughly himself when he went on: "Probably this is nothing you'll find near so interesting as geography, but Lucas brought out word today that wool is up to 12½ cents and lambs are climbing fine, too. This is the year we've been looking for, man." Rob had it right, the world and its price of wool and lambs was not what I wanted to think about, only Anna. However far gone he thought I was down romance's knee-deep road, he didn't know half of it. I was Anna dizzy, in an Anna tizzy. These days there seemed to be fresh blood in my veins, brewed by the maker of harem potions. But the relentless fact of Anna always in my mind also startled me constantly, if it can be said that way, and I will admit that it was a bit scaring, too.

At the end here of what I thought was perfectly normal lambing shed conversation, Rob cocked his head and asked: "Are you off your feed this spring, McAngus? You'd better come by and let Judith tuck a few solid suppers into you."

I said I would, soon, whenever that was, and Rob gave me one last askance glance and departed.

You could have counted the next ten days on my face. I went from remorse at how long it would be until I laid eyes on Anna again, to fevers that I wouldn't be prepared when I did. One morning I was gravely giving arthmetic when Susan Duff pointed out that I already had done so, not an hour before. And I suppose all my South Fork pupils were startled by the onslaught of Montana geography that befell them.

One thing I did know for dead-certain, and this was that my schoolhouse was going to be grandly ready to dance. At the close of class that Friday I prevailed on Davie Erskine to stay after and help me, and we moved the rows of desks along the walls and pushed my desk into a corner. Davie took out the stove ashes while I filled lanterns and trimmed wicks. There never has been a boy enthusiastic about a broom, so I next swept the floor myself in solid Medicine Lodge swamping style and put Davie to wiping the windows with old copies of the Choteau *Quill.*

"But Mr. McCaskill, it'll be dark out, why do the windows need to be clean?"

"On account of the moonbeams, Davie. You've got to let the moonbeams in on a dance, or people's feet will stick to the floor. Did you not know moonbeams are slick as soap, Davie?"

Davie gaped at me as if I already was askate on moonbeams, but he did the windows fine. Next I had him wash the blackboard, then fill our bucket with fresh drinking water from the creek. I swept and hummed, dusted and hummed, I even straightened the pictures of George and Abraham and gave them each a hum of joy, they always looked as if they needed cheer.

"Do you know this old tune, Davie?" I asked, for it seemed to me an impossibly dim prospect that anyone should go through this wonderful thing, life, knowing only songs of Texans and horses. "You don't? That's odd, for it seems to be addressed to you."

"Me?"

"Surely. Listen to it."

> *Dancing at the rascal fair,*
> *try it, Davie, if you dare,*
> *hoof and shoe, stag and mare,*
> *dancing at the rascal fair.*

Davie whipped through the last of his tasks as if afraid my lunacy might be catching. "Is there anything more, Mr. McCaskill?"

"You've more than earned supper, Davie. And thank you the world, for your help here." I fished in my pocket and handed him a coin. From the size of Davie's eyes it was more of a coin than I'd intended, but no matter.

There was a thing more I wanted done, but I needed to be the doer. I went to the freshly washed blackboard and in my best hand, which was an urchin's scrawl compared to Anna Ramsay's, wrote large the next verse to come:

> *Dancing at the rascal fair,*
> *moon and star, fire and air,*
> *choose your mate and make a pair,*
> *dancing at the rascal fair.*

By last light of Saturday, the sun behind the peak called Phantom Woman and dusk graying the valley, people came. Rob and Judith. The Duffs and Erskines. I scattered oatmeal on the floor to help the moonbeams with our gliding. George Frew as ever was our fiddler, and the night began with the high beautiful tune of *Green Glens of Strath Spey*. I took a diplomatic first turn with

George's Mavis, toward convincing her that while I might never run a school the way she did, my dancing made up for it.

The first time we earliest dancers stopped to blow, Rob glanced over his shoulder to be sure Mavis Frew née Milgrim was nowhere in hearing and declared, "This place definitely dances better since you're the schoolkeeper, McAngus. What, have you put bed springs under the floor?"

I was gazing around fondly, awaiting what—who—I knew would come. Must come. "Owe it to George, not me. He fiddles better as a married man."

Judith put in, "There's a lesson there for you, Angus."

"You mean if I married, I'd be able to play the fiddle? Judith, that's surprising. What would I need to do to be able to play the piano?"

Rob chortled and batted my shoulder while Judith mocked a huff and declared: "Angus McCaskill, you are just impossible." Ah, Judith, but I no longer was. I was purely possible. I was possibility with its wings ready, these days. "You have me right," I mollified Judith though, "yet would you dance with me anyhow? Rob, there's paper and pen in my desk there, if you'd care to jot down for yourself how Judith and I do this."

"I'm lending her to you with two sound feet, so bring her back unbroken, hear?" he stipulated.

"Unbroken, nothing. She'll be downright improved." And Judith and I swung away together, Rob's two closest people in this world, who once had kissed hotly at one of these gatherings and could grin a little rue at each other that we never would again.

Archie and Grace Findlater came. *The Shepherd's Schottische.* The Hahns and Petersons and Van Bebbers came. *The Herring Lasses' Reel.* The Roziers from down the main creek, the Kuuvuses and Sedgwicks from town, they came and came.

"Angus, lad, you can hear this schoolhouse of yours a mile down the road." Lucas! And Nancy on his arm. This major night had brought even them.

"What, did you turn the Medicine Lodge over to the customers?" I asked incredulous.

"The same as. Toussaint showed up in town today, and so he's tending the saloon for me tonight. If you can call that tending—giving away a drink to anybody who has a story Toussaint wants to hear, which is to say everybody." Nancy, brown beside Lucas's

142

ruddiness, already was making heads turn here and there in the dance crowd. "But there's more to life than what you can put in your pocket, ay?" concluded Lucas, squaring himself and casting a resolute look around my thronged schoolroom. "Good evening there, Ninian," he called as that lanky figure capered past, "you're as spry as King David up on his hind feet." I thought the beard was going to drop off Ninian when he saw Lucas here. Then Rob and Judith were beside us, a last dab of startlement on Rob's face as he said: "You didn't tell me we were going to have this pleasure, Lucas."

"I didn't want to spoil the surprise, Robbie. Nancy and I thought we'd come learn how to shake a leg."

When that didn't bring anything from Rob except a smile as neutral as he could make it, I rapidly inserted, "This is definitely the learning place and they tell me I'm the teacher. Nancy, may I have the first honor?" And next quick thing, out on the floor Lucas was paired with Judith, one handless sleeve on her back and the other meeting the grasp of her hand in the musical air, while Nancy went into the swirl with me—she did not really dance but moved quietly with me, a dark-eyed visitor from an earlier people.

After that tune, Lucas regathered Nancy and took her across to greet Sedge and Lila just as if he hadn't seen them a dozen times that day. Evening proceeded toward night. On and on the music flowed and the sweat rolled. Thank heaven George Frew's fiddling left arm was as oaken as the rest of him. Sedge taught us a square dance called *Bunch to the Middle* and we danced it until the floor would remember every step of it.

By the holy, I loved these people. This night I loved all of Scotch Heaven, the Two Medicine country, Montana, America, the sky over and the earth under. Who could not?

What I loved strongest of all entered now through my schoolroom doorway in a dark blue skirt and white shirtwaist and an ivory brooch at her throat. Anna. And her mother and father—surprisingly unprepossessing, for a pair who had given mankind such a gift—and others from Noon Creek, the Wainwrights and Egans and and Isaac Reese, all come in one wagon, and now entering our tuneful school eager for the reward of that ride.

"Welcome across the waters to Scotch Heaven," Rob called out to this delegation and drew a laugh from all. The South Fork and

North Fork and Noon Creek taken together, you could still skim your hat across.

"Brung the Ramsays along to translate for us," gruffed the rancher Thad Wainwright. "I damn well might've known, the only heaven I'd get into I need to learn to talk Scotch to do it."

Hoping for battle-axe avoidance this first night, I waited until Anna's mother and father took a dance together, then seized my chance to go over and greet Anna alone. "I see your chalk keeps talking after school, too," she said of my rascal fair verse in white on the blackboard. Which I took as approval, on the grounds that it didn't seem to be disapproval.

"That chalk must have caught the habit somewhere. Do you know, it took me by the hand as I was walking past and made me write that?"

"I suppose you objected strenuously all the while?"

"Objecting is a thing I try not to believe in, particularly the strenuous kind. Just for example, Miss Ramsay, I'm hoping you won't object to a turn around the floor with me right now? *Sir Patrick MacWhirr* wasn't meant to be stood to."

A flicker went through her steady eyes, but if that was hesitation I'll never mind a dose so small. Here came something else I'd hoped, her sidelong half-smile. Then up came her hand, writing in the air between us as if onto her Noon Creek blackboard. I waited, yes, astonished, while whatever it was got elaborately spelled into the atmosphere of my schoolroom. When done, she pronounced for me with vast amused deliberation: *"unobjectionable."* And onto the dance floor I pranced with her.

To Noroway, to Noroway!
To Noroway over the foam!
The King's fair bride from Noroway—
oh, Sir Pat, Sir Pat, Sir Pat, Sir Pat!—
'Tis thee must sail and bring her home!

"I'll need to see whether there's a floor left for my pupils, after tonight."

"If there's not, you will have to teach outside as did the ancient Greeks."

"Outside, were they. Small wonder all they ever knew how to talk was Greek. Think the tongues they'd speak if they'd gone to school to the pair of us." She had to smile fully at that, and so did my heart. Anna was alive with loveliness, she was mine in my arms for as long as I could make the moment. "And what would they think of this at the Brechin dame school?"

> *I saw the new moon, late yester e'en,*
> *with the old moon in her arm!*
> *If we go to sea, oh my dear queen—*
> *oh, dear queen, dear queen, dear queen, dear queen!—*
> *I fear we must come to harm!*

"They would think this Scotch Heaven of yours is a shameless place." My heart keeled sideways. "Cavorting in a place of learning. See up there, even your presidents think so." The jounce of the dancing had tilted Washington and Lincoln toward each other, and they did look like two old streetcorner solemns, confiding the world's latest waywardness to each other.

"I hope that's not what you think," I hoped desperately.

"If a schoolhouse is the only place big enough for a dance," she postulated, "then the schoolhouse should be used."

"My own thought, exactly. And so we'll be dancing next at Noon Creek, will we?"

I particularly meant the two of us. She only granted, "The school board has the say of any dance. But I'll not object."

> *The sails were hoist on Mononday morn,*
> *the wind came up on Wenensday!*
> *It blew and blew and blew so forlorn—*
> *oh, Sir Pat and Queen, Sir Pat and Queen!—*
> *blew Sir Pat and Queen from Noroway!*

I bided my time for a small eternity—it must have been fully the next two tunes' worth—before dancing with her again. But the wait was worth it, for during this circuit of the floor she sanctioned my suggestion that "Miss Ramsay" and "Mister McCaskill" might just as well be discarded to give "Anna" and "Angus" some wear. My aim this night was to dance with Anna enough times to begin to ratify us as a couple, yet not so many as to alarm her. So I didn't mind—much—when Allan Frew took a turn with her. From his doggish look toward me I knew that Al-

lan knew I would pound him back to milkteeth if he tried seriously to get in my way with Anna. She even went a few rounds
with Isaac Reese and made him and his drooping mustache look
almost presentable. Then Rob danced with Anna to *Brig of Dee*
while I did with Judith, and I saw Judith's eyebrow inch up at
Rob's nonstop chat there, but I knew that was just him being him. I
thanked my stars that Rob was not in the running with me for
Anna. Indeed, peer along the lovelit road ahead as far as I could, I
saw no one else who was. Which was wondrous and sobering and
exhilarating and bewildering and intimidating and sublime all in the
same pot together.

So spirited was *Brig of Dee* that it made Thad Wainwright come
by and announce, "Angus and Rob, I got to hand it to you. You
Scotchmen sure do know how to make feet move. Only one thing
missing from tonight, so far's I can tell. How come no bagpipes?"

Lord of mercy, when was the rest of mankind going to quit thinking of us as wild Highlanders? Past Thad I caught Rob's eye-rolling
look, and if Lucas hadn't been across the room trading sheep
theories with Willy Hahn, I knew he'd have given a response that
would rattle the room. The soul of moderation, I only told Thad:
"We thought there's enough wind in this country without making
more."

"It's kind of disappointing though, you know? With all you
Scotchmen here under one roof, the rest of us figured we were going
to see some real flinging." The Noon Creek rancher chuckled a regret and moved on.

*Moon and star, fire and air,/choose your mate and make a
pair,/dancing at the rascal fair,* my verse on the blackboard spoke to
me over Thad's retreating shoulder. It made me remember aloud to
Rob: "Fergus the Dervish!"

Rob roared a laugh. "Fergus and his Highland whoops! He'd
show old Thad some steps."

"Why don't we? The two of us saw Fergus enough times at the
rascal fair."

"You think we can?"

"Man, is there something we can't do?"

"We haven't found it yet, have we. You're right, you're right, it
will take Barclay and McCaskill to show these Noon Creek geezers
what dancing is."

"McCaskill and Barclay," I set him straight, "but you're correct enough other than that. See if our man Geoge can play *Tam Lin*, why not, while I tend to the rest."

Apprehensively, Judith began: "Now, you two—"

"No, love, it's we three, you're into this, too. And whoever Angus can inveigle into risking her—"

I was across the room before my feet knew they were moving. I hadn't a wisp of a clue as to how this person Anna would react to a dancing exhibition. Here was the time of times to find out.

"It's all for the cause of education, of course," I prattled to her while those direct blue eyes worked on me. "Instruction for the world at large, think of it as."

The smile I wanted began to sidle onto her face. "I'll believe you," granted Miss Anna Ramsay, and lightly grasped the arm I proffered, "but thousands would not."

With Anna gloriously beside me, I hadn't even a qualm about attempting the next impossibility across the room.

"SING?!" Lucas repeated as if I'd asked him to shed all his clothing. "Angus, what in goddamn hell"—he stoppered that because of Anna's presence, but there still was considerable flame in his next try. "Angus, lad, I hate to say that your common sense flew out the hole in your hat, but asking for singing from me . . ."

"Lucas, you're the only other one of us here who's been to the rascal fair and watched old Fergus. If Rob and I are going to step out here and show how it's done in Nethermuir, we need you to sing the tune of it."

Lucas was shaking his head vehemently when Anna spoke in firm fashion: "Mr. Barclay, we in Brechin always heard that the men of Nethermuir are brothers to the lark."

That halted his head. "Well, yes, I know that was always said," Lucas confirmed without undue modesty. "We once in a while even said something of the sort ourselves. *Tam Lin*, did you mention, Angus?" I nodded. Lucas swallowed as if to be sure he had a throat there, then looked at Nancy. If answer passed between them I never saw it, but Lucas now said: "All right, all right, if I can remember any word of it."

> *Oh, you must beware, maidens all,*
> *who wear gold in your hair*
> *don't come or go by Linfield Hall*
> *for young Tam Lin is there.*

DANCING AT THE RASCAL FAIR

Dark and deep lay the wood of night
and eerie was the way
as fair Janet with hair so bright
toward Linfield Hall did stray.

I grant that other nationalities are known to dance, but it is my
hypothesis that they must have learned how from the Scots. You
can't but admit that a land of both John Knox and Robert Burns
is nimble, and we like to think that quality comes out on us at
both ends, head and feet. Earlier that night I danced a reel with
Flora Duff, who was wide as any other two women there, and she
moved like a rumor. And now Rob and Judith and Anna and
I were the four-hearted dancer of all dancers, gliding to and
from, following the weave of the tune, answering Lucas's un-
heavenly but solid voice with the melody of ourselves, saluting
the night and life with our every motion and capping them all
with the time-stopping instant when Rob and I faced one another, each with a hand on a hip and the other arm bent high
above head, and our two throats as one flung the exultant Highland cry, *hiiyuhh!*

Her skirt was of the grass-green silk,
her cloak of velvet fine.
Around her neck so white as milk
her fox-red furs entwine.

About the dead hour of the night
she heard Tam's bridles ring.
Her maidenly heart beat with might,
her pulse began to sing.

Put away geography and numeration and the presidents from
yon to hither, pupils of mine and of my partner in whirl Anna,
and write for us books of that dance. Scissor her lovely pofile
down the left of your pages and in eternal ink say how forthright
she is even when set to music. *Miss Ramsay seems to look into the
face of the tune in the air and say, yes, you are what music should be.*
Make an exact report of the way she and I blend into a single dancing figure and then shift swiftly into two again and next meld with

Rob and Judith. You will please find a line somewhere there, too, for the heady Scotch Heaven serenade this schoolroom has never heard before tonight: *hiiiyuhhh!*

> *She heard the horseman's silv'ry call,*
> *'Come braid your golden hair*
> *in the fine manse of Linfield Hall*
> *for I, Tam Lin, am there.'*

> *She went within that hall of Lin*
> *fair Janet on her ride*
> *and now you maidens know wherein*
> *dwell Tam Lin and his bride.*
> *HiiiiYUHHHH!*

Our final whoop, Rob and I agreed, could have been heard by old Fergus the Dervish himself wherever he was cavorting in Scotland just then.

The crowd too gave us whoops and hoots and claps of commendation as we two pairs of flingers vacated the floor to merely mortal dancers and Lucas accepted bravos from all directions. Escorting Anna off—I could have made a career of just that—I asked, "Don't you suppose that changed their minds any about schoolhouse dances, over across in Brechin?"

Where she held my arm I felt a lightest affirming squeeze. "If anything could," was her voice's lilting version.

When I reluctantly left Anna's side, I saw Rob gesture for me to come over where he and Judith were catching their breath between chat with Archie and Grace Findlater. Rob had a strange distant smile on him. As I came up, he gripped my shoulder. "I have to hand it to you, Angus, you do get an idea now and again."

I must have grinned like a moonchild, for Rob's head went from side to side and he expostulated, "No, no, I don't mean her. Any man with one eye that'll open could get that idea. What I mean is our Fergus fling. Angus, it made me think back to all our rascal fairs together and Nethermuir."

"What, are you growing sentimental in your old age?"

He gave me the caught smile of a mildly guilty boy. Whatever this was about, it had put that joyous shine on him of the day we stood on the Greenock dock. But he said only, "The surprises of this thing life. A person just never does know, does he." George Frew's fiddle began *The Soldier Lad's Love's Lament.* "And now that I've danced with you, McAngus, do you mind overmuch if I take a turn with my wife?"

I got myself beside Anna one last time as the goodbyeing was going on, and began: "You know, of course, tonight was a mark your Noon Creek dance will have to match."

"We will strive," she answered.

"It'll not be easy. Much of the music of the world got used up here tonight."

"We will dust off any that's left, you needn't worry. By now I know you are not a man for standing."

"There, you see? A mere few hours in my schoolroom and you've already learned a thing." Her parents were waiting at the door, I was drawing heavy looks from that mother of hers.

"Well. Goodnight, Anna," I finally had to say.

"Yes." A bit slow from her, too, I noted with hope. "Goodnight, Angus."

But before she could turn, I blurted: "Anna, I'd like to call on you."

That direct look of hers. "Then why don't you?"

A fly buzzed uselessly against the window of the Ramsay parlor, herald of my audience thus far with Anna's parents.

"So, Mr. McCaskill, you too are of Forfar," speaks the main dragon. "That surprises me."

Margaret Ramsay, mother of Anna, looked as if she could out-general Wellington any day of the week. A drawn, bony sort of woman with none of Anna's adventurous curves, she seemed to have room in herself only for skepticism toward the male race. Beside her sat probably her prime reason for that. Peter Ramsay was a plump, placid man who sat with his hands resting on his belly, the first finger of his right hand gripped in his left, in the manner a cow's teat would be grasped. Ready to milk one hand with his other and evidently content to spend a lifetime at it. It stretched my imagination several ways beyond usual, as to how these two beings could have made Anna.

I was trying to be extra careful with my tongue, but: "I'd be interested to know, Mrs. Ramsay, in what aspect I look so different from other Forfar folk. My face, is it? I should have put on my other one."

If vinegar can smile, Margaret Ramsay smiled. "Of course I meant surprised to find someone else from Forfarshire so near at hand here in Montana." She paused a mighty moment to let me comprehend the utter justice of her viewpoint. Next she needed to know: "You were schooled where?"

"At a 'venture school in Nethermuir."

"I see. Anna and I both matriculated from the dame school in Brechin."

"So I understand." *I am a famous scholar, see./ Graddy-ated and trickle-ated, me./I've been to Rome in Germany/and seen the snows of Araby.* I swallowed that safely away and put forth: "Education is the garment that never wears, they say."

"And what of your family?"

I looked squarely at her. "Dead," I said.

Margaret Ramsay regarded me. "I mean, of course, what of them in life."

My father the ironhand, encased in his deafness; my mother the mill worker; myself the tall alone boy treading the lightless streets of old stone town Nethermuir . . . try sometime to put those into parlor speech. Anna was interested and encouraging—Anna could do me no wrong—but it was uphill all the way, trying to tell of the wheelshop years.

Sun lightened the room a half-minute, cloud darkened it, the day's weather restlessly coming and going up there on the divide of the continent. This Ramsay place all but touched the mountains. Until humans learned to hang to the side of a crag with one hand and tend livestock with the other, here was as far as settlement could go. I hoped these Ramsays knew what they were in for when winter's winter, which is to say January and February, howled down off the Rockies onto them. From where I sat I could look right up into the granite face of Jericho Reef through the curtain, the window where the fly was haplessly zizzing.

"You've seen the Bell Rock lighthouse," I thought of abruptly, "off from Arbroath?"

"I passed it close on a schooner once," spoke Peter Ramsay, his most extensive contribution to that day's conversation. "Surprising."

Well, he didn't know the half of it yet. I began telling of Alex-

ander McCaskill of the Bell Rock. Of his day-by-day fear of his
ocean workplace, of his daily conquer of the fact that a boat is a
hole in the water. Of he and the other Arbroath stonemen encircling
the engineer Stevenson as the first foundation block of the lighthouse was laid and its dedication recited, *May the Great Architect of
the Universe complete and bless this building.* Of the fog-pale day the
boat did not come and did not come, the floodtide rising to take the
Bell Rock, dry-mouthed Stevenson drinking poolwater like a dog to
try to say bravery to his men, the random pilot boat at last. Of the
three-year materializing of the round beacon tower there beside the
verge of Scotland, a single bold sliver of brightwork in the sea. And
if the impression was left that my great-grandfather had been the
right hand of the colossal Stevenson throughout that feat of bringing
fire to the sea, I didn't mind.

"Interesting," granted Margaret Ramsay. "Interesting indeed."

"I'll walk out with you," Anna said when it came my time to go.

Air was never more welcome to me. Whoof. Picklish Meg Ramsay was going to be something to put up with. But Anna was worth
all.

As soon as we were out of sight around a corner of the house, I
put her hand on the back of mine and urged, "Quick, give me a
pinch."

She lightly did and inquired, "And what was that for?"

"I needed to be sure my skin is still on me."

Anna had to smile. "You did well. Even Mother thought so, I
could tell."

"Well enough to be rewarded by my favorite teacher?"

Anna let me kiss her. Not as boundlessly as I wished, but amply
enough for a start. Then she gave my arm a squeeze, and went
back to the house.

A recess soon after that, I stepped from my classroom into the
mud room for something from my coat. The outside door had been
left open, and in from the girls' field of play was wafting the clear
lilt of Susan Duff.

> *The wind and the wind and the wind blows high,*
> *the rain comes scattering through the sky.*
> *He is handsome, she is pretty,*
> *boy and girl of the golden city.*

I smiled at all that brought back, song of every schoolyard in Scotland. I bent to my coat search and hummed along as Susan sang on.

> *The wind and the wind and the wind blows high,*
> *the rain comes scattering through the sky.*
> *Anna Ramsay says she'll die*
> *if her lover says goodbye.*

That took care of my humming. What was coming next verse, I could guess all too definitely.

> *The wind and the wind and the wind blows high,*
> *the rain comes scattering through the sky.*
> *A bottle of wine to tell his name—*
> *Angus McAsker, there's his fame.*

I wondered whether everybody on this cheek of the earth knew the future of Anna and me except the pair of us. Maybe it was time we found out, too.

Those next honeyed weeks. Anna and I, as spring wove itself around us in leaf and bud and the recess-time sounds of scamper by our unpenned school flocks. In mid-May the dance at her schoolhouse, where it all but took a pardon from the governor for anyone other than myself to be permitted a whirl on the floor with Anna. Evenings, as many as we could possibly find, of kissing and fondling and the talk that was the spring air's equivalent of those. And before I was even done wishing for it to happen, the momentous gift out of the blue, the departure of those parents of hers. They went north with Isaac Reese and a great aggregation of his workhorses—Anna said it was like seeing a lake decide to move itself, the flow of manes and the slow patterned swirl of the herd—for a summer of building railroad crossings and plowing fireguard strips along the route of the Great Northern Railway. Peter Ramsay, wherever he hid the knack for it, was to be Reese's horse tender, and Anna's mother was to cook for the crew of teamsters. The single bit of grit for me in this fine news was that it encompassed Anna. As soon as school was out, she was to go up and join her mother as second cook. "This is our chance to get something ahead at last," she told me frankly of the rare

Ramsay bonanza of three good wages at once. As I was to do much the similar myself by going into the mountains with my and Rob's sheep, there was no arguing the case, really. I put aside pangs about a summer apart as best I could and concentrated on gaining every possible moment with Anna until then.

When May granted us its last Saturday night and the end-of-school dance at my schoolhouse, it was a roaring one even for a South Fork event, as if everyone was uplifted by the green year grinning at us. The hour went to late and then rounded midnight into early, and jigged on from there.

When the dance at last called itself done at nearly three in the morning, I was to see Anna home—we were a lovely distance past that essential rung of the courting ladder—as soon as my schoolhouse had been set to rights.

"Swamping is to sweeping what whaling is to fishing," I was enlightening her as I displayed my broom style.

"And where were you so fortunate as to learn the art of swamping?" she asked from where she was closing and locking the schoolroom windows. Lovely, to see that woman stretch to the window locks, her braid swaying free as a black silk tassel when her head tilted back.

"There's a standard answer to that among swampers," I informed her, "which I'll take refuge in: 'At my mother's knee and other low joints.'" This in fact wasn't a time when I particularly wanted to recount Rob and me arriving into the Two Medicine country and my subsequent career in the Medicine Lodge. I had seen again tonight what I'd begun to notice at the other dances, that while Anna plainly prized Lucas for the rare specimen he was, she was impervious to Rob. I knew I was going to have to sort that out at some soon point, but for now it merely seemed to me Rob's hard luck.

She turned enough from her chore to throw me a bright frank look. "I do have to say, Angus, history has a strange ring to it in your schoolroom."

Broom and I veered to her, and I leaned down and kissed her quickly but thoroughly.

"Is this part of swamping?" she wanted to know.

"When it's done right."

Banter and chores went along that way together as they should, until the South Fork school was tidier than it had ever been and the one task left was to take down the coal-oil lanterns from their ceiling hooks. I stood on a chair to reach each one down to Anna, and finally I was down myself with the last lit one, so we could find our way out to where our horses were tethered.

All night until then I had not bothered to see anything beyond Anna, so the moonbeams at the windows and across the school-room floor shone new to me. "Let's not go out just yet," I suggested to Anna before we were at the door. "We need to study this." I turned out the lantern and we were in the night's own soft silver illumination. In the moonwashed windows of the schoolhouse, the wooded line of the creek loomed like a tapestry of the dark. Above the trees stood the long level rampart of benchland between the North Fork and Noon Creek, and above that firm horizon flew the sky, specked with the fire of stars.

After a minute Anna uttered, "This country can be so beautiful, when it tries a little."

With my arm around her and the moon's exhibition in front of us, she seemed in no hurry to go. I was in none myself.

"Anna," I began, trying to find how to say it the best possible, better than anyone had said the great words before, "I want to marry you. More than I've ever wanted anything, I want that. Will—"

Her fingers stopped my lips, as if they had come to trace a kiss there. "Angus, wait. Please. Wait with that—that question."

"Anna, love, I've been making a career of waiting."

"You've certainly waited in a hurry where I'm concerned," she maintained lightly but seriously. "We've only known each other a little more than a month."

Forty days! I thought indignantly, but let her go on. "What I really mean to say"—rare difficulty for her, making real meaning known—"you don't know me all that well. The person I'd be for you, I mean, Angus, for the rest of your life."

"You can let me worry about that."

"You don't show any sign of making an effort at it," she said gently. "You seem to regard me as the first woman you've ever seen."

"That's more or less the case," I vouched.

"Angus, we can see at the end of the summer. You know I need to go be with Them"—my term for her mother and father—

"for this summer, and you have your own obligations with your sheep, don't you."

"Woman," I said to her as if she truly was the first, the only, of the species, "let's say to hell with the obligations and go get ourselves married. Right now, this very morning. We'll point the horses toward Gros Ventre and go roust the minister out of bed. The man'll need to climb out soon anyway to fluff up his sermon. Anna, what do you say?"

Do you know, for a long moment I almost won her to that. I could feel the halt of all she had been setting forth until now, the stop of her thought as this new proposal opened, enormous as the future, before her.

But after that teetering moment:

"I have to say life isn't that simple, Angus. It's a stale way to say it, but there are others we have to think of."

"Anna, just tell me this. While you're being dutiful daughter this summer, will you think about what I'm going to ask you the instant you get back?"

"Yes."

"*Yes!*" I shouted and the reverberation *yes . . . es . . . es* filled the darkened school. "Do you hear that, world? Miss Anna Ramsay knows the word *yes!*"

"You great gowk," she laughed, and this time laid a single finger across my lips. "They'll hear you everywhere along the creek."

I kissed that finger of hers three times and proclaimed: "I hope they hear it down in China. I hope every ear there is knows now that at the end of the summer I have this romantic prospect to cash in—"

"Cash in?" She gave me her half-smile, her straightforward way of teasing. "Is that your idea of the language of romance?"

"—and that this timid maiden—"

"Timid! Angus, you are absolutely—"

"—will have spent her every spare moment rehearsing the word *yes*! and come to the not illogical conclusion that having said it once in her life, she can say it again. And again and again and again, as many thousand times as I ask her to be mine."

She was looking at me bright-eyed, half ready to burst into even more laughter, half ready to fondly kiss me or be kissed. We could catch up on the laughter in our old age. I reached her even closer to me.

The darkness, the moonsilver, the night-morning that was both and neither, the two of us a chime of time together and yet about to be separated for an abyss of months; maybe because everything including ourselves was between definitions just then, bodily logic began to happen. Our kisses asked ever more kisses. Our clothing opened itself in significant places. Hands and lips were no longer enough.

I whispered huskily to Anna *wait*—entire new meaning to the word she had so recently used—and went out to Scorpion and fetched my sheepskin coat that was tied behind the saddle and then the coat was under us, *us,* on the schoolroom floor. I undid more of her dress while she was slowly and wonderfully busy at my neck and back with her arms, hands, fingers. Wherever I caressed her skin it was white elegance. Except where the bold twin pink nipples and their rose circles now bloomed.

You unforgettably feel the ache, the sweet ache. The deliciousness of thighs finding their way to thighs, the soft discovery of her body's cave place, the startling silkiness my hand was stroking there at the join of her, the curly tangle and stalk where her hand was searching out my own center. There was no eyes-closed mooniness: we were both watching this.

"Anna," my voice thick. "If I'm the first, you know this may hurt a bit."

"It won't," she spoke with surprising clarity.

Atop the piled softness of the wool coat we moved as slowly as we could hold ourselves to. Anna knew things. I was not the first. I didn't care. I was the one now. Her eyes into mine. Mine into hers. All below, our locket of bodies. Slow was far too wonderful to last, now my straining to touch her as deep inside as love can thrust, her clutching to gather me in, us and the husking cries from our throats mingling.

After, I felt perfect. It seemed the perfect echo of the delirium we had just been through to murmur in a fond gabble to her beside me on the coat, "They must be wondering in China what's going on up here with the two of us this morning."

Anna laughed and perfected it with a gentle poke of me. "You do have to admit, it's unusual behavior even in a schoolroom of yours."

"I wish it was absolutely customary," I said, and kissed between her perfect breasts.

An evening of middle June, Rob poked his head in on me. "Angus, sharpen your ears. I've a proposition for you."

"It'd be news if you didn't."

"Now don't be that way. I'm here to offer you an excursion, free gratis for nothing, and all you have to provide is your own matchless self for company. What this is, I've to go up to the railroad—Judith's new cream separator came in by train. Ride along with me in the wagon, why not. It's our last chance for an outing before we turn into shearers and sheepherders."

Rob was expansive these days because commerce suddenly was. Prices of wool and lambs had sprung back to what they were before all the buckets fell in the well of 1893. With their abundance of wethers to be shorn, Rob and Lucas were looking at a real payday ahead, just as my lamb crop would raise me to comfort; to where I wanted to be for Anna and me to begin our married life.

I said my first thought: "Why don't you just have the next freight wagon bring the thing?"

"That'd be weeks yet, and I want this to be a surprise for Judith. I'm telling her you and I are going up to talk sheep with the Blackfeet Agency people. Come along, man. You've been keeping yourself scarce everywhere but Noon Creek. See some more of the world for a change. This'll be the ride of your life." Rob smiled that blame-me-if-you're-heartless-enough-to smile of his. "Well, maybe not quite. *Men*," he pulled his chin into his neck for the croaking tone of the freighter Herbert seven years before, *"there's no hotel like a wagon. Warm nights your room is on the wagon—"*

"—*Stormy nights it's under it*," I couldn't help but complete the chorus. Our first prairie night out from Helena was beginning to seem another life ago. I still wasn't ready to relent to Rob. Jaunting for jaunt's sake was not something I was in the mood for, having better moods to tend to, and to the railroad and back was a journey of three days. "So your clinching argument is the opportunity to sleep out with the coyotes, is it?"

"Angus, Angus. Trust me to carry more than one motive at a time. I thought we could spend the going-up night there on the Two Medicine at Toussaint Rennie's place. You won't pass up the chance for a dose of Toussaint, now will you? The two of you can gab history until you're over your ears in it."

As Rob full knew it would, this cast a light of interest. Visiting Toussaint on his home ground would be like seeing where they put the music into fiddles. Besides, Rob was indubitably right that after shearing next week there would be a long summer in the mountains, stretched all the longer by Anna being away. The two weeks since she left had taken at least twice that much time to pass. Anna and the railroad, though. Here now, as Lucas would have put it, was a pregnant thought. Maybe, if I had the luck that love ought to have, just maybe the Reese crew plowing fireguard strips would be somewhere on the section of railroad where Rob was headed. A bonus chance to see Anna, however slight—

"You'll come, certain sure?" Rob specified. When I agreed so, he assured me: "Herbert would be proud of you."

"You know that Nancy," said Toussaint in making the introduction of his Blackfeet wife Mary Rides Proud to us the next night. "This is another one."

I am sure as anything I saw a flick of curiosity as Mary looked at Rob. About a heartbeat's worth. Then she moved to the stove and the fixing of supper, as if she were a drawing done of her niece at that moment in the kitchen of Lucas's house, but with blunter pencil.

The household's indeterminate number of leather-dark children eyed Rob and me with wariness, but Toussaint himself seemed entirely unsurprised at the sight of us, as if people were a constant traffic through this remote small reservation ranch. I see now that in Toussaint's way of thinking, they were. In his mind, time was not a calendar bundle of days but a steady unbroken procession, so that a visitor counted equally whether he was appearing to Toussaint at the very moment or long past.

"Toussaint, this reservation opened my eyes for me today," Rob said as we sat to supper. "There's a world of grass up here."

"The buffalo thought so," agreed Toussaint. "When there were buffalo."

"Now there's a thing you can tell us, Toussaint," Rob the grazier speaking now. "Where did those buffalo like to be? What part of this country up here was it that they grazed on?"

"They were here. There. About. Everywhere." Another Toussaint chuckle. "All in through here, this Two Medicine country."

The knit of Rob's brow told me he was having some trouble with a definition of *here* that took in *everywhere.* I tried another angle for him. "What, Toussaint, were they like the cattle herds are now?" I too was trying to imagine the sight the buffalo in their black thousands made. "Some here and there, wherever you looked?"

"The buffalo were more. As many as you can see at one time, Angus."

Supper was presented on the table to us the men, but Toussaint's wife Mary ate standing at the stove and some of the children took their meals to a corner and others wandered outside with theirs and maybe still others went up into the treetops to dine, for all that Rob or I could keep track of the batch. Domestic arrangements interested me these days, but this one was baffling. So far as I could see, Toussaint and Mary paid no heed to one another. That must have had limits, though, because somehow all these children happened.

The supper meat was tender but greasy. After a few thoughtful forkfuls Rob let fall: "Now you have me asking myself, Toussaint, just what delicacy is this we're eating?"

"Bear."

Rob cocked an eyebrow to me. Then swung half around in his chair and called to Toussaint's yokemate in life, "Absolutely the best bear I've ever eaten, Mary."

"This cream separator," wondered Toussaint about our tomorrow's cargo, "is it a Monkey Ward one?"

Rob took a slow sip of coffee, in what I knew was his way of hiding a smile, then exclaimed: "The exact very make, Toussaint. See now, Montgomery Ward and anything else in the world is right out on our doorstep with this railroad. What a thing it's going to be for this country," he went on, sounding more and more like the echo of Lucas. "Homesteaders can come straight from anywhere to here, they can hop from the train into a buckboard and go find a claim without even needing to set foot on the ground. Not quite like when you and I hoofed in all the way from Augusta, Angus."

"Jim Hill's haywagons," Toussaint summed the Great Northern railroad and its builder, and chuckled. "One more way people will bring themselves."

People and what they are. As Rob and Toussaint talked I was thinking of the expanse of country-to-be-peopled that Rob and I

had come through that day, I was thinking of Anna out there somewhere under its waiting horizon, summerlong her erect presence beside the fresh steel road of rails, I was thinking of the intricate come
and go that weaves us and those around us, of how Toussaint inex-
plicably was partnered in existence with Mary Rides Proud, Rob
now with Judith, Lucas with Nancy. "The winter of '86, Toussaint," I suddenly found myself at. "What was that like, up here?"

"That winter. That winter, we ate with the axe."

Rob made as if to clear an ear with his finger. "You did which?"

"We ate with the axe. No deer, no elk. No weather to hunt them
in. I went out, find a cow if I can. Look for a hump under the snow.
Do you know, a lot of snowdrifts look like a cow carcass?"

Rob was incredulous. "Toussaint, man, you mean you'd go out
and find a dead cow to eat?"

"Any I found was dead," Toussaint vouched. "Chop her up,
bring home as much as the horse can carry. West wind, all that
winter. Everything drifted east. You had to guess. Whether the
horse could break snow far enough to find a cow." Toussaint
seemed entertained by the memory. "That winter was long. Those
cattlemen found out. I had work all summer, driving wagon for the
cowhide skinners. That was what was left in this country by spring.
More cowhides than cows."

"A once in a lifetime winter," Rob summarized, "and I'm glad
enough I wasn't here to see it. Now we know to have hay and
sheds, anyway. It's hard luck that somebody else had to pay for
that lesson, but life wasn't built even, was it."

Mary Rides Proud rose from her chair by the stove and went out,
I supposed to the outhouse, if there was one. *By now Nancy is part
us and part them,* Lucas's voice that day we arrived to Gros Ventre,
and all this, *and you never quite know which side is to the front, when.
They say when Toussaint rode into town with her, the two of them
wrapped in buffalo robes, they had so much snow on them they looked
like white bears.*

"That winter must've made it hard to get to Gros Ventre," I said
to Toussaint. He gave away nothing in his look to me. Rob glanced
over at me, curious about my curiosity, nothing more. "If you ever
had to," I added.

"When I had to, I did that ride," said Toussaint. "One time was
all."

Setting out from Toussaint's to the railroad the next morning, Rob and I traveled the brink of the Two Medicine River's gorge for several miles to where the main trail crossed it by bridge. It was as if the earth was letting us see a secret street, the burrowing route of its water.

"Now why do you suppose they put a river all the way down there, Angus? It'd save us a lot of hill grief if it was up here with the rest of the country." The Two Medicine would have needed to flow in the sky to match Rob's lofty mood this morning.

"Talk to the riverwright about it," I advised him. Below us in its broad canyon the Two Medicine wound and coiled, the water base for all the world that could be seen. The sentinel cottonwoods beside the river rustled at every touch of wind. Up where we were and out across the big ridges all around, pothole lakes made blue pockets in the green prairie. Anna, you need to see this with me, I vowed that June morning on the green high bluffs of the Two Medicine. Sometime we must come, just the two of us, and on a morning such as this watch summer and the earth dress each other in light and grass.

"No help for it that I can see," Rob announced as he peered down the long slope to the river and up the longer one on its north side. "Here's where our horses earn their oats." Down we went and across, beside sharp stark bluffs.

The buffalo cliff, Toussaint had indicated the rock-faced heights along the river here with a nod. *It was a good one. These Blackfeet put their medicine lodge near. Two times. The river got its name.* Looking at the gray cliff I could all but see the black stampede in the air as the Blackfeet drove the buffalo over. Eyes whitely mad with flight, legs stiff for shock they could never withstand, the animals would have been already dying in midair. Lucas's little recital off a tombstone that first-ever night Rob and I spent in Gros Ventre, in the Two Medicine country: *I fell through life. . . .* That had been one of the sagas here too, in a time of other people, other creatures. Maybe epitaphs were the same everywhere.

At the summit of the lofty grassy ridge above the Two Medicine, the land opened again into billowing prairie with mountains filling the western horizon. It took some looking as we rattled along in the wagon to spot our destination. This was before Browning was a town, and before it was even Browning. Willow Creek, the site had been dubbed for its stream, and what differentiated it from the absolute prairie was the depot and the buildings of the Blackfeet Indian Agency. Those and the railroad, a single thin iron trellis across all this prairie, bringing the world to Montana, taking Montana to the world. From here at wan Willow Creek, Browning-to-be, now you could go straight by train to either ocean.

Rob may have been thinking of the wool that would travel these tracks to the mills of Massachusetts in a few weeks, of the lambs that would go to Chicago at summer's end. For once he did not speak his thoughts, but sat there next to me looking royally satisfied. I was the opposite of that, for nowhere along the miles of railroad in sight was there any dark turned earth of plowed fireguards, no crew of teamsters. No cook tent. No Anna. She was somewhere east beyond the grass horizon, at Havre, Harlem, Malta, places as distant as they sounded. Had I known to a total certainty that there would be no sight of her, I would have passed up this wagon jaunt with Rob as if it was cold gravy. But even love can't see clearly over the curve of the earth. Rob clucked to the team and we headed for the depot.

Now that there was no prospect of Anna, I was anxious to head home and begin using up the days of this summer of waiting. Rob was showing impatience, too, at the lack of whoever ought to be in charge of railroad freight.

"What do they do, put coats of vanishing paint on depot agents?" he pronounced annoyedly. "McAngus, give a look for the rascal inside and I'll try the freight room, why not."

I stepped quickly into the waiting room. The sole person there was a young woman, auburn-haired and bright-cheeked, likely the out-of-place daughter or very young and trying-not-to-be-abject wife of some Blackfeet Agency clerk. A fetching enough girl, but not a fraction of Anna. "Hello," I tossed with some sympathy, still glancing around for the depotman, and then turned my eyes back to this other to ask whether she'd seen him lately. She was looking at me pertly, as if expecting answer from me instead. And then uttered:

"Hello yourself, Angus McCaskill with a mustache."

Nethermuir. Nethermuir in the voice. That shined-apple complexion and her gray eyes. She had to be, but couldn't possibly—

"Adair?" I got out. "Are you, you can't—"

Uproar burst in on us then, Rob laughing and hooting and hugging his sister and pounding me, "He never guessed! Adair, we did it to the man! It was perfect as can be, he never had a clue you'd be here! Angus, wait until they hear in Scotch Heaven how you let a slip of a girl sneak up on you all the way from Scotland!"

By now I had enough wit and wind back to enlist in the laughing, and Adair gave me a quick timid hug and asked, "Do you mind the surprise, Angus? It was this dickens Rob's doing, he insisted we not tell you."

"Mind, how could I mind. It's a thing I never expected, is all—finding you in a Montana train station, Dair Barclay. But, but what're you doing here?"

"What, you can't tell by the sight of me? Adair is a tourist," she defined herself with a self-mocking small smile. Of course I knew in my mind that Adair had grown from the scrap of a girl she was when Rob and I left Nethermuir. She was, what, twelve then. But knowing that was different from understanding, as my eyes were having me do, that she now had reached nineteen and was certifiably more than a girl in every way that I could see. "It was Rob's notion for me to come spend a bit of time. To see this famous Montana of yours."

"Rob is definitely a wonder," I said with a trickle of suspicion beginning in me. "And so how long are you here for?"

"The summer," was Adair's all innocent answer, "to keep Judith company while Rob and you are out being shepherds." But Rob had his own expanded version as he gave his sister the fifth hug of the past minute: "She's here for as long as we can keep her. The lads of Nethermuir will just have to cry at the moon."

The former lad of Nethermuir who was me looked those words over, looked over their source as thoroughly as I could and still keep a reasonably pleasant face for Adair. I had major questions to put to Rob Barclay as soon as I could get him alone and he knew it, he oh most definitely knew it.

"See now, McAngus, I did bring you along for a reason," he said brightly, "to help load Adair's things. Then we'd better make miles before dark, hadn't we?"

"One of your better thoughts recently," I told him, and set off for the luggage. As I went I heard Adair ask, "What, we won't reach Scotch Heaven by tonight?" and Rob answer, "No, not quite." So far, Dair Barclay and I were even in the day's surprises.

After we started across the prairie, Adair kept up with the first

rush of talk from Rob while I *mmm*ed and *hmm*ed in the spots between, but I could see her glancing around restlessly at the land,
the grass, the Indians, and for that matter at Rob and myself. Time
and again she turned her head toward the mountains. After a bit
she said of herself: "Forgive Adair for the amount of green in her,
but she has to ask. You don't mean those are the mountains where
the two of you will be with the sheep?" Myself, I thought the Rockies looked particularly stately this calm sunlit day, purple old
widows at tea.

"The very ones," Rob and I chorused.

"But they're nothing but cliffs and snow. Where is there even a
place for you to find a foothold?"

"Just the country for sheep and Scotchmen," Rob assured her.
"Angus and I will come down from the top of the world there in a
few months with our fortunes trotting in front of us."

Adair continued to study the vast jagged line of mountains as if
they might pounce out at us. Well, well. This sister of his whom
Rob thought was a Montanian in the making might hold a surprise
for him as well.

"Do the full recitation of them for her," Rob urged me. "Adair,
what this person on the other side of you doesn't know about the
Two Medicine country isn't worth knowing."

Adair turned to me with a wisp of a smile. "Are you guilty of all
that?"

"He's greatly worse," Rob declared. "I've only told you the top
part about him. This is a coming man, this McCaskill person. Even
I have to say so."

"I am in trouble," I agreed feelingly with Adair, "if I'm in the
good graces of our Rob. But our mountains, now, since you're keen
to know." I took her through the catechism of the peaks and crags
rising above Scotch Heaven: Jericho Reef, Guthrie Peak, Phantom
Woman Mountain, Rooster Mountain, Roman Reef, Grizzly Reef.

By the time I finished, Adair had turned from the mountains toward me again. "You say them as if they were lines of verse," she
remarked almost in a questioning way.

"Now you've gone and done it, Adair. You have to watch your
step all the time around this man," Rob enjoined, "or you'll give
him the excuse to start spouting—"

"—Burns, did I hear someone start to say?" I thrust in. "*Beware
a tongue/that's smoothly hung*, for instance? Now there's a major

piece of advice, Dair, for being around this brother of yours." Pick
the bones out of that for a while, Rob, why don't you.

Adair laughed, a pretty enough sound, fully half as melodious as
Anna's. "You mean you haven't been able to change him at all in
seven years?"

"Thank heaven I can recognize jealousy when I hear it," Rob
gave us equally, and slapped the reins lightly on the team's rumps.
"It's time to let the wheels chase the horses," he emulated our
stagecoach driver from Craig to Augusta those years ago. "Next
stop, Badger Creek."

At least I knew better than that. Any schoolteacher could have
informed Rob that unless girls of Nethermuir grew up with iron
bladders these days, a stop was imminent somewhere in the hours
before we would reach Badger Creek. Nor did Rob help his own
cause by being too busy with talking, when we crossed the Two
Medicine, to think of offering Adair a pause within its sheltering
grove. So when we topped the Two Medicine gorge's southern rim
and Adair took her first look at the naked world ahead, no conceal-
ment higher or thicker than a spear of grass for miles in any direction, I truly believe I discerned her first squirm of realization.
Forgive me this, Dair Barclay, I thought to myself, *but you may as
well meet the bare facts of this country sooner than later.* And both of us
were going to be the better off the quicker I could get Rob alone
and wring out of him what he was up to in bringing her here.

Grant Adair a good high mark, she did about as well as could be
done with the situation. "Coachman," she eventually ventured to
Rob with only a minimum tone of embarrassment, "are there any
conveniences at all along this route of yours?"

He looked startled and cast hurriedly around for a coulee. There
was one about half a mile ahead, which he promised her. "They're,
ah, they're of an airy construction in this neighborhood."

When we reached the brow of the coulee and I stepped off to
help Adair down from the wagon, I saw her nipping her lower lip
against having to ask the next question. That fret at least I could
spare her. "No snakes in this grass," I assured her.

"Except," I began on Rob the instant Adair had passed down
from view, "maybe one major one. Just out of curiosity, Mister
Rob, how long have you had this little visit of Adair's in the
works?"

"Not all that long."

"Not all how long?"

"Not long at all."

"How long is that?"

"Angus, I don't carry a calendar around in my hand."

"No, anyone with your armload of schemes of course couldn't. Just tell me this: you thought it up back this spring before I met Anna, now didn't you?"

"Angus, Angus. Which would you rather hear—yes, no or maybe?"

I could have throttled him there on the wagon seat. An instructive scene for Miss Adair Barclay of Old Scotland when she came up out of the coulee, mayhem on the wild prairie. "Your idea was to get Adair over here and marry her off to me, wasn't it?"

"If it worked out that way, I wouldn't mind, now would I. Though I do have to say, Angus, your attitude this afternoon is starting to make me have second thoughts about you as a brother-in-law."

"For God's sake, man! Do you think you can just take lives and tie them together that way?" Whatever his answer was I didn't give him a chance to polish it and bring it out. "At least why didn't you let her know about Anna and me? Why'd you let Adair come, after that? Now here she is, looking at me the way a kitten looks at her first mouse, and there's nothing in it for her."

"You and Anna, that did arrive as a surprise after I'd already written to Adair," he admitted. "But who knew, maybe you'd fall off a horse and come to your senses." Rob must have seen the incitement that was going to bring down on him, because he quickly put in, "Just joking, Angus. Man, I know how you feel about Anna. It's written all over you six inches high. But if you're not the one for Adair, there are other possibilities wearing pants in this world, aren't there. What harm can it do to bring her here for the summer and let her find out what her prospects are? You and I found our way out of that used-up life over across there. Adair deserves the chance, too, doesn't she?"

"Damn it, Rob, her chance at life here is one thing. Her chance at me is totally another. You're going to have to tell her that."

"And I will, I will. But just let me get the girl home to Breed Butte in peace, can't you? Is that so much? Whup, here she comes, looking improved. You could stand to, too, do you know."

The dusk began to catch us as we came down into the broad bottomland beside Badger Creek, and we quickly chose a willow-shel-
tered bend with the trickle of the creek close by. In the slow sunset
of that time of year, the mountains stood out like silver-blue shards
of rare stone. The western half of the sky was filled with puffy
clouds the same shade as the mountains, but with their bottoms
ember-lit by the setting sun.

"Angus and I ordered that up special for you," Rob was quick to
assure Adair.

"You're a pair of old profligates then," she retorted, gazing at the
emberglow sky and the miles and miles of mountains.

We rapidly made a fire of our own, for Montana has a chill in its
night air even in summer.

"You ought to have seen where Angus and I spent last night,"
Rob now at suppertime was reporting to Adair, about Toussaint's
household. "The crowd there was enough to make you thankful this
prairie is so empty."

"This isn't as empty as it looks," I put in purely out of peeve at
Rob. "We're camped near history here."

Rob cocked his head and peered into the last of the dusk. "What
color is it, Angus, I don't seem to see it."

"Actually it ended up red," I said, "which history seems to have
a bad way of doing."

"You mean the man Lewis that Toussaint was on about?" *Mer-
iwether Lewis. Do you know of him, Angus and Rob? He was a bad sign
for these Blackfeet. Came up the Marias, looking. Came to the Two Medicine, looking some more. There where Badger Creek runs in, he found
something, do you know. These Blackfeet. Eight in a party, horse
takers. Lewis and his were four. Lewis smokes the pipe with those Blackfeet, nothing else to do. They all camp together that night near Badger
and Two Medicine.* "Adair, this one," Rob inclined his head toward
me, "will teach at you day and night if you don't watch out for
him."

She was watching me with curiosity. "Lewis was the first white
man to explore through here," I tried to explain. If she was here to
taste Montana, she had better be aware of its darker flavors. "He
and another led a group across this part of the country almost a
hundred years ago. Burke? Not quite it. Clark, that was the other
with Lewis." *In the night, do you know, the Blackfeet grab guns from*

Lewis and his three. Everybody fights. These Blackfeet knew how to fight then. But Lewis and another get their guns back. BOOM! One Blackfeet dead. BOOM! One more Blackfeet dead. But they say that one combed Lewis's hair with a bullet first. The rest of the Blackfeet ran off, go away to think it over a while. Lucky for Lewis they did, or maybe no more Lewis.

"McAngus," Rob proclaimed, "you're a great one for yester-days."

"They've brought us to where we are," I retorted with an edge to it. Noticing Adair blinking at this session between Rob and me, I toned matters down a bit. "But Rob's right, you didn't come across the ocean for a history lesson, did you."

"No, it's all interesting," Adair insisted. "Go on, Angus." But go on to what. I gave a lame version of Lewis and the Blackfeet strug-gling in the night, then shrugged. "Toussaint has it more or less right, this reservation we're on grew out of that and these Indians have had to give way ever since."

"To the likes of us," Rob intoned. "Peaceable men of attain-ment, in pursuit of cream separators."

A round of laughter for that which I made myself join, promising Rob a time soon when he would have to laugh out the other side of himself. But then Adair said: "So much land here, and"—she sent me an apologizing look—"so empty. It's hard to think of men killing each other over it."

"A great mighty struggle," Rob said solemn as a knell, "with two casualties."

"I suppose they died as dead as any," I observed to him. *Man at war is maggots' meat/dished up in his winding sheet.* Adair at once sided with me—but then she'd have to, wouldn't she, I reminded myself—chiding Rob, "What if we were the Indians and they were us? Who'd be joking then?"

"Anyway it wasn't the Battle of Culloden, now was it, you two," Rob closed off that direction of conversation. "Angus, have you ever seen anything like this grass up here. If we could ever manage to get sheep onto this, we'd have found the front gate to heaven." He was not wrong, the grassland of the Blackfeet reservation in-deed was a grazier's dream. Led by Rob, our talk turned now to the Two country's prospects this bountiful year, our prospects as sheep-men. There but not spoken were also Adair's prospects as a Montana wife, although I doubted those more and more as I watched her try to keep a brave face to this overwhelming land.

Eventually bedtime, and Rob telling her, "The lodgings are simplicity itself, Adair. Ladies upstairs"—he indicated the wagon, with its bed of robes—"and others downstairs."

As we settled in for the night, a coyote sent its song to the moon. "We hired music for the occasion, too," Rob said up through the wagon to Adair.

"Cayuse," we heard her try very softly to herself. Then: "Coyote. Rob, Angus," she raised her voice, "is our serenade coming from a coyote?"

"Nothing else," we assured her, and then the night went still, as if the song dog had simply come by to test whether Adair could name him.

I had just begun to drowse when Rob's snoring started. Then came a cascade of giggles overhead, and my own grudging laughing as I was reminded of so many other nights of Rob's nose music, from the steerage bunks of the *Jemmy* to now.

I moved where I lay so that my head was out from under the wagon and spoke softly upstairs to Adair, "You ought to have heard him when the pair of us were on the old ocean. He drowned out the whales and all other challengers."

"Do you remember our tall narrow house, Angus?" I did, although I had not thought of cramped River Street in a long while. "When I was little and sleeping in the gable room, I would wake up and hear Rob sawing the dark below me and know that nothing had carried us off during the night," she said fondly.

And now he's carried you off here, under a misapprehension at least as big as any Scottish night. But I said only, reassuringly, "He's vital here, too. We need him to give singing lessons to our coyotes."

She giggled again, then went quiet. I was remembering now that first vast black pit of Montana night when Rob and I started for the Two Medicine country with Herbert and his freight wagon, six, no already seven years before. This time of year Adair at least ought to be safe from waking into a snowstorm as Rob and I did, although in Montana you couldn't be entirely sure ever. I hoped, too, that she would not be too hurt by the disappointment of this "visit," this bedamned misbegotten matrimonial outing Rob had got her into; I hoped that this Adair would find at the end of the dark the life she wanted, as I had now that Anna was in my life.

To be saying something in that direction without alarming
Adair, I brought out: "None of this is exactly Scotland, is it?"

"No. But then I thought that's why you and Rob are here."

"Goodnight then, Dair Barclay."

"Goodnight yourself, Angus."

The next day's miles went back and forth between fleet and
slow—the team and wagon urged snappily toward home and
Rob's confession to Adair whenever it was my turn at the reins,
lapsing into a determined saunter whenever Rob held them. At
whichever pace, our passenger between us in her clothes of
Scotland and her larklike smallness looked like someone unexpectedly being carriaged along the banks of the Congo. But true
to yesterday Adair still responded avidly to any word I said, on
those occasions when Rob managed to gouge one out of me, and
that was what led to it.

Rob had the reins when we came south out of the cattle-spotted
hills of Double W rangeland to the shallow valley of Noon Creek
and that strange bold view of Breed Butte, so gradual but so
prominent, ahead on the divide between this valley and Scotch
Heaven's, and Rob would not have been Rob if he hadn't halted
the horses to begin extolling his homestead pinnacle there to
Adair. She seemed to be listening to her brother a thousand percent, but suddenly she was pointing west along Noon Creek to
where two small white dots and a less small one stood out. This
Adair had eyes that could see. "Angus, there. Is that your
schoolhouse?" she asked as if already deeply fond of it.

"No," I answered, not looking toward her, not looking toward
Rob. "No, that one is my fiancée's."

All but true, that word *fiancée*. I propped it up with the others I
had been wanting to say into the air all of this journey from the
depot. "Her name is Anna Ramsay. We met early this spring." In
me, *And I love her beyond all the limits,* but Adair did not need that
added to this necessary revelation. At the tail of my eye I could see
her make herself hold steady, make herself keep that defending
look she had had when she first saw this land of raw mountains and
unpeopled vastness. From beyond Adair I could feel Rob's hot dismayed—betrayed?—gaze on me. But fair is fair, square is square,
Rob. I had waited with it until we were within sight of home, I had

held it in despite every doubt about when and how and if and whether you ever were going to say it to Adair yourself.

"Why, Angus," Adair managed, after a long moment. "I hadn't heard." Nothing was ever more true. "Congratulations to you. And her."

The source of guilty silence beside Adair spoke now in a strained version of Rob's voice, "Our lad Angus has had a busy spring."

Past that as if it never existed, Adair queried: "When is the wedding then?"

"We haven't named the date," I responded, and explained the circumstances of Anna's absence. "But at summer's end."

"You sound so happy," spoke Adair. Then again: "Congratulations to you." Plucky. Every Barclay ever made was that.

Done and done, at least my part of it.

"Rob," I said innocent as a choir note, "hadn't we better move on to Gros Ventre? Adair has yet to meet Lucas."

Apprehension comes in various sizes, and Rob had his next quantity of it by the time we came down off the benchland to Gros Ventre and could see past the trunks of the cottonwoods the sky-blue sign proclaiming MEDICINE LODGE.

"Adair, I'd better tell you," from him as if this was a hard day in the business of telling, "Lucas is not quite what a person expects an uncle to be."

Adair gave him a look of *what next?* "You mean because of his hands? But we at home have known about that for years."

"No," answered Rob, "I just mean Lucas."

"So now Montana can boast another Barclay!" boomed Lucas when Rob fetched him out of the Medicine Lodge. I swear, Lucas had figured out the situation to the last zero, just by the look on Rob's face, and for Dair's sake was being twice as hearty as usual. "Come down here for a proper hug, lass!" and she did, stepping gamely from the wagon into an embrace between Lucas's arm stubs. "Adair, welcome to Gros Ventre," he bestowed on her with enough hospitality for several towns this size. "By Jesus—excuse my Latin—you can't know how pure glad I am to lay eyes on my very own . . . niece!"

If Lucas hadn't been facing down the street toward Wingo's; if his last word hadn't shot out with an unexpected ring as the years of habitual talk about Wingo's "nieces" chimed in him; if Lucas hadn't started roaring, I never would have laughed. And Rob wouldn't have reddened into resemblance to a polished apple if it hadn't been for the uncontrollably chortling two of us.

Adair blinked in mystification.

"Nothing, nothing, lass," Lucas assured her. "Just a private joke. Maybe Robbie can explain it to you when he has time, ay, Robbie?"

There ensued a fast stew of family chitchat, ardent questions from Lucas and mettlesome tries at response from Adair and infrequent mutters from Rob, which I carefully stayed out of. If I knew anything by now I knew that the Barclays were going to be the Barclays, and the rest of the race may as well stand back.

"Now you have to come around to the house," Lucas ultimately reached, "and meet Nancy."

"Nancy?" responded Adair, further bewildered.

"Sometime, we can," Rob inserted rapidly. "But we need to head home just now, Angus and I have chores and more chores waiting."

"No matter." Lucas waved an arm stub that Adair's eyes could not help following. "We'll be out to see you shear next week. It's past time all of us in the sheep business got a chance to watch something that'll make us money instead of taking it from us. We can have a Barclay gathering and welcome you proper then, Adair. In the meantime, make this awkward squad treat you right."

"And how is Adair taking to Scotch Heaven?" I sweetly asked that famous matchmaking brother of hers a few days later when he and I had to begin readying the sheep shed for shearing.

"Fine, fine," Rob attested stoutly. "She's having just a fine time."

"Getting used to the wind, is she?" I asked with solicitude. The last of our wagon journey home from Gros Ventre after Adair's niecehood coronation by Lucas had been into a bluster which steadily tried to blow the buttons off the three of us, and at the creek crossing sent Adair's sunhat sailing. I had gallantly held the team's reins while Rob waded to retrieve the hat from its port of willows fifty yards downstream.

"She never even notices the old breeze any more," Rob re-

sponded, and impatiently waited for me to lift my end of the next
shearing-pen panel to be carried into place.

"I imagine seeing shearing will be a major thrill for her," I went
on, straight as a poker but enjoying myself immoderately, "don't
you think?"

"I'm sure as anything it will," responded Rob as we grunted and
carried. "And that reminds me of a thing," he galloped to the new
topic, "the Leftover Day. I'm going to keep back a bunch of yearling wethers for it, enough to make a real day of shearing. Why
don't you pair with me?"

This startled me twice at once. First, that Rob was asking me to
pair-shear, so soon after making myself less than popular with him
by unfurling my news of Anna to Adair before he could prepare.
But one of the problems of a partnership is the difficulty of staying
steadily angry at someone you have to work side by side with, and I
supposed Rob's peeve at me simply had worn out in a hurry. The
further unexpectedness, though, was that Rob intended a big event
of what was usually merely the do-whatever-is-left-to-be-done final
day of shearing. It of course had been Ninian Duff, back when we
all entered the sheep business, to discern that if we ourselves did
the last odds and ends of shearing—the lambless ewes who hadn't
borne that spring, our bellwether Percy and the handful of less fortunate wethers destined to be mutton on our own tables, the crip-
pled sheep and the lame sheep and the ill sheep and the black
sheep, all the "leftovers" there ever are at the fringe of raising
sheep—if we ourselves did Leftover Day we saved a full day of
paying the hired shearing crew. Too, Leftover Day had come to be
not just the finale of shearing but also as much of a bit of a festival
as you can make from an occasion such as the undressing of sheep,
with four of us taking up the wool shears ourselves, and the rest of
Scotch Heaven to wrangle the sheep remnant and provide commen-
tary. But this was new, that some of Rob and Lucas's fine healthy
yearling wethers would be in with the hospitalers and other rag-
gletaggles of Leftover Day.

I studied Rob. It was a clear economy for the Barclays, to get
those wethers shorn free by neighbors instead of the hired crew.
But as to how Rob was going to justify this to those neighbors—

"What it is," he enlightened me without delay, "I thought maybe
Adair would enjoy seeing a real shearing contest. So I challenged

George and Allan Frew to one on Leftover Day. They went for that like a pair of fetching pups."

I had to hoot. "You're a generous man, to show your sister how you get the whey beat out of yourself"—and myself too; I didn't miss that interesting implication—"shearing against the Frews. I can hear Allan crow now." I could, too. Other shearing times Rob and I had paired to try, Ninian and I had tried, Ninian and Rob had tried, every set of Scotch Heaven men with any contest blood in them had tried and fully failed to tally more sheep than the Frew cousins on Leftover Day. The damn man Allan simply was a wool-making machine and George was almost as bad.

"This is the year we'll put a plug in Allan Frew," maintained Rob. "What do you say to that?"

"I'll say the plain fact, which is that we've never even managed to come close yet. Rob, the two of us have about as much chance of outshearing the Frew boys as we have of jumping over this sheep shed."

He smiled and then shook the smile at me. "This year, we've got a card in our hat."

"Do we. And what's that?"

"These."

Rob stepped over to where his coat was hanging, reached under, and with a beam of triumph brought forth two gleaming sets of wool shears.

I had seen my share of wool shears before. But not these. Each of these shears had a pair of elongated triangular blades which faced each other with sharp expectancy, their bottoms linked in graceful loops of handle.

"Just listen to these lovelies sing," Rob urged me. Experimenting dubiously I put my hand around the grip of the shears he'd handed me and squeezed the hafts of metal. The faces of the blades moved across each other like very large scissors that had just been dipped in oil, steel crooning ever so gently against steel. *Zzzing zzzing,* they chimed a soft chorus with the identical blades Rob was clasping and releasing, *zzzing zzzing.* Truly, here was a shears that seemed to coax my hand to keep working it, keep discovering the easy buttered whet of the blades as they met. Here was just the thing to make wool fly, right enough. I made my hand stop eliciting the whicker of the blades, so that I could read their tiny incut letters:

175

MANUFACTURED IN SHEFFIELD, ENGLAND.

"Finest steel in the known world," proclaimed Rob. "Sheffield stuff holds an edge like a razor."

"These don't grow on trees. Where'd you get them?"

"I had Adair bring them. See now, McAngus, these're our ticket over the Frew boys."

I saw, and then some: saw through Rob here as an open window. The winning shearing team were the heroes of Leftover Day, which was to say, stolid and effacing as George Frew was, Allan Frew was the perpetual hero of Leftover Day. But this time, this time Rob wanted me up there on the woolly cloud of triumph, for Adair to see up at. The damn man was still trying to fan up ardor between her and me, exactly as if Anna did not exist. You had to credit him for persistence, moments when you didn't want to wring his stubborn Barclay neck. But rather than spend the rest of the day in steaming argument with Rob, I held myself to pointing out the hole in the bottom of his scheme:

"Rob, it's a clever notion and all. But I can't say I'm going to be that much faster a shearer even with blades such as these. Allan came out of his cradle shearing faster than I can even dream about."

"Fast isn't it, man. Come on now, think sharp." He paused significantly. "The afternoon recess. Do you see the idea now, or am I going to have to paint it red for you?"

I saw again, this time with my every pore, down to the small of my back. I can swear that there was not a shearing muscle in me not alarmed by what Rob was proposing. Yet it might work. Outlandish enough, it just might. More than that, even. Gazing at Rob there in the shed, as innocently luminous with scheme as he had been when he lured me to the depot and Adair, I had the thought that Allan Frew was not the only one eligible for getting a plug put in him, come Leftover Day.

Life missed a major step in efficiency by putting fleece onto sheep instead of directly onto us. There is no other harvest like shearing, the crop directly from the living animal, panting and squirming, the shearers stooping daylong in sweat and concentration as they reap greasy wool. Everyone had work. Most often I was gate man, scurrying to operate all the waist-high swinging doors in the cutting chute that sluiced the sheep into the shearers' catch pens six at a time, each penful the pantry the shearer went to for sheep, so to say. Behind me, Rob and Allan Frew customarily were the wranglers, wrangling consisting of steadily shoving the band of sheep to the end of the corral where they funneled single file into my cutting chute, but as Rob and Allan performed it, lengthy wrangles about theories of sheep and sheepdogs and sheepherders also went on between them as if it was coffee-time conversation. If you think of shearing as an hourglass of work, Rob and Allan and I and the unshorn sheep were the supply bell of sand grains at the top. The hired crew of shearers who traveled from job to job of this sort—my back ached to think of their season of stooped-over labor—made the neck of the hourglass: from the shearing floor where twelve or fifteen of them did their clipwork, naked sheep and fleeces of wool steadily trickled. Then on the other side of the shearing crew, the catch-chamber of all this effort of shearing: Archie Findlater the tallyman, Donald Erskine the brander who daubed the sheep owner's paintmark onto each ewe's newly naked back, one boy or another as doctor—Davie Erskine had just enough concentration to manage it—who swabbed on disinfectant whenever a sheep was nicked by the blades; and finally, ultimately, Ninian Duff as wooltromper, stomping the fluffy fleeces down into the long woolsack hung like a giant's Christmas stocking through a hoop in the high little tromping tower. It always seemed to me fittingly festive that as each woolsack filled with its thirty-five or forty fleeces, Ninian within the sack gradually emerged out its top like a slow, slow jack-in-the-box.

All this to undress a sheep, you may say. But it wasn't the naked affronted ewe, stark as glass knickers, that was the product of this. No, it was the rich yellow-white coat she had been separated from. Wool. The pelt that grows itself again. I for one could readily believe that when man started harvesting his clothes from tamed animals instead of shopping wild for furs, then true civilization began. The wool of our sheep went off to eastern mills with abracadabra names such as Amoskeag and Assabet and transformed into cloth for shirts, dresses, trousers, everything. You cannot overlook the marvelous in that.

"Man, this is the year we've been looking for under every rock." Rob was built on springs, this shearing time. A tremendous wool crop at a good price, Adair on hand, the Sheffield shears waiting to trim Allan Frew down to size—every prospect pleased.

"The sky is about to rain gravy," I agreed with him, and grinned. I was in great spirits myself, Anna and our future always right there at the front of my mind. Adair I was aware of only at meals, when the entire shearing gang of us trooped into my house to eat off the long plank-and-sawhorse table Rob and I had put up. Odd to see, there in my kitchen, her and Judith— particularly Judith, whose presence there always reminded me that with a small veer of fate those years ago she might be in my kitchen all the time—but odd is part of life, too. Yet I wondered what Adair made of all this, our Two country and its infinity of sheep and its mountains the size of clouds.

I had my one chance to find out midway through that shearing time. We had just finished with the Erskine band and I was helping Davie drive them west from the shed, toward the start of their summer in the mountains. As we shoved them past my house and buildings, the bare sheep blatting comparisons of indignation to each other and Davie and I and our dogs answering them in full, out from the house came Adair to empty a dishpan. She stopped to witness the commotion, as who wouldn't. Once the sheep were past the buildings I called out, "They're yours, Davie," and dropped away to return to the shearing shed. But my spirits were so thriving, with how well the shearing was going and, yes, with thoughts of Anna someday standing there in my yard where Adair now stood, that I veered over to Adair to joke: "Whatever you do, don't count these sheep as they go past or you'll be asleep a year."

"They look so—so forlorn without their wool."

"They'll have a fine fresh coat of it by the end of summer. By the time you go back to Scotland, you won't recognize these ladies." Or by the time, Dair Barclay, I am the husband of Anna and you're married to some Montanian conspicuously not me. One or other. But not that result which Rob dreamed up and still was trying to puff life into, not that result for which he brought you innocent from Nethermuir: not the altar halter tying together Angus and Adair, thank you just the same.

"Yes, I know they'll get new wool," Adair answered. "It's just that they're so plucked right now. Like poor old chickens ready for the pot.''

I noticed she was flinching from the wind trying to find its way into her through her eyes. "What you have to do, girl," I instructed as I moved around to stand between her and the breeze's direction, "is learn to get in the lee of it. I make an A Number One windbreak, if I say so myself.''

"That helps," Adair concurred. "Thank you.'' She took the chance to look past me to the mountains, high and clear in the June air, and then around at my house and outbuildings and down the creek to the sheep shed. While she was at that I did my own bit of inventory. Not so bad a looker, this Adair, actually. Slim and small-breasted, but I had seen less consequential examples. Then those Barclay rosettes in her cheeks, and the auburn crinkle of her hair, like intricately carved ornamentation. Anna of course was an Amazon cavalcade all by herself, but in the rest of womanhood's rank and file this Adair was no worse than midway. Something I had forgotten from her face when she was a Nethermuir tyke; under each eye she had a single dark freckle, specks that repeated the pupils just an inch above. As if there had been an earlier near-miss try at siting her eyes in her face. Interesting. Odd. Now in that recital way of hers, as if providing information to herself, Adair was saying: "You and Rob have built all this, here and at Breed Butte.''

"And the others their own places, Ninian there and Donald and Archie." I thought to scrupulously add, "And the Frew boys, they're as solid as people come, too. But yes, we had to build ourselves.''

"For you it must be like being born a second time, is it? Coming into the world again, but already grown.''

"Something of that sort, I suppose. If you can call me grown.'' Standing a foot taller than she did, I meant this to cheer her with a chuckle. She only smiled the minimum and went on, as if still trying to get to the fact of the matter: "I don't see how you could do all this, you and Rob.''

"Main strength and ignorance," I said. "Dair, I hope you're taking to Scotch Heaven all right.''

She gave me a glance in which she seemed to be seeing

something of herself instead of me, not a Barclay declarative look at all. "Adair is not to be fretted about," she quietly advised.

Leftover Day. The morning of it was sheer hospital work, George and Allan and Rob and I laboring our way with our clippers through ill and lame sheep, trying to be as tender as they were fragile, poor old dears. Life perked up measurably just before noon, when we reached the first few of Rob and Lucas's big yearling wethers. It was always the case, that older sheep who had been through the shearing process before knew what lay in store for them and did not like it one least bit. Even that morning's wheezers and geezers squirmed and writhed to the best of their ability. Yearlings on the other hand, virgin wool on their broad young backs, were greatly easier to shear because of their undefiled ignorance. Even as you held a yearling wether down and began working the shears over his body, he had a dazed disbelief that what was happening could be happening. And being wethers they had on them no hazards of udder and teats for us to be extra careful of; the easy of the easy, these innocent sheep who now were meeting our shearing blades.

"Those were just enough to get us going," Rob announced to the world and Frews at large, and with a wink to me, when we halted for noon dinner, "Barclay and McCaskill can hardly wait until we start counting." I grinned, but only half meant it. Already shearing was taking a toll on my back and whatever other parts of me it could reach. The afternoon ahead looked long.

Allan Frew of course was as fresh as froth. "You're ready for the shearing lesson this afternoon, then?" he piped out, with a particular glint my way to remind me I was a schoolteacher. But it wasn't news to me that Allan had beef where his brains ought to be, and so I let pass everything of that noon hour except the constant thought that my shears were going to have to do a lot of talking the rest of the day.

"Ay, you're ready, both pairs?" declaimed Ninian from on high, atop his woolsack platform. "As you know, Archie will tally and call out the totals of each team every hour. Set then, are you, Allan and George? Angus and Robert?"

Receiving our four nods, Ninian lowered himself into the

woolsack until just his head and half his beard showed, and boomed his starting call:

"MORE WOOL!"

We dove to the work. Four amazed sheep emerged from the woolsack curtains between our catch pens and the shearing floor, being dragged by us and then before they knew it being half sat up, half held against our bodies, like stunned cats press-ganged into a children's game. Worse came next, as the suspicious sound of snipping started circling their bodies and did not stop. Here was the moment for each sheep to declare its character. Some bleated in consternation and tried to wriggle free, which earned them only a tighter clamp of the shearer's legs and a possible gash if they did their worming while the blades were moving to meet them. Others seemed to try to sink through the shearing platform, ooze away from the alarming problem. Either case, the unfleecing relentlessly proceeded to happen to them, and their eyes became like doublesize marbles, hard glaze of fatal acceptance there now. As the yellow-white wool, oily and rich, began to fall away like a slipping gown, you could all but feel the young sheep's innocence of life sliding off with it.

Both Allan and George were left-handed. With them opposite that way to Rob and myself, the two pairs of us down in labor must have been like a mirror reflection. Except that the left-side image little by little, inexorably and inevitably, produced a greater number of shorn sheep than did my and Rob's version. Leave the pairs of us there shearing for centuries and it would go on and on that way, always the left-side Frews manufacturing a few more naked sheep than we ever could. From experience and all else, Rob and I knew this would be the case. I am overtall to be any kind of an ideal shearer, having to get through the endless stoopwork in whatever spurts I could manage. Rob, as a person lower to the ground, could go about it much more ably, and with his deft hands he was a proficient workman with the shears, fine to watch. But George Frew was as relentlessly regular as do-re-mi-fa-so-la in disposing of a catch pen of six sheep, while the damnable Allan had several rhythms, all of them casually swift, for undoing the fleeces off his animals. Spirited infantry in the attack on wool, Rob and myself; the saber cavalry, those damn Frews.

As was confirmed by Archie Findlater's tally at the end of the first hour: "The Frew boys, ahead by two sheep." Actually, Rob and I could take heart from that. Other times, they outsheared us by twice that in the opening hour.

"We've got them just where we want them," Rob imparted to me in an undervoice as he dragged his next wool victim past me. Maybe so, but my muscles had elsewhere they wanted to be.

The next hour Allan and George gained another two sheep on us, again a heartening loss for Rob and me in that it could have been so much greatly worse. By now the women were arriving from the house to watch the finale. Rob tossed a wave to Judith and Adair between finishing one wether and diving into his catch pen for the next. I wasn't sure I could lift an arm high enough for a wave, so I called out—panted out, really—my greeting. Long since had these big broadbacked wethers, absolute fields of wool, stopped being the easy of the easy of shearing.

"By Jesus, lads, we could see the wool flying from a mile off," Lucas called out, now arriving grandly, Nancy's brown inquisitive face beside his broad bearded one. "Angus and Robbie, a little faster if you can stand it, ay?" Not even Rob could muster the retort that deserved. It had to come instead from the squirmy dismayed sheep between my knees: BLEAGH!

Half an hour until the momentous mid-afternoon recess. My arm and wrist and hand were becoming a sullen rebel band from the rest of my body. I wondered how many other parts of myself there were to be contended with in the half of an afternoon still ahead.

At last, it seemed days, Ninian climbed up out of his wool-sack and called, "Recess, both pairs. Time to see to your blades."

From the corner of my eye I could see Allan and George stretch and arch their backs, then walk over to the grindstone to bring an edge back onto their blades, while Rob and I labored to finish the sheep we were on. A streak of sparks flew as a Frew bladeface met the whirling stone, *kzzzkzzzkzzz*. Rob released his shorn sheep, straightened for a glance at the Frews in their leisure of shear-sharpening and a quick cocked glint of reassurance at me, then dove to his catch pen and brought out a next sheep. I swallowed hard and followed his example.

"Angus, Robert, have you lost your ears?" came the next call from Ninian. "It's afternoon recess. Time to take a rest halt and sharpen your blades."

"Work is all the whetstone we need, Ninian," Rob answered in gulps of breath as he clipped rapidly around his sheep. I saved air and wordlessly labored ahead on my own wether. The Sheffield shear in my hand still felt nearly as sharp and gliding in its clipping as when we'd started.

Here now was the famous card in the hat, the bone for the craw of those Frews. Now we were gambling, Rob and I, that by forfeiting the stop to rest and sharpen we could gain enough sheep to offset George and Allan's skill and speed. The thought was that by keeping stoplessly at it we might just eke in ahead of them—one sheep, a half a sheep, any portion of a sheep would be pure victory—by the end of the day. The thought was that Barclay and McCaskill were hardy enough specimens to withstand a recessless afternoon. The thought was . . . I tried not to think further about our forfeit of blessed rest.

From beside the skreeking grindstone Allan Frew hooted to us. "You pair had better hope your fingernails are sharp, so you can use them when those shears get dull as cheese."

"Up a rope, Allan," Rob gritted out, sulphurous for him, the rest of that phrase involving an unlikely hydraulic feat by Allan.

We sheared like fiends. Meanwhile George and Allan with apparent unconcern went on with their blade-sharpening, interrupting to refresh themselves with swigs of water, which from Allan's lip-smacking testimonial you would have thought was the king's brandy.

At recess end, Archie announced the new tally: "Rob and Angus are ahead by three sheep." I thought I saw Allan's eyebrows lift a fraction of an inch at that, but immediately he was mauling wool off a sheep and George was, too, and Rob and I set ourselves to be chased.

But across the next hour the Frews not only did not catch us, they gained only a sheep and a half. With one last hour of sheep left, that pace by both pairs of us would make the outcome as narrow as a needle. Rob was shearing valiantly, even-steven with George's implacable procession of fleeces. I wasn't faring that well with Allan, or rather my hand wasn't. Going into this day I thought my hands were hard as rasps, toughened by every kind of homestead work since I took off my winter mittens months before. But shearing is work of another magnitude and I was developing a blister the size of a half dollar where the haft of the Sheffield shears had to be gripped between my thumb and first finger. Between sheep I yanked out my handkerchief and did a quick wrap around my palm to cushion the blistered area—Allan seemed to gain half a dozen swooping strokes on me in just that time—and then flung myself back to shearing.

In the effort of that final hour, I swear even my mustache ached with weariness. My shearing arm grew so heavy that the labor of dragging each fresh sheep from the catch pen was perversely welcome. Even through the wrap of the handkerchief I could still feel the hot blotch of pain that was the blister. And I noticed Rob lurch a little—yes, you can imbibe too much work just as you can too much liquid leisure—in his trips past me to his catch pen. Our salvation was that the Frew cousins were having the blazes worked out of them, too, challenged more mightily this day than they had ever been before.

The afternoon and the supply of sheep drew down together. Our audience beyond the shearing floor had not uttered a word for many minutes. The snick of four sets of blades was the only sound now. *I thought maybe Adair would enjoy seeing a real shearing contest.* She was seeing, right enough, Rob. Nethermuir eyes were going to get a Montana education this day, if it killed me. Which it just maybe was about to.

Finishing with yet another mammoth sheep, I lurched groggily to my catch pen. The fog of work was so heavy in me that I had an instant of muddle when wool did not meet me everywhere there in the pen. Only one sheep, looking defiant and terrified and indignant and piteous, was there. Rob's pen next to mine was empty. George's next to his was empty. Allan's had one sheep left.

Dear God. This close. This far.

I sucked breath. Grabbed the lone last sheep and dragged.

As I burst out through the woolsack curtain with my sheep, I saw Allan hurl past me to catch his final wether.

I had mine's head shorn and was working desperately along the top of his back when I heard the coarse slicing sound of Allan's blade go into action.

"Good, good, Angus," from Rob with hoarse glee. "You're almost there, man. Just keep on and you've got it made."

My yearling seemed vast, long as a hog, enough wool on him to clothe an orphanage. Sweat streamed into my eyes. My hand seemed to work the clippers without me.

I turned the sheep for the final side. Only moments later, I heard Allan grunt as he turned his own sheep.

Now I had to do this just so.

Hand, keep your cunning. Do as bid. Slow yourself just enough, while seeming to speed for all you are worth. Work less than you know you can, aching faithful hand, for the first time this day.

As my shearing hand was performing its curtain scene, the tail of my eye caught a movement of Allan's head—he was throwing a desperate glance to see how much wool was left on my sheep. I met his eye with mine, and did what I could not have resisted for a thousand dollars: I gave Allan the briefest instant of a wink. And then nearly regretted it, for it made him falter in surprise between his mighty strokes with the shears. But hand, you were in on the wink, too, you were ever so little less busy than you made yourself seem, and now, there, cut air instead of wool, now the fleece again, what little is left, drive the blades but not too—

A scrape of steel on steel. No wool between in that noise. Allan's shout of it, "Done!"

As his word finished in the air, my own blades shaved free the last of my wether's fleece.

I stood up, as far as my outraged skeleton would let me, and met the face of supreme disappointment that was Rob.

"Angus, Angus," he shook his head in a mix of consternation and commiseration. "I'd have bet every nickel that lummox wasn't going to catch you on that last sheep."

"You'd be on your way to the poorhouse if you had, then," I managed to provide, trying to look properly downcast. Now that we were being joined by the Duffs and Erskines and Findlaters and Lucas and Nancy and Judith and most of all Adair, I spoke out with what I wanted in all their minds and that last one in particular: "Did you ever see a man shear the way of that Allan? He can't be beat, I'm here to tell you." I caught the instant of regret, condolence, in Adair's gray eyes as I waved widely to my conqueror. "Come over here, man. Let me shake that hand of yours."

Which I did, blister and all, with the last shred of fortitude in me. Allan by then had convinced himself he hadn't seen a wink from me, I must have been merely blinking sweat from an eye, and by the time I found an excuse to get away from the throng, much was being made of him, not a little of it by himself.

And so it went later, too, at the dance that put away Leftover Day for another year, where I assiduously romped the floor with Judith, with Flora Duff, with Jen Erskine, with any and everyone other than Adair. Not that I maybe had to be that circumspect, for by then she was being squired to the hilt by Allan.

Dearest Anna— Although they are no competition to a certain lovely product of Brechin, I can tell you that a few thousand ewes and lambs do provide absorbing company. In point of fact, they absorb time from me as if it was water and they were sponges. One minute the band will be grazing on the mountainside as peaceful as picnickers and I think to myself, now here is the way herding is done—the sun mothering the fresh grass, the ewes butting and nuzzling their lambs in an epidemic of affection. Then the next minute, reality intrudes when one of the rearmost sheep is spooked by her own shadow, she bolts in alarm, alarming the next few around her, they race pell-mell into the others, and before I can say an appropriate word or two, the tail-end of the band is wrapped around its lead, a sudden colossal knot of sheep . . .

Dear Angus— Here where we are is called the High Line, in deference to the Great Northern as the northernmost, "highest," of railroads. The towns along the railroad have been named out of a gazetteer: Havre, Malta, and such. Considerably eastward there is even a prairie version of Glasgow. . . .

Try as I did to give them their due for scenery and the healthy hermit life, the days of that mountain summer were merely stuffing between the too-short time Anna and I had had together and the rest of our life together that would begin in autumn. In telling her goodbye, I made her pledge that we would write copiously to each other throughout the summer. "A number of times a day," I stipulated earnestly. "As often as possible," she concurred, and with one last kiss—remarkable how much more a kiss means when the two of you have done all it promises—we had gone our ways for the vast months of summer.

Dearest Anna— I have been doing my utmost to make this a monumental summer. By now I have built several of them— sheepherder's monuments, cairns about as tall as I am, to serve as landmarks and boundary points between the area of the mountain where I graze my band and the one where Rob is herding his wethers. So, Miss Noon Creek Schoolkeeper, the topic is history: did old Alexander McCaskill, stone mason of the Bell Rock, ever have the thought that a great-grandson of his would be piling stones into miniature towers in far America? . . .

Dear Angus— It would be gratifying to tell you that I can look out from this cook tent to the distant Rockies and imagine you there at work on your monuments, but the actuality is that the mountains are not within sight from this section of the High Line. All is prairie here. This is quite another Montana from your Scotch Heaven or my Noon Creek, and I wonder how many Montanas there are, in all . . .

Everything of life we ever find or are given ends up in the attic atop our shoulders, it is said. I have no cause to doubt it. During those high summer weeks my head stored away new troves all the time. My final season alone, this. The point at which the trade was to be made, my solitary wonderment at life and where it was taking a person, for becoming half of two. *You, I'd say, need the right partner in this old life, Angus.* You spoke it first, Lucas, and now it was on its way to happening. Even after the marriage there would be the everlasting astonishment of how Anna and I had coincided, from a handful of miles apart in Scotland, where we had not met and may well never have, to coming together in this far place. And now there would be McCaskills derived of Nethermuir and Brechin. I could imagine waking beside Anna every morning the rest of our lives and gazing at her face and thinking, how did this come to be? And then she would blink awake—

"McAngus, do you let a visitor onto your cloud?"

Rob had ridden so near he could have tossed his hat onto me, that noontime in early August, without my noticing.

"Some of us are intent on our flocks," I maintained, with a

gesture to my band serenely shaded up in a stand of lodgepole pine, "while others of us have nothing better to do than go around sneaking up on people."

"A choir of geese could sneak up on you these days," he said with a mighty smile down at me.

I doubted that he had ridden all the way across the mountainside just to test my alertness. No, he admitted, he saw this as an errand of mercy. He had come to see if I wanted to take a turn at camptending. "Man, from the look of you, you'd better go down for air," Rob urged.

Well, why not. The day's ride down to Breed Butte and back up with a pack horse laden with our groceries would stir the blood around in me, right enough. When I told Rob I'd do it, he suggested with a straight face that I take along a second pack horse for my High Line mail.

When I rode in to Breed Butte that next day, it didn't take a bushel of brains to figure out that mine wasn't the only well-being Rob had in mind when he suggested I come instead of him. Ordinarily Judith wasn't the kind to get nettled unless she sat in them. But one look at her told me she had been storing up opinions for Rob about his absence from the homestead's remorseless summer tasks. All she said to me—it somehow sounded like a lot more—was: "How quick will you two be bringing the sheep down?"

"Another three weeks," I proffered as if it was overnight, and began lugging groceries out of range of her. And almost waltzed over Adair, coming up onto the porch as I was starting to step off it.

"Hello you," I sang out brightly, and received a lot less than that in exchange. As I went on over to the pack horse, she stood on the porch steps and watched.

"So. How are you liking this country of ours by now?" I asked her across the yard.

"It's—different," I heard back.

"Getting acquainted some, are you, with this Scotch Heaven tribe?"

"A bit." Not exactly bright as a bangle, a report of that sort. I sallied on anyway:

"Seen or heard anything of our champion shearer?"

Those gray eyes of hers sent me a look as direct as a signpost. "Angus," she said levelly, "you know as well as I do that Allan Frew is stupid as a toad."

I made my retreat from the Breed Butte garrison of women and headed gratefully back to mountains and sheep. The Barclays. What an ensemble. Rob ought to have his head examined for plopping Adair over here from Nethermuir in the first place. It would be saner all around when she wrote off this visit of hers as one of Rob's follies and returned to Scotland at summer's end. Well, I at least had done what I could to pair Adair with a Montana mate, so long as it wasn't me. I couldn't help but agree with her about Allan Frew, though.

The last day of August, down I came from the mountains with fat lambs and plump profit everywhere in front of me, and beyond those the precious prospect that waited for me at Noon Creek. As soon as the sheep were putting their noses to the first bouquets of grass on the slope above my homestead, I aimed Scorpion north as fast as he could trot. On hunch, I went not to the Ramsay place but to the Noon Creek schoolhouse. With the beginning of school so near, I'd have bet hard money, Anna, that you would be readying your classroom. And I'd have won, three times doubly. I patted your sorrel saddlemare rewardfully as I stepped past and toward the schoolhouse door.

"Is this where a person comes to learn?" I called in.

You turned around from the blackboard so quickly your braid swung forward over your shoulder, down onto the top of your breast. "Angus! They said you were still in the mountains, I wasn't expecting you yet!" I'll tell you again now, that braid was the rope to my heart.

"Yet?" I answered. "It's been forever, whatever the calendar says." I went to you and held you at arm's length and simply looked, drank you in. Your gaze was steady on mine, then you put your face against my shoulder. "You look as if the mountains agreed with you," you said warmly. After my summer of not hearing it, your voice was as rich as a field of buttercups.

"They were good enough company, but I desperately need to hear a Brechin voice."

"You do, do you."

"I do. And I want it to tell me every minute of itself since I last heard it, back in Napoleon's time."

"That's an extravagant expectation," you said, giving me the half-smile.

"A mighty word, extravagant. What's the spelling for it? Write it for me, Miss Noon Creek Schoolkeeper."

"You are the Angus McCaskill who can read the air, are you? We shall see." You began tracing lovely maneuvers of alphabet before my eyes.

"An unfair advantage," I protested. "You can't expect me to read your old word backwards."— I moved around behind you, peering down over your right shoulder, my cheek against the black silk of your hair, my hands along the twin bone thresholds so near to where your breasts began. "Now then. Write your utmost, Anna Ramsay."

You stood stock-still. Then, "Angus . . ."

Suddenly what we were saying to each other was with lips, but words were nowhere involved. Our kissing took a wild blind leap. The next thing I knew my lips had followed your neck down, the top of your dress was open and the feminine undergear was somehow breached—your breasts were there, bare as babes, and I was kissing the beautiful whiteness and twin budding nipples. Your hand was under my shirt, your fingers spread and moving back and forth on my spine.

I looked up at you and your other hand came to my face, to the corner of my mouth. You looked intent, Anna, ready to say something. My urge was to keep on with the kissing and the divesting of clothing, and yours evidently was, too. But instead, "Angus, we can't. Not—not here."

"We can," I answered gently. "And sooner or later we will. But for now just let me hold you." Your hands hesitated where they had begun to close the front of your dress; and then they were clutching my back again, the two of us snug together, just being there clasped. We rocked gently against each other or the schoolroom floor was swaying on a gentle tide, we didn't care which. Out of my spell of sheer happiness I heard myself say: "Talk, we were mentioning. It seems to me a poor second-best to this, but yes, let's talk some more. I'll even begin. Anna, marry me now."

I felt you tighten even more against me, the twin globes of your breasts wonderful in their pressure. You said into my shoulder: "I have to tell you, Angus, you're not the first to ask."

"I suppose not. If the male half of the world has any sense at all, it's been trooping to you in regimental file with that question since you were the age of twelve. But Anna, love, first isn't what I had in mind—I just want to be the last."

While I was saying it all you pushed yourself just far enough away to look me in the eye. You didn't smile, not even the half-smile I loved so. "Isaac has asked me."

I nearly chuckled and asked how many words of how many different tongues he did it in. But your face stopped me. Lord of mercy, Anna, had you been so overkind as not to tell Isaac Reese outright no?

"Angus," you said.

"Angus," you said, "I've told Isaac yes."

I rode away doomed.

Not around Breed Butte toward home, because I could not face the new everlasting canyon of emptiness waiting for me there. Down the Noon Creek road toward Gros Ventre I reined Scorpion. In ordinary times it was a pleasant straight-as-a-rope route along the benchland, roofs of the Noon Creek cattle ranches below, but this day I wouldn't have given them a glance if they were the castles of the moon. The tatters that were left of me had all they could do to cling there onto Scorpion's back, hang in the saddle and be a sack for the disbelief. *Angus,* Anna saying, there in the schoolhouse and endlessly in my mind, *I am fond of you, I enjoy you. You know I find you attractive*—the memory of her open dress came into the air between us. *You know how we were, Angus, that last night there in your schoolroom. I have to tell you. Isaac and I have been that way together all this summer.* The moment of pause as that news pierced every inch of me. Then even worse words. *Angus, I'm afraid it's Isaac I feel actual love for.*

Scorpion's ears pricked, his horse view of life alert to the stark lone outline standing ahead of us on the benchland. The pole gateframe of the Double W ranch, gallows-high. As we passed the lofty gate I turned my head to the other side and looked back to where the misery began. The Noon Creek schoolhouse was a square white speck now, under the mountains with their evening roof of cloud and beside the longsail rise of Breed Butte and nearest of all to a spacious creekside ranch that was Reese horseland.

Angus, I'm afraid it's Isaac I feel actual love for. Just that way. As if we two men were jars of jam on the table and she was saying, this is strawberry, this is plum, I'll have plum from now on. Anna was marrying him for the sake of those parents of hers, to tie the leaky boat of Ramsay finances to the ark of Isaac. She was marrying him because she felt sorry for him, damned Dane gabbler him. She was marrying him because she had temporarily lost her mind. Amnesia. A blow on the head she couldn't recall. The instant she came out of this sad mad drift of her senses . . .

She was marrying Isaac because she chose to. Because she wanted to. Because some form of the love infection that had happened to me had now happened to her. I knew that, to the bone. Knew it indelibly and with no possible mistake because Anna Ramsay in her honesty made plain the difficulty of her decision. *Angus, you are a rare man. Maybe the rarest I've ever met.* Her half-smile seemed wistful, or did I imagine. The frank faction of her, though, the Not Proven verdict-giver, went right on to say: *But I think you don't know yet what you want of life.* But I did, did, did. Everything I wanted was standing here telling me she was marrying someone else.

And you do, I raged, *and his name is Isaac?*

How can I ever say it as well as you deserve? Angus, you are one who wants to see how many ways life can rhyme. I just—I just want it to add up as sensibly as I can make it do. And while I didn't at all intend it to, this summer told me how much I want to be with Isaac. Her perfect face looked at me with steady regret. *Angus, I'm so sorry. I am sorrier for you than can ever be said.* She put her hand gently on my wrist, half a grasp which she must have thought was better than none. *I can tell you this. If I ever see that Isaac and I are not right for each other, I'll know where to turn for better. Any woman would do well to marry you, Angus.*

Scorpion was snorty and nervous, our shadow a restless one on the road in front of us from his head-tossing and twitching. If truth could show itself as sunlight throws down our outlines, there would have been a third form there in our composite shadow—the dread that rode me. There is nothing else to call it, a dread as harsh and bottomless as the smothering one I had felt in the steerage bunk those first Atlantic nights out from Scotland. For what was tearing at me was not simply that Anna had turned me down. No. No, the greatly worse part was that even now I could not stop myself from siding with her, defending her against myself even as I derided her reasons in favor of mumblejumble Isaac. I still loved that woman. And if this day had not changed that fact, what ever could?

"By Jesus, Angus, you look as if the dog ate your supper."

I gave Lucas an answering eyeshot that sent his stubs reaching for a large glass for me. Lucas Barclay, author of my homesteading venture, commandant of the Medicine Lodge and the tall house behind and Nancy in that house. All this without even having hands. Isaac Bedamned Reese barely had approximate English. Yet here was I, supposedly complete but womanless. Less the exact one woman I wanted.

I explained to Lucas in the one word: "Anna." Misunderstanding the situation as something that could be mollified he said: "A spat, ay? Don't be so down, lad, you're not the first—"

"She told me to go chase myself," I told him. I told him about the Anna–Isaac wedding-to-be, told him my bafflement, told him a couple of rapid drinks' worth.

"Bad," he agreed. "But you will mend, you know."

I wanted to blaze to him that this wasn't like Rob being infatuated with Nancy, he'd sing a different tune if he were me right now. For that matter, something of the sort must have flared, because Lucas now was steering me to the weaning corner of the bar and casting keep-away looks at the few other customers as they drifted in. "Another glass or so will do you more good than harm, Angus, but that's the end of the night for you then."

Harm, did I hear him say. From that day when Rob and I walked into this Medicine Lodge and Lucas laid his lack of hands before us to see, I had wondered what so harmed a life was like, how Lucas must feel, true and deep, about enduring the rest of existence as less than he had been. Now Lucas was the one who did not, could not, know anything near the full sum of damage I felt. Come put on my bones, Lucas. Come and wear Angus McCaskill like borrowed clothes, let our hearts pump in tune, our eyes sight together at this rascal thing life. Come stand here under my skin and find what this is like, I will learn your loss and you mine.

"Angus, Angus. Take it slow, now. Both on this whiskey and yourself."

Slow, is it. My whole life is slow as anything can be now, indeed it's halted, bogged, stranded . . . This was my Bell Rock. My time of stone, with obliteration all around. The ocean was coming to cover me, ready to put salt pennies on my eyes, and it may as well, why live if this was what living amounted to. *I'm here to tell you. No boat on the reef and none in sight anywhere.* Land stood a dozen miles distant from the Bell Rock; yes, that was the ever same unswimmable distance, from here in the Medicine Lodge to that Noon Creek schoolroom where Anna had told me no, Isaac yes.

"Angus, man, you're full. No more of the wet stuff for you tonight. Sedge and Toussaint, each grab an end of him, can you, and take him around to the house. Angus, here now, just let the lads lift you, there's the way. You'll be different in the morning."

Let the tide come. The Atlantic, the Annalantic. Take my ankles, shins, knees, rise, damn you, bless you, sweep me off this reef, blanket me with water, arms and throat and eyes and higher yet, the whole hopeless thing I am.

What followed, an exact month from that day Anna said no to me, even yet seems the kind of dream a puppet must have, each odd moment on its own string of existence, now dangled, now gone, no comprehension allowed between. Around the wedding pair a cloud of faces, high nimbus and low, years-married couples remembering with faint smiles and their children curious but fidgety. Inevitable breeze, blowing the few strands of the Gros Ventre minister's gray hair down into his eyes as he begins to read the ceremony, *We are gathered* . . . Mountains up over the valley in their eternal gather. The couple, in voices as brave as they can make them, reciting vows for life. The thought caught up with me: *Life. That could be a long time.* Then moved on through my slowly registering mind. Here the last of the dreambead instants, this tardy and this soon, the ring being handed by the brightfaced best man.

I shifted slightly, turning to the woman beside me. Onto Adair's finger I slipped the ring warm from Rob's grasp and it was done. We were wed.

The minister gave out that last intonation to us. "You may kiss the bride." Leaning my head down to Adair's, I saw she had her eyes closed, as if casting a wish. It all revisited me, the pieces of time that had never really passed, simply drifted from corner to corner within me, dreamlike yet never with a dream's innocence. Rob's voice beginning by saying *Her Highness gave you a flick of her handkerchief, I hear,* when I rode home the morning after my night of forlorn souse and found him there, crossing the yard to feed my indignant chickens. *Those Ramsays think they're God's first cousins, though where they get it from I can't see. Angus, she's not the only woman in this world.* No. There was another. In three days, when I hoped I was some semblance of a human again, I rode to Breed Butte, asked Adair to walk with me to the brow of the butte, and there my words came out with cloppety boots on, but they came out. *Dair, you know what's happened with me.* She: *I know about Anna, Angus, and I'm sorry for you.* She did not entirely know, though, nowhere nearly all. Could not know how thoroughly the lovespell for Anna still gripped me, that neither disappointment nor anger nor reason nor laughing at myself nor crying with myself nor anything else among the storms going through me seemed to loosen at all. Nor did I dare even try to bring out my hopelessness for Adair to see, because the bargain we needed to make could not withstand full truth. I spoke fact instead: *That's the past now, Dair. And I'm asking you not to go back to Scotland. I'm asking you to stay and marry me.* Further fact silent but plain behind each line aloud: I no longer could stand to face life by my solitary self, could not reverse myself into the awaiting watcher I was before Anna changed me; Adair who had come across an ocean believing I was awaiting her did not want to return empty-handed to a stone Scottish town: we two together at least were a different sum than either of those awkward results. *She made her choice, more pity to her,* Adair said softly without touching Anna's name. Then said the rest in that lofty little way as if outside herself, speculating. *And Adair has made hers. Angus, I'll marry you any number of times over.* I: *We can start with once.* And Rob again, exultant: *McAngus, man, this is the best news in the world! Have the wedding here on Breed Butte, what do you say? We'll throw you two a shindig that'll not be forgot.*

Someone of the crowd calling out now, "That kiss ought to more than do the job, you two. You'll be married a couple of hundred years on the strength of that!"

Adair looked as if I had taken every bit of breath from her, she looked as if she'd heard a wild rumor prove true. In front of us the minister hemmed and hankered as he wished us well. Faces of my pupils had been astounded into giggles.

"I thought all the kissing had to be done at once," I alibied to the world at large and drew Adair snug against my side. "You mean to tell me there's more of that to come, Dair Barc—" I stopped and laughed with the rest until I could manage the correction—"Dair McCaskill?"

I heard more giggles, shushes, whispered bulletins, as if echoing ghostly up the butte from my schoolroom. Then unmistakably Susan Duff announcing, "We have a song for Mr. and Mrs. McCaskill." I turned and Adair with me, to the every-sized choir that had crept behind us; my pupils in slicked-down hair and stiff Sunday clothes, descending in grinning disorder around the central figure of Susan Duff, Susan long and tall, Susan princess of my classroom, Susan of that silvered voice that now soared out and coaxed the wavery others:

> *Dancing at the rascal fair,*
> *Adair Barclay, she was there,*
> *gathering a lad with red hair,*
> *dancing at the rascal fair.*
> *Angus McCaskill, he was there,*
> *paired with a lass named Adair,*
> *dancing at the rascal fair.*
> *Feel love's music everywhere,*
> *fill your heart, fill the air,*
> *dancing at the rascal fair.*

"Some people," I declaimed after the applause died and Adair and I thanked Susan Duff to the limit, "will try anything to get on the good side of their teacher." Laughter met that, Adair met my pupils one and all, and after them it would be their parents and everyone. The song had helped, I told myself. Maybe I did know what I was doing, maybe Adair did, too, maybe we were going to be a good fit. But tell myself whatever I would, the other refused to leave my mind. I tried and tried not to think any of it, which only incited the factions up there all the more. *Anna, come today. No, don't come, not this day that is by every right Dair's day.*

Married life was proceeding from there. Congratulations from the men filling my ears, Adair receiving bushels of advice from the women about how to perfect me. Lucas at one point provided me brief rescue with a generously full glass captured between his stubs. "Have a drop of angel milk," he directed. "You look as though you need it, ay?"

It was a lovely whiskey, like drinking the color off a ripe wheat field. "This is the house brand in the Medicine Lodge now, is it?" I advocated.

"Don't get wild ideas, lad. It happens to be a bottle that's a precious commodity. Only the advent of good sense in you, marrying a Barclay, makes me crack it open."

Lucas's face did not live up to our banter, either; he was eyeing me in a diagnosing way. And so he knew, knew for certain that my tongue had just vowed for one woman but my thoughts still chose another.

I waited for words from this man who always could see through me and out the other side. For once, there were none. Lucas gravely nodded—was it simply acknowledgment? or lodge greeting of the maimed?—and left Adair and me to our congratulators.

Scotch Heaven was here without exception, and nearly everyone from the South Fork and down the main creek as well, and many from Gros Ventre and several from Noon Creek, although not the two most on my mind. Seven days ago, Anna and Isaac had gone through this same ceremony at Fort Benton on one of his horse-merchant trips. *Anna, come. No, stay away. Anna, I just want to see you, before Adair and I make our life, to ease you from my mind. No, I want to see you because that is what I always want, the hunger I always have, and so Anna, don't—*

I felt Adair startle, startling me. A round walnut-colored face, crinkles of amusement permanently at the corners of its eyes, regarded the two of us as if we held the secrets it had forever wanted to know.

"I came to see the cream separator," spoke Toussaint. "She looks like the good kind."

All simultaneously I was exclaiming in relief and shaking hands hello with Toussaint and introducing him to Adair, who was looking as if she'd encountered a feathered Zulu. When Toussaint had paid us his chuckling respects and gone she asked, "Who on earth was that?"

"The king's remembrancer, except that the Two Medicine country doesn't have the king. I'll try to explain Toussaint later."

As much to herself as to me she said softly, "Adair has much to get used to in your Montana."

"And she will," I said with a heartiness based on my own need to believe that. "First, though, she has to meet all these Montanians who admire my taste in wives." Countless more introductions were undergone to the tune of *Angus, we wondered who you've been waiting for.*

When the next chance came I asked her, low, "Dizzy with names yet?"

"At least," she said, close to breathless again. She looked a bit abstracted, too, as if having stepped off a sudden little distance from the proceedings. Deciding that since I was now a husband I'd better undertake to be husbandly, I announced to our assemblage: "Time for our first war council. We'll be back before you can get your whistles wet." I led her up the butte a little way, just far enough to be by ourselves.

Adair asked in wonder, "Do people flock out this way for every wedding?"

"Only the ones I'm in," I vouched.

"Angus." She put her hand on my arm. "Angus, I'll try with whatever's in me to be a good wife. I don't want you disappointed in me."

"Dair, what's this about?" The unexpected note of doubt in her voice hit deep in me, colliding with my own fears. But I made the words light enough to float away. "It's been most of an hour already since the vows and I'm not ready to trade you in yet."

"I want you to know. I'll be all I can for you."

"Then that ought to be more than enough."

"A person just doesn't know . . ." Her words faltered. "Or least this one doesn't know."

In my chest the sound thudded in echo: *know . . . know . . . know . . .* or was it *no . . . no . . . no . . .* I made the fatal little round sound become her word again: "Know? Know what, Adair?"

"I don't know how I'll be. Amid all of this." She swerved from my staring quiz of her, and the two of us looked out over as much of all as eyes can ever see. The homesteads along the creek, the unpopulated miles all around, the cluster of wellwishers for this occasion, our occasion—Rob with Judith, Lucas and Nancy, Ninian Duff and Flora, Toussaint, the children of my school, people and people and people—and the mountains patiently propping the sky.

"We have the rest of our lives to find that out, Dair," I at last offered. "Let's not worry about ourselves until we have to."

Our public was calling to us from the tables of wedding supper. *Here now, the lovey-dovey stuff just will have to wait a bit . . . Angus, you've got the ring on her finger now, you can afford to share her with us . . .* Rob's voice emerging over the others: *We're moving on to*

*important matters such as food and drink, you two, so bring yourselves
on down here.*

"Hadn't we better?" Adair said, and tried to give me a smile. I
manufactured one in return and confirmed, "By popular demand."
And in me that desperate double chorus I could not be rid of. *Anna,
come. No, don't.*

Anna.

And Isaac. Just arriving. The sight of Adair and me coming down
the butte to join the wedding crowd halted the two of them at the
far edge of the throng as though it was a wall.

There wasn't a chance in this world to know what Isaac Reese
was thinking above that drooping mustache, behind those horse
trader's eyes. As well go read a fencepost as try to decipher that
Dane. But Anna registered on me exactly, instantly as a mirror
reflection. I saw in Anna a great judiciousness, a careful holding
back as she met my gaze with hers, and understood at once that this
was the total of our meeting today, these exacting looks across the
wedding crowd: a man beside his yet-to-be-known bride, casting
every glance he can toward the woman he knows every inch of.
Propriety was delivered now by Anna and Isaac being here, now
there could be no behind-back talk as to why schoolkeeper Anna
was absent the day of schoolkeeper Angus's wedding, *weren't they
seeing one another, for a time? You don't suppose . . .*

And now I had my private answer as to whether the sight of Anna
here, unattainable, the past in a glorious glossy braid, would begin
to heal my pang for her or make it worse. Seeing her did absolutely
neither. Not a candleworth of difference one way or the other in the
feeling for Anna that burned like a sun in me. That heartfire had
persisted past her choice of Isaac for a husband, it was persisting
past my vow to this new presence at my side, my wife. But it
couldn't persevere on and on in the face of all the rest of life to
come, could it? Could it, Angus? I drew breath. I had to hope not. I
had to make it not.

I put my hand in a reassuring clasp over Adair's, where it held
hard to the corner of my arm. "That brother of mine," she was
saying, "you never know the next from him."

Rob had climbed onto a chair. He stood amidst all of us of the
wedding crowd, half again as tall as anyone. A glass of Lucas's
magic whiskey was raised in his hand. "A toast!" he called out. "In

fact, many more than one toast before this day is nearly done, but this one first."

Rob turned toward Adair and me, his eyes met mine and our looks locked as they had so many times. Of everyone there on Breed Butte—Adair, his own Judith, Lucas, Nancy, the many of Scotch Heaven and Noon Creek and Gros Ventre—of this day's entirety of people, Rob was speaking straight to me. "Angus, man, you and I have been all but family." He held his glass as high in the air now as he could reach, as if toasting the sky, the earth, all. "And now we're that."

THE 'STEADERS

The Great Herdsman Above must have thrown up his hands over the territory of bald plains between here and North Dakota and ordained it to be eternally stampede country. First of all, He turned loose the buffalo there; next the cattle herds in the days of open range; and now the homesteaders are flocking in by the thousand. Nearest us, a Paris of the prairie called Valier already exists on the maps the irrigation company is providing to hopeful immigrants, and there can even be found in the townsite vicinity occasional buildings which, if rounded up and bedded down, may constitute some sort of a town eventually.

—GROS VENTRE WEEKLY GLEANER,
MAY 13, 1909

I MEAN this better than it will sound. Adair was the biggest change my life had known since sheep came into it.

"Dair? You don't snore."

She stopped the work of her fork, that breakfast time in the early weeks of our marriage, and gazed across at me curiously. "Such high praise so early in the day."

"All I meant was—it's a nice surprise." Surprise and cause for wonder, this small woman silent in the dark as if she wasn't there in the bed beside me. My years of alone life had made me think that adding a second person to a household would be like bringing in a crowd. Whenever you looked up, there would be a presence who hadn't been, now at the stove, now at the window, now in the chair across from you, now in the blanket warmth next to you. But not so, with Adair. She was not what could be called a throng of wives. No, instead she was proving to be a second solitude on the homestead, a new aloneness daily crisscrossing my own. Constantly now I had to try to fathom this sudden young gray-eyed woman with my name joined onto hers. This quietly-here newcomer from the past. This afterthought bride in the lane of time where I foresaw only Anna.

That was the parallel I meant with the sheep: the saying is that to be successful with sheep, even when you're not thinking about them you had better be thinking about them a little. Now that I was coupled into life with Adair, even when I was trying not to wonder I had to wonder whether I was up to this.

I was letting this be seen bald by remarking to the presence across the breakfast eggs from me about her snorelessness, wasn't I. Figuring I had better get out of the topic before damage was done, I deployed: "You're sure you're related to Rob Barclay, the Scotch Banshee?"

"Would you like me to ask Rob for lessons in sawing with my nose?" she said back, lightly enough.

"No, no, no. I can step out and listen to the coyotes whenever I feel too deprived."

My wife lifted her chin at me and declared softly, "Adair has the same news for you, old Angus McCaskill. You aren't a snorer, either."

"Where do you get the evidence for that?" For if she was asleep as she seemed while I lay there searching the night—

"I wake up early, well before you do. And you're there, quiet as a gatepost."

So Adair and I were opposite wakefulnesses, were we, at either end of the night. The dark quiet between, we shared.

"I always knew marriage would agree with you," Rob accorded me. "You don't have that bachelor look on you any more." He sucked his cheeks into hollows and meanwhile crossed his eyes, just in case I didn't happen to know what abject bachelorhood looked like.

Adair had barely come across the threshold when Rob and I had to trail his wethers and my lambs to the railhead for shipping. Quick after that, school began again and I was making the daily ride from homestead to the South Fork and then back. In weekends and other spare minutes, winter had to be readied for.

It sometimes seemed I saw more of Scorpion than I did of my new wife.

She said nothing of my here-and-gone pace, just as I said nothing of her beginning attempts at running a household. Accustomed to tea, Adair applied the principle of boiling to coffee and produced a decoction nearly as stiff as the cup. Her meals were able enough, but absentminded, so to speak; the same menu might show up at dinner and at supper, then again at the same meals the next day, as if the food had forgotten its way home. Courage, I told my stomach and myself, we'd eventually sort such matters out; but not just yet. There already was a problem far at the head of the line of all others. Adair's lack of liking for the homestead and, when you come all the way down to it, for Montana.

Again, her words were not what said so. I simply could see it, feel it in her whenever she went across the yard to fling out a dishpan of water and strode back, all without ever elevating her eyes from her footsteps. The mountains and their weather she seemed to notice only when they were at their most threatening. I counted ahead the not many weeks to winter and the white cage it would bring for someone such as Adair, and tried to swallow that chilly future away.

Before winter found its chance to happen, though, there was a Friday end-of-afternoon when a session of convincing Ninian on the need for new arithmetic books—*ay, are you telling me there are new numbers to be learned these days, Angus?*—didn't get me home from the schoolhouse until suppertime. During my ride, I had watched the promise of storm being formed, the mountains showing only as shoals in the clouds by the time I stepped down from Scorpion.

"Sorry, Dair," I said, providing her with a kiss, and headed sharp for the washbasin while she put the waiting food on the table. "It's just lucky I didn't end up arguing with Ninian by moonlight."

"The old dark comes so early these days," she said, and took the glass chimney off to light the lamp wick.

"We get a little spell of this weather every year about now," I mollified her as I craned around to peer out the window at the clouds atop the mountains, hoping they would look lessened, "but then it clears away bright as a new penny for a while. We'll be basking in Indian summer before you know what's hap—" The sound of shatter, the cascade of glass, spun me to Adair.

She was staring dumbstruck at the table strewn with shrapnel of the lamp chimney, shards in our waiting plates and in the potatoes and the gravy and other food dishes as if a shotgun loaded with glass had gone off. In her hand she still held a glinting jagged ring of glass, the very top of the chimney.

I went and grasped her, wildly scanning her hands, arms, up the aproned front of her, up all the fearful way to her eyes. No blood. *Mercy I sought, mercy I got.* Adair gazed back at me intact. She did not look the least afraid, she did not look as if she even knew what the fusillade of glass could have inflicted on her. Tunnels of puzzle, those eyes above the twin freckle marks. She murmured, "It just— flew into pieces. When I went to put it back on the lamp."

"That happens the rare time, the heat cracks it to smithereens. But what matters, none of it cut you? Anywhere? You're sure you're all right, are you, Dair?"

"Yes, of course. It surprised me, is all. And look at poor supper." Adair sounded so affronted about the surprise and the stabbing of supper that it could have been comical. But my heart went on thundering as I stepped to the shelf where I kept a spare lamp chimney.

In the morning I said what had lain in my mind through the night.

"Dair? You need to learn to ride a horse today."

She thought it was one of my odder jokes. "I do, do I. What, do I look like a fox-hunting flopsie to you? Lady Gorse on her horse?"

"No, I mean it. As far back in here as we are, no one else near around, it'd be well for you to know how to handle a horse. Just in case, is all." In case lamp chimneys detonate in innocent moments, in case any of the accidents and ailments of homestead life strike when I am not here with you, I was attempting to say without the scaring words. "I'm living proof that riding a horse isn't all that hard. Come along out, Scorpion and I'll have you galloping in no time." I got up from my breakfast chair and stood waiting.

"Now?"

"Now. Out to the barn." I put my arm in hers, ready escort. "Scorpion awaits."

Her gaze said *all right, I will humor you, show me what a horse is about if you must.*

At the barn I demonstrated to her the routine of saddling, then unsaddled Scorpion and said: "Your turn."

"Angus. This is—"

"No, no, you don't do it with words. Hands and arms are unfortunately required. They're there at the ends of your shoulders if I'm not wrong." No smile from her. Well, I couldn't help that. "Just lift the saddle onto him and reach slowly under for the cinch."

Beside the big gingerbread-colored horse, Adair was a small pillar of reluctance.

"Now then, Dair," I encouraged. "Saddle him and get it over with."

She cast me a glance full of *why?*

"Please," I said.

The saddle seemed as big as she was, but she managed to heave it onto Scorpion. Then in three tries she struggled the cinch tight enough that I granted it would probably hold.

"There," she panted. "Are you satisfied?"

"Starting to begin to be. Now for your riding lesson. *Over Pegasus I'll fling my leg/ and never a shoe will I need to beg.*" Verse didn't seem to loft her any more than the rest of my words. "What you do is put your left foot in the stirrup," I demonstrated with myself, "take hold of the saddle horn, and swing yourself up this way." From atop Scorpion I sent my most encouraging look down to Adair, then swung off the horse. "Your turn. Left foot into stirrup."

"No." She sounded decisive about it.

"Ah, but you've got to. This isn't Nethermuir. Montana miles are too many for walking, and there are going to come times when I'm not here to hitch up the team and wagon for you. So unless you're going to sprout wings or fins, Dair, that leaves you horseback."

"No, Angus. Not today. I have this dress on. When I can sew myself a riding skirt—"

"There's nobody around to see you but me. And I've glimpsed the territory before, have I not?" I hugged her and urged her, wishing to myself that I knew how to snipper Barclay stubbornness into five-foot chunks to sell as crowbars. "You can do this. My schoolgirls ride like Comanches."

"I'm not one of your wild Montana schoolgirls. I'm your wife, and I—"

"I realize that makes your case harder, love, but we'll try to work around that handicap." She didn't give me the surrendering smile

I'd hoped that would bring, either. By now I realized she wasn't being stubborn, she wasn't being coy, she was simply being Adair. At her own time and choosing, riding skirt newly on, she might announce her readiness. Fine, well, and good, but this couldn't wait. "I'm sorry, Dair, but there's no halfway to this. Come on now," I directed. "Up."

"No."

I suppose this next did come out livelier than I intended.

"Dair, lass, you came across the goddamned Atlantic Ocean! Getting up into a saddle is no distance, compared. Now will you put your foot here in the stirrup—"

"No! Angus, I won't! You're being silly with all your fuss about this." Adair herself wasn't quite stamping that foot yet, but her voice was. She sounded as adamant as if I'd wakened her in the middle of the night and told her to go outside and tie herself upside down in the nearest tree.

The only thing I could think of to do, I did. I stepped to Adair and lifted her so that she was cradled in my arms. Surprised pleasure came over her face, then she giggled and put her arms rewardfully around my neck. The giggling quit as I abruptly took us over beside Scorpion.

"Angus, what—"

"Upsy-daisy, lazy Maisie," I declared. "Whoa now, Scorpion," and with a grunt I lifted Adair, feet high to clear the saddle horn and I hoped aiming her bottom into the saddle.

"Angus! AnGUS! ANGUS, quit! What're you—"

"Dair, let yourself down into the saddle. Whoa, Scorpion, steady there, whoa now. Don't, Dair, you'll scare the horse. Just get on, you're all but there. Whoa now, whoa—"

Her small fists were rapping my back and chest, and not love taps, either. But with no place else but midair to go, at last she was in the saddle, my arms clasped around her hips to keep her there. Scorpion gave us a perturbed glance and flicked his nearest ear. "Dair, listen to me. Sit still, you have to sit still. Scorpion isn't going to stand for much more commotion. Just sit a minute. You have to get used to the horse and let him get used to you."

She was gulping now, but only for breath after our struggle; her tears were quiet ones. "Angus, why are you doing this?"

"Because you have to know how to handle a horse, Dair. You just absolutely do, in this country." I buried my face in her dress while the sentences wrenched themselves out of me. "Dair, I'm afraid for you. I could never stand it if something happened to you on account of marrying me. An accident, you here alone, this place off by itself this way . . ." The ache of my fear known to both of us now. I had lost one woman. If I lost another, lost her because of the homestead— "But this place is all I've got. We've got. So you have to learn how to live here. You just have to."

A silent time, then I raised my head to her. She was wan but the tear tracks were drying. "Hello you, Dair Barclay. Are you all right?"

"Y-yes. Angus, I didn't know—how much it meant to you. I thought you were just being—"

I cleared enough of the anxiety out of my throat to say: "Thinking will lead to trouble time after time, won't it. Now then, all you need do is to take these reins. Hold them in your right hand, not too slack but not too tight either, there's the way. Don't worry, I'll be hanging tight onto Scorpion's bridle and first we'll circle the yard. Ready?"

You won't find it in the instructions on the thing, but for the first year of a marriage, time bunches itself in a dense way it never quite does again. Everything happens double-quick and twice as strong to a new pair in life—and not just in the one room of the house you'd expect.

Here, now, in the time so far beyond then, when I see back into that winter after Adair and I were married, it abruptly is always from the day in May. The day that stayed with us as if stained into our skins. Take away that day and so much would be different, the history of Adair and myself and—

Even on the calendar of memory, though, winter must fit ahead of May, and that first winter of Adair and myself outlined us to one another as if we were black stonepiles against the snow. After the first snowfall the weather cleared, the air was crisp without being truly cold yet. Being outside in that glistening weather was a chance to glimpse the glory the earth can be when it puts its winter fur on, and Rob and I tried any number of times to talk Adair into bundling up and riding the haysled with us as we fed the sheep. "Come along out and see the best scenery there is. They'd charge you a young fortune for an outing like it in the Alps." But nothing doing.

Adair quietly smiled us away, brother as well as husband. "Adair can see the winter from where she is," she assured us.

For a while my hope was that she was simply content to be on the inside of winter looking out, the way she paused at any window to gaze out into Scotch Heaven's new whiteness. That hope lasted until a choretime dusk soon after the start of the snow season when George Frew, quiet ox in a sheepskin coat and a flap cap, trooped behind me into the house. "Anything you'd like from town besides the mail, Dair?" I asked heartily. "George is riding in tomorrow."

"Yes," she responded, although you couldn't really say it was to George or myself. Times such as this, conversing with her was like speaking to a person the real Adair had sent out to deal with you. Wherever the actual mortal was otherwise occupied at the moment, the one in front of us stated now: "Adair would like a deck of cards."

George positively echoed with significant silence as he took those words in. Flora Duff might want darning thread, Jen Erskine might want dried peaches for pie, but what did Adair McCaskill want but a—

"You heard the lady, George," I produced with desperate jollity. "We're in for some fierce cribbage in this household, these white nights. Kuuvus's best deck of cards, if you please. I'll ride down and pick it up from you tomorrow night."

Thereafter, Adair would indeed play me games of cribbage when I took the care to put my reading aside and suggest it in an evening. But her true game was what I had known she intended. Solitaire. After the deck of cards arrived, I began to notice the seven marching columns of solitaire laid out on the sideboard during the day. Aces, faces, and on down, the queues of cards awaiting their next in number. Adair amid her housework would stop and deal from the waiting deck to herself, play any eligible card where it belonged, and then go on about whatever she had been doing, only to stop again her next time past and repeat the ritual.

But I soon was repeating my own silent ritual that winter, wasn't I. My own solitary preoccupation. Against every intention in myself, I was soon doing that.

The schoolhouse dances brought it on. At the first dance in my schoolroom, fresh silver of snowfall softening the night, I was in mid-tune with Adair when I caught sight of Anna and Isaac Reese

entering. The sensation instantly made itself known within me, unerringly as the first time I ever saw Anna. Toussaint Rennie once
told me of a Blackfeet who carried in his ribcage an arrowhead from
a fight with the Crow tribe. That was the way the feeling for Anna
was lodged in me: just there, its lumped outline under the skin same
and strong as ever. *Dair, here in my arms, what am I going to do with
myself and this welt inside me? Marrying you was supposed to cure me
of Anna. Why hasn't it?* Until that moment of Anna entering from
the snow-softened dark, not having laid eyes on her since the day
Adair and I were married, I was able to hope it was my body alone,
the teasing appetite of the loins, that made me see Anna so often as
I waited for sleep. *I am not inviting any of this, Dair, I never invited
it.* Her in the midst of this same music, that first night of glorious
dancing here in my schoolroom. Her in the Noon Creek school,
turning to me under a word in the air, her braid swinging decisively
over her shoulder to the top of her breast. *Dair, I wish you could
know, could understand, could not be hurt by it.* Anna beneath me,
watching so intently as we made the dawn come, arousing each
other as the sun kindled the start of morning. Double daybreak
such as I had just once shared with a woman, not the woman I had
wed. Night upon night I had been opening my eyes to explode
those scenes, driving sleep even farther away. Beside me, Adair
who slept as if she was part of the night; there in the dark was the
one place she seemed to fit the life I had married her into. But this
other inhabitant of my nights—I knew now, again, that whether she
was Anna Ramsay or Anna Reese or Anna Might-Have-Been-Mc-
Caskill, every bit of me was in love with the woman as drastically as
ever.

How many times that winter, to how many tunes, was I going to
tread the floor of my South Fork schoolroom or her Noon Creek
one, glimpsing Anna while Adair flew in my arms? I couldn't not
come to the dances, even if Adair would have heard of that, which
she definitely would not have. To her, the dances were the one time
that Montana winter wasn't Montana winter.

"She's another person, out there in the music." This from Rob.
He meant it to extol, but that he said anything at all about an odd-
ness of Adair was a surprise.

"She is that," I couldn't but agree. Dancing with Adair you were
partnered with some gliding being she had become, music in a
frock, silken motion wearing a ringleted Adair mask. It was what I

had seen when she danced with Allan Frew after the shearing, a tranced person who seemed to take the tunes into herself. Where this came from, who knew. At home she didn't even hum. But here from first note to last she was on the floor with Rob or me or occasional other partners, and it was becoming more than noticeable that she never pitched in with the other wives when they put midnight supper together. To Adair, eating wasn't in the same universe with dancing.

"Angus, you look peaked," Adair remarked at the end of that first schoolhouse dance. "Are you all right?"

"A bit under the weather. It'll pass."

But then the Monday of school, after that dance. A squally day, quick curtains of snow back and forth across the winter sun, the schoolroom alight one minute and dimmed the next. By afternoon the pupils were leaning closer and closer over their books and I knew I needed to light the overhead lanterns. Yet I waited, watching, puzzled with myself but held by the mock dusk that seemed to find the back of the schoolroom and settle there. Davie Erskine in the last desk gradually felt my stare over his head toward that end of the room. He turned, peered, then at me. "Is something there, Mr. McCaskill?"

"Not now there isn't, Davie." Of all the tricks of light, that particular one. Slivers of cloud-thinned sunshine, so like the moonsilver when Anna and I lay with each other on the floor there. *You've got to let the moonbeams in on a dance, Davie.* The silvered glim had come and gone in the past half-minute, a moment's tone that I had seen in this schoolroom any number of times without really noticing, that now I would always notice.

"Davie!" I called out so sharply his head snapped up. "Help me light the lanterns, would you please."

That winter, then. Adair and I so new to each other, and the snow-heavy valley of the North Fork so new to her. I at least believed I could take hope from the calendar. Even as the year-ending days slowed with cold and I fully realized that Adair's glances out into the winter were a prisoner's automatic eye-escapes toward any window, even then I still could tell myself that with any luck at all she would not have to go through a second Scotch Heaven winter with only cards for company. Any luck at all, this would be our only childless winter. Children, soon and several, we both wanted. Adair seemed to have an indefinite but major number in mind—it came with being a Barclay, I supposed—while I lived always with the haunt of that fact that my parents had needed to have four to have one who survived. It would be heartening to think the world is growing less harsh, but the evidence doesn't often say so, does it. In any case, the next McCaskill, the first American one, was our invisible visitor from the winters to come.

It was a morning in mid-March when Rob and I declared spring. Or rather when the sheep did, and he and I, fresh from the lambing shed, came into the kitchen bearing those declarations, a chilled newborn lamb apiece.

"Company for you, Adair," sang out Rob.

She gave a look of concern at our floppy infants, who in their first hours of life are a majority of legs, long and askew as the drone pipes of a limp bagpipe. "But whatever's wrong with them?"

"A bit cold, is all," I told her. "Bring us that apple box, would you please."

"Poor things." She went and fetched the box. "What are you going to do with them?"

"Put them in the oven, of course."

"The oven?"

"A cold lamb's best friend," vouched Rob.

"In—this oven? The oven of my cookstove?"

"It's the only oven there is," I replied reasonably.

"But—"

"They'll be fine," I provided instruction to her as I dropped the oven door and Rob arranged his little geezer in the box next to mine, "all you need do is set the box behind the stove when they come to. In you go, tykes." With their amplitude of legs out from sight under them, the lamb babes in the open oven now looked like a pair of plucked rabbits close to expiration, their eyes all but shut in surrender and the tips of their tongues protruding feebly. "They're not as bad off as they look," I encouraged Adair. "They'll be up and around before you know it."

"But, but what if they climb out of the box?"

"In a situation like that, Adair," Rob postulated, "I'd put them back in. Unless you want designs on your floor."

"How long are they going to be in here?"

Rob gawked around studiously. "Do you have an almanac? I can never remember whether it's the Fourth of July or Thanksgiving when we take the lambs out of the kitchen. McAngus, can you?"

"You know better than to listen to him," I counseled her. "He'll be up to get these lambs when they thaw out in an hour or so. Dair, the lambs are our living. We've got to save every one we can, and when they're chilled, as a lot of them are always going to be, this is the only way to do it."

"How long did you say lambing goes on?"

"Only about six weeks."

So May was a double event for Adair, an end to lambs in the oven and the beginning of weather that wasn't winter. Her spirits rose day by day, taking mine with them. Compared with how we had wintered, Adair and I were next things to larks the afternoon when we were to go to Gros Ventre for provisions.

"You're ready for town, are you?" I called in through the doorway to her. "Or can you stand to be away from the company of lambs for that long?"

"Adair is more than ready for town," she informed me.

"If she's that eager she can practice her driving, can't she. I'll go see whether Jupiter and Beastie are agreeable to you handling their reins."

"Tell them they'd better be if they know what's good for them."

The day was raw, despite the new green of the grass and the fact that the spring sun was trying its best. We were a bit late starting because I'd had to take a look at the last bunch of ewes and lambs that had newly been put out to graze. Even so, how fine it felt to have a change from the muck of the lambing shed.

"This must be what they mean by the civilized life," I said with my arm around Adair as she handled the reins. "A carriage and a driver and the kind of day that makes poets spout. Have you heard this one: *My life your lane, my love your cart/Come take my rein, come take my heart?*"

"I've heard it now, haven't I. Depend on you and your old verses." We were almost at the side road up to Breed Butte. "Had we better see if Rob and Judith want anything from town?"

"Rob was in just yesterday, there'll be no need. Let's make up the time instead. Poke the team along a little, Dair, what about. Then I'll take a turn driving after we cross the creek."

Jupiter and Beastie stepped along friskily as we passed meadow after meadow of half-grown hay beside the North Fork. I never tired of reviewing Scotch Heaven, the knob ahead where I first gazed down into this valley, Breed Butte and the south ridges on either side of us and the plains opening ahead through the benchland gap made by the creek.

"A halfpenny for them," spoke up Adair eventually. "Or are you too lost in admiration for my driving to have any thoughts."

"Actually, I've been watching that horse." Considerably distant yet, the stray animal was moving along the fenceline between the Findlater place and Erskines' lower pasture. It acted skittish. Going and stopping, going again. Shying sideways. Too early in the season for locoweed. Odd.

"Dair, stop the team. I need to see over there."

With the buckboard halted, I stood up and peered. The distant horse shied once more, and the inside of me rolled over in sick realization. That stray horse had a saddle on.

"Angus, what—" Adair let out as I grabbed the reins and slapped the team into a startled run.

"Something's happened over there, we've got to go see what. Hang on, Dair." She did, for dear life. We left the road behind and went across the Findlater pasture at a rattling pace.

The wire gate into the Erskine field was closed: it would be. I saw the scene in my mind as Adair held the team and I flung the gate aside. The rider starting to remount after having come through the gate and closed it, his foot just into the stirrup, the horse shying at the sudden flight of a bird or a dried weed blowing, then in alarm at the strange struggling thing hanging down from its stirrup . . .

I swerved our team from the worst rocks and dips in the ground but we could not miss them all and keep any speed, so we jolted, banged, bounced, Adair clinging part to me and part to the wagon seat, closer and closer ahead the antsy saddlehorse and the figure dragging below its flanks.

By the time I got our own horses stopped they were agitated from their run.

"Dair, you've got to get down and hold them by their heads. Don't let go, whatever happens. Talk to them, croon to them, anything, but hold onto those halters. We can't have a runaway of our own."

"Good Beastie, good Jupiter, yes, you're good horses, you're good old dears . . ." Her words came with me as I slowly approached the restless saddlehorse, my hands cupped as if offering oats. I was halfway when there was a sharp jangle of harness and a clatter behind me; I looked fearfully around to where our team had jerked Adair off her feet for a moment, but she still clung to their heads, still recited "Beastie . . . Jupiter . . . be good horses now," still bravely holding a ton and a half of animals in her small hands.

"Are you all right there, Dair?" I called with urgent softness, not to startle the saddlehorse off into another dragging of its victim.

"Yes," she said, and resumed her chant to Jupiter and Beastie.

"Easy now," my voice added to Adair's horse chorus as I turned back to the saddlehorse, "easy now, fellow, easy, easy, easy . . ."

The false offer of oats got me to within a few steps before the saddlehorse snorted and nervously began to turn away. I lunged and caught the rein, then had both hands clinging to his bridle.

"Whoa, you son of a bitch, whoa, you demented bastard, whoa . . ."

The worst wasn't done yet, either. Somehow I had to hold his head rock-firm and at the same time sidle along his side until I could reach the stirrup and the ankle and foot trapped in it. For once I was glad of the long bones of my body as I stretched in opposite directions to try this rescue.

When I managed to free the ankle and foot I had time to look down at the dragged and kicked rider.

The battering he had undergone, it took a long moment to recognize him.

"Dair," I called. "It's Davie Erskine. He's alive, but just. You'll have to lead the team and wagon over here. Slow and easy, that's the way."

Adair caught her breath when she saw how hooves and earth had done their work on Davie. "Angus. Is he going to live?"

"I don't know that," I answered, and tried to swallow my coppery taste of fear for poor Davie. He was a bloodied sight it made the eyes pinch together in pain just to look at. "He looks as if he's hurt every way he can be. The best we can do is get him home to Donald and Jen."

Now our ride to the Erskine homestead had to be the reversal of the careening dash we had just done; as careful as possible, our coats under Davie in the back of the wagon while Adair held his head steady, the saddle horse docilely tied to the tailgate.

By the time the doctor had been fetched to the Erskine place and delivered his verdict of Davie to white-faced Donald and Jen, his news was only what Adair and I expected. Oh, it is hindsight, there is no way she and I could have known as we conveyed him home in the creeping but still jolting wagon, that the places of shatter in Davie could never entirely true themselves, that he would lead the limping half-atilt life he had to afterward. But I still feel we both somehow did know.

Two days after that, Adair had the miscarriage.

"Angus, you dasn't blame yourself."

Seeing me silent and long-faced, Adair herself brought the matter into words. "We had to help Davie. That's just the way it happened. You heard the doctor say it's not even certain the wagon ride caused it. Maybe so, maybe no. Isn't that the way everything is?"

I had heard. And as best I could divine, Adair entirely meant it when she said there was no blame on me. As well blame the rocks for jarring the wagon wheels, or the wheels for finding the rocks. No, I knew where Adair put the blame. On Scotch Heaven itself, on Montana, on a land so big that people were always stretching dangerously to meet its distances and season-long moods. Not that she came out and said so. Another case of dasn't; she did not dare lay open blame on our homestead life, for she and I had no other footing of existence together.

You would have to say, then, Adair took the loss of our child-to-be as well as a person can take a thing such as that. Not so, me. To me, a double death was in that loss. The child itself, the packet of life, we had withheld from us; and the miscarriage also had cost us a possible Adair, Adair as she could be, Adair with the son or daughter she needed to turn her mind from the homestead, the isolation. I had lost my own best self when Anna spurned our life together. How many possibles are in us? And of those, how many can we ever afford to lose?

"Angus." Adair by me now, touching me, her voice bravely bright. As if the ill person had climbed from bed to dance and cheer up the mourning visitor, she was doing her best to bolster me. "We'll have other children," she assured me. "You're definitely a man for trying."

That December, Adair miscarried again. This time, four months into her term.

I see that second winter of our marriage as a single long night. A night in the shape of the four walls of a bedroom. The man Angus with thoughts hammering at him from the dark. *How has it turned out this way? I saw where my life ought to go, to Anna. Why then this other existence, if that is what it is, of Adair and me not able to attain the single thing we both want?* The woman Adair this time the one staying grievous, silent as the frost on the window and as unknowable. A pair patternless as the night, us.

I turn onto my side, to contemplate again the sleeping stranger who is my wife. And am startled to meet her awake, her head turned toward me.

"Angus. Angus, what—what if we can't have any children."

Silence of darkness, our silence added into it. Until she says further: "If *I* can't have any children."

"You don't seem anything like a stone field to me." I move my hand to her. "Or feel like one either."

"I need to know, Angus. Do you still want me for a wife, if?"

How to answer that, in the face of *if?*

"Dair, remember what the doctor keeps saying. 'There's not that much wrong; as young and strong as you are, there's every chance . . .'"

"Every chance. But none has come yet, has it." She didn't add but it is there anyway: *will it ever?*

Suddenly I was angry with life. Not in the spit-against-the-wind way of exasperation, but vexed all the way up from my core, from whatever heartpit of existence I have. For life to be against this marriage of ours was one matter. Adair and I could answer for that, we *were* answering for it. But why begrudge us our child, life? A child would be the next link of time, the human knot woven from all McCaskills and Barclays there ever have been, the new splice of Scotland and America and Montana and what was and what needs to be. But here where our child ought to fit—by your own goddamn logic of us, life—the only strands of time in sight to us were the old harsh ones of winter and night. Well, you haven't done us in yet, I vowed silently to the winter thorns of frost on the window and the faceless night, we will stave you off a while yet. Adair did her

utmost to bolster me after the wagon ride cost us our first child. My
turn now.

"Dair, listen to me." I touch to her, stroking the gentle horizon of
her body. "Dair," I say with the kind of declaration that can be
said only in bed, "we'll get you a baby."

We . . . I rise over her and kiss her lips . . . *will* . . . next kiss for
the point of her chin . . . *get* . . . now down to her throat for the
next kiss and the tender unbuttoning . . . *you* . . . this kiss on her
breastbone . . . *a* . . . kissing back and forth on her breasts now . . .
baby . . . as she lifts to me with her quickening breath.

It was one of those May mornings which could have just as well
saved itself the trouble of posing as spring and simply admitted it
was leftover February. A wash day, too, and Adair was hard at it
when I pecked her cheek and went out into the day. In the gray
chilliness of the barn I had untied my sheepskin coat from behind
Scorpion's saddle and gratefully put it on, and was ready to swing
onto the horse when I heard Adair, calling from the house: "Angus!
Come look!"

I wrapped Scorpion's reins and hurried out of the barn. Snow had
begun to fall, a fat and feathery May squall, so that I saw Adair as
if through cloud tufts. I strode across the yard calling to her,
"What's happened?"

"Just look around you! It's snowing!"

I peered at her, then had to laugh. "Either that or it's awful early
for dandelions to fly."

Laugh was the least thing this wife of mine was in a mood to hear.
She was the closest I had ever seen her to despair when she fas-
tened her gaze on me and demanded: "But how can it snow? This is
May! Almost summer!"

"Dair, in this country it snows any time it takes a sweet notion
to."

She scrutinized me as if I'd told her the sun was due to go cold.
Then she was reminded of her basket of wet laundry. "My poor
wash, though. What'll I do about—"

"Hang it as usual. If nothing else it'll freeze dry."

"Angus, you really don't care that it's snowing in May?"

If I couldn't say truth about the weather, then what could I.
"Worse than that, Dair. I'm glad to see it."

"Glad?" As if I'd said treason. "But what will this do to the grass? And the lambs?"

"I was on my way to shed up the ewes and newest lambs. They'll be fine, under roof. And a spring snow is just exactly what the grass wants. After an open winter such as we had, the country needs the moisture."

Adair blinked steadily against the snowflakes as we stood looking at each other. "A strange way to get it," she told the country and me.

The next did not surprise me. I had only wondered when it would come.

Two days after the snow, when slush and mud were everywhere and spring was reluctantly starting over, Adair asked:

"Angus, do you ever have any feeling at all to see Scotland again?"

"No, Dair. It never occurs to me." We might as well have the next into the open. "But it does to you, doesn't it."

"I don't mean going back for good. But for a visit."

"If it's what you want, we can get the money ahead some way for you to go."

"But you won't come?"

"No."

"Is it the ocean? Adair doesn't really like the old Atlantic, either."

"No, it's not the ocean, at least not just. Dair, everything I have is here now. Scotland is an old calendar to me." To hear that from me who once stood pining up the Clyde to yesterday. *Angus, are we both for it?* And to have the sister of Rob the America prophet turning back like a compass needle toward Nethermuir and all its defeats. Straight paths simply are not in people.

Adair at least deserved to have the terms between us made clear, here. "If you feel you want to, you can go—for however long you like."

She did the next clarifying. "Do you want me to, Angus?"

"No." The full answer was greatly more complicated than that, but that was the uppermost edge of how I felt. I wanted not to be alone in life, and whatever else marriage with Adair wasn't, it was not utter aloneness. My way of saying so came out now as: "What would I do without you?"

She answered as simply as those gray eyes gave their knowledge of me: "You would still have a life to look ahead to."

Time to be honest, said the thief in the noose. Since the moment of my wedding vow to this inexplicable woman, I had spent four-thirds of my time imagining how I might ever be found out, and here when it happened, it was nothing at all like the rehearsed versions. Time and again in those, out of somewhere it would come, Adair's question *Angus, after all this while, haven't you been able to forget Anna?* There we would be at last. On the terrible ground of truth that I had hoped we could avoid. Adair would be staring at me in appeal. *Convince me otherwise,* her look would be saying. And I would ready myself to begin at it. *Dair, you are imagining. There is nothing between Anna and me any more, there has not been for—for years. You are my wife, you are the one woman I hold love for.* The disclaiming would marshal all of itself that way in my head, ready to troop along my tongue. And instead I would look at Adair and in eight words give up all I had. *Dair, you're too right. I still love Anna.*

But now it had happened, and not that way at all. Whether Adair saw it in the manner I tried not to watch Anna at the dances, or whether it simply stuck out all over me as I tried to be a husband, she knew my love for Anna was not changing. More than that. In her distance-from-all-this way of doing so, Adair had just told me she knew that Anna maybe was possible for me yet, in time. And more than that again. By invoking Scotland, Adair was saying that our marriage need not be a lasting barrier keeping me from Anna.

Straight paths are not in people: amidst all my relief that Adair knew, and granted, my helplessness about Anna, I was sad that the knowing had to cost her. She was carefully not showing so, she was staying at that slight mocking distance from herself as she calmly answered my gaze with her gray one. But cost surely was there, in her and in our marriage from here on.

Our marriage, if that was what it was going to continue to be. Wedding vows are one thing; the terms of existing together are another language altogether. "Dair, where are we coming out at here? *Are* you going back to Scotland?"

My wife shook her head, not meaning no, she wouldn't like to go, just that she wasn't deciding now. "I'll see." We both would.

"Adair seems a bit drifty lately," Rob remarked when he rode by the next day.

"Does she," I acknowledged without really answering.

His head went to one side as he studied me. "Angus, you know I only ask this because Adair is my sister and you're all but my brother. Is life all right between you two, these days?"

"Right as ever," I provided him, and managed to put a plain face over my quick moment of irk before I added: "But you didn't come all the way to take the temperature of Adair and me, I know."

"You're right, you're right, there's other news. I've been up looking at the grass"—he gave a head toss toward Roman Reef, where we grazed our sheep each summer—"and there's no reason we can't trail the sheep in a week or so." A good early start toward fat lambs in the fall, and I nodded in satisfaction with his news. Or rather, with that much of it. "We've got a new neighbor up there," Rob went on. "The Double W."

My turn to cock a look at him. "With how many cows?"

"No more than a couple of hundred head, is all I met up with. I gave them a dose of dog and pushed them north off where we've been pasturing. But that damn Williamson," Rob said in what almost might have been admiration. "The man has already got cattle on every spear of grass he owns on Noon Creek, he 'borrows' on the reservation, and now he's putting them up in the mountains. Old Wampus Cat must have invented the saying, 'all I want is all I can get,' ay?"

"We'd better hope he doesn't make a major habit of putting cattle up there."

Rob shook his head. "They're big mountains. No, Angus, I don't like having Double W cows within mouth distance of our summer grass any better than you do. But Williamson will have to put enough cows up there to tip over the world, before he makes any real difference to us. That's what brought us here, wasn't it—elbow room when we need it?"

True enough, Rob. But as you gave me a lifted hand of goodbye and rode away that day, Montana even then did not seem to me the expanse it had been.

At first I thought it was bad pork. Just an evening or two after our inconclusive circle of Scotland, Adair took her opening bite of supper and then swiftly fled outside, where I could hear her retching as if her toenails were trying to come up.

I pushed my plate back. Even our meals could not go right.

When a marriage begins to come apart, the stain spreads into wherever it can find. The thunder between my father and mother within the stone walls of River Street. The worse silences between whatever Adair sought of life and the unattainable, the Anna shadow, that I wanted. Those mindblind days before Adair and I said the vow there on Breed Butte, why had I ever, why had she ever—

The screen door slapped again. Adair leaned against the doorway, one hand cupped onto her stomach. She still appeared a bit weatherish, but strangely bright-eyed, too. Fever next?

"Dair, are you all right?"

Her heart of a face had on the damnedest expression, a smiletry that wasn't anything like a Barclay smile; a nominated look that seemed a little afraid to come out. Adair gazed at me with it for a considerable moment. Then she moved her cupped hand in a small arc out and down over the front of her stomach, as if smoothing a velvet bulge there.

I can only hope my face didn't show the arithmetic racing through me before I stood and went to my wife-with-child. *May-June-July-August-September-October-November?-December?* That calendar of pregnancy could not have been worse. If we lost this child as we had the other two, it would be with Scotch Heaven winter staring Adair in the face again.

"McAngus, the third time is the charm," Rob proffered with a hearty smile but worried eyes.

"Something grand to look forward to, Angus, pure grand," from Lucas, his eyes not matching his words either.

We count by years, but we live by days. Rightfully, we should do both by seasons. Even now, looking back, it makes greater sense to me to recall how that springtime, when the baby was yet invisible in her, nurtured Adair's hope along cautiously, as a sun-welcoming tree unobtrusively adds a ring of growth within itself. That summer, when the creekside meadows became mounded with haystacks, Adair began to round out prominently. Then as autumn came and remorselessly wore on toward worse weather, a gray strain began to show on Adair as well. But so far so good, we said to each other in our every glance. Each season in the procession had handed her along without jolt, without fatal jostle to the life she was carrying.

Drawing ever nearer to the birthtime, I cosseted her every way I could think of. The oldest Findlater daughter, Jenny, for months now had been on hand as hired girl to do our washing and other work of the house. Adair was the first to declare of herself, "Adair has the life of a maharanee these days." I knew it was put somewhat differently by others in Scotch Heaven. "Adair is still feeling delicate, is she?" I was queried by Flora Duff, who marched babies out of herself as if they were cadets. Elbows of the neighbors I didn't care about; Adair and her inching struggle to bring us a child were all that counted. She had become a kind of season herself, a time between other times. I noticed that once in a while now she would lay a game of solitaire, but only seldom. Almost all of her existence now was waiting. Waiting.

One single day of that time stands out to be told. The day of Isaac.

It came courtesy of Ninian Duff. "I am here to borrow a favor," he announced straight off. "We have a wagon of coal coming for the school." Ninian stopped to glance sternly at the sky. This was late October now; first snowfall could come any hour. "But Reese's man can only deliver Sunday or never. Ay, he's busy as the wind these days. Everyone in Gros Ventre has caught the notion they can't live without coal now. A Sunday, though. You see my dilemma, Angus."

I did. Any hard breathing on Sunday that wasn't asthma was frowned upon by the Duffs and Erskines.

"Angus, I will trade you whatever help you need around your place when Adair's time comes, if you'll handle this."

I agreed to be the welcomer of Sabbath coal, and on the day, the big wagon and its team of horses were no sooner in sight on the road from Gros Ventre than I knew. Isaac Reese himself was the teamster today.

"Annguz," he greeted when he had halted the wagon. "You vish for coal?"

"Isaac," I reciprocated, my throat tight. "I'll see if your shovel fits me."

Not much more was said as we began unloading the coal. I suppose we were saying without words, letting our muscles talk. Coal flew from our two shovels. I wondered if he had any least idea of my love for his wife. Of those words of hers to me, *If I ever see that Isaac and I are not right for each other, I'll know where to turn for better.* Those were words with only the eventual in them, though. The ones with the actual in them had been the ones that counted: *You know how we were, Angus, that last night there in your schoolroom. Isaac and I have been that way together all this summer.* I sent a glimpse at him as we labored. Since when did Denmark manufacture Casanovas? Isaac Skorp Yun Reese. Scarecrow of sinew and mustache and unreadable face. If you had tried to tell me the day I bought Scorpion from him how this man was going to figure in my life, I would have laughed you over the hill. Yet, maybe Isaac in turn was living in silken ignorance of me and what I might some-day—in the eventual—do to his life with Anna. Wasn't that more than possible? With an ordinary human, yes, but with a horse dealer . . . I would have given a strip of skin an inch wide to know what Anna's mate in life knew. In that mustached face, though, there was no sign I ever would. Through everything, I had never managed to hate Isaac Reese. Not for lack of trying; with him as a target my despair about Anna would have had a place to aim. But Isaac was not a man who could be despised. Calm, solid, entirely himself in the way a mountain is itself; that, and nothing else, so far as could be seen. I had might as well despise the coal we were shoveling. No, all I ever felt when I was around Isaac was a kind of abrupt illness. An ache that I was myself instead of him.

Exertion greatly warmed the chilly day, and as soon as Isaac stopped to peel off his coat, I did, too. As we stood and blew, he asked, "How are your missus?"

I told him Adair was fine, hoping as ever that our history of misfortune wasn't making a liar of me at that precise moment. Then I was privileged to ask: "And your better half. How is she, these days?"

Isaac Reese gave me a probable smile under that mustache, nodded skyward and gabbled out:

"Ve got a stork on de ving."

I held my face together not to laugh, and cast a glance into the air around for the hawk or heron that Isaac was trying to name. Then his meaning came.

"So, congratulations," I got our, trying not to swallow too obviously. Anna now with child, now of all times? Now as I watched Adair grow with our own creation, Anna with this man's—"When does the baby arrive?"

"Sometime of spring." He gave me a twinkling look, unquestionably grinning under his handlebars now. "Foalz, calfs, lamps," he recited, as if the busyness of the animal kingdom then was contagious. I stooped to more shoveling, more pondering. But Isaac's hand came down onto the haft of my shovel. When I peered up at him I found he had something more he wanted to say. It came out: "Ve vill be feathers of our country, Annguz."

I had to hope Isaac was right even if his corkscrew tongue wasn't. I had to hope he and I indeed would be fathers of children whose dangerous voyages into life somehow would do no harm to the women we were each wed to.

On the eleventh of November, 1899, Adair's baby came—weeks early but alive, whole, healthy, squalling for all he was worth.

"It's a wonder a son of yours didn't come out spouting verse," Flora Duff tendered to me when she had done the midwifing.

In our bed with the tiny red storm of noise bundled beside her, Adair was wan except in her eyes. I leaned over her and said low and fervent, "He's the finest there ever was. And so is his mother." She smiled up while I smiled down. Our son found higher pitch. We didn't care. He could yell for a year, if that was the fanfare it took to bring us a child. Softly Adair asked, "Whatever time of day is it?"

"Early. Flora is fixing breakfast and right after I'll need to feed the sheep. And you're going to have a feeding of your own to do, with a prettier implement than a pitchfork."

When I went out into that day and its start-of-winter chores I felt as exultant as any being ever has, I felt that this was the morning the world was all possibilities. Adair and I and in the frosty November daybreak this miracle of a baby, our son of the sun.

To balance this boy of ours, Adair and I gave him a name from each side of the family. *Varick* because it was her father's, and then the traditional McCaskill *Alexander* for a middle, in spite of it being my father's.

I measure the next span of years by you, Varick. You who were born into one century, one era of Scotch Heaven and the Two Medicine country, and by the time you were approaching eight years of age, a different epoch and place had been brought around you. Or so it very much seemed to me, as sentinel called father.

You were not past your first birthday before your mother and I knew by doctor's verdict that you were the only child there was going to be for us. You weren't past your second before our hearts ticked on the fact that keeping you in life was never going to be simple. Every winter from then on you worried us, coming down with alarming coughs and fevers and bouts of grippe, as influenza was called then, for which spring seemed to be the only cure. Strange, the invalid ghost of yourself that you became as soon as cold weather cooped you in the house. As if your vitality dwindled when the length of daylight did. But in your hale seasons you more than made up for that; you sprouted long and knobbly, like me, and rapidly you were out and roaming into every corner of the homestead. The first major talking-to I ever had to give you was about wanderlust, the spring afternoon I found you in the barn: down under the workhorses at their oat trough, crooning happily amid those hooves that with a casual swipe could have smashed you as if you were a pullet egg. Had your mother seen you there innocent among the feet of death, she would have forfeited years of her life. My own heart pounded several months' worth before I managed to sidle among the big horses and snatch you. Snatch only begins to say it, for I also gave three-year-old you a shake that rattled your eyeballs, and the appropriate gospel: "If I ever again catch you anywhere, ANYWHERE, around the hoof of a horse, I'll lather you black and blue! DO YOU UNDERSTAND ME? Varick? DO YOU?" You looked downright shocked—at me rather than realization of your peril. But you piped apologetically, "I unnerstand," and lived up to it.

You went on, in the next year or so, to your lasso period of trying to rope the chopping block, the dog, the cat, the chickens, and fortunately got over that. But horses you did not ever get over. By the time you were five you could ride as well as I could, and by six you were twice the person I was on the back of a horse. The more horseman you became, the more worrisome it was for your mother; that hauntful day of our finding Davie Erskine bloody as a haunch of beef was ever there in her eyes when she watched you rollicking full-tilt across a meadow aboard Scorpion or some other mount. But she braced herself, as a person will when there seems nothing else to be done, and like a person who has simply decided to suffer— there is no less way to say it—she watched you out of sight the school morning when you proudly set off toward the South Fork on the back of your own pony Brownie now.

To say the truth, I had my own overwhelming fret about you. The dread deep as the bloodstream in me. What I feared for you, from the time you began to toddle, was what I had until then always prized. The water of the North Fork and its easy nearness to the house. I who would never swim was determined for you to become complete tadpole; water and the McCaskills were already several generations late in coming to terms with each other. And so the minute you were old enough I got Rob to teach you the water, your small strokes dutifully imitating his there in the North Fork's beaver ponds beneath Breed Butte, until he was saying, and meant it: *See now, McVarick, they couldn't drown you in a gunnysack.*

Did it lead on from there, the alliance between you and Rob? "Unk" as you called him from the time you were first persuaded to try your tongue on "uncle." No, even without the swimming you and he would have doted on one another, I have to believe. The two of you made a kind of inevitable league against your girl cousins, Rob's daughters Ellen and Dorothy and Margery and Mary, who for all that he treasured them like wealth were unmistakably four versions of Judith. Your tenet of those years, *girls are bossy,* fit snugly with his customary joke about unexpectedly running a convent on Breed Butte, and it was your Unk more often than not who enlisted you into riding the gutwagon with him during lambing time or a buckrake during haying, you little more than a tyke but the reins taut in your small hands as Rob taught you to tug the work-horses into their necessary routes.

You just don't know how lucky you are, Angus, I heard from your Unk regularly in that time, *having a Varick.*

I maybe have some idea of it, Rob.

I did not take the school that first South Fork year of yours, on the doctrine that you ought to be spared the awkward load of having your own parent everlastingly up there at the teacher's desk. But when that first year produced as little in you as it did, I tossed away doctrine and became schoolmaster as quick as the annual offer came again from Ninian. And found out for myself that as a pupil, you were reminiscent of the fellow who declared that his education simply hadn't happened to include reading, writing and 'rithmetic. Oh, you could do well enough to scrape by in the schoolroom, and did, with prods from me. But the main parts of you were always outside the walls rather than in. Riding beside you to and from the schoolhouse, I saw day by day what made you absentminded above a book. Absent to the mountain canyons like crevices in the wall of the world, absent to the warm velvet back of Brownie, absent to the riffles and trout holes of the North Fork—you already were a fishing fiend—absent to anywhere your volition could be your own, rather than an arithmetic book's or a teacher father's. Those were points at which, as maybe all parents ever have, your mother and I wondered where we got you. Except in the lines of your body, there was much about you that did not necessarily seem to be my son. Except in your annual war with winter and a certain habit of drifting quietly into yourself, there was considerable about you that did not seem to be your mother's son. You seemed to be the Two Medicine country's son. Your chosen curriculum, even then, was with Rob and me in the year's rhythm with our band of sheep, lambing-shearing-summering-shipping-wintering. With us as either Rob or I rode up atop Roman Reef once each summer week to tend the camp of our sheepherder, Davie Erskine, whom I had hired as soon as he grew from twisted boy into twisted man. With us as we more and more discussed—*cussed and discussed,* as Rob put it—the jumping total of Double W cattle on the mountains' summer grass after the Blackfeet reservation finally was fenced against the Williamsons of the world. With us, jackknife in your earnest small hand, skinning the pelts off our bad loss in the winter of 1906, when almost a quarter of our sheep piled up and smothered during a three-day blizzard. With us to every extent a boy could be in his greenling years.

A last thing that needs saying of those earliest years of yours, Varick. In all that was to come, I hope it was not lost to you that some supreme truces were made of those years. Your mother's with the homestead. Mine with the everpresence of the shadow between your mother and me, the shadow named Anna; Anna now with children of her own, Lisabeth born half a year after you and Peter a few years after that, children who might have been mine, instead of you. Truce, yes: your mother's and mine with each other, for I believe—I hope with all that is in me—that you grew through these years without yet having to know that a truce is not a full peace.

In the spring of the year that Toussaint Rennie ever after spoke of as *that 19-and-7,* you at rambunctious seven-going-on-eight. A Saturday morning amid lambing time you were helping me at the sheep shed, watering the jugged ewes with as much as you could carry in a bucket while I suckled a freshborn lamb onto its reluctant mother. As you were making one of your lopsided trips from the creek, outside the shed door I heard a voice with Missouri in it say to you:

"Hullo, mister. Funny how water turns heavy when you put a bucket around it, ain't it."

"Uh, yeah, sure is, I guess." I could hear, too, the startlement in your question back to the Missouri voice: "Who is it you're looking for, my dad?"

"If he's the sheep boss of your outfit here, yeah, I'd kind of like to talk to him about something."

You plunged into the shed as nearly running as a person can with a bucket of water tilting him sideways. "Daddy!" you called out, your face still lit from having been mistered for the first time in your life, "Daddy, there's some man—"

"I hear, son. As soon as little Fiddlesticks here gets his breakfast, I'll be there. Tell our visitor so, will you please?"

But you lurched on toward me with your water bucket until near enough to whisper in scared thrill, "Daddy, he's wearing a badge!"

An added fact such as that does take the slack out of a person's behavior. I finished with the lamb quicker than I'd have thought possible and stepped out of the shed, you close as a shadow to my heels, Varick.

And both of us very nearly tromped on the nose of a chestnut-colored saddle horse with so much white on his head he was the sort called an apron face, chewing the tall new grass beside the shed.

"Hullo," the figure atop the big horse greeted. "Sorry to pull you off of your work this way." The man wore a campaign hat and a soft brown leather vest, and was lazing on the horse with one knee hooked over the saddle horn in an easy way I knew I would never learn. His face had good clean lines but only a minimum of them: a sparse, almost pared look to this rider. And while the badge on his vest seemed to say he was a lawman, he was more casual about it than any I'd ever seen. He was asking me now, "You the gent of this enterprise?"

"I am."

"Myself, I carry the name Meixell. Stanley Meixell." He put down a hand and I responded with mine and my own name. The restlessness behind me was close enough to feel, and I added: "This bundle of fidgets is my son Varick."

"Him and me has met just now, though we didn't get quite as far as names. Pleased to know you, Varick," and the rider put down his hand again. While your small one was going into his large work-brown one I snatched the chance to look hard at the man Meixell's badge. Not a law star; not anything I had ever seen: a shield with a pine tree embossed in its middle.

Stanley Meixell moved his head to take in the ridgeline above the creek valley, the summit of Breed Butte above that. "This's a pretty valley in here. Kind of up toward the roof of the world, though. Get some snow in the winter, do you?"

"A bit," I submitted. "Then a few feet more for sauce on that."

"Winter," he repeated, as if it were an affliction of the race. Meanwhile the chestnut saddle horse chewed on at the high grass, the only one of us getting anything accomplished. Whatever this Meixell's business was he seemed to have forever to do it in, but I had a maternity ward of sheep waiting.

"Your badge isn't one I'm familiar with. What, have the trees elected you sheriff?"

"Not exactly the trees. A character named Theodore Roosevelt. I'm what's called a forest ranger." He went on in his same slow voice, "The country up west of you here is gonna be made a national forest." Meixell shrugged in what seemed a mildly regretful way. "They sent me to make it."

"Mr. Meixell, I have to ask you to trot that past me again. A which forest?"

"A national one." He began giving me an explanation of the new United States Forest Service, and then I remembered that what were called forest reserves existed a number of places, mostly west of the Divide where trees grew big enough to be made into lumber.

"Mr. Meixell, I'm afraid you've got your work cut out for you if you're looking for timber to reserve anywhere around here. It reserves itself on this dry side of the mountains. No self-respecting logger would bother with these little pines of ours for anything but kindling, now would he?"

Meixell's gaze had been all around our valley and up the pinnacle of Breed Butte and back and forth across the mountains we were talking of, and now it casually found me, and stayed.

"No, I don't guess he would, Angus—if I can go ahead and call you that?"

I had to nod; civility said so.

"But actually it ain't just the trees I'm supposed to be the nurse-maid of," Meixell went on, "it's the whole forest. The soil and water, too, a person'd have to say."

He contemplated me and added in a slower voice yet:

"Yeah, and the grass."

I felt as if a tight rope suddenly was around my insides. It was then I blurted to you, Varick, "Son, you'd better get on with your watering, before those ewes come looking for you."

"Aw." But you went as promptly as a reluctant boy ever can. And I have regretted since that I sent you, for if you had stayed and heard, the time ahead might have come clearer to you. You who were born in the Two Medicine country with its rhythms and seasons in you had a right I did not manage to see just then, there in the welter of apprehensions instantaneously brought on me by Stanley Meixell's words, a right to witness what was beginning here. We both knew it was not the worst you could ever hold against me, but if I had that exact moment back . . . Instead, as soon as you were out of earshot, I spun around to the man Meixell. "But we summer our sheep up there. Everybody here, on both forks of the creek. That's free range and always has been."

"Always is something I don't know that much about, Angus. But I just imagine maybe the Blackfeet who used to have free run of this country had their own notion of always, don't you suppose? And if there was anybody here before them, they probably knew how to say always, too." Meixell shook his head as if sorry to be the herald of inescapable news. "As I get it—and I'm the first to admit that the Yew Ess Forest Service ain't the easiest thing in the world to savvy—the notion is we can't go on eating up the land forever. As the lady said to the midget, there's a limit to everything."

I could feel the homestead, seventeen years of labor, hours incalculable spent on the sheep, all slip beneath my feet as if I were on a 160-acre pond of ice. With surprising quickness now, the forest ranger spoke to my wordless dismay:

"Don't take on too hard about the national forest, though. More'n likely you're still gonna be able to summer your sheep up there. There's gonna be grazing allotments and permits I'll be doling out, and prior use is something I'm supposed to take into account." Up there on his chestnut horse he began outlining to me how the permit system was to work, every inch of it sounding reasonable in his laconic tone, but I was still unready to let myself skid back to hope. I broke in on him:

"But then, if we can still use the range, why bother to—Mr. Meixell, just what in holy hell is it you and President Teddy have in mind for us?"

"The idea ain't to keep the range from being used," Meixell said as if it was a catechism. "It's to keep it from being used to death."

Now the summer mountains filled my mind, the rising tide of Double W cattle we sheep graziers were encountering in each grass season up there, Wampus Cat Williamson's chronic imperial complaint, *You people would sheep this country to death.* The awful echo of that in what this—what was the word for him, *ranger?*—had just said. Prior use. But *whose* prior use of that mountain range? Suddenly cold with suspicion, I studied the hardworn lean face above the badge, beneath the campaign hat: had he come as agent of the Wampus Cat Williamsons of the world, those who had the banks and mills and fortunes in their white hands? *Ruin's wheel drove over us/in gold-spoked quietness.* I had thought it wouldn't be like that in America. I clipped my next words with icy care:

"I hope while you're so concerned against grass being sheeped out, you'll manage to have an eye for any that's being cattled out, too."

From his saddle perch Meixell gave me a look so straight it all but twanged in the air. "Yeah," he spoke slowly, "I figure on doing that."

Maybe so, maybe no. I kept my gaze locked with his, as if we were memorizing each other. Say for this Meixell, he did not look like anyone's person but his own. Yet even if he was coming here neutral, that eternal seep of Double W cattle to wherever Williamson's eye alit . . . "You may as well know now as later," I heard myself informing the man in the saddle, "there'll be some who have their own ideas about your government grass."

"Oh, they won't have no real trouble telling the difference between the forest grass and their own," Meixell offered absently. "There's gonna be a bobwire fence for the boundary. And I'll pretty much be on hand myself, if the fence ain't enough." Still absently, he tacked on: "And if I ain't enough, then Assistant Ranger Windchester likely'll be." The butt of his Winchester rifle stuck out of its scabbard as casually ready as this forest ranger himself.

"Fellow there in the saloon in town," Meixell resumed as I was striving to blink all that in, "he told me you're the straw boss of the school up here. I wonder if I could maybe borrow your schoolhouse for a meeting, just in case anybody's got any questions left over about the national forest." Meixell paused and scanned the long stone colonnade of Roman Reef atop the western horizon. "The Yew Ess Forest Service is great on explaining. Anyway, next Saturday wouldn't be any too soon for me about your schoolhouse, if it wouldn't for you."

I answered, "I'll need to talk to our school board," which meant Ninian. "But I can tell you the likelihood is, people here are going to have questions for you, yes."

Meixell nodded as if that was the fairest proposition he'd heard in years. "Well," he concluded, "I better get to getting. Figured I might as well start here at the top of the valley with my good news and work on down. Noticed a place on that butte." He inclined his head an inch toward the summit of Breed Butte. "I suppose you maybe know the fellow's name up there?"

Only as well as I knew my own. And although this forest ranger was a stranger to me, and maybe a dire one, I felt impelled to tell him at least the basic of Rob Barclay. "He has a mind of his own, especially where his sheep are concerned."

Meixell cast me another look from under his hat, a glance that might have had a tint of thanks in it. "There's some others of us that way. Be seeing you, Angus." Before he swung the chestnut saddle horse away, he called into the shed to you: "Been my day's pleasure to meet you, Varick."

While the man Stanley Meixell rode away, I stood staring for a while at the mountains. National forest. They did not look like a national anything, they still looked just like mountains. A barbed wire fence around them. It did not seem real that a fence could be put around mountains. But I would not bet against this Meixell when he said he was going to do a thing. A fence around the mountains not to control them but us. Did we need that? Most, no. But some, yes. The Double W cattle that were more and more. It bothered me to think it in the same mental breath with Wampus Cat Williamson, but even Rob's penchant for more sheep was a formula the land eventually would not be able to stand. And without the land healthy, what would those of us on it be? The man Meixell's argument stood solid as those mountains. But whether he himself did . . . Not Proven.

I heard you come out of the shed with your bucket and start your next dutiful journey to the creek. When I glanced around at you, I found that you had taken a sudden new interest in your hat. You were wearing it low to your eyes as the forest ranger did. I registered then, Varick, that from the instant he reached down to shake your hand, you looked at Stanley Meixell as if the sun rose and set in him. And I already was telling myself that you had better be right about that.

"What in goddamn hell"—Rob, full steam up—"are we going to do about this national forest nonsense?"

"You're of the opinion there's something to be done, are you."

"Man, you know as well as I do that's been our summer grass up there ever since we set foot into this country. We can't just let some geezer in a pinchy hat prance in here and tell us how many sheep we can put on this slope, how many on that one. What kind of a tightfart way is that to operate, now I ask you?"

"There's maybe another piece to the picture, you know," I had to say. "Those grazing allotments could mean Williamson can't pour every cow on earth up there any more, too."

"Williamson has never managed to crowd us off those mountains yet."

"Yet."

"Angus, are you standing there telling me you're going to swallow the guff this man Meixell is trying to hand us? Just because he wears a goddamn tin badge of some kind?"

"I'd say it's not the worst reason to pay the man some attention. And no, I'm not swallowing anything, just yet. I do think we all need to do some chewing on the matter, though."

Rob shook his head slowly, deliberately, as if erasing Meixell and the heresy he called a national forest. "I'll tell you this: I can't stand still and accept that any sheep I own has to have a permit to eat grass that doesn't belong to a goddamn soul."

"Rob, there's a fair number of sheep you own one side of and I own the other."

That drew me a sharp look. I had not seen Rob so het up since our ancient debates over how many sheep we ought to take on.

Yet why wouldn't he be; this matter of the national forest grass was the same old dogfight, simply new dogs.

Rob must have realized we were fast getting in deep, for he now backed to: "All right, all right, I might've known you're going to be as independent as a red mule. If it'll keep peace in the family, you can go around daydreaming that we can run sheep with reins on every one of them." He cocked his head and made his declaration then and there: "But if that forest ranger of yours thinks he's going to boss me, and a lot of others around here, he has his work cut out for him."

When I made a quick ride down to the Duffs' after supper, Ninian was bleak, even for Ninian. "Ay, we can open the schoolhouse next Saturday and give a listen to the man Meixell," he granted. "But if what he has to say isn't against our interests as sheepmen, I'll be much and pleasantly surprised."

That night at bedtime, I told Adair: "I think we'd better make a trip to town, after school Monday."

She glanced over at me in surprise. Any town trip other than a periodic Saturday was rare for us, and during lambing time it was unheard of.

"Davie can handle the lambing shed until we get back," I elaborated. "That way, we can take our time a bit, have supper with Lucas and Nancy."

She still gazed at me. She knew as well as I did that my elaboration was mere fancywork, not revelation.

"Dair, I need to talk to Lucas about this national forest."

"Rob has made his opinion clear."

"Rob isn't Lucas."

At least that turned off her gaze. "No," she said. "No one is anyone else."

Gros Ventre these days was a growing stripling of a town, all elbows and shanks. The main street was beginning to fill in; fresh buildings for the *Gleaner* newspaper, for a new saloon that called itself the Pastime, for the stagecoach office next to Dantley's stable, for an eating place that had opened beside the Medicine Lodge— *pure convenient,* as Lucas put it, *whenever the notion of a meal happens to strike one of my customers.* But it still had plenty of room to go.

In every conceivable way, though, I was assured by Lucas in the next breath after I stepped into the Medicine Lodge, the town was advancing grandly. "We're even about to get ourselves a bank, Angus. It's bad business to let such places as Choteau and Conrad keep our money in their pockets." All this he tendered to me as I was noticing that now that a bridge of bright new lumber hurdled the creek ford, by weathered comparison the Northern Hotel looked as if it had been in business since Lewis and Clark spent the night there. And Rob and I preceded the Northern, and Lucas preceded us . . .

I took a sip from the glass Lucas had furnished me, and speculated, "Then if we were to put the royal mint next to the bank, with a chute between for the money to flow through, and spigots on the front of the bank . . ."

Lucas had to laugh. But he came right out of it with: "Angus, you'll see the day this town of ours is the county seat, and of our own county, too. Gros Ventre is a coming place."

I could agree with that. It had been coming for nearly twenty years that I knew of personally. Before I could say anything to that effect, Lucas produced a glass for himself, between his stubs, then the whiskey bottle, freshening my drink after he had poured his own. "But enough progress for one day. Lad"—for a change that was not me but Varick, who had wanted to tag along with me rather than endure while his mother and Nancy were fixing supper—"what would you say to a fine big glass of buttermilk?"

"Uh, no thanks," uttered Varick with that eloquent dismayed swallow only a boy can perform.

Lucas peered over the bar at him. "It's a known fact that buttermilk will grow a mustache on you practically overnight. How do you think this father of yours got his? I'm telling you, this is your chance to get yourself a cookie duster." Varick grinned up at him and gave out a skeptical "aw."

Lucas shook his head as if dubious. "If you're going to pass up perfectly good buttermilk, I'm afraid the only choice left is root beer." That resolved, while Varick happily started into his rich brown glassful, Lucas remarked all too casually in my direction: "It's not usual to see McCaskills in town on a school night."

"I thought we ought to talk, Lucas. You just maybe can guess what about."

"Angus, Angus." Lucas's great face behind the bar, his bald

dome and his kingly beard, and those gray Barclay eyes regarding me; how many times had I known this moment? "Life was a lot simpler before this man Meixell, wasn't it," Lucas was saying.

"You've met up with him, I understand."

"The day he hit town. I believe this was the exact next place he found after the Northern."

"And?"

"And once I'd picked my jaw up off the floor after hearing the words *national forest* and what they meant, I stood him a few drinks while I tried to figure him out. That, I have to say, didn't even come close to working." It was an admission chipped in stone, the chilly way Lucas said that, then this: "Our Meixell definitely is a man with a hollow leg, and by the time he strolled out of here I was the one wobbling."

Lucas stopped and cocked a look Varick's direction. Then, soul of discretion, said: "That was Meixell's first half hour in town, Angus, and his second was a visit to Uncle Bob," which was to say Wingo and his "nieces." A fellow who attends to priorities promptly, this Meixell, ay, Lucas?

All of this Varick was taking in avidly. The first Montana McCaskill, trying to hear beyond his years. Even to myself I couldn't have specified why, but I now wanted my son to know as many sides as there were to this thing called the Two Medicine National Forest, this matter of the land and us on it, and the sudden forest ranger on whom our future pivoted. I asked Lucas straight: "Other than Meixell's social capacities, what've you concluded about him?"

To my surprise, Lucas Barclay hedged off to: "The talk I hear, this national forest notion is about as popular around here as a whore in church."

"I've heard similar, just recently. But unless our conversation walked out the door while I wasn't looking, Lucas, we're talking now about Meixell himself and what we can expect from him."

"Angus, Robbie is not wrong about what this national forest can do to us and the way we're used to going about things. I know as well as you do that Robbie can be the quickest in the world to get a wild hair up his"—Lucas's eye caught the attentive face of Varick below—"nose. But this notion of divvying the grass as if it was the oatmeal and we were the orphans. By Jesus, I don't know why that should have to be, Angus, I just don't. What I do know is that we've always run whatever sheep we could manage to, up on that grass, and we've built ourselves and Scotch Heaven and Gros Ventre and the entire Two country by doing it, ay?"

"That's been the case, yes," I had to agree. "But how long can any piece of ground, even one the size of those mountains, keep taking whatever sheep get poured onto it?" I studied Lucas to see how he would ingest this next: "Or cattle either, for that matter."

Lucas rubbed a stub across his beard as if reminded of an untidiness there. "You mean Williamson. Our dear friend Wampus Cat. I don't have the answer there either, Angus, any more than I do this geezer Meixell. I'm as fuddled about this as the old lady when she was told that astronomers had found planets named Mars and such up there among the stars. 'I've nae doubt they can see those things with their long glasses and all,' she said, *'but how did they find out their names?'*"

And that proved to be Lucas's say on planetary matters this night. Even after the lilt of that joke, though, I was certain of this much: certain that I saw come back into Lucas the same bleakness I had found in Ninian Duff two evenings ago. *Ay*, the one of them beginning dourly about Meixell, and the other concluding dourly, *ay?* Not pleasant to be squeezed between, Ninian and Lucas. If these two old stags of the country set their minds and horns against Meixell; if they led the many others who would listen to them into rank behind Rob's anger . . . A fence could be built around a forest, but a fence could be cut, too. Grass could be allotted, but sheep could forever stray onto the unallotted, too. A forest ranger could be sent to us, but that forest ranger could rate early replacement if everything he touched turned to turmoil.

I looked down at my son and had the sudden wish for him to be twice or three times his not-quite-eight years, to be old enough, grown enough, to help me think through what I ought to do. To bring his native attunement to the land into my schoolmasterly mind.

Lucas, too, now put his attention on the inquisitively watching boy. Leaning across the bar, he announced:

"Varick, I happen to know for a fact that Nancy has ginger cookies in oversupply at the house. Go tell her I said to give you the biggest one, ay?"

Varick couldn't help blurting his astonishment at such unheard-of fortune: "This close to supper?"

"I know just who you mean by that, lad," sympathized Lucas.

"But tell that mother of yours that I've known her since she was just an idle notion up my brother's leg"—I'd wanted Varick to have full education tonight, had I—"and I don't want to hear any whippersnap arguments out of her about when a cookie can be eaten. Tell her that for me if she needs it, ay?"

Varick scooted out of the saloon for the house and I sat wondering if the Barclays maybe constituted an entire separate human race. It would explain a lot. Lucas now turned his magnanimity my way and proclaimed: "We've just time to top off these drinks before supper." He poured and toasted, "Rest our dust."

As we put our glasses down, Lucas asked: "And how is life treating its schoolkeepers?"

Schoolkeepers. That *s* whispering *more than just yourself and you know who I mean by more, Angus.*

I studied my glass while all the other whispers of Anna whizzed in me, years of accumulated echoes of not having her, a chorus of whispers adding and adding to themselves until they were like the roar of a chinook wind. *Angus, I've told Isaac yes . . . Angus, Angus, take it slow now, both on this whiskey and yourself. . . . Angus, man, this is the best news in the world! . . . Angus, I'll try with whatever's in me to be a good wife. . . . Annguz, ve got a stork on de ving.* And ever around to first words again: *I am called Anna Ramsay. And it is Miss Ramsay.*

The swarm of it all was too much. If I ever once began letting it free . . . Even here now to Lucas, I could stand only to say the utter minimum of my Anna situation:

"We get by, Lucas. That seems to be the story of schoolkeepers."

"And that's enough, is it?"

"I try to make it be."

George and Abraham traded their eternal stoic stares along the schoolroom wall, and the bunch ranged below seemed to have caught their mood. If faces could somehow be said to be sitting there with crossed arms, these of Scotch Heaven's sheepmen on Saturday morning were.

Stanley Meixell half-perched half-leaned on the corner of my big desk in front of us. By years, he was the youngest person in this gathering. But with his hat off, the start of a widow's peak suggested itself there in his crow-black hair, and the lines webbed in at the corner of his eyes by wind and sun and maybe personal weather as well made his face seem twice as old as the rest of him.

Having just given us the full particulars of the land he was boundarying to create this Two Medicine National Forest of his, Stanley paused to let it all sink in, and it definitely sank.

"Why don't you just arrange your goddamn boundaries to the North Pole and the Atlantic Ocean while you're at it?" spoken lividly by Rob.

To say the truth, the empire of geography the forest ranger had delineated to us was stunning. Grizzly Reef. Roman Reef. Rooster Mountain. Phantom Woman Mountain. Guthrie Peak. Jericho Reef. Anywhere in the high stone skyline to our west, name a rimrock bow of mountain or a sharp flange of peak, and it sat now within the Two Medicine National Forest. And its foothills below it, and its neighbor crags behind it, all the way up to the Continental Divide. All the way up to the moon, may as well say. And Stanley hadn't only tugged his indelible boundary west to the Divide and north to the Two Medicine River. To the startlement of us all, he already had put a Forest Service crew to building his ranger station here on the east edge of Scotch Heaven, at the juncture where the North Fork and the South Fork met to form the main creek. The narrow panhandle of national forest boundary he had drawn from the mountains down here to the station site took in only hogback ridges of rocks and stunted pine that could never be of use to anyone, but still. Everyone of Scotch Heaven and the South Fork both would need to pass by the ranger station and the bold flag atop its pole, whenever they traveled to or from town. Like having an unexpected lodger living on the front porch of our valleys, although I knew from Stanley's own lips why he had done it: *You're asking me if I absolutely have to bring the national forest all the way down to the forks of the creek, Angus, and yeah, I figure I do. If I hide the ranger station way to hell and gone out of sight somewheres, that's not gonna do either side of the situation any good. This station and the forest have got to be facts of life around here from now on. People might as well get used to them as quick as they can.* My answer, *Some aren't going to like your station out there so prominent.* I didn't much myself. *Me and the forest got plenty of time*, said Stanley, *for them to change their minds.*

Changing of minds wasn't the fad yet, if this schoolroom audience was any evidence. In the seat next to me Rob was tight-jawed, fired up as a January stove. On the other side of him, Lucas was the definition of skeptical. Around us, a maximum Ninian frown and variations of it on Donald Erskine, Archie Findlater, the two Frews . . . the only unperturbed one in the room was Stanley.

He wasn't going to stay that way if Rob had anything to do with it. "Christ on a raft, man! You're taking every goddamn bit of the country we use for summer range!"

"I ain't taking it anywhere," Stanley responded quietly. "It's still gonna be there."

"What makes you think," Rob spoke up again, "you can parade in here from nowhere and get us to swallow this idea of a national forest and like it?"

"I wouldn't necessarily say you got to like it, Bob," answered Stanley. "If you just got used to it, that'd be plenty to suit me."

"But man, what you're asking of us"—pure passionate Rob, this—"is to get used to limiting our sheep on all that mountain grass. That's the same as limiting our livelihoods. Our lives, too, may as well say."

"I'm not here to fool you any," Stanley responded. "You're probably not gonna be able to put any more sheep into those mountains than you've already had up there, and maybe some fewer." Glower from Rob, on that. His look changed to bafflement as he realized the ranger didn't intend to expand that response. Rob burst out:

"You mean you're flat-out telling us there isn't anything we can do about you and your goddamn grazing allotments?"

"Me personally," Stanley said to Rob, "I guess you could get rid of someway. Or at least you could try." The schoolhouse filled with consideration of that. "But about the grazing allotment system, no, I don't really see nothing for you to do."

Before Rob's fury found a next tangent, the forest ranger went along us from face to face with his eyes. "But none of what we been saying so far here today goes through the alphabet all the way from A to Why, does it. I've told you what the national forest is gonna be, you've told me what you think about it. Seems to me we both better take a look at just why I got sent here to make the Two Medicine National Forest."

I shifted drastically in my chair, not just for the exercise. Was this going to work? Was I several kinds of a fool for abetting Meixell as I had? The night after my visit to Lucas in town, another visit, this one in the lambing shed after supper: Stanley Meixell appearing again where Varick and I first laid eyes on him. *Found your note under my door, Angus.* I almost hadn't gone to the Northern and left that message, when I announcedly got up from Lucas and Nancy's table to go harness the team for our drive home to Scotch Heaven. Yet I did, yet I had to make the effort to give Stanley the words, the thoughts, for fitting this national forest onto the Two Medicine country with as little woe as possible to all concerned. My words to him there in the lantern light of the shed, that the national forest was actually the pattern of homesteading, the weave of land and utility, writ large: lines of logic laid upon the earth, toward the pattern of America. A quiltpiece of mountains and grass and water to join onto our work-won squares of homestead. The next necessary sum in trying to keep humankind's ledger orderly. Those words of mine, Stanley's tune of them now to listening Scotch Heaven: "I guess you're all familiar with the term public domain. It's the exact same bunch of land you were all able to homestead on . . ." Land, naked earthskin. America. Montana. *We can be our own men there,* the Rob of then to the me of then. Maybe so, maybe no. What can you have in life, of what you think you want? Who gets to do the portioning? Stanley's voice going on, low, genuine: "The national forest is a kind of pantry for tomorrow, for your youngsters when they grow up and inherit all this you've got started . . ." In the lambing shed as Stanley and I met, our one witness: Varick. *Your mother doesn't need to know about this, son;* one more item put into that category, sorry to say. But Rob and Lucas already were more Barclays than any sane man ought to have to contend against, without an Adair salient, too. I hated for Varick to see me sneak. But I wanted him there that night, to absorb whatever he could of the words of the land as Stanley and I knew them.

"My life maybe don't count up as much in years as some of yours, but I been quite a number of places in it." No one of us in his audience could doubt that. Stanley definitely had the look of a man with a lot of befores in his life. "Every one of those places," he went on, "I seen some pretty sad behavior toward the country." I watched him twice as carefully as I had been. There was none of me in these words, this was undiluted Stanley now. "I used to ask people about that. What was gonna happen when the land wore out. And they always said that when they'd used the country up, they'd just move on. But I don't know of anything you can just keep on using up and using up and using up, and not run out of. And that's all the Forest Service is saying with this Two Medicine National Forest. You can use it, but not use it up."

The schoolroom was quiet. Stanley was finished with that part of the task. But now the next.

I wanted not to be the one to ask it. Yet no one else was. I would have to; Stanley had to have the chance to answer. Before I got my mouth to agree, though, I heard my intended words coming out of Lucas:

"What about cattle? Do your grazing allotments take in the fact that cattle eat grass, too?"

"I guess I know what you got on your mind, Mr. Barclay. Its initials are Double W, ain't they." Stanley paused to gather his best for this. "I went and did some riding around in the mountains, taking a look at the ground wherever the snow was off. Trying to figure out for myself just what the country up there can carry. How many sheep. And how many cattle." *There's one thing you've utterly got to do,* my last words to him in the shed those nights ago. *Somehow prove you're going to put a rein on Williamson as well as on the rest of us. If you're going to have people of Scotch Heaven accept the notion of this national forest, prove to them it's not just going to be another honeypot for the Williamsons of the world.* Prove it to me, for that matter. And Stanley easing away then out of the lantern light, saying only, *Been a interesting evening. Good night, Angus, and thanks.* And to the watching boy not much higher than our waists: *My pleasure one more time, Varick.* Now I waited with the rest, waited for proof.

"Arithmetic never was my long suit," Stanley was saying unpromisingly. "But I do savvy that old formula, which I guess all of you know better than I do, that you can run five sheep on the same ground it takes for one cow. Now, each of you in this room has got a band of a thousand sheep, by yourself or in partner with somebody"—here a Stanley glance along the line from me to Rob to Lucas—"or whatever. So, the fairest thing I can think of to do is what I went ahead and did. Let Williamson know I'm allotting him a grazing permit the equal of a band of sheep. Two hundred cows."

A massive thinking silence filled the schoolroom.

Stanley spoke again. "If it'll help your own arithmetic along any, I figure he's been running a couple of thousand cows up there the last summer or so. Fact is, I came across some bald places around springs and salt licks where it looks like he's been running a couple

million." Came across such places, yes, with my guidance. It would
take a man weeks to ride an inspection of those mountains, and
Stanley had had only days; I'd cited him chapter and verse, where
to see for himself the overuse and erosion from Williamson cramming the land with Double W cattle. "Manure to your shins, and
the grass worn away just as deep," as Stanley was saying it now. "I
asked our friend Williamson about behavior like that. He told me
any overgrazing up there was done by you sheep guys. I kind of
hated to have to point out to him I do know the difference between
cowflops and sheepberries when I see them on the ground."

Ninian now, starkly incredulous—it was worth being here today
just for this. "Ay? Am I hearing you right, that you've already instructed Williamson you're cutting him to just two hundred head of
cattle in those mountains?"

"Yeah." Stanley peered out the window toward the mountains,
as if for verification.

"And then—?" demanded Ninian.

"Some other stuff got said, is all. Mostly by him." Stanley still
studied the mountains. "As long as I'm the ranger here, though, he
ain't gonna get treated any different than the rest of you."

Now Stanley Meixell looked out among us.

"None of us needs any more trouble than we already got," the
man at my desk with a face older than himself offered. "For my
part, I can always be worked with if you just keep one thing in
mind. It's something they"—the jerk of his head eastward, to the
invisible church of the Forest Service in Washington—"claim President Roosevelt himself goes around saying. 'I hate a man who skins
the land.'"

Deep silence again. Until Stanley cleared his throat and said:
"Just so we all know where we're coming out at here, can I get a
show of hands on how many of you go along with the idea of grazing
allotments the way I intend to do them?"

I raised my hand.

No other went up.

Indecision was epidemic in the room. Stanley had said much
sense. But the habit of unrestricted summer grass, the gateless
mountains, the way life had been for the two decades most of these
men had put into their homesteads, those said much, too. Skepticism and anger and maybe worse weren't gone yet. I could feel

Rob's stiff look against the side of my head. My hand stayed lonely in the air, and was getting more so.

Then, from the other side of Rob:

"Will a slightly used arm do?"

Lucas's right sleeve, the stub barely showing out its top, slowly rose into the air.

The next assent that went up was that of Ninian Duff. Then Donald Erskine's hand vaguely climbed. Archie Findlater's followed, and George Frew's, and Allan Frew's. Until at last Rob's was the only hand not up.

The expression on Rob was the trapped one of a man being voted into exile. I felt some sorrow for him. The horizon called Montana was narrower for Rob after today.

But you never wanted to be too quick to count Robert Burns Barclay out. As if by volition of all the other assents there in the air, Rob's hand at last gradually began to rise, too. For better or for worse, in trepidation and on something a bit less than faith, all of Scotch Heaven had taken the Two Medicine National Forest for a neighbor.

There was not a one of us who stepped out of that South Fork schoolroom into the spring air and put a glance to the mountains of the new Two Medicine National Forest who didn't think he was looking at a principal change. But those of us that day weren't even seeing the first wink of what was coming. In the next few years, change showed us what it could do when it learned the multiplication table. Change arrived to the Two Medicine country now not in Stanley Meixell's mountain realm west of us but onto the prairies everywhere to our east, it arrived wearing thousands of farm boots and farm dresses, and it arrived under the same name we ourselves had come with, homesteaders.

Overnight, it seemed, the town Lucas had always said Gros Ventre was going to be was also arriving. But it was arriving twenty miles away, at a spot on the prairie which had been given the name Valier. A town made from water, so to speak, by a company fueled by water. *Irrigation* was the word wetting every lip now. The water-flows coursing from the Rockies would be harnessed as if they were clear-colored mares, and made to nurture grainfields. Dam to canal to ditch to head of wheat was going to be the declension. And soon enough it began to be. Scotch Heaven simply watched, because the valley of the North Fork was narrow and slanted to the extent that only a smidgen of hayfield irrigation could be done, or, honestly, needed doing. But a water project such as the one around the townsite called Valier, seventy-five thousand acres of irrigation being achieved and homesteaders pouring off every train, was reason enough to rethink the world and what it was quick becoming.

Yet you have to wonder. If someone among those prairie homesteaders, Illinoisan or Missourian or Belgian or German, if some far-eyed soul of 1908-9-10 who had come to plaid himself or herself into this Montana land could have taken an occasional moment to watch Scotch Heaven, would even we up here have seemed as fixed in a rhythm of life as we assumed we were? Riffle through us in those years, and you find Scotch Heaven's first automobile—Rob's Model T Ford. *See now, McAngus, I haven't laid eyes on one of these contraptions yet that has a wheel worth the name. But the thing is an amazement, am I right? To be able to go down the road without horses . . .* You find a fresh new wire atop the fenceposts beside the road to town, the Forest Service telephone line from the ranger station to the world. You find in my schoolhouse a long-boned boy named Samuel Duff, son of inimitable Ninian and brother of inimitable Susan—Samuel, my first pupil whose dreams and passions are of airplanes and wireless messages that fly between ships at sea.

So, no, even spaces of time that seem becalmed must be riding a considerable tide.

I knew I was. Season by season, those nearest around me were altering. Varick was ever taller, like a young tree. His quiet beyond-the-schoolbook capabilities grew and grew; he had a capacity for being just what he was and not caring an inch about other directions of life. A capacity that I could notice most in one other figure, when I did my wondering about it. Was it in any way possible that Varick somehow saw the knack he wanted for his own, began to practice it in himself even then, that first time the two of us laid eyes on Stanley Meixell?

My son, then, was steadily becoming some self that only he had the chart of. And as he did, my wife just as surely began glimpsing ahead to the time when Varick would leave us. Several years yet, yes, but Adair saw life the way the zoo creature must see the zoo; simply inexorably there, to be paced in the pattern required. The requirement beyond raising Varick through boyhood was losing him to manhood, was it? That being life's case, she would go to the only other manner of pacing that she knew. She was preparing herself to be childless again, while I watched with apprehension. Not that Adair was in any way ending, yet, the companionable truce that was our marriage. We had our tiffs, we mended them. We still met each other in bed gladly enough. The polite passions of our life together were persevering. But in the newly watchful gazes she sent to the mountains now, in how the deck of cards occasionally reappeared and she would be absorbed into the silent game of solitaire, I could more than notice that this was beginning to be the Adair of our first winters of marriage again, the Adair of *Angus, I don't want you disappointed in me.* The Adair of *A person just doesn't know . . . Or at least this one doesn't know.*

So there were shades of change anywhere I looked in those years—except within me. This person me, permanent in the one way I ought not to have been: in silent love with a woman not my wife, not the mother of my son; seeing her at dances, thinking across the divide of the North Fork and Noon Creek to her. Angus the Hopeless. If I could have changed myself from that, would I? Yes, every time. For it was like having a second simultaneous existence, two sets of moments ticking away in me at once, one creating the Angus who was husband to Adair and father to Varick and partner to Rob in sheep and schoolmaster to my pupils and all other roles to the community, the other the mute Angus who did nothing but love Anna Reese. One existence too many, for the amount of me available. It was cause enough to wonder. Was everyone more than the single face they showed the world? It periodically did seem so. The side of Adair I could not get to. Angles within Rob that could catch me by surprise even after twenty years. And were these divisions in people relentlessly at war with each other, as mine were? Or did I alone go through life in the kind of armistice that my South Fork pupils used as time-out in their games at recess, thrusting up crossed fingers and calling out *King's X?*

Nineteen-ten was our year of fire. A summer that would have made the devil cough. We of Scotch Heaven had seen hot before, we had seen dry before, we had even seen persistent forest fire smoke before. But this. This was unearthly.

What seemed worse than the acrid haze itself was that the great source of it lay far beyond the horizon to the west of us, all the way over in the Bitterroot mountains along the Idaho border, halfway to Seattle. Every splinter of that distant pine forest must have caught aflame, for its smoke seeped east to us day after day as if night was drawing over from the wrong side of the world. Somebody else's smoke, reaching across great miles to smear the day and infect the air, it rakes the nerves in a way a person has never experienced before.

And next, as if our own mountains were catching the fire fever from the Bitterroot smoke, in mid-August a blaze broke out in the Two Medicine National Forest. From the shoulder of Breed Butte the boil of gray-black cloud could be watched, rising and spreading from the timber gulches north of Jericho Reef. Stanley Meixell rounded up crews and fought that fire for weeks, but it burned and burned. *We'd might as well been up there spitting on the sonuvabitch, Angus, for all the goddamn good we ended up doing,* Stanley told me after. With the Two Medicine smudge added into the Bitterroot smudge, the sky was saturated with smoke. The day the Northern Hotel caught fire and burned like a tar vat—by a miracle of no wind, not quite managing to ignite the rest of Gros Ventre along with itself—none of us in Scotch Heaven even noticed any smoke beyond usual in the murky direction of town.

On the homestead we went through the days red-eyed, throats and noses raw, nerves worse yet. I felt a disquiet in myself even before the season of smoke honestly arrived. Somehow I had smelled the smoke coming, a full day before the sky began to haze. An odor of char, old and remindful of something I could not quite bring back into mind. No other aroma so silky, acidic. . . . It hung just there at the edge of being remembered, pestering, as each dusklike day dragged past.

By turns, Varick was wide-eyed and fretful—"It can't burn up all the trees, can it, Dad?"—and entranced by the fire season's un-dreamt-of events—"Dad, the chickens! They went back in to roost! They think this is night!"

Adair looked done in. How else could she look, these days of soot, of smoky heat seeming to make the air ache as the lungs took it in?

A suppertime in our second or third week of smoke, she said across the table to me:

"How long can this last?"

At first I thought her words were ritual exasperation, as a person will wonder aloud without really wondering, *Isn't this day ever going to end?* But then I saw she was genuinely asking.

"Dair, I'd rather take a beating than tell you this. But a couple or three times since I've been in this country, it didn't rain enough in August to disturb the dust. And it'll take a whopping rain to kill fires as big as these." I had delivered that much bad news, I might as well deliver worse. "They might go on burning until first snow in the mountains, Labor Day or so."

"Really?" This out of Varick, as he tucked away yet another un-heard-of prospect. After he went outside to his daily woodpile chore, his mother turned her face to me again. "And yet this is the one place you want to be."

"Times like this, I could stand to be somewhere else a minute or two."

"Angus. I don't want this to sound worse than I mean it. But this country never seems to get any easier."

And anywhere else in life does, does it? Famous places of ease, Adair, such as Scotland and Nether—

Abruptly I knew the smell, the disquieting connection that had been teasing in my mind these weeks of the forest smoke. *Angus, is your sniffer catching what mine is?* That unvarying question from Vare Barclay, Adair and Rob's father, to me there in the Nether-muir wheelshop. *It is,* I reply. *Better see to it, Angus, best to be sure than sorry.* Out I go into the woodyard to inspect for fire, the wheel-shop's worst dread. But as ever, the sawyers merely have halved an ash tree. It is the black heart of an ash when it is split, an inky streak the length of the tree, that gives off the smell so much like burning; like a mocking residue of char. And now in the air of Scotch Heaven and much of the rest of Montana, that old odor from Nethermuir. I wondered if Adair, daughter of that wheelshop, somehow was recognizing the freed aroma of the ash's heartwood, too, in this latest dismay of hers against Montana. I was in no mood to ask.

Instead, levelly as I could:

"Dair, this isn't a summer you can judge by. I know the country is so damn full of smoke you can cut it with scissors. But this is far out of the ordinary. None of us has ever seen a worse fire season and we're not likely to."

"I'm trying not to blame the country for how awful these days are, Angus. I truly am."

I wonder if you are, ran in my mind. It'd be new of you. But that was smoked nerves squeaking. I made myself respond to her:

"I know. It's just a hard time. They happen. You're perfectly entitled to throw your head back and have a conniption fit, if it'll help."

"Adair would do that," she went that mocking distance from herself, from the moment, "if she thought it would help."

It helped matters none either that a few days later I had traveling to do. With school to begin in not much more than a week and the flood of pupils from the homestead influx that was upon us, the county superintendent was calling all country-school teachers to a meeting in new Valier.

"I'll be back the day after tomorrow," I told Adair. "Any stray rain I see, I'll bring home with me."

"Varick and I will do our best not turn into kippers in the meantime," she gave me in return.

Riding into Gros Ventre just before nightfall—although it was hard to sort dusk from haze any more—I stayed over with Lucas and Nancy, and in the small hours got up and resaddled Scorpion and rode eastward.

The face of the land as dawn began to find it took my breath away. The land I had ridden across so gingerly when Rob and I first came to Gros Ventre, the bald prairie where I had met only the one Seven Block rider in my three days of scouting, now was specked with homestead cabins. Built of lumber, not our Scotch Heaven logs. This was as if towns had been taken apart, somewhere distant, and their houses delivered at random to the empty earth. *The rainbow eyes of memory/that reflect the colors of time.* My remembering of a hawk hanging on the wind, steering me with his wings to this prairie that was vacant of people then; these people now in these clapboard cabins, would they in twenty years be recalling when their plump farms were just rude homesteads? And the memories-to-come of the next McCaskill: what tints of any of this change in the land were waiting to happen in Varick's mind? For that matter, if people continued to flock in, if the scheme of earth called Montana grew ever more complicated, where was there going to be room, land, for Varick to root his life and memories into?

With more and more light of the morning, which was tinted gray-green even this far from our smoke-catching mountains, I could see the upsloping canal banks of the irrigation project, and machinery of every kind, and then, not far from the Valier townsite, the whitish gray of several tents near a corral.

As I passed that encampment the many colors of horses grew apparent, muted a bit by the hazy air but still wonderfully hued; big workhorses standing like dozens of gathered statues. Quickly I began to meet and greet men walking in from homesteads to their day's work of teamstering, another session of moving earth from here to there in the progress of canals.

I rode on trying not to dwell on those tents and the brand on the hips of those workhorses, Isaac Reese's Long Cross.

At Valier, or what was going to be, a three-story hotel of tan brick sat mightily above the main intersection of almost houseless streets, as though lines had been drawn from the corners of the world to mark where the next civilization was to be built. The other main enterprises so far were lumberyards and saloons. There was something unsettling about coming onto this raw abrupt town sprung from the prairie, so soon after Gros Ventre nestling back there in its cottonwood grove. Valier did not possess a single tree—no, there, one: a whip being watered from a wash tub that a tan-faced woman had just carried out and dumped. I touched my hat brim, the washerwoman gave me a solemn Toussaint-like "Morning," and we went our ways. Say this for the fledgling town, Valier was only half as smoky as anywhere else I had been in recent history; the other half of its air was an enthusiastic wind. Squinting, I saw through the scatter of buildings to where the schoolhouse sat alone, and directed Scorpion that way.

The rural teachers from nearer were already there and of course the Valier ones, six in total, more than Gros Ventre's school had. The rounds of hello revealed that four of the Valier contingent were young single women, none so pretty as to make a man break down the door but each unhomely enough that in all likelihood four marriage proposals were around not very distant corners.

If the Valier maiden teachers wanted a lesson in loveliness, she was the next to arrive after me. Anna.

I knew she had been spending the summer here where Isaac's horsework was. For how many years now had I had ears on my ears and eyes on my eyes with the sole specialty of gathering any news of Anna, and the early-June item in the Gros Ventre *Gleaner* had shot out of the page of print at me: *Anna Reese has joined Isaac at*

Valier. Isaac's crew will be the fortunate beneficiaries of her provender the duration of the summer, as they engage in canal construction on the irrigation project and grading streets in the forthcoming metropolis. She was in the cook tent of that corralside assemblage I rode past, she was here in front of me now as the county superintendent solemnly joked, "Mrs. Reese, you and Mr. McCaskill maybe already have made each other's acquaintance. If not, it is past time you did." For the benefit of the Valier teachers, he further identified us: "These two have been the pillars of education at Noon Creek and the South Fork ever since the foundations of the earth were laid."

"Angus, how are you?" Her half-smile, glorious even when she was being most careful with it.

"Hello again, Anna." *And you know how I am. We both know that, Anna.*

I but half-heard the morning's discussions of school wagons to bring children from the nearest homestead farms into Valier, of country schools to be built east and south of town for the more distant pupils, of the high school to be begun here next year. My mind was ahead, on noon.

When that hour came, picnic dinner was outside in the wind because every new Montana town tries to defy its weather. I got myself beside Anna as we went out the door into the first gust.

"Wouldn't you say we've eaten enough wind at our own schools," I suggested, "without having to swallow this place's?"

The truth of that brought me a bright glance from her, and then her words: "I could say that even without any prompting."

We stepped around the corner of the schoolhouse out of the wind and seated ourselves on the fire-door steps there. Promptly a high-collared young man, more than likely a clerk at the hotel or a lumberyard, strolled by with the most comely of the Valier teachers. There went one.

As Anna and I began to eat, we resorted to conversation confined to our schools.

"Three of my pupils this year are children of some of my first pupils," she noted.

"I have that beginning to happen, too." *And after them will it be these children's children in our schoolrooms, and the two of us still separate? By all evidence.* I stood up abruptly. Seeing her look, I alibied, "Just a cramp in my leg."

I drew a breath and hoped it had as much resolve in it as it did smoke and dust, then sat down beside Anna Ramsay Reese again. Even from our low set of steps, Valier and the irrigation future could be seen being built, a steam dragline shovel at continuous work in the near distance. It was like a squared-off ship, even to the smoke funnel belching a black plume at its middle. Its tremendous prow, however, was a derrick held out into the air by cables, and from the end of the derrick a giant bucket was lifting dirt, swinging and dropping it along a lengthening dike for the lake that would store irrigation water. Handfuls of earth as when a child makes a mud dam, except that the handfuls were the size of freight wagons.

"People come from miles just to watch it work," Anna said.

"It does dig like a banker who's lost a nickel down a gopher hole," I had to grant. "Turning a prairie into Holland. You need to see it to believe."

"Yes. A town built from a pattern," she announced as if storing away the spelling of a fresh word. "They say they are planning for ten thousand people here."

"They've got a ways to go."

"And you don't think they'll get there?" Not disputing me, merely curious to hear so minority an opinion; her instinctive interest in Not Proven.

"Who knows?" Things are famous for not turning out the way I think they will, aren't they. "Maybe all this time we've been living in the Two Medicine grainfield and never realized it."

I forced my attention back into my plate. It was as much as I could do not to turn to Anna, say *Here's something ten thousand Valierians ought to be here to cheer for*, wrap her in my arms and kiss her until her buttons burst.

"Isaac thinks you are right."

I instantly was staring at her, into those direct eyes.

"To have stayed with sheep as you and the others in Scotch Heaven have and not be tempted off into farming or cattle," she went on. "He tells our Noon Creek neighbors that if they want to go on being cowboys, they had better buy some sheep so they can afford their hats and boots."

"Isaac"—my throat couldn't help but tighten on the name—"has always been the canny one."

Now Anna's plate was drawing diligent attention. After a bit she gazed up again and offered, carefully casual: "With Isaac out and around in his work so, we don't see much of Scotch Heaven any-

more. Except at dances, and there's never any real chance to visit
during those. I don't feel I even much know Adair and Varick."
She paused, then: "How are they this fire summer?"

"They're as well as can be. Varick gets an inch taller every
hour."

Her voice was fond of the thought. "Lisabeth and Peter, too.
They're regular weeds at that age." But when she turned her face
directly to me to ask this next, I saw she was starkly serious. "And
you yourself. You really didn't answer when I asked this morning.
How is Angus?"

"The same." We looked levelly into each other's eyes, at least we
always were capable of honestly seeing each other. "Always the
same, Anna."

She drew a breath, her breasts lifting gently. Then:

"How much better if we had never met." What would have been
simpering apology in any other woman's mouth was rueful verdict
from hers. "For you, I mean."

"Anna, tell me a thing. Do you have the life you want?"

She barely hesitated. "Yes. Given that a person can have only
one, I have what I most want. But you don't at all, do you."

I shook my head. "It's never as simple as do and don't. The
version I walk around in, there's nothing to point to and say, 'this is
so far wrong, this can't be borne.' Adair and Varick, they're as good
as people generally come. It's the life I don't lead that is the hard
one."

I turned to her, that face always as frank as it was glorious. She
had hesitated, before answering my question about her life. There
was something there, something not even the remorseless honesty
of Anna wanted to admit. More than the accumulated firesmell of
this summer was in the air around the two of us now. A feel, a tang,
of sharpest attention, as if this moment was being devoutly watched
to see how it would result.

Anna's intent stillness told me she was as aware of it as I was. I
needed to know. Was I alone in the unled life of all these years? Or
not alone, simply one separate half and Anna the other?

"I wonder when I'll get used to it," I suddenly was hearing Anna
say. But this was not answer, I hadn't yet asked, she had slipped
her eyes away from my gaze, past my shoulder to a chugging noise
down the street. "Every automobile still is a surprise," she continued. If this coming one was any standard, Valier was going to be a

clamorsome town. With no patience I waited for the racketing machine to pass by the school.

It didn't pass. The automobile yanked to a stop and sat there clattering to itself while the driver flung himself out. And with a lift of his goggles became Rob.

"Angus!" he tumbled his words out as he came, "there's been— you have to come. There was an accident."

Anna and I were onto our feet without my having known we'd done so, side touching side and her hand now on my arm to help me stand against Rob's words. He stopped halfway to us, the realization of Anna and me together mingling with what he had to report. Dumbly I stared all the questions to his tense bright face: Adair or Varick, Varick or Adair, how bad, alive or—

"It's Varick. He was chopping wood. We got him in to Doc Murdoch. You have to come." He jerked his head almost violently toward the chattering automobile.

"I'm coming." But to what. I pressed Anna's hand in gratitude for her touch, in gratitude for her. "Goodbye."

"One of Isaac's men will bring your horse home for you," Anna said before echoing my goodbye. I climbed into one side of the Ford while Rob banged shut the door of the other, and in a roar we hurled away.

On the rattling ride to Gros Ventre Rob provided me the basic about Varick's accident, and then we both fell silent. In those miles of fire haze and dust from the Ford's tires, I seemed already to know the scene at the homestead that morning, before Adair's words told it to me. *I was just ready to bake bread, before the day got too hot. And I heard the sound.* An *auhhh*, a low cry of surprise and pain. Then the awful silence in her ears told her Varick's chopping at the woodpile had stopped. *I ran out,* the screen door flying open and crashing shut behind her like a thud of fear. She knew there would be blood somewhere, but she was not ready for the scarlet fact of it on our son's face, on the edge of the hand he was holding over his left eye as he stood hunched, frozen. *Varick, let me see, I've got to see,* Adair lifting his red wet hand far enough away for the eye to show. *Hold still, darling. Perfectly still.* The blood was streaming from the outer corner of the tight-shut eye, there was no telling whether the eyeball was whole. *The stick of wood,* Varick was gasping. *It flew up.* She carefully put his hand back in place to staunch the flow. *Sit. Sit right here on the chopping block, Varick, and don't touch your eyeball at all while I go*—with water and clean rags she tended the bloody mess, then half-led half-carried the boy big as her into the house. *Listen to me now. You have to lie here on the bed until I get back. Hold the rag there against the cut, but don't touch your eye itself. Varick, no matter how it hurts, don't touch that eye.* Varick ice-still as she left him on the bed holding back the red seep, as she went to the barn silently crying and saddled Varick's mare Brownie and swung herself up and still was silently crying when she halted the horse on Breed Butte in front of Rob. Then the Ford journey to Gros Ventre with Varick, past the fenceline where she and I had found Davie Erskine being dragged by his horse, where she and I first learned of the impossibly unfair way life can turn against its young.

"We'll just have to wait," judged Doc Murdoch to Adair and me that night. "To see whether those eye muscles are going to work. I do have to tell you, there's about an even chance they won't." Precisely what we wanted not to hear: flip of the coin, whether Varick would be left with one powerless eye, a staring egg there in its socket. "But the eyeball looks intact," the doctor tried to relent, "and that's a piece of luck."

Luck. Was there any, and if so, where? Had the chunk of wood flown a fraction farther away Varick would have only a nicked cheek or ear, one quick cry and healed in a few days. But a fraction inward and the eyeball would have been speared. The tiny territory between, the stick struck. That must be luck, the territory between.

In the big guest bed at Lucas's house, the same bed where Rob and I had spent our first dazed night in Gros Ventre, Varick lay as still as an eleven-year-old boy ever has for a week. Then the doctor lifted the bandage to examine the left eye and its eyelid as Adair and I and Lucas and Nancy wordlessly clustered to watch.

"Blink for us now," the doctor directed. And Varick did. "Open wide. Close it now. Excellent. Look this way. Good. The other. Good again. Now bat your eyes, that's the boy." All those, too, Varick performed.

"If that eye was any better, my boy," the doctor eventually stepped back and announced, "you'd be seeing through these walls."

Varick regarded him, and the others of us, with his two good eyes. This can only be retrospect, but I swear I already was seeing a Varick considerably further in years than the one I left when I rode off to Valier the week before; a boy who knew some of the worst about life now, and who was inserting some distance, some gauging space, between it and him. Because, when all at once Varick was grinning up at the doctor, the smile maybe was as boyish as ever but that left eyelid independently dropped down to half-shut. As it ever did thereafter when something pleased him; my son's wise wounded squint of amusement and luck.

"Varick is twice the son you deserve, McAngus," Rob acclaimed when I went by Breed Butte to tell him and Judith of Varick's mend. More, he clapped me on the shoulder and walked out with me to the gate where I'd tied Scorpion.

"The fact is, I wish I'd managed to sandwich in a son along with the girls," Rob went on confidentially when we were far enough from the house not to be heard. He gave a laugh and added in the same low tone: "I still could, of course, but I'd have to do it without Judith, she tells me."

"Man, think of all the husky sons-in-law ahead," I assuaged him. "Pretty soon you'll have them wholesale." His and Judith's oldest girl, Ellen, already was out in the world of swains, working at the millinery shop in Choteau.

"They aren't the real item, though, are they," Rob mused in a lamenting way that wrote off any future husbands of Barclay daughters. I was opening my mouth to point out that he and I were real enough in-laws, of the brother-in-law sort, when he went on: "Whether or not you know it, there's no substitute for having a Varick."

"I at least know that much," I affirmed to him lightly. Rob could brood if he wanted to, but on a day such as this my mood was top-notch. I stood there at the gate a moment with Rob beside me, just to enjoy all around. *I didn't come all the miles from one River Street to live down there on another.* This day supported those lofty home-stead-building words of Rob's. The first fresh fall of snow shining in the mountains had sopped the forest fires, the air was cleansed and crisp with autumn now, and the view from Breed Butte was never better nor would be. My own outlook was just as fresh as the moment. Varick's restored eye, another year in my schoolroom about to begin, the Valier minutes spent with Anna so significant in my mind—I felt as life had shed a scruffy skin and was growing a clean new one.

Absorbed, I was about to swing up onto Scorpion when Rob stopped me with:

"Angus, I think it's time you had a talking to."

I turned to him with the start of a grin, expecting he had some usual scold to make about my taking the school again.

"About Anna Reese," he said, destroying my grin.

"Rob. She's not a topic for general discussion."

"But she's one that's generally on your mind, isn't she. Angus, this is no way to be."

"Is that a fact?" It was and it wasn't. By choice I would not be the way I was toward Anna, carrying this love through the years. But choice was not in this. "Rob, who the hell do you think you are, my recording angel?"

Rob had the honesty to look uncomfortable. "I know you maybe think I'm poking my nose in—"

"You're right about that, anyway."

"—but Angus, listen, man. Adair is my sister. I can't just stand by and see you do this to her."

"You're going to have to." My eyes straight into Rob's eyes six feet away, suddenly a gap the size of life. "Dair and I are managing to live with it, it shouldn't be a major problem for you."

"Living with it, are you? That's what you call this, this infatuation you won't let go of?"

I wanted to shout in his face that there had been a time when he was the expert on infatuation, right enough. That if Lucas had not outwitted him and sent Nancy out of reach and us here to the North Fork, Robert High-and-Mighty Barclay would have taken his own uncle's woman. What had been a quick infection in him had escaped every cure I could try on myself but it was the same ill. Why couldn't he of all people see so, why—

Rob was resuming, "I kick myself—"

"You needn't," I tossed in on him, "I'll be glad to help you at it."

"—Angus, serious now. I kick myself that I didn't see this earlier, why you and Adair aren't more glad with each other. It wasn't until I saw you with Anna there in Valier that I put two and two together."

"Rob, you have a major tendency, when you put two and two together, to come out with twenty-two."

Rob surged on: "I've known you forever but I can't understand this Anna side of you. How is it that you're still smitten with her?" Smitten? I was totally harpooned, and this man was not willing to make himself understand that. Rob stood planted, earnest, waiting. "All I'm asking is how you can let a thing like this go on and on." He meant for this conversation to work as a poultice, I knew. But it wasn't going to.

I had to be sure: "Do you hear any complaints out of Adair about me?"

"She's not the kind to. But—"

"Let me understand this, Rob. You're telling me I owe you more about this than my own wife is content with?"

"Adair is not content with this, how can she be? You moping like a kicked pup, another man's wife always on your mind. What woman can accept that?"

What Barclay? was his real question, wasn't it. Now that I saw where this storm had come from I was sad as well as angry. The old great gulf, life as it came to the McCaskills and as the Barclays expected it to come to them.

But Rob, you. You who indeed had known me forever. You, now, who would not listen and then say, *yes, I see, you have a friend in me for always, if I can help I will and if not I'll stand clear.* You who instead stood here in-lawing me relentlessly. I got rid of sad in a hurry and stayed with angry.

"Rob, I'm telling you. This isn't yours to do. You can't interfere into my life and Adair's this way. So don't even start to try."

"Interfere? Angus, you're not taking this in the spirit it's meant. All I want is for you and Adair not to come apart over—over Anna. Can you at least promise me that?"

"Promise—? Where in all hell do you think you get a right like that—that I have to promise you anything about my own marriage? Listen to yourself here a minute. This is idiots out at play, the pair of us yammering on and on at this, is what this is."

I swung up onto Scorpion and looked down at Rob. "If it'll close you on this topic, I'll tell you this much: Adair and I are not coming apart over Anna Reese. All right?"

Rob as he studied up at me was a mixture of suppressed ire and obvious discomfiture. I at least thought the decent side, discomfiture, won out when he spoke:

"All right, Angus. We'll leave this at what you just said."

I let my breath out slowly over the next several days. But it seemed to have passed, that notion of Rob's that he had a say in how Adair and I were to manage our marriage. Rob being all he was to me, I was able to forgive him the incident, although not forget it.

One last waft of that summer of smoke did not pass. Instead, it began to spread in the benchland country to the south of Scotch Heaven and Gros Ventre; the wind-blown and slope-skewed landscape where Herbert's freight wagon tilted its way through, twenty years earlier, while a pair of greenlings named Angus McCaskill and Rob Barclay trudged behind. The dry and empty bottom edge of the Two country, which now, who would have ever thought it, was drawing in people exactly because it was dry and empty.

They were a few families at first, and then several, and then more. Homesteaders who were alighting on dry-land claims instead of the irrigated acres of Valier and the other water projects. It took Stanley Meixell to dub them so sadly right. After riding past one or another of their shanties optimistically sited up a wind-funneling coulee or atop a shelterless bench of thin soil and plentiful rock, Stanley bestowed: "Homestead, huh? Kind of looks to me like more stead than home." And that is what they became in Scotch Heaven's askance parlance of them. The 'steaders.

Settlers who were coming too late or too poor to obtain watered land and so were taking up arid acres and trusting to rainfall instead.

Men and women and children who had heard of Montana's bonanza of space and were giving up their other lives to make themselves into farmers instead.

Investors of the next years of their hopes into a landscape that was likely to give them back indifference instead.

Watching the 'steaders come, the first few in 1910 and more in the next summer and the summer after that, I couldn't not ask, if only to myself: Was this what that dry land was meant for—plowed rows like columns on a calendar, a house and chicken coop every quarter of a mile? In homesteading terms, it indubitably was. But

when can land say, *enough?* Or *no, not here?* We of Scotch Heaven
believed we were doing it as right as could be—you can't live anywhere without some such belief, can you—but then we had the
North Fork, water bright and clear on the land. At Valier and the
other irrigation projects, those settlers too had water, ditch water.
But these ones out on the thirsty benchlands . . . I grant that Rob
and I knew next to nothing about homesteading when we came to
undertake it. But we were royal wizards compared to many of these
freshcomers. Here were people straight from jobs in post offices and
ribbon stores, arriving with hope and too little else onto the
benchlands and into the June-green coulees. Entire families down
to the baby at the breast, four-five-six people living in a shanty the
size of a woodshed or in a tent while they tried to build a shanty.
And meanwhile were struggling too to break the sod and plant a
crop, dig a well, achieve a garden. I suppose these 'steaders had to
be as Rob and I were when we began in Scotch Heaven, not daring
to notice yet that they were laboring colossal days and weeks for a
wage of nothing or less. I suppose there is no other way to be a
homesteader. Yet, bargaining yourself against the work and the
weather is always going to turn out to be greatly more difficult than
you can ever expect. Even in Scotch Heaven we had the absences
around us, the Speddersons and Tom Mortensen, to remind how
harsh and unsure a bet homesteading was. Yet and again, agog as I
might be at the numbers of these incomers and aghast as I often was
at how little they knew of what they needed to, I could not deny
that the 'steaders on their raw dry quarter-section squares were
only attempting the same as we had, trying to plaid new lives into
this proffered land.

This was bright June. Winter waited four or five months away
yet. Nonetheless I began saying a daily prayer to it: be gentle with
these pilgrims.

Not many days later, Rob and Lucas waylaid me when I was in
my lower meadow making a peaceful reconnaissance of the hay
prospect there. Angling a look into the Ford as it halted briskly
beside me, I couldn't help but put the query:

"What's this, now—a war council of Clan Barclay?"

Out they climbed, here they were. "Mark this day, McAngus,"
Rob proclaimed, Lucas equally sunny beside him. "We're here with
the proposition of a lifetime for you."

"Wait. Before I hear it"—patting each appropriate neighborhood of my body I recited: *"Testicles, spectacles, wallet, watch.* There's proof I had all my items before the two of you start in on me, just remember."

"Angus, Angus," chided Lucas. "You're as suspicious as one deacon is of the other. Just hear what we've got in mind, ay?"

"That shouldn't take all day. Bring it out."

"There's hope for you yet, Angus," Rob averred with a great smile. "Now here's the word that's as good as money in the bank: 'steaders." He cocked his head in that lordly way and waited a moment for my appreciation before proceeding. "You know as well as we do that they're starting to come into this end of the Two country by the hatful and they can barely recognize ground when they're standing on it."

"And?"

Rob's smile greatened more yet. "And we can be their land locators."

Lucas broke in: "Angus, it's something I ought to've listened to when I first came, when I was mining." Into his coat pockets went his stubs, as if he was whole again there at the start of Montana life. "Someone asked old Cariston there in Helena, the same geezer you worked for in his mercantile, Angus, what he did for a living. Do you know what he said? 'I mine the miners, there's where the real money is.' And it's pure true. Every word of it and then some. In a new country the one thing people need is supplies. And what's the supply every homesteader needs first of any? Land, Angus. You and Robbie know all this land around here by the inch. You're just the lads to supply homestead sites."

I studied from Lucas to Rob, back to Lucas again. Usually Lucas was as measuring as a draper, but Rob plainly had him entirely talked into the gospel of land locating. Rob alone I would have given both barrels of argument at once, but for Lucas's sake I went gentler. "Just how does this rich-making scheme work?"

"Simple as a dimple," Rob attested. "I'll meet people right at the depots, in Valier and Conrad and Browning—you know they're pouring in by the absolute trainload." They were that. Just recently an entire colony of Belgians came to the Valier land; men, women, children, grandparents, babes, likely cats and canaries, too. The Great Northern simply was throwing open the doors of freight cars in St. Paul, and Montana-bound families were tossing in their belongings and themselves. "I'll ferry them out to here in the Lizzie," Rob strategized, "and here's where you come in, Angus. You're the man with the eye for the land. You'll locate the 'steaders onto the claims, mark the claim for them, tell them how to file on it, all but give them their homestead on a china plate. Lucas just said it, really. What we'll be is land suppliers, pure and simple."

The arguing point to all this couldn't be ignored any longer. "If we had the goods, I could see your supply idea," I told Rob. Then with a nod toward the south benchlands: "But what land is left around here is thin stuff for homesteading." I paused and gave him a look along with this next: "Concentrate a bit and you'll maybe remember what we thought of it ourselves, when you and I walked into this country behind Herbert."

"By our lights, maybe it isn't the best land there ever was," Rob granted. "But to these 'steaders it's better than whatever to hell they've had in life so far, now isn't it? Man, people are going to come, that's the plain fact of the matter. Whether or not we lead them by the hand, they're going to file homestead claims all through this country. They might as well be steered as right as possible, by knowledgeable local folk. Which is the same as saying us. In that way of looking at it, McAngus, we'll be doing them a major favor, am I right?"

"And charging them a whack for it," I couldn't help saying of Rob's version of favor.

"Are you so prosperous you can do it for free?" came back at me from him. "Funny I don't notice the bulges in your pockets."

"Lads, now," Lucas interceded. "Angus, we're not asking for your answer this very minute. Just put the idea on your pillow for a few nights, ay?"

Had they been asking my answer right then, it would have been No, in high letters. But. The prosperous problem. The perpetual problem with homesteads, with livestock, or maybe just with McCaskills. Working yourself gray, year after year, and always seeing the debt years eat up most of the profit years. To now, Adair had never said boo about the fact that where money was concerned we were always getting by, hardly ever getting ahead. So the dollar thoughts were delaying my No a bit, and I decided to leave matters with the Barclays at: "I'll need to do a lot of that pillow work, and to talk it over with Dair."

"You can save your breath there," Rob tossed off. "She's thoroughly for it."

I gave Rob a look he would have felt a mile away. "You know that already? From her?"

"I happened to mention it to Adair, yes. Angus, she is my sister. I do talk to her once in a blue moon. Not that I'd particularly have to in this case. She's bound to be for anything that'll fetch money the way this will. Who wouldn't be?"

"Angus, I know how you feel about this country and the 'steaders," Adair said that night. By then we had been thoroughly through it all. Adair's point that here was a plateful of opportunity on Varick's behalf, as easy a chance as we would ever have at money for his future, his own start in life and land in the years not far ahead now. My lack of any way to refute that, yet my unease about the notion of making myself into a land locator. "But change always has to happen," she was saying, "doesn't it?"

"The big question is whether it happens for the better or the worse."

"Either case, what can you really do about it?" she responded. "You and Rob came here as settlers. So are all these others."

"If they were bringing their own water and trees and decent topsoil, I'd say let everybody and his brother come. But good Christ, this dry-land craziness—Dair, they say there are 'steaders on the flats out north of Conrad now who haul all their water a couple of miles, a barrel at a time on a stone boat. They strain that cloudy water through a gunny sack as they bucket it into the barrel. My God, what a way to try to live. And these have been wet summers and open winters. What are those people going to do when this country decides to show them some real weather?"

"I suppose some will make it and some won't," she answered in all calmness. "It's their own decision to come here and try. It's not ours for them." The deep gray eyes were steady on me, asking me to reason as she was.

I could do that. What I wasn't able to manage was the waiting conclusion: that I ought to join in, bells, tambourines and all, with Rob and Lucas in putting people onto land that ought not to have to bear any people.

"There's something more, Angus," my wife offered now. "It's not just Varick we need to plan for. It's each other as well."

Her silence, my waiting. Then from her:

"Adair doesn't know if she can stay, after Varick is grown and gone."

So here it was, out. Adair and how long she would reconcile herself to Scotch Heaven, once it became a childless place to her again, had been in my mind with Anna at Valier and so I could not call this an entire surprise. Stunning, yes, now that it was here, openly said. But all the years since *Angus, do you ever have any feeling at all to see Scotland again?*, since *Do you still want me for a wife, if?*, all those years led here, if you were Adair.

I reached her to me, but there was too much in me to speak straight to what she had just said. Adair herself, myself, Anna, past, future, now. It all crowded in me beyond any saying of it. No, only the one decision, the one I had to do at once rather than let the next years take care of, came to my tongue. If there were three McCaskill lives ahead that needed finance—mine of Scotch Heaven, Varick's of the Two Medicine country, Adair's of Scotland or wherever—then I had to find money.

"All right, Dair," I whispered. "We're in business with a couple of Barclays."

Squint as hard as you will, you can't see to tomorrow. Had I been told in the wheelwright shop in Nethermuir, *Angus, the day will arrive when you trace the hopes of homesteaders onto the American earth with a wagon wheel . . . when the turns of that wheel become the clock that starts dew-fresh families on years of striving . . . when the wheel tracks across the grass single out another square of earth for the ripping plow . . .* I would have looked around from my own dreams and said skeptically, *You have the wrong Angus.* Yet there I was, that summer and the next, on the wagon seat with a white handkerchief tied around a wheelspoke to count revolutions by, counting the ordinations of wheelspin. *Fifty.* Seeing the craft of my unhearing father, the band of iron encircling the spokes, holding all together to write the future of 'steaders onto prairie acres. *That's a hundred.* Conveying, in a single day, lives from what they had abandoned to where they had dreamed of being. *A hundred fifty.* Here is your first corner of your claim, Mr. and Mrs. Belgium. Mr. Missouri bachelor. Miss Dakota nurse. Mrs. Wisconsin widow. Then to the next corner, and the next, and the next, and the square was drawn, here was your homestead utter and complete: *SE¼ Sec. 17, Tp. 27 N, Rge. 8 W: the land has been made into arithmetic.* A sort of weaving, wasn't it, these numerated homestead squares, the lives threaded in and out. But these bare dry-land patches amid the mesh of homesteading . . . It was said there were twice as many people in Montana now as five years ago. The growth, the 'steader-specked prairies and benchlands and coulees, the instant towns, they were what Lucas dreamed of and Rob calculated on, and I was earning from. If I could dance ahead into time yet to come, what would I see in this procession of 'steaders that ought not have been let to happen, and what ought to have been encouraged instead? But we never do dance ahead into time; every minute is a tune-step of ours to the past. Say it better, the future is our blindfold dance, and a dance unseen is strangest dance of all, thousands of guesses at once. That was what my 'steaders amounted to, after all. Say that each of these people beside me on the wagon seat was a flip of the coin. Half would turn up wrong. And so for two summers I watched the 'steaders, Rob and Lucas's 'steaders, my 'steaders, and wondered just which of them were wrong tosses, which would meet only distress and failure and maybe worse here on this dry land which was free but not costless, not nearly.

It was a Saturday early the next May that there was the Hebner occurrence.

The family of four was Rob's first delivery to me in this new season of 'steaders. As Rob and the Ford receded back down the road to further depot duty, the newcomers and I sized each other up.

The man was loose-jointed, shambly, with a small chin, a small mouth, small nose, and then a startlingly high and wide forehead. The woman was worn, maybe weary after their journey from wherever to Montana, maybe just weary. Two children thin as sticks, the boy a replica two-thirds the size of his father, the girl small yet. Both children and the man stared at me as openly as hawks. As to what they saw in all this eyework on me, I do not really know, do I.

I introduced myself, and received from the man in just less than a shout: "Our name's Hebner, but you got to call me Otto."

I invited them into the wagon, and after an odd blank little pause
while the rest of the family glanced at him and he fidgeted an un-
trusting look at me, up they came.

The ride into the south benchlands was a few miles, and would be
longer than that without conversation. I inaugurated:

"Where is it you're from?"

The man peered at me in dumb dismay. Hard of hearing, the
poor pilgrim must be. Deaf and a 'steader too ought to be more
hardship than any one soul rated. I squared around to the fidgeting
Hebner and repeated my question louder and slower.

Relief came over him. In a braying voice, he responded:
"Couldn' cut through your brogue, there that first time. A feller
gets so used to hearin' American he gets kind of spoiled, I reckon."

I gazed at Hebner, hoping that was what passed for a joke wherever to hell he had been spawned, but no. He rattled on: "Anyhow,
we come from Oblong, Illinois. Ever hear of it?"

"Illinois, yes."

Having had my fill of conviviality Otto Hebner style, I whapped
the team some encouragement with the reins. Delivering this man
and his wan family to their 160 acres of delusion couldn't come too
soon for me.

Atop the rim of the benchland, I halted the wagon. Beside me
Hebner kept his head turned in a gawk toward the mountains and
the North Fork for so long that I truly wondered if he and I both
belonged in the human race. Now he gesticulated for his family's
benefit to the hay-green valley of the North Fork, the newly
lambed bands of sheep on its ridges around, the graceful wooded
line of the creek and its periodic tidy knots that were our houses
and outbuildings.

"Hannah, honey, those're what I been tellin' you about," he resounded to his wife. Noticing that the boy's stare was still fixed in
my direction rather than onto the Scotch Heaven homesteads,
Hebner added sharp to loud in telling him: "Garland! You listen up
to what I'm sayin' here, you hear?" The boy's gaze slowly drifted
from me to the North Fork. His father by now had reached his
proclamation point: "Those're what our homestead is goin' to be
like before you know it."

Bring that moment around to me again and I would utter what I
furiously kept myself from uttering at the time. *Hebner, you major
fool, you're looking at twenty years of stark work down there. Twenty*

years of building and contriving and fixing and starting over again.
Twenty lambing times, twenty shearings, twenty hayings. Twenty Montana winters, each of them so long they add far beyond that. You're
looking at the stubborn vision of Ninian Duff, you're looking at the
tireless ambitions of Rob Barclay, you're looking at the durable routes
Scorpion and I have worn into the ground back and forth between sheep
and schoolchildren, you're looking at choreworn wives who put up with
more isolation and empty distance than anyone sane ought to have to.
You cannot judge this country by idle first glance. I am here to tell you,
you cannot. But no, I was there to guide the Hebners of the world to
available acres, such as they were now. Try to dike this 'steader
flood with myself and all I would get was reputation for being all
wet.

I drew a steadying breath. My own gaze down into Scotch
Heaven helped. On the shoulder of Breed Butte between Rob's
homestead and mine, a rider had come into motion: Varick, on his
way up to check our sheep, while I was in the midst of this Heb-
nerian episode. Varick on a horse now looked as big as a man. Already his first year of high school was nearly behind him. His school
year of boarding in town with Lucas and Nancy and returning to
Adair and me only on weekends was his first footprint away from
home, and this summer would bring his next. He had asked Stanley
Meixell for, and received, the job of choreboy at the ranger station
until school began again in the fall. Not many years now, not many
at all, Angus, until this son of yours would need to find his own
foothold in this country, and so I swung back to the task of delving
with 'steaders.

"Those of us in Scotch Heaven do have a bit of a head start on
you, Mr. Hebner, so there's—"

"Otto," he corrected me with a bray.

"Otto, then. As I was setting out to say, there's no real resemblance between a settled creek valley and a dry-land homestead. So I don't want to startle you, but here we are at the
available land for you to have a look at."

Hebner hopped down and gawked south now, across the flat table
of gravelly earth sprigged with bunchgrass, his son duplicating the
staring inspection while I took the girl down from his wife and then
helped her out of the wagon. We stood in a covey at the section
marker stone, the wind steadily finding ways to get at us under and
around the wagon, until Hebner strode off twenty or so paces to-

ward the yawning middle of the benchland as if that was the fa-
vored outlook. After a long gander and kicking his heel into the soil,
what there was of it, a number of times, he marched back and took
up a stance beside me. Still scrutinizing the benchland, the shanties
and chicken coops and pale gray-brown furrows of the Keever and
Reinking and Thorkelson homesteads, he demanded: "You're
dead-sure this here is the best piece of new ground?"

Anyone with an eye could see that the benchland was equally
stark, stony, unwelcoming, wherever a glance was sent. "None of it
is fair Canaan, is it," was all I could answer Hebner. "But if here in
this dry-land end of the Two country is where you truly want to
homestead, right where we're standing is as good as any."

Not a lot of satisfaction for him to find in my words. He leaned
away from me and turned a bit so his silent wife would see the
shrewdness of what he asked next: "How deep is it to water?"

The question I had been dreading. "I can only tell you this
much. The Keevers and the Reinkings and the Thorkelsons all dug
about forty feet to get their wells."

"*Forty!* Back in Illinois we could dig down ten feet anywhere and
get the nicest softest vein of wellwater there is!"

"Then you ought to have brought one of those matchless wells
with you." I faced around to his wife, on the chance she might not
be so hopeless a case as him. "Mrs. Hebner, you had better know,
too—the water up here is hard." She made no reply. "Just so you
know, come first washday," I tried to prompt, "and you won't cuss
me too much." Still nothing from her except that abject or defeated
gaze at her husband. By the holy, if she could stand here wordless
and let this Hebner commit her to a homestead eternity of clothes
washed out stiff as planks and of a sour grayness in every teaspoon
of water she ever used, why then—

"Seems like you ain't overly enthusiastic about this here
ground," Hebner now gave me with a suspicious frown.

"Mr. Hebner, listen—"

"Otto," the man insisted thunderously.

"Otto, then. Listen a minute. None of this is going to be easy or
certain, for you and your family. Even at its best, homesteading is a
gamble, and it's twice that in these benchlands. A dry-land homestead is just what it says it is, dry."

"I didn' notice as how you left us any room back down there

along the creek," he retorted, making only small attempt to smile around the resentment.

Roust yourself twenty years ago from Lopside or wherever it is that spawned you, and there was room along the North Fork, along the South Fork, room everywhere across the Two Medicine country. And in the same thinking of that I knew that I would not have welcomed Otto Hebner even then; that anyone who did not come accepting that the homestead life was going to be hard, I did not want at the corner of my eye.

"Let's call this off," I said abruptly. "We're not doing each other any good here."

"Call it off!" Hebner blinked at me, thunderstruck. "This's a funny doggone arrangement you're pullin' on us, seems like," he brayed. "Leadin' us out to this here ground and then givin' us the poormouth about it. This's doggone funny exchange for the money we paid, is what I say."

"I thought you might want to know what you're in for, trying to homestead country such as this. I was obviously wrong. I'll give you your money back and take you in to Gros Ventre. If you're still set on finding a site, someone in town can do your locating for you."

"Nothin' doin'." Hebner did not look toward his wife and children, did not look around at the land again. He fixed his gaze onto my face as if defying me to find any way to say him nay. "This here's what I'm goin' to claim, right where we're at."

"Even against my advice, you want me to mark off the claim?"

"That's what we come all the way out here for."

I wrote HEBNER on four corner stakes, climbed into the buggy and counted the one hundred and fifty wheel revolutions south, east, north, and finally west to the section stone again.

By the time that day was done, I knew my craw could not hold any more Hebners, ever. All 'steaders from here on were going to have to dry-land themselves to death without my help.

In bed that night, I said as much to Adair.

"We're back where we started, then," she said as the fact it was. "Back to just getting by, and putting nothing ahead."

"There may be a way we can yet," I offered to her in the dark. "Dair, if I'm going to get us and Varick anywhere in life, it's going to have to be some way where I savvy and believe in what I'm doing. Something I know the tune of." I could feel her waiting.

"Sheep," I announced. "If we were to take on another band of sheep, the profit from that we could set aside for Varick."

Silence between us. Until Adair spoke softly: "You've never wanted to take on more than the band you and Rob run."

"I'll need to try stretch my philosophy, won't I." Try, for Varick. For you, Dair. For myself?

"Do we have the money for another band of sheep?"

"No. Half enough, maybe."

"Lucas would have it," she contributed.

"Lucas took his turn in backing me with sheep, long since. Besides, he's in up to his neck in land dealings these days. No, I think I know who would be keener than Lucas for this." Although I didn't look forward to hearing it from him: *I never thought I'd see the day, McAngus, when you'd start sounding like me—'More sheep, that's the ticket we need.'* "Dair, I thought I'd see if Rob will partner with us on another band."

Adair spoke what I was counting on, from her, from her brother. "He will."

What I had not counted on was Rob's notion of where we ought to put a new band of sheep. "Angus, I won't go for putting any more sheep up there in Meixell's hip pocket, even if the damn man would let us." If not on the national forest, then we'd have to rent grazing somewhere else, I pointed out to him. Maybe in the Choteau country, not that there was that much open range left there or anyplace, for that matter.

"Give me a couple of days," Rob said. "I just maybe know the place for those sheep, where Meixell or some Choteau geezer either one won't have a hoot in hell to say about them."

The couple of days later, Rob's announcement was pure jubilation.

"The reservation! Angus, you remember that Two Medicine grass. Elephants could be grazed on it! The Blackfeet don't know anything to do with it but sit and look at it."

I stirred. "Rob, hold your water a minute here. You know as well as I do why the Agency fenced the cow outfits out. That old business of 'borrowing' reservation grass—"

"'Borrowing,' who said anything about 'borrowing'? We'll be paying good lease money to the Blackfeet. You can ask your pocket whether there's any 'borrowing' to this. No, this is every-dot legal, Angus. The agent will let us on the big ridge north of the Two Medicine River with the sheep the first of the month. Man, you can't beat this with a stick! A full summer on that grass and we'll have lambs fat as butter."

I gave it hard thought, sheep on the Blackfeet grass. Sheep were not plows that ripped the sod; sheep with a good herder were not cattle casually flung Double W style. Prairie that had supported buffalo herds vast as stormclouds ought to be able to withstand a careful load of sheep. If Rob saw this band as a ladle to get at the cream of reservation grass, so be it. With Davie Erskine as herder, I could see to it the summer of leased grazing was kept civil and civic. I wanted it begun right, too.

"Those are some miles, from here to the Two Medicine," I pointed out. Forty or more, in fact.

"Sheep have feet," retorted Rob. As I knew, though, the days it would take to trail the sheep were not going to be his favorite pastime. "I hate like the dickens to lose that many days from the locating business. But I suppose—"

Without needing to think, I said: "I'll take the sheep up. Varick and I can, with Davie along."

I felt Rob study me. Probably it was all too plain that I didn't want to see his next crop of 'steaders. Then from him:

"Angus, you're made of gold and oak. If you can handle the reservation band until shearing, I'll make it right to you when we settle up this fall."

They were a band of beauties, our new sheep; the top cut of ewes and their eight-week lambs from the big Thorsen sheep outfit in the Choteau country. And confident grazers, definitely confident. The morning Varick and Davie and I bunched them to begin the journey from Scotch Heaven to the reservation, making them leave the green slopes above the North Fork was sheer work. You could all but hear their single creed and conviction in the blatting back and forth, *why leave proven grass for not proven?* That first hour or so it seemed that every time I looked around, a bunch breaker was taking off across the countryside at a jog trot, her lamb and twenty others in a scampering tail behind her. Relentlessly Varick and

Davie and I dogged that foolishness out of them, and the band at last formed itself and began to move like a hoofed cloud toward the benchland between the North Fork and Noon Creek, toward the road to the Two Medicine River.

Telling Varick and Davie I'd be with them shortly, I rode back down to the house.

"Varick and I ought to be no more than a week, Dair. Four days to get the sheep there, a day or two to help Davie settle in, and then the ride home."

"I'll look for you when I see you coming," she said.

"We're going a famous route, you know. A wife of mine came into this country by way of it," I said from high spirits. "My expectation is that there'll be monuments to her every mile along the way."

Adair smiled and surprised me with: "I hope there's not one at a certain coulee south of the Two Medicine River." *Coachman*, a so-young Adair to Rob at the reins, *are there any conveniences at all along this route of yours?* Myself ready to throttle Rob as she disappeared to piddle: *Your idea was to get her over here and marry her off to me, wasn't it?* The inimitable Rob: *If it worked out that way . . .* Rob's was the way it had worked out, although whether life after the wedding vow was working out for Adair and me seemed ever an open question.

"Dair?" The impulse of this felt deeper, truer, even as I began to speak it. "Come along with us, why not. To the Two Medicine."

Now the surprise was hers. "To christen the monuments?" she asked lightly.

"I'm talking serious here. You can ride the wagon with Davie, or have a turn on Scorpion whenever you feel like. But just come, why don't you. See all that country again." With me who is your husband, even if the country and I are not what you came expecting. With our son of this country and its namesake Two Medicine River. Come and make us the complete three, the McCaskills of Montana, America.

She watched me as if sympathetic to what I was saying, but then shook her head. "I suppose I think I saw the country as much as I am able to that first time, Angus. No, I'd better stay." She lifted her head in the self-mocking way and pronounced: "Adair will take care of here while you and Varick have to be there."

"Well, I tried. But if you can't be budged without a crowbar—"

Surprising again, how strong my pang that she wouldn't be sharing this Two Medicine journey with me. "Goodbye, Dair."

This wife of mine came up on tiptoes and kissed me memorably. "Goodbye yourself, Angus McCaskill."

The bell of the lead wether, the latest Percy, led us all. A thousand ewes and their thousand lambs, and Varick and Davie and I and two sheepdogs to propel them across forty miles to the northern grass. By all known rules of good sense there was much that I ought to have been apprehensive about. Weather first and last. The very morning we started, the mountains looked windy, rain-brewing; one of those restless days of the Rockies when a storm seems to be issuing out of every canyon, too many to ever possibly miss us. Well, we of Scotch Heaven had seen weather before. The under-the-sky perils that sheep invite on themselves were another matter. Fatal patches of death camas or lupine could be hiding ahead amid these grass miles that neither Davie nor I had local knowledge of. Alkali bogs that lambs could wander into, which would be their last wander. Of course, coyotes. *Cayuse . . . Coyote. Rob, Angus, is our serenade coming from a coyote?* Badger Creek two days ahead, and Birch Creek a day before that, creeks usually lazily fordable but if spring runoff was still brimming them . . . Things left, right and sideways all could go wrong, but they were going to have to do it over the top of me. I had never in my life felt so troubleproof. *This I know the tune of,* conviction sang in me from the first minute of that sheep drive. This band of sheep was Varick's future, his foothold into Two Medicine life when he would need it. For his sake, if it ended up that I had to carry each and every last wonderful woolly fool of a sheep on my back these forty miles, *this I know the tune of.*

As the first hard drops of rain swept onto us we were shoving the sheep across the short bridge over Noon Creek. In less time than it takes to tell, Varick and Davie and I in our slickers were wet yellow creatures, the ewes and lambs were gray wet ones, as we pressed across creek water through storm water. But the rain was traveling through so swiftly that the lambs did not stay chilled and begin to stiffen too much to walk, and there was the first woe we hadn't met.

This I know the tune of. All of life seemed fresh, sharp, to me as we spread the sheep into a quick grazing pace. The mountains from an angle different than the one I had known every day for more than twenty years were somehow an encouraging chorus up there, news that the world is more than the everyday route of our eyes. I could even look west to the Reese ranch nestled in the farthest willow bends of Noon Creek and not crush down under the weight of what my life and Anna's could have been, much. After a last glance west I swallowed away the thought of her, at least away as far as it would ever go, and dogged my wing of the band of sheep into quicker steps, and pointed us north.

Now the rise of the long hills beyond the Double W, their pancake summits the high flat edge of the Birch Creek country ahead. I called out to Davie, and to Adair in my imagination, that these bare ridgelines were in dire need of our sheepherder monuments. But there are monuments not just of stone, aren't there. When the sheep were topping that first great ridge north of where the buildings of the Double W lay white and sprawling, there on that divide I climbed off Scorpion, unbuttoned my slicker, and pissed down in the direction of Wampus Cat Williamson.

Overnight at Birch Creek, and then across the ford of the creek at dawn and through the gate of the reservation fence and into the first of the Blackfeet reservation and a land immediately different. Drier, more prairielike, the benchlands flatter and more isolated. Here toward the northern heart of the Two country, every distance seemed to increase, as if giving space to the Blackfeet grassland. The mountains no longer were head-on and near, but marching off northwestward toward the peak called the Chief, which stood out separate as if reviewing them. Benchlands here were bigger and higher and more separate than we were used to, so that cattle and horses looked surprisingly small in the Indian pastures we passed, and when I rode ahead a mile or so to be sure of water for noon, our band of sheep was hard to spot at all.

This I know the tune of. But did I. At the end of that day, bridgeless Badger Creek. Bridgeless and brim full. Time to turn sheep into fish. I had Varick lead Percy across, the wether uneasy about the creek water up to his belly but going through with his leadership role. His followers were none. For an endless hour there on the brink of dark, we relearned that making sheep wade water is a task that would cause a convent to curse in chorus. At last by main strength Varick and I half-led half-hurled enough sheep into the water to give the others the idea, and the community swim began. There was a last mob of lambs, frantic about not being across with their mamas but also frantic about the rushing water. Varick and Davie and the dogs and I fought them into the creek, lambs splashing, thrashing, blatting, and when there were no more kinds of panic to invent, swimming. *This I know the tune of.*

From dawn of the next day, with not a stormcloud in the Blackfeet sky and a fine solid bridge ahead of us at the Two Medicine River, I could feel our great journey as if it already had happened, as if now we, Varick and I and our poor bent Davie, we incomparable three had only to walk steadily in its tracks. Hour on hour, life sang out to me. Any moment that my eyes were not on the sheep and the land, they were on Varick. More and more he was growing to resemble me. The long frame, the face that was a mustacheless version of mine, probably of all McCaskills back to old Alexander hewing the Bell Rock lighthouse into the sea. *The job was there . . . it was to be done.* We still were living resemblances of old Alexander McCaskill in that, too, this son of mine born attuned to this country's work and I who had spent every effort I knew to learn it. Time upon time that day, I stood in my stirrups and gazed for the sheer pleasure of gazing. The land rolled north with grassy promise in every ridge. The pothole lakes we were passing, with clouds of ducks indignantly rising at the sight of us, seemed a wondrous advent. Even old Scorpion under me seemed more interested in being a horse. By the holy, I was right. Right to have brought these sheep, for Varick's sake. Right, even, to have married Adair and persisted through our strange distanced life together if this strong son was our result.

We came to the Two Medicine River in sunny mid-afternoon and were met by gusts of west wind that shimmered the strong new green of the cottonwood and aspen groves into the lighter tint of the leaves' bottom sides, so that tree after tree seemed to be trying to turn itself inside out. In the moving air as we and the sheep went down the high bluff, a crow lifted off straight up and lofted backwards, letting the gale loop him upward. I called to Varick my theory that maybe wind and not water had bored this colossal open tunnel the Two Medicine flowed through. And then we bedded the sheep, under the tall trees beside the river.

When morning came, I was sorry this was about to be over. All the green miles of May that we had come, the saddle hours in company with Varick, the hand-to-hand contest with the sheep to impel them across brimming Badger Creek, yesterday's sight of the Two

Medicine and its buffalo cliffs like the edge of an older and more patient planet. Every minute of it I keenly would have lived over and over again. This I knew the tune of.

The sheep crossed the bridge of the Two Medicine in a series of hoofed stammers. Up the long slope from the river Varick and Davie and the dogs and I pushed them. When they were atop the brow of the first big ridge north of the river, we called ourselves off and simply stood to watch.

On the lovely grass that once fed the buffalo, the sheep spread themselves into a calm cloud-colored scatter and began to graze, that first day of June of 1914.

TWO MEDICINE

With water projects abounding from the Sun River in the south to the Two Medicine River in the north, it is evident that the current creed of our region of Montana is "we'll dam every coulee, we'll irrigate every mountain." But the betterment of nature goes on apace in other ways as well. Anna Reese and children Lisabeth and Peter visited Isaac Reese at St. Mary Lake for three days last week, where Isaac is providing the workhorses for the task of building the roadbed from St. Mary to Babb. Isaac sends word through Anna that the summer's work on this and other Glacier National Park roads and trails is progressing satisfactorily.

—GROS VENTRE WEEKLY GLEANER,
JULY 2, 1914

"*PRRRRR PRRRRR.* Right along, Percy, that's the way, into the chute, earn a brown cracker. *Prrrrr prrrrr.* Bring them for their haircut, Percy. *Prrrrr.*"

It stays with me like a verse known by heart, that first ever Two Medicine day of shearing and all it brought. Our site of pens and tents atop the arching grass ridge above the river was like being on the bald brow of the earth, with the sunning features of the summer face of the land everywhere below. Three weeks before, Varick and I had left Davie here with his browsing cloud of sheep; when I returned with its shearing crew, the reservation grass had crisped from green to tan, the pothole lakes now were wearing sober collars of dried shore, the bannerlike flow of the Two Medicine River had drawn down to orderly instead of headlong. Even the weather was taking a spell of mildness, a day of bright blue positively innocent of any intention to bring cold rain pouncing onto newly naked and shelterless sheep, and with that off my mind I could work at the cutting gate with an eye to other horizons than the storm foundry of those mountains to the west.

A long prairie swooped from our shearing summit several miles north to Browning and its line of railroad, iron thread to cities and oceans. The chasm of the Two Medicine River burrowed eastward to graft itself into the next channel of flow, the Marias, and next after that the twinned forces of water set forth together to the Missouri. Every view from up here was mighty.

Not that any scenery short of heaven's was ever going to ease the hard first hours of shearing. The crew of shearers laboriously re-learning the patterns of the work from the year before. The sheep alarmed and anarchic. But I could grin at all that and more. The troubleproof mood I brought here to the Two Medicine when Varick and Davie and I trailed the sheep was still in command of me, still the frame of all I saw and thought as the swirling commotion of a thousand ewes was being turned into the ritual of wool. Life and I still were hand in hand, weren't we, life.

Past noon, whenever I found chance to gaze up from my cutting gate, it was south, the direction of Scotch Heaven and home, that needed my watching. Up from the great trench of the Two Medicine River the Gros Ventre-to-Browning road wove itself in a narrow braid of wheel tracks worn into the ground, but Rob still had not appeared on that road as promised. *First thing after breakfast that first day, Angus, I've got a 'steader to take out to see his claim. But I'll drive up in the Lizzie the minute after that's done. You can get the shearers under way and then I'll be there by afternoon to pitch in. You and the sheep can gimp along without me for that long, can't you?* Aye, yes and yea, Rob. We could do that and were. It was plain as noonday that these Two Medicine sheep were nowhere near Rob's central enthusiasm this summer, but I didn't mind. In the eventual, these sheep were not for his benefit anyway nor for mine, but for Varick's. I thought of my son, man of employment now at the ripe age of fifteen, somewhere beside Stanley Meixell there on distant Phantom Woman Mountain or Roman Reef or other venue of the Two Medicine National Forest, hard at the tasks of summer. *He'll have misfortunes great and small/He'll be a credit to us all.* In summers to come, if Adair and I could make our financial intention come true, Varick could have his own sheep in those mountains, could be as much a master of flocks as Rob or I ever were. So it was befitting that I was here amid earnful sheep, seeing across the miles from the Two Medicine to Varick's future.

What I still was not seeing any clue of was Rob. This was unlike

Rob Barclay, to not be where he said he would. As time kept passing, it more than once brought the thought, Rob, is that automobile of yours on its side in a gully somewhere and you under it? I would give him until suppertime, and then serious searching would need to commence.

"*Prrrrr*, Percy, bring them, that's the lad. Follow Percy, ladies. Time to get out of those winter coats. *Prrrrr*."

As the end of the afternoon neared I at last saw a wagon begin to climb the road from the river toward our shearing operation. This now was possibly Rob, resorting to hoof and wheel if his automobile had disgraced itself in some way, and so I kept watch between my chute duties. Before long, though, I could make out that there were three people on the wagon seat. Most likely a family of Blackfeet going in to Sherburne's trading post at Browning. I dismissed my attention from the ascending wagon and went back to sluicing sheep into the shearers' catch pens.

When I happened to glance down the ridge again, the wagon was less than a quarter of a mile away and it was no Blackfeet rig, not with that pair of matched sorrels and the freshly painted yellow wheelspokes. A gaping moment before I could let myself admit it, the shoulders-back erectness of the driver made me know definitely.

Anna at the reins. Her daughter and son on either side of her.

She brought the wagon to a stop near the shearing pen. I went over to her flabbergasted.

"Anna!" I greeted with more than I wanted to show in front of Lisabeth and Peter, but couldn't help. They were just going to have to take my warm tone as surprised hospitality; in their lack of years, how could they know it as anything more? I made myself speed on to: "You're no small distance from Noon Creek."

"Angus, hello again." Anna provided me her life-giving half-smile. "That husband of mine is even farther," she divulged. "Isaac is building roads in the national park. He'll be away most of the summer, so we're going up to St. Mary to spend some days with him." Except for the light veil of time that had put a few small wrinkles into her forehead and at the edges of those forthright eyes, she could have been the glorious young woman gazing back at me that first instant I stepped into her schoolhouse. Except for whatever propriety that had managed to find me now that I was a husband and a father, I still was the surprised smitten caller who was perfectly ready to rub my nose off kissing her shadow on that schoolroom wall.

Our eyes held. Was I imagining, or were we both watching this moment with greatest care?

"Angus"—how many thousands and thousands of times, across the past seventeen years, had I missed her saying my name—"how far is it into Browning for the night?"

Eight or ten miles, and I of course put it at ten. This sudden wild chance thumped in me as I said what civility would say but with greatly more behind it: "That's a lot of wagonwork yet, before dark. You're welcome to stay here, do I even need to say." I indicated the shearing camp, our impromptu little tent town, oasis amid the grassy miles if she would just see it that way. "Mrs. Veitch is cooking for the crew. You could share the cook tent with her and have proper company for the night, why not."

"Mother, let's!" from the boy Peter, craning his neck toward the hubbub of the wrangling corral and the rhythmic motions of the shearers at work.

Anna cast her look north across the expanse of prairie to Browning, the girl Lisabeth so much like her in face and bearing as she gauged the miles to Browning, too.

Anna, stay. That same desperate chant in me from the day when Adair and I were wed, yet not the same. This time there was no division in the chorus. This time it wanted only one outcome. *Stay, Anna. I want to see you, here, now, in this least likely place.*

When Anna stated, "It is a distance—I suppose we had better stay here for the night," Lisabeth nodded firmly, a separate but concurring decision. I breathed a thanks to Montana's geography for its helpful surplus of miles. Young Peter yipped his pleasure and asked to go watch the shearing, could he please, and was away.

I helped Lisabeth down from the wagon, then her mother, aware as deep as sensation can go that I was touching the person who might have been my daughter and then the person who might have been my wife.

"We'll of course lend Mrs. Veitch a hand with supper," Anna was detailing to Lisabeth now, "but I don't feel we should impose on her for the night. Under the wagon served us perfectly fine last night and there's no reason why it won't again." Anna sent her gaze around the shearing camp, her eyes eventually coming back across my face and lingering a bit there. Or was I imagining? "Beth," she spoke to her daughter, "why don't you go see the shearing with Peter, before we pay our respects to the cook tent. Mr. McCaskill can help me with our things from the wagon."

The girl's eyes, the same direct sky-source blue as her mother's, examined the bedrolls and other travel gear in the back of the wagon, then Anna and myself as if weighing the capability of adults in such matters. Evidently satisfied that the tasks were not beyond us, she gave that decisive nod again and went to join Peter at the shearing pen. I watched her go in a gait of grace that was more than a girl's. Lisabeth was, what, fourteen now, and womanhood had its next priestess arriving.

As I lifted out the Reese traveling larder, a venerable chuckbox with cattle brands singed into every side of it, I said to Anna, "She resembles you so much it must be like meeting yourself in the mirror."

"People think we're as alike as eggs, yes. Beth has a mind of her own, though." Anna glanced at me. "But then I suppose there are those who would say an independent child serves me right."

"Send me anybody who says so much as word number one against you and I'll pound the tongue out of him for you."

Her gaze stayed on me. "You would, too, wouldn't you, Angus. In spite of everything, you would."

Yes and then some. I would defend her in any arena, even the one within myself. Every instant of the next few minutes, as I helped Anna unhitch the sorrel team and situate her family's night gear under the shelter of the wagon, and then accompanied her to the shearing pen a discreet adult distance from where Lisabeth and Peter were engrossed in watching the clipwork, it was beyond belief to me that, yet and now, this still could be so. But I felt as thundershook by love for this woman as that first giddy ride home from the Noon Creek schoolhouse when it was all I could do not to fall off the back of Scorpion. Not to fall off the planet, for that matter.

Like a dozen marionettes, the shearers made their patterned motions, stooping, clipping, rising to begin over again. The sheep, betrayed and dismayed, gave up their buttery fleeces with helpless blats. While I was there beside Anna assiduously spectating the shearing pageant, my mind was everywhere else.

I knew I had only moments in which to contrive, before she gathered Lisabeth and they marched off to the cook tent. Yet she wasn't showing great sign of going, was she. Watching wool depart from sheep seemed the most absorbing activity either of us could imagine.

"Anna," I finally began, then found nowhere to alight next but onto: "The times we meet up are few and far between."

"Yes, they are. And now you're busy here. I mustn't take up your time, Angus."

"No, I thoroughly wish you would." I signaled to Davie to come up and work the cutting gate for the next batch of ewes into the catch pens. "I've had my fill of wool today, the crew can get along fine without me a bit." As I said it I wondered: did she know I would be here, handy beside her road north? By now everyone in the Two country above nipple age would have heard of the Mc-Caskill-Barclay advent of sheep onto the Blackfeet reservation. But granting that Anna knew, did she come because I would be here on her plausible route to Isaac? Or in spite of it?

I tried to test that water now. "It's glorious to see you. But what's Isaac going to think of you"—I didn't want to say spending the night—"stopping over here?"

"Isaac knows me." I questioned how thoroughly true that could be. How much any skinsack of existence ever can know of what is in another. She went on: "If it'll relieve your conscience, he'll at least know nothing out of order could happen with so many people around." Yes, two of them his own—your and his—children. That was unfortunately so, my yearning told me. Yet I was aware there was something else here with us. Her tang of interest toward me. The air's taste of about-to-happen, that I had caught so clearly during our noon hour together the time in Valier. I was every inch conscious of it again, and so was Anna. She was making every effort to say lightly: "Counting the sheep into the situation, Angus, we have chaperones by the hundred, don't we."

Sheep or not sheep, sentinels were going to have to get up before early to stop me from seeing this woman. *The liquid fire/of strong desire.* I gathered it all behind my words and asked her rapidly:

"Anna. Will you do a thing for me?"

She scrupulously kept her eyes on the wool brawl in front of us. "If I can, I will. You know that, Angus. What?"

"See the dawn with me tomorrow."

A blue flash of eyes from her, quicker than quick, then away. I reasoned to her profile: "It'd be our one time to talk alone."

There was that same narrow hesitation she had shown when I asked her four years before, *Do you have the life you want?* Now her answer:

"Yes. Show me a Two Medicine dawn."

Rob pulled in just before suppertime, the automobile gray with mud halfway up itself like a pig that has been wallowing, Rob himself more than a little dirt-freckled as well.

"See now, McAngus," he called out, "I'm the only land merchant who carries his real estate on his person."

I had to grin a bit. Even when he was abominably late, the man arrived the way olden travelers might have been announced by a drum.

Rob waved a hand toward his automobile.

"Badger Creek," he explained ruefully. "The Lizzie got stuck in the crossing and I had to troop off and find the nearest Blackfeet to pull me out. You can just about guess how involved an enterprise that turned out to be, Angus. A person might as well dicker with the creek, at least it has some motion to it. How those people manage to—" He broke off. The girl Lisabeth was stepping out of the cook tent with a kettle to fill from our milk cans of drinking water. Like the wraith of Anna stepping out of years ago.

Rob rid himself of his look of confoundment as fast as he could, then offered speculatively: "Company, have we. I thought Isaac was somewhere north, contracting roads or some such."

"He is," I affirmed.

Rob scanned around until he found the Reese wagon, plainly parked for the night, and for once seemed not to know what to say. Which of course did not stop him from coming out with: "A girl that age isn't kiting around the country by herself, I hope."

"No," I solemnly assured him.

He gave me a close look that had me on the verge of answering him by hand. By the holy, how did this man think he was the clerk in charge of my life?

"Angus," he began, "I don't savvy what in the hell—" and I didn't want to hear the rest.

"Her brother is with her, Rob. And her mother. She's thoroughly chaperoned," as if I still meant Lisabeth, although we both knew that I meant Anna. I enlightened him about their journey onward to

Isaac in the morning, and he unruffled considerably. But couldn't help adding:

"It's just a bit odd to have overnight guests in a shearing camp, is all I meant."

"Don't worry about your reputation, Rob," I gave him. "I'll vouch for you."

He cocked his head and ajudged, "You're a trifle touchy, McAngus," which I thought made two of us by that description. "Well, I'd better wash this Blackfeet real estate off me. Supper guests and all that, a person needs to keep up his appearance, doesn't he?"

Steel on grindstone and whetstone, the keen-edged chorus of the shearers sharpening for the day. A wisp of wind, the grass nodding to it.

I leaned over into the corral where the sheep had been wrangled up against the chute mouth by Davie and the shearing crew's choreboy, and felt the wool on three or four ewes' backs for dew. Dry enough to shear, now that the sun had been up for a few hours.

But before beginning the shearing day I cast a look to all the directions, lingering on north and the road to Browning that had taken a wagon with bright yellow wheels and a team of sorrel horses from sight a bit ago. The morning was bright as yesterday and so was I.

"*Prrrrr*, Percy, you're ready to bring them through, are you? Let's start making wool, Percy, what do you say."

The bellwether blinked idly at me in reproach and stayed where he stood in the mouth of the chute. Well, he was right. I needed to live up to my end of the proposition if I expected him to enter into his, didn't I. Life has its rules of bargaining.

"Here you are, Percy, half a brown cracker. *Prrrrr*, Percy, come get the rest here at the cutting gate. *Prrrrr*, sheep, follow Percy, that's the way. Everybody into the chute, *prrrrr, prrrrr*."

All the while that I was shunting sheep from the chute into the shearers' catch pens, all the while that the crew was taking their places and beginning the snipwork of taking the fleeces off the ewes, all the while I was not truly seeing any of it, but the scene at dawn instead. The barest beginning of light in the east, and Anna materializing from the direction of the shearing camp and joining me under the brow of the ridge, out of sight to all but each other.

Anna, you need to see this with me, that vow from another June morning, the first time I saw this green high bluff above the Two Medicine River, the precipice of the buffalo cliff, the prairie heaven of grass emerging from the sky's blue-and-silver one. Then as the warming colors of morning came, our words back and forth, my hope and her ver—

I felt the hand drop onto my shoulder just as I finished filling the catch pens. The clamping touch alone told me this was Rob, back from his start-of-day chore of spreading yesterday's shorn sheep along the slope of the ridge to graze. I glanced around at him inquisitively, for I'd assumed he would be taking his place behind the sheep to help Davie with the wrangling.

The face on Rob Barclay was thunderous. He grated out: "What in Christ's name is it between you and her, man? Out there this morning, like a couple of slinking collie dogs."

Again, was this. Rob patrolling my life again, Rob the warden of my marriage again. And again no more able than ever to understand the situation between Adair and me, and therefore Anna and me.

"Put it in the poorbox, Rob," I told him flatly.

But plainly he didn't intend to be dissuaded from giving me what was on his mind. He persisted: "You're not answering—"

"Oh, but I am. I'm telling you what I told you before, Anna isn't a topic of discussion between us. So just save yourself the trouble of trying, all right?" Save us both it. The two of us had been through this backwards and forward, after Valier. That outbreak of in-law from you was more than enough, Rob. Neither of us had one damn least iota of a thing to gain by—"Neither of us has a thing to gain by getting into this again," I kept to. "You know my opinion by heart, and yours is stamped all over you."

"You'd like the trouble saved, all right, wouldn't you. Well, not this time. You're going to hear me on this, goddamn it." Beyond Rob I saw that Davie was watching us wide-eyed, Rob's words loud enough to carry anger above the sounds of sheep and shearing.

"Then it better be away from here," I informed Rob, and I went off enough distance from the chute and corral, him after me.

We faced each other again. Still determined to carry me by the ears, Rob began: "You just won't make yourself stay away from her, will you. Even after that last talking-to I gave you—"

"Try giving me a leaving-alone, why not," I answered. "Anna

and I are still none of your business, Adair and I are still none of your business, and climbing out of your bed this morning to spy on me was none of your business either, Rob." Oh, I had known even while it was happening that Anna and I were seen. But not by these Barclay gray eyes that were auguring into me now. No, it was when Anna returned first from our dawn, went to the wagon and had a look at her sleeping children, and then headed on toward the cook tent to begin helping toward breakfast; and I meanwhile came up over the ridge from a deliberately different direction. Beneath the wagon, Lisabeth's head suddenly was up out of the bedroll. She watched her mother go. Then she turned enough to watch me come. Across that distance, I knew she knew. The steady attitude of her head, the gauging way she looked at us both, and then conclusion. That lovely young face in its frame of black hair, like a portrait of Anna gazing from the past, seemed to have seen through the ridge to where her mother and I were together. And there was no explaining I could do to the girl. It was a situation I would make worse if I so much as tried to touch it; Anna would have to be the one to handle it if Lisabeth brought out the question. The truth would have to handle it. The truth, Lisabeth, that I had asked your mother: *Anna, when Lisabeth and Peter and Varick are grown and gone . . . if Adair takes herself back to Scotland then . . . if and when, Anna, is there the chance then of our lives fitting together? Of you answering my love with yours, if and when?* And her, *Angus, you know how I am. Beyond anyone else, really, you grasp the kind of person I am. So you know all too well, I can only decide as far as I see a situation.* The judging hesitation, the click as she gauged. *But I can't see ahead to forever, can I. Whether Isaac is there in my life, after the children go—or whether . . .* Her eyes honestly telling me the same as her words. *I'm sorry the words aren't any better than they were, those years ago. You more than deserve better ones from me. But they're the same, Angus. If I ever see that Isaac and I have become wrong together, I'll know in the next minute to turn to you.* Again and yet and still: Isaac was not lastingly innocent of the hazard of losing Anna: I was not irredeemably guilty of loving her hopelessly. Not Proven, the verdict one more time. Well, we had life ahead yet to see if proof would come, didn't we. I had lost no ground since our meeting in Valier, I could stay on the compass setting Adair and I had agreed to, getting on in life as best we could for Varick's sake, hers, mine, ours.

"You've utterly got to stop this infatuation of yours," Rob was delivering urgently to me now. "It was one thing when you were just mooning around like a sick calf over her. But this is the worst yet. Meeting her out there to go at it in the grass."

I stared at Rob as if some malicious stranger had put his face on. *Go at it in the grass?* On the one hand, this slander was the worst thing that had come out of him yet today, which was saying a lot. On the other hand, the random stab of what he had just said showed that at least he hadn't slunk out after us this morning close enough to count our pores. All during our meeting of dawn, Anna and I had not so much as touched. We knew we didn't dare. Starved as I was for her—and I recognized, from another morning, long ago, that she was more than a little hungry for me—we didn't appease those cravings. Anna was still Isaac's, I was still Adair's; until those facts managed to change, we did not dare make the remembered touches we wanted to on each other's body, for families and lives would tumble with us.

"Rob," I uttered flat and hard. "You're going way too far."

"Somebody finally has to tell you what a lovesick sap you're looking at in the mirror every morning," he retaliated. "Adair has been too easy on you, all these years."

"Who made you the world's expert on Dair and me?" I burst out. "Man, just what is it you want from the two of us—doves and honey every blessed minute? She and I have what life together we can manage to. And we have Varick. Those are worth whatever Dair and I have cost each other."

The Barclay face bright with anger wasn't changed by my words. I took a last try.

"Rob. Will you just remember that your sister and I are a pair in life you devised yourself. Dair and I knew from early that we weren't perfect for each other, and it's damn far past time for you to accept that fact, too."

"I'm not accepting that you can sniff off after her"—he jerked his head north toward Anna's route to Isaac—"whenever you get the least little chance. Angus, how is it you can't see that when you're the way you are about Anna, you're only half a husband to Adair. And that's not enough."

"ANGUS AND ROB!" Davie had limped halfway our direction to call out worriedly to us. "The shearers are hollering for more sheep."

I gave Davie a wave of reply. And then I answered Rob, one last time. "It'll have to be enough. It's as good as I can ever do."

Rob shook his head stonily, at me, at my answer, at the existence of Anna. Each of us had said our all, and we hadn't changed each other a hair. That was that, then. I turned from him to go to the shearing pens, but had to let him know this useless argument couldn't go on perpetually.

"Rob, don't ever give me any more guff about something that's none of your business, all right?"

Behind me, his tone was tighter than ever. "I'm telling you this. I'll give you more than guff if you don't get her out of yourself."

For the rest of the shearing, speaking terms between us were short and narrow. When Rob announced, as soon as we were done loading the woolsacks for hauling to the depot at Browning, that he'd like to get on back to Breed Butte immediately, I nodded and silently applauded. The three or so days before I finished the wool-hauling and made my ride back to Scotch Heaven would give us both some time to wane from the argument about Anna. I just wondered what year it would be on the calendar when Rob Barclay decided he had to get huffy in a major way again.

The third day later, I was atop the divide between Noon Creek and the North Fork when I decided to veer past the ranger station on my way to home and Adair. There was no telling how soon I'd see Varick if I didn't snatch this chance to drop in on him at his summer employ, and I much wanted him to hear the news that as far as our Two Medicine sheep and shearing was concerned, the world was wagging its tail at us.

When I rode over the crest into sight of the ranger station, I was double glad I'd come by. Varick was out behind the building boiling fire camp utensils in a huge tub of lye water, a snotty job if there ever was one, and good news would sound even better amid that.

By the holy, I swear the son I was seeing ahead of me had put another inch on himself during the week and a half I'd been at the Two Medicine. Growing so fast his shadow couldn't keep up with him.

Varick's fire under the lye tub was crackling crisply—odd to hear, this warm almost-July afternoon—and he was judiciously depositing into the boiling murky water a series of camp pots as black as tar buckets. I got down from Scorpion and went over to him. With a grin I said, "When the Forest Service washes dishes, it really means it, ay?"

My tall son stayed intently busy with his lye cauldron until all the pots were drowned, then turned around to me. And delivered:

"You and Mrs. Reese. Is that true?"

The inside of me fell to my shoetops.

Varick's face showed all the strain behind the asking, all the confoundment of a fifteen-year-old not wanting to believe the world was askew. I made myself look back at him steadily before I said: "I suppose that depends on what you've heard."

"What I hear is that you and her get together any chance you can. Out in the grass along the Two Medicine, say."

Mercy I sought, mercy came not. Where had this squall dropped on us from, besides out of the vasty blue? Abruptly my mind saw again the face of the girl Lisabeth, up out of the bedroll beneath the wagon, gazing levelly toward her mother, turning that gaze toward me. No accusation in her look, only judgment: choosing among the three verdicts, innocent or guilty or not proven. But even if she accounted me guilty, why would she have sought out Varick with poison such as this? *Your father and my mother* . . . A person with any of Anna in her, destructive and vindictive to this degree? In that young Anna-like face beneath the wagon, I just could not see—

Accusation still stood here staring at me, waiting, wearing its painful mask of Varick. Pushing the echo of that question at me: *Is that true?*

"Son," a confused sound I added to the thudding of my heart, "I did see Anna, yes, but not—"

Varick's next was on its way: "Is that why you put sheep on the reservation? So you'd have a way to sneak off to her?"

"For Christ's sake, no!"

"Unk says it was."

Disbelief filled me now.

And in a sick terrible surge after it, belief.

The voice I knew as well as any but my own, following me across the Two Medicine prairie. *I'll give you more than guff if you don't get her out of yourself.* But Rob, why this? Why drag Varick into the middle between Anna and my helpless love for her? Why in all hell did you ever resort to this, Rob?

I struggled to concentrate through my fury at Rob and my anguish toward Varick, fight one welter of confusion at a time.

"Varick. You've heard the worst possible version. Nothing anywhere near wrong happened between Anna and me at the Two Medicine."

"Then what were the two of you doing out there alone that morning?"

"I asked her to watch the dawn with me."

Varick's look said this confounded him more than ever. He swallowed and asked shakily, "What, are you in love with her?"

Truth, were you going to be enough in this situation? Maybe so, maybe no.

"Yes." An answer that needed to go back seventeen years had to start somewhere. "This is hard to find the words for. But yes, I've always been in love with her, in spite of myself. Varick, this goes back farther in my life than you. Farther than your mother, even. She's known how I feel toward—"

"She *knows?* Mother *knows?*"

"Ask her. If you're intent on the history of this, you'd better get all sides of it." Not just that meddling bastard Rob Barclay's version. I tried again to swallow Rob away and say what was needed to make Varick understand. "Son, your mother and I—"

"I don't savvy any of this!" he blurted.

"Listen to me half a minute, will you. What—"

"You and Mother aren't—" the words broke out of him. "You don't—"

"If you're trying to say your mother and I don't love each other, all I can tell you is we come close enough. Otherwise you wouldn't be here." Wouldn't be here challenging the years we had spent trying to have you, and then to raise you, Varick. "Let's get a grip of ourselves here, and I'll try again to make you see how this is. What I feel for Anna Reese has nothing to do with your mother. That's the utter truth, son. It began before her, and nothing she or I have ever been able to do has changed it any. It's something I have to live with, is all. And I pretty much do, except when that goddamned uncle of yours shoves his size twenty nose into the situation."

My words didn't have effect. There wasn't a semblance of under-standing on Varick's face. A hurt bafflement instead. My son who could so readily comprehend the land and its rhythms and its tasks, could not grasp my invisible involvement with a woman not his mother. Those stormy countries of the mind—love, loss, yearn-ing—were places he had not yet been. And what words were strong enough to bring him there, make him see.

"Varick, there is just no way to undo the way I've always felt for Anna. I know you're upset about your mother and me, you've every right in the world to be. But we'll go on as we have been. She and I will stay together at least until you're grown and gone from home, I promise you that on all the Bibles there are."

But I could see I was losing. I could see from Varick's pained stare at me that whatever I said, my son was going to look on me from here forward as someone he had not really known. Even that realization, though, nowhere near prepared me for what came now from him.

"You don't have to stay together on my account. Not any more, you don't."

I eyed Varick and tried not to show how his words made me come undone inside. "Meaning what, son?"

"I'm not coming home at the end of this summer. Or any other time."

The clod of realization choked my throat. Any other boy-man, man-boy, whichever this son of mine was, might have been pre-tending the determination behind that statement. But you could col-lect all the pretense in Varick on an eyelash; he was like Adair in that. He meant his declaration.

He had gulped in enough breath for the rest, and now was rush-ing it out: "I'll board in town for school, but weekends and summers I'm going to be working here for Stanley."

"Varick, you're making this a whole hell of a lot worse than it needs to be."

"I'm not the one who started making it worse, am I. I don't want to be"—his gaze said *be around you*—"be part of this situation, as you call it."

If only the tongue had an eraser on the end of it as a pencil does, this terrible set of minutes wouldn't need to be called anything. Rob would unsay his monstrous slur, Varick would never need to blurt, *Is that true?* I would not have to frantically search for how to keep what little was left after my son's declaration. "You can't just walk out on your mother"—I swallowed miserably—"and me."

"I don't see how you're going to stop me from it."

"By stirring your head with a stick, if I have to. Varick, behave toward me the way you feel you need to. But not your mother. Go to her and tell her you take her side in all this, tell her you're on the outs with me, tell her whatever the hell. But don't pull away from her." I tried to will into him the urgency of what I was saying, tried to hold in the loss this was costing me. "If you'll keep on terms with her, stay the same as ever with her, you can ignore me or throw rocks at me when you see me coming or whatever will make you feel any better. If you'll do that, I won't stop you from staying on with Stanley as much as you want." Until you get your dismay at me out of your system. If you ever do.

With a wordless nod, my son took that bargain. And turned away from me to his boiling task.

He was on his porch waiting when I rode to Breed Butte.

I climbed down from Scorpion and tied his reins to the gate while Rob came across the yard to me.

"McAngus, you've got a face on you that would curdle cream," he began on me. "But man, something had to hammer it home to you about your foolishness over that woman. Maybe this will finally do the job."

The *job?* As if the life of my family was some task for him to take into his hands, bang us this way and that, twiddle our parts around—

"If I know you," his words kept soiling the air, "you're going to drag out that old argument of yours that I don't have any right to do anything about the mess you're making of your marriage. But I told you before, and I'll tell you till the cows come home. Adair is my sister and she's my right to stop you from making a fool of yourself, any way it takes to do that."

Any way? Even by costing me my son? Was that the crazy gospel you still believed, Rob—sonless yourself, you were wishing on me the worst spite you could by tearing my son out of my life? After you had returned from the Two Medicine and hotly spilled your words to Varick, didn't you want them back, want them unspoken? Want yourself not to have been the tool of anger that jealously ripped between Varick and me? I stared into you, needing to know.

Your face again now had as much anger as it could ever hold. But Rob, your eyes did not have enough of red emotion. Or of any other. Your tranced look, your helmeted mood when you had put yourself where it all could not but happen. And so I knew, didn't I. Your own belief in your sabotage wasn't total now, you had to trance yourself now against the doubt. Not let yourself bend now, from the angle you had talked yourself into. And now was too late. Doubt and trance didn't count in your favor now. Nothing did.

"You sanctimonious sonofabitch." My fist following my words, I swung to destroy that Barclay jaw.

Rob was ever quick, though. My haymaker only caught him pulling away, staggering him instead of sending him down. Which only meant he was still up where I could hammer at him. The single message thrummed in me, it had built in my blood from the instant I left Varick to come here and fight Rob. *Will I kill him? How can I not, deserving as he is.* He tried to set himself to return my blows, but I was onto him like fire, punching the side of his head, his shoulders, forearms, any available part of him. I beat that man as if he was a new drum. He took it grimly and struck back whenever he could manage. We struggled there, I see now, and fought through the years into our pasts, into the persons we had been. A Rob stands lordly and bright-faced on the Greenock dock, and my Angus of then pummels him in search of the being who hides inside that cocked stance. Rob on the sly with Nancy, and in Lucas's behalf the me whirling in from my first-ever North Fork day pounds him with the hands for both of us. The exultant Rob of the depot at Browning, *He never guessed! Adair, we did it to the man!* and the Angus who only ever has wanted Anna smashes the words back down his throat. The Rob of his homestead site aloof above the rippling North Fork, of ever more sheep, of the 'steaders, I at last was finding them all with my fists. The final one, the monster Rob who had betrayed by turning my son against me, I wanted to butcher with my bare hands. In that Rob's eyes, here, now, amid the thuds of my blows bringing blood out of him, there was the desperate knowledge that I was capable of his death.

How many times Rob Barclay went down from my hitting of him, I have no idea. Not enough for my amount of rage against him and what he had done. Eventually he stayed down, breathing brokenly. The sound of him, ragged, helpless at last, came up to me as if it was pain from a creature trapped under the earth.

A corner of my mind cleared and said, "You're not worth beating to death. You're worse off living with yourself."

I left him there in the dirt of his Breed Butte.

"I wish Rob hadn't bothered."

"Bothered? Dair, bothered doesn't begin to say it. The damn man has set Varick against me. Nobody has the right to cost me my son."

"I suppose Rob thought he was doing what he did for my sake." Her glance went from me to the rimline of mountains out the window. "As when he brought me over here from Scotland."

"That's as may be." I drew a careful breath. "In both cases he maybe thought he had you at heart, I give him that much. But he can't just glom into our lives whenever something doesn't suit him. We're not his to do with."

"No." She acknowledged that, and me, with her gray eyes. "We're our own to do with, aren't we." She stayed her distance from me across the kitchen, but her voice was entirely conversational, as if today's results were much the same as any other's. I almost thought I had not heard right when she quietly continued: "I'll have to live in town with Varick when school starts." Then, still as if telling me the time of day: "We'll need to get a house in town."

Her words did worse to me than Rob's fists ever could. On every side, my life was caving in. Varick. Rob. Now her. Our marriage had never been hazardless, but abrupt abandonment was the one thing we had guarded each other against.

Suddenly my despair was speaking. Suddenly I desperately had to know the full sum against me, even if it was more severe than I had imagined.

"Dair. Are you leaving me? Because if you are, let's—let's do the thing straight out, for once."

"Leaving?" She considered the word, as if I had just coined it. "All I've said is that I had better live in town with Varick during the school year." She looked straight at me now. "Angus, in all these years you've never really been able to leave Anna. So do you think leaving is something that can be done, just like that?"

"What do you call this, then, whatever it is you intend?"

"I call it living in town with our son while he goes to school, so that he has at least one of us in his life."

My wife, the ambassadress to my son. How does a family get in such kinks? Trying to keep the shake out of my voice, I asked Adair next: "And summers?"

"Summers I'll come back here with you, of course." Of course? Seventeen years with Adair and I still didn't recognize what she saw as the obvious. She was adding: "If you want me to."

"I want you to," I answered. And heard myself add: "Of course."

Lucas tried to invoke peace. The first time I stopped in at the Gros Ventre mercantile after Rob and I divided, the message was there that Lucas needed to see me. That didn't surprise me, but his absence at the Medicine Lodge when I went across to it did. "Luke just works Saturday nights now," I was told by the pompadoured young bartender. Around to the house I went for my next Barclay war council.

"Angus, I'll never defend what Robbie did to you. We both know there was a time he was half into the honey jar himself."

Lucas inclined his head to the kitchen doorway. Nancy could be heard moving about in there, the plump woman of middle age who had been the curvaceous girl at the stove when I walked in on Rob and her. Her lifted front lip, inquiring my verdict on them. Rob quick to ask my hurry, to blur the moment with his smile. So long ago, yet not long at all. "That lad needs some sense pounded into him every so often," Lucas was going on, then paused. "As I hear you undertook to do, ay?"

"I was too late with it."

"Maybe more of it sank in than you think," Lucas speculated behind a puff of his pipe. Does humankind know enough yet, Lucas, to determine what has and hasn't sunk into a Barclay skull? Enough of that thought must have come out in my gaze at him, for Lucas now went to: "None of this has to be fatal, Angus. It's one pure hell of a shame Varick got dragged into this, but he'll get over it sooner or later, I hope you know."

"I don't know that at all. Nothing I've tried to say to him does a bit of good. He has that edge to him. That way of drawing back into himself, and the rest of the world can go by if it wants."

"But in the eventual, Angus, he'll—"

Lucas, Lucas. *In the eventual* was time I could not spare. *In the eventual* lay the only possible time-territory of Anna and myself, when our lives would find their way together if they were ever going to. No, it was in the *now*, in these years before the possibility of Anna and myself, that I had to regain my son. To have him grow up understanding as much of me as he could. But the impossibly knotted task of that, so long as Varick refused to come near me in mind or self. My father, in his iron deafness. Myself, encased in my love for Anna. They look at us, our fleeceless sons do, and wonder how we ever grew such awful coats of complication. To understand us asks so much of sons—and for all I knew, daughters—at the precise time when they least know how to give.

"Angus, I know that what's between you and Varick, the two of you will have to work out," Lucas was onto now. "But maybe I'm not without some suasion where Robbie is concerned. Or where you are either, I hope." He peered at me in his diagnostic way, and wasn't heartened by the signs. "By Jesus, lad"—Lucas threw up his hands, or what would have been his hands at the empty ends of those arms—"I tell you, I just don't see how it helps the situation any for you and Robbie to be reaming the bones out of each other this way."

I shook my head. No, it helped nothing for Rob and me to be in silent war, and no, I would do nothing to change it. The hole in my life where Varick had been was a complication I wouldn't have but for Rob. In exchange, he could have my enmity.

Lucas's last try. "Angus, all those years of you and Robbie count for something."

I looked steadily at Lucas, the age on him gray in his beard and slick on his bald head. Here was a man who knew time, and I wanted to answer him well about those years of Rob and myself: our lives, really.

"The trouble is, Lucas, they don't count for the same in each of us. Maybe they never have, with Rob and me. He sees life as something you put in your pocket as you please. I never find it fits that easily."

"That's as may be, Angus," he said slowly, deliberatingly, when I was done. "But those differences weren't enough to put you at each other's throats, in all the time before." He gave me one more gaze that searched deep. "I just can't think it's forever, this between the two of you."

"If it's not forever, Lucas," I responded, "it's as close as can be."

In less time than is required to tell it, Rob and I took apart twenty-four years of partnership.

With Adair and Judith, each of them silent and strained, on hand to restrain us, everything went. He took my share of the Two Medicine sheep, I took his share of the band we had in the national forest. I bought his half-ownership in the sheep shed we had built together at the edge of my homestead nearest his. Oh, I did let him know he still had watering freedom on my portion of the North Fork whenever he had sheep at Breed Butte—my grudge was not against his animals, after all—if he wanted, and while he most definitely did not want so, he had no choice when the situation was water or no water. But of all else, we divvied everything we could think of except Scorpion. There, Rob would not touch the money I put on the table for his long-ago grand insistence that he stand half the price of my saddle horse. Bruised and scabbed as he was from my beating of him, Rob still wore that disdainful guise. There could not be more contempt than in the wave of his hand then, and his banishing words: "Keep your goddamn Reese horse, as a reminder."

Or so I thought, about the limits of disdain, until that September. When there was the morning that I looked up from my ride to school and saw teams of horses and earth equipment coming across the shoulder of Breed Butte. It seemed too many for road work, but then who knew what royal highroad Rob Barclay had to have to travel on.

Riding home at the end of that schoolday, I saw what the project was. The soil was being scraped, hollowed, beneath the spring at the west edge of Rob's homestead.

"Rop's ressavoy," Isaac Reese confirmed to me when I went up to see closer. "Ve build him deep."

Rob had always said I would see the day he would build a reservoir here. As I stood beside Isaac, watching the fresnoes and teams of big workhorses with the Long Cross brand on their sides as they scraped the hillside down into a dam, it seemed to me one last barrier was going up between Rob and myself. Spurning my offer that he could use my portion of the North Fork for his sheep, he was choosing to store up the spring's trickle instead. Choosing to create water of his own. That was Rob for you.

As the reservoir rose, it changed the face of the North Fork valley. A raw dirt pouch beneath the silver eye of the Breed Butte
spring; a catchment inserted into a valley built for flow. Then when
Rob brought the Two Medicine sheep home from the reservation
for the winter, each few days I would see him on horseback pushing
the band back and forth across the top of the earthen dam to pack
down the dirt, a task which the sharp hooves of sheep are ideal for.
Him and his gray conscript column, marching back and forth to im-
prison water. I know I had an enlarged sense of justice, where Rob
Barclay was concerned. But that private earthen basin of his up
there on Breed Butte only proved to me, as if I needed any more
proof, the difference in the way he saw the planet and the way I
did.

As those sheep tamped and tamped the Breed Butte reservoir
into permanence, I tried to settle myself into the long seasons without Adair and Varick that Rob had inflicted on me. Back across
time's distance, when America and Montana began for me at the
Greenock dock, I thought the Atlantic was worth fear. But the Atlantic was a child's teacup compared to the ocean that life could be.
The unexpected ferocities of family I now was up against, their unasked hold on me, were as implacable in their way as the seawater
ever was. This too was a sick scaredness of the kind that gripped me
in the steerage compartment of the *Jemmy*, down in the iron hole in
the water. Suddenly again my life was not under my own control,
now that everyone I had tried to stretch myself toward had yanked
away from me. I felt so alone on the homestead that if I had
shouted, I would have made no echo. When I tried to occupy myself with tasks and chores, even time was askew. Hours refused to
budge, yet days went to no good use. I did not even have the usual
troublesome company of sheep, for after Rob and I went our separate ways, that autumn at shipping time I sold my band of the
sheep to provide for Adair and Varick living in town; somehow two
households cost three times as much to run as one did. I told myself
I would soon have heart enough again to go back into the sheep
business, but I did not. Back there in my ocean fear, the worst that
could happen was that my life might promptly end that way. Now
the worst was that my life, without Varick at all, without Adair most
of the time, without Anna yet, my so-called life might go on and on
this way.

I believe this: my South Fork schoolhouse saved my sanity, gave me a place to put my thoughts and not have them fly back shrieking into my face. Day after day I was mentally thankful for the class-room distraction of Paul Toski and his tadpoles in a jar; thankful, too, that he hadn't quite figured out how to jug up skunks, coyotes, bears. There was the slow circling intelligence of Nellie Thorkelson to watch, and to wonder where it would alight. There was Charlie Finletter's war cry at recess-time disputes with Bobby Busby, *you whistledick!* There was the latest generation of Roziers, none as le-thal as Daniel but formidable enough, formidable enough.

During that school year and then next after that, Scotch Heaven saw Adair ensconced in a rented house in town with Varick and of course assumed that she and I had had a falling out and Rob was aloof to me because of that. But then glance out some sunny start-of-summer day and here Adair was, like the turn of the calendar from May into June each year, at the homestead with me again, wasn't she. And Varick nearby, working for Stanley at the ranger station or up in the national forest.

The McCaskills dwelt in some strange summer truce, did they? I knew not much more of it than you did, Scotch Heaven. I turned my brain inside-out with thinking, and still none of it came right. Varick, Adair, Rob, Anna as ever—each had extracted from my life whatever portions of themselves it suited them to, and I knew noth-ing to do but try to trudge along with whatever was left.

These were years, 1915 and 1916, when it seemed downright un-patriotic not to be thriving. I could stay as sunk as a sump if I wanted, but the homestead boom was rollicking along. 'Steaders were not only retaining those dry-land footholds of theirs that I thought were so flimsy and treacherous, they were drawing in more 'steaders; Montana in these years attracted like a magnet amid iron filings. And while the dry-land acres of farming extended and ex-tended, even the weather applauded. The winters were open and mild. Each spring and summer, rain became grain. There was even more to it: thanks to the endless appetite of the war in Europe, the price of anything you could grow was higher than you had ever dreamed. I had been dubious about whether prairie and benchland ought to be farmed, had I? Obviously I didn't know beans from honey.

The other person who did not join in the almost automatic pros-perity was named Rob Barclay. Not for lack of trying, on his part. But to my surprise, he sold the Two Medicine band of sheep even before lambing time of the next spring after our split. Rob's decision, I learned by way of Lucas, was to put all his energy into land-dealing. *See now, there's just no end to people wanting a piece of this country:* I could hear him saying every letter of it. His misfortune in deciding to become a lord of real estate was that the buying multitudes had their own ideas. When Rob took the plunge of purchasing every relinquished homestead he could lay his hands on, under the notion of selling land to 'steaders as well as delivering them onto it, he then found that the next season's seekers were seeking elsewhere, out in the eastern sweeps of the state where there still was fresh—"free"—land for homesteading. When he decided next to enter the sod-breaking business, buying a steam tractor half the caliber of a locomotive and the spans of ripping plows and hiring the considerable crew for the huge apparatus, that was the season he discovered he was one of many new sodsters, so many that there wasn't enough 'breaking business to go around. No, the more I heard of Rob's endeavors in these years, the more he sounded to me like a desperate fisherman trying to catch a bait grasshopper in his hat—always at least one jump behind, and sometimes several.

Hearsay was my only version of Rob Barclay now, and that was plenty for me. He and I had not spoken to one another since the day of severing our partnership, we tried not even to lay eyes on each other. This was the other side of the mirror of the past twenty-five years; the two of us who had built ourselves side by side into the Two Medicine country now were assiduously separate existences.

"Angus, it's not for me to say so," Ninian began once, "but it seems unnatural to see Robert and you—"

"—then don't say it, Ninian," I closed that off.

"Angus, lad," from Lucas toward the end of that time, "Robbie is losing his shirt in his land dealing, and he'd go all the way to his socks if I'd let him. By Jesus, I don't mind telling you it's time I straightened his head around for him again. So I'm going to back him in buying maybe fifteen hundred head of prime ewes. These prices for wool and lambs are just pure glorious. If I can talk Robbie into it, I wonder if you'd consider coming in with us on the deal."

"You can stop wondering, Lucas," I said, "because I won't do any considering of that sort."

And then it was our own war year, 1917. Wilson and America had been saying long and loud that they never would, but now they were going into Europe's bloody mud with both feet. That first week of April, I put down the *Gleaner* with its declaration-of-war headline, I thought of the maw of trenches from Belgium all across France, and I felt as sick as I ever had. This was the spring Varick would finish high school in Gros Ventre. If the war did not stop soon, a war that had so far shown no sign it would ever stop, Varick in all soldier-age inevitability would go to it or be sent to it.

"Angus?" from Adair, one of that year's first summer evenings, the dusk long and the air carrying the murmur of the North Fork flowing high with runoff from the mountains. Her first evening at the homestead with me, now that the school year was done. Now that our son no longer had the safety of being a schoolboy. "I need to tell you. There's something terrible I wish. About Varick."

This was new. I have to truthfully say that each other June, Adair reappeared here in this house just as if she had never been away from me. The homestead simply seemed to take on a questioning air, the same as it had when she first came here, straight from our Breed Butte wedding. But this was open agitation of some sort.

"What's this now, Dair? I don't believe the terrible in anything you could—"

"I wish he'd lost that eye." She gazed at me steadily, her voice composed but sad. "When the stick of kindling flew up, that time, I wish now it had taken his eye, Angus."

"Because, because of the war, you mean."

"Is that wrong of me, Angus?" To wish a son saved, from the army, from the trenches, from metal death? When Samuel Duff enlisted, Ninian subscribed to the daily newspaper from Great Falls and the war news came to us in that, the battle for some French hill in one headline, the sinking of half a convoy in another, in pages worn from reading as they traveled up the North Fork valley. As if tribes were fighting in the night, and messengers were shouting guesses at us. A person had to wonder. Was this what all the effort, the bringing of yourself around the bend of the world to another life, the making of homesteads, raising of children, was this what it all came to? Our armies trading death with their armies?

"No," I answered my wife. "No, I can't see that you're wrong at all, Dair. You brought him into the world. You ought to have every right to wish the world wouldn't kill him."

Only a night later, Adair and I had just gone to bed when the scuff of hooves arrived in the yard, then the creak of a saddle being dismounted from. I pulled clothes on, went and opened the door. To Rob.

Our stiff looks met one another. "I have something to say to Adair," was as much as he let me know.

From behind us, Adair's voice: "Anything you ever say to me, you say to Angus as well."

Rob stepped in around me, toward his sister. He began huskily, "Lucas—"

His voice cut off, swallowed by the emotion of his news. He did not really need to wrench out the rest; Adair and I knew the sentence.

"Do you know, Angus," Lucas's death spoke itself in Toussaint's words the afternoon of the funeral, "we thought he was funning us. Saturday night, everybody in the Medicine Lodge. Luke pouring drinks left, right, sideways. All at once, he says: 'My hands hurt. They're like fire.' We didn't know. To laugh or not. He rubbed both his stubs slow on his chest, like so. Then he fell. Doc was right there. But no use. Luke's heart went out, Doc says."

Lucas's funeral brought everyone. In its way, Gros Ventre itself seemed to attend, the town and its tree columns of streets at a respectful distance from the green graveyard knoll. Around me at his graveside, the years' worth of faces. Anna and Isaac. Rob and Judith. Duffs, Erskines, Frews, Findlaters, Hahns, Petersons, the rest. Varick arrived with Stanley Meixell, a faded but clean workshirt on each of them, and strode across to join his mother and me, saying nothing to me. Nancy with us, too, not wearing widow's weeds . . . All of us, except the one whom death had chosen for this first whittle into us, Lucas's slit in the earth.

I blinked when Ninian Duff stepped from amid us to the head of the grave.

"I have asked Robert whether I may say some words over Lucas," he announced. The feedbag beard looked even mightier now that it had cloudswirls of gray in it. I could see in my mind how that asking went. Not even Rob could turn down Ninian.

"It is no secret that Lucas and I did not see eye to eye about all of life." *Lad,* Lucas's voice to me in the Medicine Lodge that year

Rob and I arrived to Gros Ventre and the Two Medicine country, *how many Bibles do you suppose old Ninian's worn the guts out of?* "I bring no Bible here today," Ninian was all but thundering now, "yet there is one passage that I believe even Lucas would not overly mind to hear, if said in its proper light. It is of sheep, and those of us who make them our livelihood. One of the most ancient livelihoods, for as you will remember, Adam's first son Abel was a keeper of sheep." *Ninian, you're as spry as King David up on his hind feet.* "The old treasured words come to us from ancient Israel, where the tending of sheep was a work far different from the sort we know. The flocks of that ancient time were small in number and each sheep possessed its own name, and answered to that name when the familiar voice of his shepherd called forth." *May we all go out with the timbre of a Ninian accompanying us; a voice such as that would shut down Hell.* "Ay, and a shepherd of Israel did not herd his little flock from behind, as we do with our bands of a thousand and more. Rather, that shepherd of old went before his flock, finding out the safer ways, and his sheep followed him in confidence, depending upon him to lead them to safe watering places and to good pasturage." *The North Fork there, that's sinfully fine country. I'll tell you lads what may be the thing, and that's sheep. As sure as the pair of you are sitting here with your faces hanging out, sheep are worth some thinking about.* "And too, that same shepherd of Israel carried certain items necessary to the guarding and care of his sheep. His rod was a club of some heft, nailed through at one end, and was used for fighting off wild creatures and robbers. His staff was a longer, lighter tool, used to beat down leaves from trees and shrubs for his sheep to eat when the grass was short, and it had too a crook in one end, for the rescuing of sheep caught in the rocks or tumbled in a stream. Ay, very like our own sheephooks, they were." *I'll go with you on them. I'll partner the two of you in getting sheep. What do you say to the idea, Angus? Can I count on you both?*

Ninian paused, as if to let the wind carry his words where it wanted before he gave it more to transport. Then he resumed:

"Lucas was stubborn as a stone. They seem to be like that in Nethermuir. But he was no bad man. And like the others of us, all of us who draw breath, he is part of the flock who in one way or another speak through time in the words of the Twenty-third Psalm." Ninian's beard rose as he put his head back to recite:

"The Lord is my shepherd. I shall not want. He maketh me to lie down in green pastures. He leadeth me beside the still waters . . . Yea, though I walk through the valley of the shadow of death, I will fear no evil; for Thou art with me. Thy rod and thy staff, they comfort me."

By Jesus, the woollies do make a lovely sight. If we could just sell them as scenery, ay?

As the funeral crowd began to disperse, and Adair was taking condolences, I singled out Rob. I would rather have been made to pull my own toenails out one by one, but this I needed to do.

"Rob," I stepped in while several others were around him and his family, so that he had no private chance to ignore me, "see you a minute, I need to."

He aloofly followed down the slope of the graveyard after me, far enough where we wouldn't be heard.

I began with it. "I've a thing to ask of you."

"You can always try," issued back from him, wintry.

"The remembrance of Lucas for the *Gleaner*. I, I'd like to write it."

"You would, wouldn't you." It didn't come from Rob as any kind of commendation. "When all is done, you come prissing around wanting to have the saying of it, don't you. That's been a failing in you since—" Since the dock at Greenock, Rob, do you mean? Since the moment you and I put foot into Helena? Gros Ventre? Scotch Heaven? Where and when did I become something other than the Angus you have known the length of your life? Specify, Rob. If you can, man, specify. I'm here waiting.

He didn't finish, but went to: "Well, you've asked. And I'm telling you no, in big letters. I'll write that remembrance myself. It's for a Barclay to have final say about a Barclay. And Christ knows, you've never even come close to being one."

Two days from then, in the lawyer Dal Copenhever's office up over the First National Bank of Gros Ventre, Rob sat at one end of the arc of chairs in front of the lawyer's desk, I at the other with Adair and Nancy between us. Gros Ventre's streets of cottonwood trees had grown up through the years until they now made a shimmering green forest outside this second-story window, and I stared out into the lace of leaves while trying to collect my mind. The reading of Lucas's will was just over, and its effect was beginning.

"Dal, is this some sort of joke lawyers make?" Rob broke out. "To see if they can rile up the audience? If so, you've damn well succeeded in that."

The lawyer shook his head. "I've only read you what's on the paper. It's an unusual document, I'm the first to admit."

Unusual, he said.

I, Lucas Barclay, being of sound and disposing mind and memory and mindful of the uncertainty of human life . . . do hereby make, publish and declare this to be my last will and testament . . .

First: I give and bequeath to Nancy Buffalo Calf Speaks my residence in Gros Ventre, Teton County, Montana, and all my household furniture, linen, china, household stores and utensils, and all personal and household effects of whatsoever nature. Further, I direct that my business property, the Medicine Lodge Saloon, shall be sold, at public or private sale, by my executor; and that said executor shall pay over the proceeds of that sale, together with all funds on deposit under my name in the First National Bank of Gros Ventre, to Nancy Buffalo Calf Speaks in such monthly sums as may reasonably be expected to sustain her for the remainder of her life . . .

Well and good, Lucas. Even Rob, after his involuntary grimace at the news of all that was being bequeathed to Nancy, did not seem unduly surprised. But the rest of that piece of paper.

Second: I direct that my share of the sheep, approximately one thousand five hundred head, either owned outright by me or with my personal lien upon them, that are operated in partnership with Robert Burns Barclay, shall be conveyed thusly: said sheep I give and bequeath to Robert Burns Barclay, Adair Sybil McCaskill née Barclay, and Angus Alexander McCaskill, share and share alike, provided that they operate said sheep in partnership together for three years from the effective date of this will. I expressly stipulate that within that same period of time said sheep cannot be sold by the beneficiaries, nor the proceeds of any such sale derive to them, unless all three beneficiaries give full and willing agreement to such sale. In the event that said beneficiaries cannot operate in partnership and cannot agree unanimously to sell said sheep, my executor is directed to rescind said sheep and all rights thereunto from said beneficiaries and sell said sheep forthwith, with all proceeds of that sale to be donated to the municipality of Gros Ventre, Montana, for the express purpose of establishing a perpetual fund for the care and upkeep of the Gros Ventre cemetery.

. . . I hereby nominate and appoint Dalton Copenhaver to be the executor and trustee of this my last will.

"The three of us couldn't pet a cat together," from Rob now, thoroughly incredulous, "and Lucas full well knew that! So how in the hell are we supposed to run fifteen hundred head of sheep?"

With the supreme patience of a person being paid for his time, the lawyer stated: "If it's indeed the case that you can't cooperate in a partnership, then Lucas left you the remedy here in plain sight. The three of you only need to agree to sell, and the money from the sheep holdings can be split among you in equal shares."

From his face, Rob evidently didn't know which to be at this prospect of getting only a third of what he'd been anticipating, enraged or outraged. But at least he could be quickly rid of me by agreeing on sale of the sheep. "That's readily enough done," he spoke with obvious effort not to glare in my direction. I nodded sharp agreement. With all that lay between us, there was no way known to man by which the two of us could work as sheep partners again.

"No."

That from Adair. Rob cast her an uncomprehending glance and asked what my mind was asking too: "No what?"

"Just that." She returned Rob's gaze, gray eyes to gray eyes. "No."

Silence held the law office. Then the three male tongues in the room broke into wild chorus.

"Dair," I chided—

"Adair," Rob blurted—

"Mrs. McCaskill," the lawyer overrode us, "we must be very clear about this. You refuse to divide these sheep?"

Adair gave him a floating glance as if he was the biggest silly in the world, talking about dividing sheep as if they were pie pieces. "I refuse, yes, if that's what it has to be called."

In any other circumstance, I would have sat back and admired.

My wife looked as though she had a lifetime of practice at being an intractable heiress. Small, slim, she inhabited the big round-backed chair as if it were a natural throne. Not a quiver in the ringlets above her composed face. How many times had I seen this before. Wherever Adair was in that head of hers, she was firmly planted there. But as rich as the value was in watching Rob goggle at his sister, this was going to be expensive entertainment. Unless her *no* could be turned around, neither she nor I nor Rob was going to get so much as a penny from the sale of Lucas's sheep.

Rob gamely began on her. "Adair, what's this about? Unless you agree, the cemetery gets it all when the sheep are sold." Try his utmost, the look on Rob and the strain in his voice both told what a calamity he saw that as. *Robbie is losing his shirt in his land dealing, and he'd go all the way to his socks if I'd let him.* Well, well. The skin of Rob's feet were closer to touching disaster than I'd even thought. He was urging Adair now, "And surely to Christ that isn't what you want to happen, now is it?"

"Of course it isn't," she responded. "And you don't either." She regarded Rob patiently. "We can keep that from happening by the three of us running the sheep."

That brought me severely upright. Rob and I exchanged glances of grim recalcitrance.

"See now, Adair"—credit him, Rob sounded valiantly reasonable under the circumstances—"we can all grant that Lucas intended well with this piece of paper of his. But you know better than anyone that Angus and I—we'd just never jibe, is all. The two of us can't work together."

"You did," she said, cool as custard. "You can learn to again."

"Dair, it'd be craziness for us to even try," I took my turn at reasoning with her, past my apprehensions that reasoning and Adair weren't always within seeing distance of each other.

"Trying is never crazy," she reported as if telling me the weather. "Lucas wished us to try this together, and that's what we're going to do."

Rob shifted desperately around in his chair to confront the lawyer again. "Give us a bit of mercy here, why not. All that rant in the will about 'sound mind' and what is it, 'disposing memory' and such; surely to Christ this sheep mess Lucas came up with can't be called sane, am I right?"

"It was up to Lucas to dispose of those sheep as he saw fit," responded Copenhaver. "All I can tell you is, this will is plainly legal in its language." He pushed the paper toward Rob. "And here's Lucas's signature validating it." Even from where Adair and I and Nancy sat, that royal coil of signature could be recognized. Lucas's stubs propelling a pen, proudly saying to Scotland, *This place Gros Ventre is a coming town,* leading Rob and me from Helena with its loops and swirls. *Why did I write it, after these years? Matters pile up in a person. They can surprise you, how they want out.* They were out now, weren't they, Lucas. You saying with this last signature of yours that Rob and Adair and I must make ourselves look at reconciliation, must face it if only to reject it.

"Moreover," the lawyer was asserting to Rob, "the will has been attested by the requisite two witnesses"—he glanced closer at the pair of much smaller ragged scrawls—"Stanley Meixell and Bettina Mraz."

Rob shot the accusatory question to Adair and me, but neither of us knew the name Bettina Mraz either.

"Bouncing Betty," said Nancy quietly.

The other four of us swung to Nancy in stupefaction. Her dark eyes chose Rob to look back at. The lifted middle of her lip made it seem as if she was curious to know what he would make of her news to him. "Wingo's 'niece,' once. A year, two, ago. Stanley's favorite. Young. Yellow hair. And—" Nancy brought her hand and arm up level with her breasts, measuring a further six inches or so in front of them. "Bouncing Betty," she explained again.

Rob was out of his chair as if catapulted now, his knuckles digging into the lawyer's desktop as he leaned forward to half-demand half-plead: "Dal, man, a will witnessed by a forest ranger and a whore can't be valid, can it?"

Adair faced around to Rob reproachfully. "Really now, Rob. Just because Stanley Meixell is a forest ranger doesn't give you reason to question—"

"Mrs. McCaskill," the lawyer put up a hand to halt her, "I imagine your brother has reference to the competency of Miss"—he checked again the bottommost signature on the will—"Mraz as a witness. But unless she has ever been convicted of practicing her purported profession, she is as competent to witness as any of us. And convictions of that sort are hardly plentiful in Montana, I would point out to you. No, there really isn't much hope of contesting this will on the basis of its witnesses, in my opinion. Nor on any other that I'm aware of."

Rob looked as if he'd been kicked on both shins. "Adair," he intoned to her bleakly, "you've got to get us out of this sheep mess Lucas put us in."

"You know how much I hate to admit it, Dair," I chimed in at my most persuasive, "but for once in his life Rob happens to be right."

She stated it for us once more. "No."

There was a long moment of silence except for the rattle of the breeze in the cottonwood trees. But everything in my mind was as loud as it could be and still stay in there. *Adair*, it banged again and again, *what now?*

"Gentlemen," the lawyer summed, "Mrs. McCaskill is entirely within her rights. If and when you three heirs decide to divide the sheep, I can draw up the necessary papers. But until that decision is reached, you are in the sheep business together."

At home that night, I tried again.

"Dair, I don't know what it is you want, in this matter of Rob and me."

"I want the two of you to carry out Lucas's wish."

"It's not as if I want to go against something Lucas had his heart set on."

"Then you won't," she said.

"If you want us back in the sheep business so badly, I'll find the money somewhere to buy a band of our own."

"We already have sheep," she instructed me, "as of today."

"Dair. Dair, you know as well as I do that there's every reason under the sun for me to say a *no* of my own." *No* to her hopeless notion that Rob and I together could ever run that band of sheep, *yes* to the perpetual upkeep of the green bed, ay, Lucas? *Yes* to a ruination of Rob, as glad a *yes* as I could utter.

"I'm hoping you won't. I'm asking you not to."

"Because why?"

"Because this is another chance, for each of the three of us. Angus, I've never asked you these words before, but I am now. Will you do this for me?"

Put that way, this notion of hers resounded. Put that way, it had an inescapable echo. Here was the other end of the bargain she quietly broached to me those years ago: *You would still have a life to look ahead to.* Her acceptance, her grant, all through our marriage that I still loved Anna. And now this asking, that I make a demented try to partner with Rob again. Because why? Because for better or worse, Adair and I had each other, our marriage, until time told us otherwise. The Atlantic itself was a field of battle now; there could be no Scotland for Adair until the war wore itself out. Anna's Lisabeth was grown now, I had heard that she was going away to the teachers' college at Dillon in the fall, but Peter was still a few years from homeleaving. All the hinges that life turns on. And in the meantime Adair at last asking a thing of me, repeating it gently as if wondering aloud to herself:

"Will you, Angus?"

How many times had I seen this, now. A Barclay locked into an iron notion. Lucas becoming a builder of the Montana that had torn his hands from him. Rob so outraged toward me about Anna that he pried my son away from me. And now Adair bolting Rob and me into impossible partnership.

"Dair, I don't even want to be around the man. How under thunder am I supposed to run sheep with him?"

"The sheep won't care whether you and Rob have anything to say to one another."

I studied her. "Does Adair? Do you care?"

"In my way, I do."

I went to Breed Butte to begin lockstep sheep-raising.

The sheep were grazing complacently on the shoulder of the butte nearest Rob's reservoir. As I rode Scorpion across the narrow top of the dam I saw that Rob had been packing its dirt down again with the sheep, their small sharp hoofprints leaving every inch of it as pocked as a grater. The damn man and his damn dam.

Rob came out into his yard looking baleful in the extreme. I planted myself to face his harsh silence.

Nothing, from either of us.

Then some more of it.

Eventually I asked:

"How are we going to do this, by signal lamp?"

"Don't I wish."

"Rob, wishing isn't going to help this situation."

"You're one to tell me not to toss away life by wishing, are you. Surprising."

"We'd better stick to the topic of sheep."

Rob looked bleakly past me, down the slope of Breed Butte to the sheep shed that had been ours and now was mine. Then he shifted his gaze to the contented cloud of sheep. I followed his eyes there with my own. At least neither of us was new to the sheep part of this; after nearly thirty years, we could be said to have commenced at starting to make a stab at a beginning toward knowing a thing or two about the woollies.

After enough stiff silence, he made himself say it. "What brings you? Shearing?"

I confirmed with a nod.

He rapped back, "You know my thoughts on it. Or at least you goddamn ought to, after all these years."

"That doesn't mean I agree with them a whit," I pointed out. "I'm for shearing at the end of this month, to be as sure as possible of the weather."

"That's just the kind of pussyfoot idea you'd have, right enough. I say shear now and get the sheep up on the forest grass."

"You've said it, and I don't agree."

The next jerked out of him savagely, not simply at me but at the situation. "Goddamn it all to hell, this can never work. We both know Adair means well, but a half-assed situation like this, neither of us able to say a real yes or a real no—how to hell are we ever going to settle anything about the sheep?"

He was right about one matter. Nothing he or I could provide was going to ordain anything to the other. I reached in my pocket and showed him what Adair had handed me before I left the house.

Rob stared down at my hand, then sharply up into my eyes. "What's this, now?"

"What it looks like. A deck of cards. Adair says when we can't agree, we're to cut for who gets to decide."

"Jesus' suffering ass!" Rob detonated. "We couldn't run a flock of chickens on that basis, let alone fifteen hundred goddamn sheep!"

"Adair has one more stipulation," I informed him. "Low card always wins."

You never know. Adair's second stipulation so dumbfounded Rob that his howl of outrage now dwindled to the weary mutter, "It'd take that sister of mine to think of that."

"Anyway it's a change from letting magpies decide," I reminded him. Turning around to Scorpion, I used the seat of his saddle to shuffle the cards on three times, then held the deck toward Rob: "Your cut."

He produced the five of diamonds.

Grabbing the deck as if he wanted it out of sight of him, he shuffled it roughly, then thrust it out to me.

I turned up the ten of clubs.

"Well, then," Rob ground out. "We'll shear now, won't we."

I nodded once, and left.

The summer went that way. The thousand and a half sheep and Rob and I and our goddess of chance, also known as Adair. To ask myself how I had got swallowed into all this was to bewilder myself even more, so I tried instead to set myself to wait it through. Waiting was what I had practice in by now.

The deck of cards did me one inadvertent favor. In early August, when I was trying to finish the last of haying, Rob and I cut cards to see who had to camptend Davie that week, and I lost. Nothing to do but pocket my exasperation and begin the journey on Scorpion up into the national forest with the pack horse of Davie's supplies behind.

It was one of those mornings of Roman Reef looming so high and near in the dry summer air that my interest wandered aloft with it rather than toward the barbwire gate of the boundary fence I was nearing. When I came to earth and glanced ahead and discovered the person off his horse at the gate, performing the courtesy of waiting for me to ride through too before he closed it, at first his brown Stetson made me hope it was Varick. I saw in my next minute of riding up, no, not quite that tall and far from that young. Stanley Meixell.

"Hullo, Angus," the ranger spoke up as I rode through and stopped my horses on the other side of the gate. "What do you know for sure?"

Never nearly enough, Stanley. But aloud: "I know we could use rain."

"That we could. There's never enough weather in Montana except when there's too much of it."

Both of us knew I had stopped for more than a climate chat. I threw away preamble and asked:

"How's Varick doing for you?"

"Just topnotch. He's about a man and a half on anything I put him to. Regular demon for work, and what he can't do a first time he learns before a next time gets here. I tell you, the Yew Ess Forest Service is proud of him." Stanley paused, then casually tacked on: "You maybe heard, he's getting to be just quite a bronc stomper, too."

I had heard, unenthusiastically. The Sunday gatherings of young riders at the Egan ranch on Noon Creek were no longer complete without Varick atop a snorty horse, the report was.

Stanley studied me, then Roman Reef, as if comparison was his profession. "I guess you'd kind of like to know his frame of mind about you, Angus. It ain't real good."

"I wish that surprised me." What I went on to say did startle myself: "You know what it's about, this between Varick and me?"

"I do, yeah. Him and me had a session right after the blowup first happened between you two." Stanley regarded me thoughtfully for a moment before saying: "The ladies and us. Never as tidy as you'd think it ought to be, is it."

Definitely not for some of us, Stanley. Others of us, and I could name you one quick, the Bouncing Bettys ricochet soundlessly off of and never leave a whisper in the world.

"Angus, I've tried and tried to tell Varick to let it drop, the ruckus between him and you. And I'll keep on trying. But I've got to say, Varick ain't easy to budge, wherever he gets that from." Stanley paused again, then: "This probably don't help none, but my guess is it ain't just you that's burring him, Angus. It's him wanting to be away from home, get out in the world a little."

"He can be out in the world and still have a father."

"Yeah, I suppose. It's a whole hell of a lot easier for you and me to see that than it is for him, though."

It was my turn to glance away at Roman Reef. This deserved to be said, Stanley in his Stanley way had earned the hearing of it:

"Stanley. If I can't have Varick around me at this time of his life, there's nobody I'd rather he was with than you."

The only answer from under the brown hat was a brief session of throat-clearing. After a considerable moment: "Yeah, well, I better get on up the mountain. See you in choir practice, Angus."

At shipping time that fall, for once in our yoked partnership Rob and I did not need to cut the cards to find a decision.

"Ones like these, I'm going to take leave of my senses and go up to 17½ cents on," the lamb buyer offered. "However you Scotchmen manage to do it, you grow goddamn fine lambs."

While keeping a careful straight face Rob glanced at me. I was already glancing implacably at him. When we both nodded and got out ritual admissions that we supposed we could manage to accept such a sum of money, the flabbergasting deal was done. Eighty-five pounds per lamb × 1500 lambs × 17½¢. In the years of '93, Rob and I and all other sheepmen would have gone through life on our knees to get three cents a pound for our lambs instead of two, and now these unasked lofty prices of wartime. Life isn't famous for being evenhanded, is it.

"This doesn't mean one goddamn bit that I want to go through another year of this with you," Rob lost no time in imparting to me outside the stockyard as we were pocketing our checks. "If you had the least lick of sense, you'd go home right now and ask Adair if she won't let us sell the ewes this fall, too."

"I already asked," I gave him in identical tone. "She won't."

The next two months of numbers on the calendar, I hated to see toll themselves off. Why can't time creep when you want it to instead of when you don't. I stood it for half the toll, then on a mid-October Sunday afternoon I told Adair I was riding up into the foothills to see where our firewood was for this winter and instead rode across the shoulder of Breed Butte to Noon Creek.

Elderly Scorpion being pointed now to the country where I bought him: *Skorp Yun, lad, what about that?* What about it indeed. A woman looking up from the teacher's desk, a woman with the blackest of black hair done into a firm glossy braid, a glory of a woman: *I am called Anna Ramsay.* How long had it been in horse years, Scorpion? How long since Anna, at her schoolhouse or at the old Ramsay place, began being my automatic destination at Noon Creek? My destination anywhere in life, for that matter. But not now, not today, not yet, when I was reining Scorpion instead toward the round corral at the Egan ranch.

He was there atop a corral pole with the other young Sunday heroes when I arrived. Varick, whom I had come to lay eyes on before the eleventh day of the next month made him eighteen years of age. Before he became war fodder.

He saw me across the corral as I dismounted. I gave him a hello wave, he nodded the minimum in return, and with public amenities satisfied, we left it at that. Maybe more would eventuate between us later, but I did not really expect so. No, today I simply was bringing my son my eyes, the one part of me he could not turn away from on such a public afternoon as this.

As I tied Scorpion where he could graze a little, I heard a chuckle from the passenger on a horse just arriving. "You are here to ride a rough one, Angus?"

I looked up, at the broad-bellied figure in the saddle. "That I'm definitely not, Toussaint. A bronc has to bring me a note of good behavior from his mother before I'll go near him. But you. What fetches you down from the Two Medicine?"

"The riding. The young men riding." As if such a sight was worth traveling all distances for. Well, I had come no small way myself, hadn't I, to peruse Varick.

I chatted with Toussaint about the fine green year, his job as ditch rider on the reservation's new Two Medicine irrigation canal—"Did you know a man can ride a ditch, Angus?"—the war in Europe—"those other places," he called the warring countries—until I saw the arrival of a buckboard drawn by a beautiful team of sorrels. My breath caught. But this time the Reese wagon was not driven by Anna but by Isaac, with the boy Peter beside him. I might have known that wherever horses were collected, here would be Isaac.

"Toozawn, Annguz," he greeted us benignly, and headed on toward the corral. Peter's eyes registered me but didn't linger, flew on to the happenings within the circle of poles. I felt relief that he didn't dwell on me. Yet some pang, too, that the immensity of the past between his mother and me did not even generate a speculative gaze from this boy. Add inches to him for the next year or two, 1918, 1919, and he would be out into life. About the time when

Adair and Rob and I would have done our duty to Lucas's will and could all go our separate ways. I had thought through the arithmetic of these next few years a thousand times: the Reese nest would be empty and Anna would be able to judge just on the basis I had waited so long for, Isaac or me.

"That Isaac," declared Toussaint. "He knows."

I could feel my face going white or red, I couldn't tell which. I stared at Toussaint. "Knows?"

"He knows horses like nobody's business, that Isaac."

I recovered myself, told Toussaint it was time I became a serious spectator and found a place along the corral. Men *hello*ed and *An-gus*ed me in surprise as they passed. Quite a crowd in and on the corral by then. Besides Varick and Pat Egan's son Dill and other local sons, riders from the Double W and Thad Wainwright's Rocking T abounded here today, and just now, the last one they had been waiting for before starting was arriving with a whoop and a grin, young Withrow from the South Fork.

"Angus, good to see you here," Pat Egan called out as he came over to me. "Heard about the special attraction, did you?"

When my blank look said I'd heard no such thing, Pat told me that after the bronc riding there was to be a bucking exhibition of another sort. "Some guy from Fort Benton brought over this critter of his. Claims he's trained the thing to toss any rider there is. Our boys are going to have to show him how real riding is done, don't you think?"

Away went Pat, as he said, to get the circus started. Across the pole arena from me, the Withrow lad had climbed onto the fence beside Varick. "How you doing, Mac?"

"Just right, Dode. How about you?"

"Good enough, if they got some real horses here for us."

"They're rank enough, probably. I see you're dressed for the worst they can do, though." Withrow was always the dressiest in a crowd, and for today's bronc riding he sported a pair of yellow-tan corduroy trousers with leather trim at the pockets, new as the moment. Except for his habit of dressing as if he owned Montana, he was an engaging youngster, of a sheep-ranching family that had moved to the South Fork from the Cut Bank country in the past year or so. I perched there, watching Varick and Dode, listening to their gab of horses. Aching at the thought of how much of Varick I had not been able to know, these years of his climb into manhood.

Shortly the afternoon began to fill with horsehide and riders. Even just saddling each bronc was an exercise in fastening leather onto a storm of horse. The animal was snubbed to a corral post by a lasso tight around his neck while the saddlers did their work. Any too reluctant horse or a known kicker was thrown onto his side in the corral dirt and saddled while down. The rider would poise over him and try to socket himself into the saddle and stirrups as the horse struggled up. It looked to me like a recipe for suicide.

My throat stoppered itself when I saw that Varick had drawn one of the saddle-in-the-dirt rides.

"Watch out for when this sonofabitch starts sunfishing," I heard Dode counsel him, "or he'll stick your head in the ground."

Varick nodded, tugged his hat down severely toward his eyes, and straddled with care across the heaving middle of the prostrate pinto horse. Then said to the handlers: "Let's try him."

The pinto erupted out of the dirt, spurts of dust continuing to fly behind his hooves as he bucked and bounced, querously twisting his spotted body into sideway crescents as if determined to make his rump meet his head. While the horse leapt and crimped, Varick sat astride him, long legs stretched mightily into the stirrups. My blood raced as I watched. What son of mine was this? Somehow this bronc rider, this tall half-stranger, this Sunday centaur, was the yield of Adair and me. I was vastly thankful she was not here to see our wild result.

When Varick had ridden and the other braves of the saddle tribe had taken their turns at rattling their brains, Pat Egan hollered from beside the corral gate: "Time for something different, boys!"

Pat swung the gate open and in strolled a man and a steer.

At first glimpse, the Fort Benton critter looked like a standard steer. Red-brown, haunch-high to a horse, merely beef on the hoof. But when you considered him for a moment, this was a very veteran steer indeed, years older than the usual by not having gone the route to the slaughterhouse. An old dodger of the last battle, so to say. He was uniquely calm around people, blinking slow blinks that were halfway toward sleep as the onlookers gathered around him. The circle gave way considerably, however, when he lifted his tail like a pump handle and casually let loose several fluid feet of manure.

For his part, the Fort Benton man was a moonface with spectacles; a sort you would expect to see behind the teller's wicket in a bank instead of ankle deep into a corral floor. The fiscal look about him was not entirely coincidental. He was prepared, he announced, to provide twenty-five dollars to anyone who could ride this steer of his. He also would be amenable, of course, to whatever side bets anybody might care to make with him about his steer's invincibility.

At once, everybody in the corral voted with their pockets. All the young riders wanted a turn at the steer, or professed to. But the Fort Bentonian shook his head and informed the throng that was not how steer riding worked, it was strictly a one-shot proposition. One steer per afternoon, one rider per afternoon: what could be more fair? Then he set forth the further terms of steer riding, Fort Benton mode: the rider had to stay astride the steer for a total of three minutes in a ten-minute span. Naturally this Sunday assortment of bronc conquerors was free to choose the best rider among them—the bland spectacles suggested there had been a lot of other claims of "best" that came and went—and if the rider could stay on the steer the required sum of time, the twenty-five dollars was his.

Somebody spoke up: surely the steer impresario didn't mean three minutes straight, uninterrupted, aboard the animal, did he?

He did not. The rider could get off and on again any hundred number of times he wanted to during the overall time span. Did he need to add, he added, that the steer would be glad to help the rider with the offs.

What about a hazer, to even the odds for the rider getting back on?

The eyebrows lifted above the moonface in surprise. But the Fort Bentonian allowed that one man hazing on foot maybe wouldn't do lasting harm to his cherished pet.

I saw Isaac come into the corral, stoop, sight along the steer's backbone—I could all but hear him mentally compare it to a horse's—and then step over and gabble something to Varick, Dode Withrow and the others. They surveyed the territory for themselves, then somebody put it to the Fort Bentonian. How were they supposed to saddle something with as square a back as that?

Any old which way they desired, came the answer.

The young riders conferred again. Discussion bred inspiration. Could they tie on the saddle as well as cinch it?

They could entwine the steer a foot thick in rope if that was their way of doing things, the steer's spokesman bestowed, but they had better decide soon, as darkness was only hours away.

At last the terms of the contest were as clear as tongue could
make them, and all bets were laid. Someone called out the next
conundrum:

"Who's gonna climb on the thing?"

Faces turned toward Varick and the Withrow lad. Varick looked
at young Withrow, and young Withrow at him. "Toss you for him,
Dode," offered my son.

"Heads, Mac. Let her fly."

The silver dollar that spun into the air, I tried to exert to come
down heads; not to send danger toward another man's son, simply
away from my own. Name me one soul who could have done different. But I had my usual luck where Varick was concerned.

"You got on the wrong pants for riding a male cow anyway,"
Varick consoled Dode after the coin fell tails. Then, "I guess I'm
ready for this if your steer is, Mister Fort Benton."

Varick and his adherents gathered around the steer. The steer
blinked at them. As Dode Withrow approached with the saddle,
someone moved from behind the steer to watch. The steer's right
rear leg flashed, the hoof missing the pedestrian by an inch.

"Now, now, McCoy," the Fort Bentonian chided his pet. "That's
no way to act towards these boys." He scratched the steer between
its broad eyes as if it were a gigantic puppy, and it stood in perfect
tranquility while Dode and the others saddled and trussed. The
kick had done its work, though, as now both Varick and Dode, who
was going to be his hazer, knew they would have to avoid the steer's
rear area during the corral contest.

When the saddlers had done, a rope ran around the steer's neck
and through the forkhole of the saddle. Two further ropes dupli-
cated the route of the saddle cinch encircling, if that was the word
for such a shape, the steer. And it had been Dode Withrow's ulti-
mate inspiration to run a lariat around the animal lengthwise, chest
to rump and threaded through the rigging rings of the saddle, like
the final string around a package. "You people over here sure do
like rope," observed the Fort Bentonian.

Dode Withrow gripped the halter with both hands at the steer's
jaw while someone passed the halter rope up to Varick. He took a
wrap of it in his right hand and put his left into the air as if asking
an arithmetic question in my classroom. He called to Pat Egan and
the Fort Bentonian, the two timekeepers: "Let's try him."

The moonface boomed out, "GO, MCCOY!" and the steer writhed

his hindquarters as if he were now a giant snake. A giant snake with horns and hooves. Varick's head whipped sideways, then to the other side, like a willow snapping back and forth. Then the steer lurched forward and Varick whipped in that direction and back.

MURRRAWWWW issued out of McCoy, a half-bellow, half-groan, as he and Varick began storming around the circle of the corral. It was like watching a battle in a whirlwind, the steer's hooves spraying the loose minced dirt of the arena twenty feet into the air.

I watched in agony, fear, fascination. So I wanted to know about Varick's Sunday life, did I. We spend the years of raising children for this, for them to invent fresh ways to break their young necks?

At about McCoy's dozenth MURRRAWWWW, Varick continued left while the steer adjourned right.

"That was fifty-one seconds!" Pat Egan shouted out as Varick alit in the corral earth.

His words still were in the air when Dode dashed beside the steer to grab the halter rope. As he reached down for it, the animal trotted slightly faster, just enough to keep the rope out of reach. Dode speeded up. McCoy speeded up even more, circling the corral now at a sustained pace that a trotting horse would have envied. As the seconds ticked by in this round race between Dode and McCoy, it became clear what they used for brains in Fort Benton. Before the considerable problem of climbing onto McCoy and staying on, there was going to be the trickier problem of catching him each time.

Varick by now had scrambled to his feet and joined the chase. "I'll cut across behind the sonofabitch, you run him around to me," Dode strategized in a panting yell.

He started his veer behind McCoy. Sudden as a clock mechanism reaching the hour, McCoy halted in his tracks and delivered a flashing kick that missed Dode by the width of a fiddlestring.

But while McCoy was trying to send his would-be hazer into the middle of next week, Varick managed to lay hands on the halter rope and hold the steer long enough for Dode to gain control of the halter. Time sped as Dode desperately hugged McCoy by the head and Varick remounted, then the writhing contest was on again. The steer bounced around the arena always in the same direction, with the same crazy seesaw motion, and I thought Varick was beginning to look a bit woozy. Then MURRRAWWWW again and my son flew into the dirt another time.

"Another forty-six seconds!" shouted Pat. "That's five and a half minutes," chimed the Fort Bentonian. Away went McCoy, away went the puffing Dode after him, in a repeat race until Varick managed to mount again and the bucking resumed.

They rampaged that way, McCoy and McCaskill, through three further exchanges, man onto steer, steer out from under man. Each time, Varick's tenancy atop McCoy was briefer; but each time added preciously toward the three minute total of riding, too.

Now McCoy sent Varick cloudchasing again, and I half-hoped my stubborn son would find enough sense to give up the combat, half-wished his heavy plummet into the arena would conk him hard enough that he had to quit. But no, never. Varick was one long streak of corral dust, but he was onto his feet again, more or less. Gasping as if he'd been running steadily in tandem with McCoy ever since their bout began, he cast a bleary look around for his adversary. Over by the corral gate Dode Withrow had McCoy by the halter again, snugging the animal while urging Varick: "Now we got the sonofabitch, Mac! One more time!"

The steer casually studied young Withrow, then tossed his head and slung Dode tip over teakettle into the expanse of fresh green still-almost-liquid manure he had deposited just before the riding match commenced. The dazzling corduroy trousers and most other fabric on Dode abruptly changed color. While he slid and sloshed, the steer started away as if bored. But Varick had wobbled close enough to grab the halter rope as it flew from Dode, and now somehow he was putting himself aboard McCoy again.

The steer shook him mightily, but whatever wild rhythm McCoy was cavorting to, Varick also had found. The clamped pair of them, creature and rider, MURRRAWWWW and gritting silence, shot around the corral in a steady circle, if up-and-down isn't counted. Varick grasped the halter rope as if it was the hawser to life. McCoy quit circling and simply spun in his tracks like a dog chasing its tail. Varick's face came-went, came-went . . .

"Time!" yelled Pat Egan. "That's three minutes' worth! And still half a minute to the limit!"

"Whoa, McCoy," the Fort Benton man called out sourly. At once the steer froze, so abruptly that Varick pitched ahead into its neck. With a great gulp of air, Varick lowered himself from McCoy's back, held out the halter rope and dropped it.

Blearily my son located the figure, manure-sopped but grinning, of young Withrow.

"Dode," Varick called out, "you're awful hard on a pair of pants."

1918

It is now one year, a year with blood on it, since
America entered the war in Europe. Any day now,
the millionth soldier of the American Expedition-
ary Force will set foot into France. Nothing would
be less surprising, given the quantities of young
men of Montana who have lately gone into uni-
form, than if that doughboy who follows the
999,999 before him in the line of march into the
trenches should prove to be from Butte or from
Hardin, from Plentywood or from Whitefish—or
from here in our own Two Medicine country. We
can but pray that on some future day of signifi-
cance, a Pasteur or a Reed or a Gorgas will find
the remedy to the evil malady of war.
                    —GROS VENTRE WEEKLY GLEANER,
                                        APRIL 11, 1918

"*A*s SURE *as thunder falls into the earth and becomes stone,*"
cried the king the next morning, "I am struck dumb by what you are
saying, Remembrancer! You can stand there in truth's boots and say
time will flee from us no matter what we do? The sparks as they flew
upward from the fireplace last evening were not adding themselves
into the stars? The whipperwhee of the night bird did not fix itself
into the dark as reliably as an echo? The entire night that has just
passed is, umm, past? Where's the sense in all this remembering busi-
ness, then?"

"Those things yet exist, sire. But in us now, not in the moments that
birthed them."

"If that is so, we'll soon overflow! Puddles of memory will follow
us everywhere like shadows! Think of it all, Remembrancer! The calm
of a pond lazing as it awaits the wink of a skipping stone. The taste

*of green when we thumb a summer pea from its pod. The icicle
needles of winter. The kited fire of each sunrise. How can our poor heads
hold the least little of all there is to remember? Tell me that, whoever
can."*

"Let's stop there for today, Billy, thank you the world," I called
out from my perch at the rear of the classroom to the boy so earnestly reading aloud at my big desk.

Blinking regretfully behind his round eyeglasses, like a small owl
coming out of beloved night into day, Billy Reinking put the place
marker carefully into the book of stories and took his seat among
my other pupils. "Now tomorrow," I instructed the assortment of
craniums in front of me, "I want your own poor heads absolutely
running over with arithmetic when you walk into this schoolhouse,
please." Then out they went, to their saddle horses or their shoe-
worn paths, Thorkelsons and Keevers and Toskis and the wan
Hebner girl and the bright Reinking boy to their 'steader families in
the south benchlands, the Van Bebber and Hahn girls up the South
Fork, the Busby brothers and the new generation of Roziers and
the Finletter boy down the main creek.

After watching them scatter like tumbleweeds, I picked my own
route through the April mud to my new mount, a lively bay mare
named Jeannette. Scorpion I'd had to put out to pasture, he was so
full of years by now. I felt a little that way myself—the years part,
not the pastured one—as I thought of the lambing shed duties waiting for me before and after supper. Of Rob, scowling or worse, telling me in fewest words which of the ewes were adamant against
suckling their newborn and needed to be upended so their lambs
could dine. I would like to see the color of the man's hair who could
look forward to ending his day with stubborn ewes to wrestle and
Rob Barclay as well.

Prancy Jeannette and I entered the wind as soon as we rounded
the base of the knob hill and were in the valley of the North Fork,
but it was not much as Montana breezes go. Reassuring, in a way.
The waft felt as if it was loyally April and spring, not a chilly leftover of winter. My mood went up for the next minutes, until I rode
past the Duffs', where Ninian was moving a bunch of ten-day lambs
and their mamas up the flank of Breed Butte onto new grass. Across
the distance I gave him a wave, and like a narrow old tree with one

warped branch Ninian half-lifted an arm briefly in return and let it drop.

I rode on up the North Fork, in the mix of fury and sorrow that the sight of Ninian stirred in me. Scotch Heaven now had its first dead soldier, Ninian and Flora's son Samuel. Long-boned boy fascinated with airplanes and wireless. Little brother of the immortal Susan. Heir to all that Ninian and Flora had built here in the North Fork the past thirty years. Corpse in the bloody mud of France. *A life bright against the dark/but death loves a shining mark*. Samuel was our first casualty but inevitably not our last. Suddenly every male in Montana between milkteeth and storeteeth seemed to have gone to the war. Was it happening this drastically in all of America? A nation of only children and geezers now? Why wouldn't Europe sink under the Yankee weight if our every soldier-age man was arriving over there? Of my own generation, only Allan Frew was young enough to enlist, and he of course figured on settling the war by himself. But our sons, our neighbors, boy upon boy upon boy who had been pupils of mine, were away now to the war. Maybe that was my yearfull feeling, the sense of being beyond in age whatever was happening to those who were in the war. Yet, truthfully, who of us were not in it? Here at our homestead that I was riding into sight of, Adair would be in her quiet worry for Private Varick A. Mc-Caskill of Company C, 361st Regiment, 181st Brigade, 91st Division, in training at Camp Lewis in the state of Washington. And Anna, invisible but ever there, on the other side of Breed Butte from me Anna was doubtless riding home now from the Noon Creek school just as I was from mine, maybe with her own thoughts of pupils who already were in the trenches of France but definitely with the knowledge that her own son Peter was destined into uniform, too, if the war went into another year. Like the inescapable smoke of the summer of 1910, the war was reaching over the horizon to find each of us.

"Hello, you," I gave to Adair as spiritedly as I could when I came up from the lambing shed to supper.

She knew my mood, though. She somehow seemed to, these days. The winter just past was the first that Adair and I had spent together since Varick turned his face from me. The first, too, of trying to live up to this horn-locked partnership with Rob. To my surprise, when he and I had begun feeding hay to the sheep, she insisted on getting into her heavy clothes and coming with us. *I can drive the sled team for you,* she said, and did. Of course the reason was plain enough. She was putting herself between the slander Rob and I could break into at the least provocation. And it had worked. Seeing her there at the front of the hayrack, small bundled figure with the reins in her hand, seemed to tell both her brother and me that we may as well face the fact of her determination and plod on through this sheep partnership. At least that was my conclusion. I could never speak for Rob these days. By midway through the winter I was able to tell Adair she could abstain from her teamstering. *Rob and I are never going to be a duet, but we can stand each other for that long each day.* She scrutinized me, then nodded. *But you'll let me know if you need me again?* I hoped it would never be again that I needed her between myself and Rob, but I answered, *Dair, I'll let you know. I most definitely will.*

"How many today?" Adair asked as she began putting supper on the table.

"Forty," I gave the report of the day's birth of lambs.

She gave me a smile. "I'm just as glad you didn't bring them all in for the oven at once." I had to laugh, but I was still hearing her *how many?* question. This was the first lambing time Adair had ever asked that, night after night, the first time she had shown interest in the pride and joy of any shedman, his daily tally of new lambs. A new ritual, was this. Well, I would take it. Anything that emphasized life, I would gladly take.

At the end of May came our news of where Varick would be sent next by the army.

It's going to look just a whole lot like where I've been, he wrote in the brief letter to Adair. *Maybe because it's the same place.*

He was staying stationed at Camp Lewis, he explained, in a headquarters company. *They think they found something I can do, without me jeopardizing the entire rest of the army, so for now they're going to keep me here to do it. So here I stay, for who knows how long. I sure as h——don't, and I think maybe the army doesn't either.*

As they did each time, Varick's words on the paper brought back the few that had passed between him and me before he went off to the army. He had ridden into the yard just after I had come home from the school. I stepped out of the house to meet him. He dismounted and said only, *I came to see Mother.*

Unless you close your eyes quick, you'll see me, too, I tried.

No grin at all from him. Well, that could be because of the war rather than just me. But for three years it hadn't been.

Your mother's out at the root cellar, I informed him. But I couldn't stand this. Since time out of mind, Varick was the first McCaskill to wear the clothes of war. A ticket of freedom had let my great-grandfather shape the blocks of stone at the Bell Rock rather than face the armies of Napoleon. Neither my Nethermuir grandfather nor my deaf father were touched by uniform, nor was I. Which led inexorably to the thought that Varick was bearing the accumulated danger for us all.

*Varick. Son. Can't we drop this long enough to say goodbye? Who knows when—*if, I thought—*I'll see you again.*

Sure, we can say that much. And that was going to be all, was it. Varick held no notion that this could be our last occasion. He was at that priceless age where he thought he was unkillable. He drew a breath, this man suddenly taller than I was, and came to me and thrust out his hand. *Goodbye then.*

Goodbye, Varick. Your mother . . . and I . . . you'll be missed every moment.

I saw him swallow, and then he went off around the house to the root cellar. I felt my eyes begin to stream, tears that have been flowing since the first man painted blue fought the first man painted green and still have not washed away war.

Now Adair was putting Varick's letter in the top drawer of the sideboard with his others. Without turning, she asked, "And which do we hope for now, Angus? That they keep him and keep him in that camp, or that they ship him to France?"

I knew what was in her mind, for it was abruptly and terribly at the very front of mine as well. The army camps were becoming pestholes of influenza. Generally that was not something to die of, but people were dying of it in those camps. We had heard that the oldest son of the Florians, a 'steader family south of Gros Ventre, was already buried at a camp in Iowa before his parents even had word that he was ill. And now there in the midst of it at Camp Lewis was going to be our son, the child who came down with something in even the mildest of winters; Varick would be a waiting candidate for influenza as the months of this year advanced. But to wish him into the shrapnel hell of the fighting in France, no, I never could. Twin hells, then, and our son the soldier being gambled at their portals.

In earliest June, Rob and I met to cut the cards for a shearing time. This year mine was the low card, contradictory winner in Adair's order of things, and so we would shear later in the month, when I thought the weather was surest. Rob looked as sour as usual at losing, but before I could turn away to leave, he broke out with: "Any word from the Coast lately?"

By that he meant the Pacific Coast and Camp Lewis and Varick, and I stood and studied him a moment. We would never give each other the satisfaction of saying so, but he and I at last did have one thing we agreed on, the putrid taste of the war. *They're rabid dogs fighting in a sack, England and Germany and France and all of them,* I had heard him declare in disgust to Adair. *Why're we jumping in it with them?* Yet I knew, too, that the war's high prices for wool and lambs were the one merit he found in this partnership of ours. Well, nobody ever said Rob Barclay was too insubstantial to carry contradictions.

"Nothing new," I said shortly, and turned from him.

In the Fourth of July issue of the *Gleaner* was published the Two Medicine country's loss list thus far in the war.

THE MEN WHO GAVE ALL

Adams, Theodore, killed in action at Cantigny.

Almon, John, fought in the taking of Boureches, died of wounds.

Duff, Samuel, killed by a high explosive shell in the Seicheprey sector.

Florian, Harold, contracted influenza and died at Camp Dodge, Iowa.

Jebson, Michael, while returning from a furlough, was killed in a train wreck between Paris and Brest.

McCaul, George, saw service in France, taken ill with influenza, died in hospital of lobar pneumonia.

Ridpath, Jacob, killed in action at Château-Thierry.

Strong Runner, Stephen, entered the service at Salem Indian Training School in Oregon, died of tuberculosis at the Letterman General Hospital, San Francisco.

Zachary, Richard, killed in action at Belleau Wood.

A hot noon in the third week of August, the set of days that are summer's summer. I had my face all but into the washbasin, gratefully swashing off the sweat of my morning's work with cupped handfuls of cool well water, when Adair's hand alighting on my back startled me.

"Angus," she uttered quietly, "look outside. It's Rob coming. And Davie."

The first of those was supposed to be taking his turn at camptending our herder with the sheep up in the mountains, and the other was that herder. They could not possibly both be here, because that would leave the sheep abandoned and—yet out the west window, here they both came, slowly riding.

I still was mopping myself with the towel as I flung out to see what this was, Adair right after me. At the sight of us, Rob spurred his horse ahead of the lagging Davie and dismounted in a hurry almost atop Adair and myself.

"Davie's come down ill," he reported edgily. "I didn't know what the hell else to do but bring him out with me. It's all he can do to sit on that horse." Rob looked fairly done in himself, showing the strain of what he'd had to do. His voice was rough as a rasp as he went on: "Davie has to be taken on home to Donald and Jen, but one of us has got to get up there to those sheep, sharp. Do we cut to see who goes?"

"No, I'll go up. You tend to Davie." I stood planted in front of Rob, waiting for what he would be forced to tell me next.

"The sheep are somewhere out north of Davie's wagon, a mile or so more. I threw them into the biggest open patch of grass I could." He told it without quite managing to look at me. If you ever wanted to see a man cause agony in himself, here he was. Leaving a band of sheep to its own perils went against everything in either of us. I could all but see the images of cliff, storm, bear, mountain lions, coyotes, stampeding in Rob's eyes; and for a savage moment I was glad it was him and not me who'd had to abandon that band to bring Davie.

I went over to the sagging scarecrow on the horse behind Rob's. "Davie, lad, you're a bit under the weather, I hear."

His feverish face had a dull stricken look that unnerved me more than had his bloody battered one beneath the horse's hooves, the day of that distant spring when Adair and I jolted across the Erskine field to him; that day. Now Davie managed in a ragged near-whisper, "Couldn't . . . leave the . . . sheep."

"I'm going up to them this minute. The sheep will be all right, Davie, and so will you." If saying would only make either of those true.

As Rob and his medical burden started down the valley toward Davie's parents' place, I headed for the barn to saddle the bay mare. I hadn't gone three steps when I heard: "Angus. I'm coming with you."

I turned to my wife, to the gray eyes and auburn ringlets that had posed me so many puzzles in our years together. "You don't have to, Dair. I'll only be a day or so, until Rob can fetch another herder up."

"I'm coming anyway."

I hesitated between wanting her along and not wanting her to have to face what might be waiting up there, a destroyed band of sheep. The wreck of all our efforts since the reading of Lucas's will. "The sheep are a hell of a way up onto the mountain, Dair." I jerked my head to indicate Roman Reef standing bright in the sun, its cliffs the color of weathered bone. "It's a considerable ride."

"Adair knows how to ride, doesn't she."

True. But true enough? The saddle hours it would take to climb Roman Reef, through the sunblaze of the afternoon heat, to the grim search for adrift sheep—I recited the reasons against her coming, then asked: "Do you still want to?"

I swear she said this, as if the past twenty-one years of her avoidance of the Two Medicine country's mountainline were unceremoniously null and void. She said, "Of course I want to."

All afternoon Adair and I went steadily up and up, not hurrying our saddlehorses but keeping them steady at the pace just short of hurry. At midpoint of the afternoon we were halfway up Roman Reef, the valley of the North Fork below and behind us, Scotch Heaven's log-built homesteads becoming dark square dots in the distance. Our own buildings looked as work-stained as any. Then a bend of the trail turned us north, and the valley there was Noon Creek's, with the Reese ranch in easy sight now. Easy sight to where Anna was. Anyone but me would not have known the years and years of distance between.

At the next climbing turn of the trail I glanced back at Adair. She had on Varick's old brown Stetson he had left home when he went away to the army, and her riding skirt, and a well-worn blouse that had begun as white and now was the color of cream. My unlikely wife, an unlikely mote of light color against the rock and timber of the mountain. I wondered if she at all had any of the division of mind I did on this journey of ours. Part of me saw, desperately, that if the sheep had found a way to destroy themselves since Rob left them atop this mountain, Adair and I would possess what we had on our backs and that homestead down there and the rest you could count in small coins. Yet if the sheep were gone, stampeded all over the hemisphere, eaten, dead a myriad of ways, that also would mean the end of my teeth-gritting partnership with Rob. As we climbed and climbed, there was a kind of cruel relief for me in the fact that the sheep in their woolheaded way were doing the deciding, whether this enforced pairing of Rob and myself was to be the one thing or the other.

Atop, with the afternoon all but gone, Adair and I urged our horses toward where Davie's sheepwagon showed itself like a tall canvas igloo on wheels. Rob had shut Davie's dog in the sheepwagon so that he wouldn't follow down the mountain. When I unjailed him he came out inquisitive as to why I was not Davie, but otherwise ready to participate. I climbed back on my horse, leaned down from the saddle and called, "Come up, Scamp. Come up, boy."

The dog eyed me a moment to see if I really meant such a thing, then crouched to the earth and sprang against my leg and the stirrup leather, scrambling gamely as I boosted him the rest of the way into my lap. There across my thighs between the saddle horn and my body he at once lay quiet, exactly as if I had told him to save all possible energy. If the sheep were not where Rob had left them, this dog was going to have to work his legs off when we found them. If we found them. If we found them alive.

Adair and I and my border collie passenger in about a mile found what I was sure was the meadow Rob had described, and no sheep. An absence of sheep, a void as stark as a town empty of people. We sat on our horses and listened. Except for the switching sounds of our horses' tails, the silence was complete. I put the dog down. "Find them, Scamp." But the sheep had been over so much of the meadow that the dog could only trace out with his stymied dashes what I already knew, that some direction out of this great half-circle of grass they had quit the country.

Below us the last sunshine was going from the plains, the shadow of these mountains was now the first link of dusk. This meadow in the fading light looked like the most natural of bedgrounds for sheep. Tell that to the sheep, wherever the nomadic bastards had got to. Here Rob had made his decision that flung the sheep to their own wandering. Now I had to make mine to consign them to their own perils for the night.

"We'll take up the looking in the morning, Dair. It won't help anything for us to tumble over a cliff up here in the dark."

Back at the sheepwagon, Adair began fixing supper while I picketed our horses and fed Davie's dog. Then I joined her in the round-topped wagon, inserting myself onto the bench seat on the opposite side of the tiny table from the cooking area. That was pretty much the extent of a sheepwagon, a bench seat along either side, cabinets above and below, the bunk bed across the wagon's inmost end and the midget kitchen at its other. I suppose a fastidious cook would have been paralyzed at the general grime of Davie's potwear and utensils. Adair didn't seem to notice. She gave me a welcoming smile and went on searing some eggs in a black-crusted frying pan.

I sat watching her, and beyond her, out the opened top half of the wagon's Dutch door, the coming of night as it darkened the forest trees. So here we are, Dair. The McCaskills of Montana. After twenty-one years of marriage, cooped in a mountaintop sheepwagon. Sheepless. All the scenery we can eat, though. Not exactly what you had in mind for us when you contrived that will of yours, ay, Lucas? Somewhere out there in the prairie towns, Rob was scouring for a herder in these hireless times, at Choteau or Conrad if none was to be had in Gros Ventre, as there likely wasn't. Everyone in the war effort, these days. It was an effort, they were most definitely right about that.

After we had eaten, I leaned back and looked across at this wife of mine. Those twin freckles, one under each eye, like reflections of the pupils. Flecks of secondness, marks of the other Adair somewhere within the one I was seeing. I asked, "How do you like sheepherding, so far?"

"The company is the best thing about it."

"You have to understand, of course, this is the deluxe way to do it. Usually there are a couple of thousand noisy animals involved." *Sheep sound like the exact thing to have,* Rob responding to Lucas's suggestion of our future in my newfound valley called the North Fork. *Now if we only had sheep.*

"Tomorrow will tell, won't it," she answered my spoken and unspoken disquisitions on sheeplessness.

Well, if today was its model for revelation, it would. Adair volunteering herself into these mountains: I could have predicted forever and missed that possibility.

My curiosity was too great to be kept in. "Dair, truth now. Coming up here today where you could see it all, what did you think of it?"

In the light of the coal-oil lantern, her eyes were darker than usual as she searched into mine.

"The same as ever," she told me forthrightly, maybe a bit regretfully. "There is so much of this country. People keep having to stretch themselves out of shape trying to cope with so much. Distance. Weather. The aloneness. All the work. This Montana sets its own terms and tells you, do them or else. Angus, you and Rob maybe were made to handle this country. Adair doesn't seem to have been."

"For someone who can't handle that"—I inclined my head to the sweep of the land beneath our mountain—"you gave a pretty good imitation today."

"Such high praise," she said, not at all archly, "so late at night."

"Yes, well." I got up and stepped to the door for one last listen for the sheep. The dark silence of the mountains answered me. I turned around to Adair again, saying "Night is what we'd better be thinking about, isn't it. That bed's going to be a snug fit."

Adair turned her face toward me in the lanternlight. She asked as if it was the inquiry she always made in sheepwagons: "Is that a promise?"

The buttons of that creamy blouse of hers seemed to be the place to begin answering that. Then my fingers were inside, on the small pert mounds of Adair's breasts, and eventually down to do away with her riding skirt. Her hands were not idle either; who has said, *the one pure language of love is Braille?* If no one else, the two of us were inscribing it here and now. We did not interrupt vital progress on one another even as I boosted Adair into the narrow bunk bed and my clothes were shed beside hers. Two bodies now in the space for one, she and I went back and forth from quick hungers of love, our lips and tongues with the practice of all our years together but fresh as fire to each other, too, to expectant holidays of slow soft stroking. Maybe the close arch of canvas over us cupped us as if in a shell, concentrating us into ourselves and each other. Maybe the bachelor air, the sheepwagon's accumulated loneliness of herders spending their hermit lives, fed our yearning. Maybe the desperation of the day, of the marriage we somehow had kept together, needed this release. Who knew. It was enough for Adair and me that something, some longing of life, had us in its supreme grip. Something drives the root, something unfolds the furrow: its force was ours for each other, here, now.

As ever, Adair's slim small body beneath mine was nothing like Anna's the single time it had been under mine; as ever, our lovemaking's convulsion was everything like Anna's and mine. Difference became sameness, there in our last straining moments. This was the one part of life that did not care about human details, it existed on its own terms.

At first hint of dawn, we had to uncoil ourselves from sleep and each other. No time for a breakfast fire, either; the two of us ate as much dried fruit from Davie's grocery supply as we could hold, and then we were out to our saddle horses and the eager dog. As we set off into a morning that by now was a bit fainter than the darkness of night, my hope was that we were getting a jump on the sheep of maybe an hour.

That hour went, and half of another, before we had sunrise. Adair and I tied the horses and climbed up to an open outcrop of rock where we could see all around. As we watched, the eastern sky converted from orange to pink. Then there was the single moment, before the sun came up, when its golden light arrived like spray above a waterfall. The first hot half of the sun above the horizon gave us and the rock outcroppings and the wind-twisted trees long pale-gray shadows. Scrutinize the newly lit brow of the mountain as we did, though, there were no shadows with sheep attached to them.

"All this," Adair said as if speculating, "you'd think something would move. Some motion, somewhere."

I took her arm to start us down from the vantage point. "We're it, Dair. Motion is our middle name until we catch up with those goddamn sheep."

We worked stands of timber. Sheep sifted out of none of them.

We cast looks down over canyon cliffs. No wool among the harsh scree below.

We found at least three meadows where the grass all but shouted invitation to be eaten by sheep. All three times, no least trace of sheep.

Two hours of that. Then another. Too much time was passing. I didn't say so, but Adair knew it, too. The day already was warm enough to make us mop our brows. If we didn't find the sheep by ten o'clock or so, they would shade up and we would lose the entire hot midpart of the day without any bleats of traveling sheep to listen for.

Now Adair and I were ears on horseback, riding just a minute or two and then listening. How could there be so much silence? How could the invisible ligaments that bound the sky to the earth not creak in tense effort at least once in a while?

But nothingness, mute air, answered us so long and so steadily that when discrepancy finally came, we both were unsure about it.

I shot a glance to Adair. She thought she had heard it, too, if you could call that hearing. A sliver of sound, a faintest faraway *tink*.

Or more likely a rock dislodging itself in the morning heat and falling with a *clink*?

The dog was half-dozing in my lap. One of his ears had lifted a little, not enough to certify anything.

Adair and I listened twice as hard as before. At last I had to ask, low and quick, "What do you think, Dair?"

She said back to me in a voice as carefully crouched as my own: "I think it was Percy's bell."

By now we were past mid-morning, not far short of ten. We could nudge our horses into motion toward the direction where we imagined we'd heard the *tink* and risk losing any repeat of it in the sounds of our riding. Or we could sit tight, stiller than stones, and try to hear through the silence.

With her head poised, Adair looked as if she could sit where she was until the saddle flaked apart with age. I silently clamped myself in. I say silently. Inside me my willed instructions to the bellwether clamored and cried. *Move, Percy,* I urged. *Make that bell of yours ring just once, just one time, and I promise I'll feed you graham crackers until you burst. If you're up, don't lie down just yet. If you're down, for Christ's sake get up. Either case, move. Take a nice nibble of grass, why not, make that bell—*

The distant little clatter came, and Davie's dog perked up in my lap. I put him down to the ground and away he went, Adair and I riding after him, in the direction of the bell.

But for the dog, we still would have missed the sheep. They were kegged up in a blind draw just beneath a rimrock, as if having decided to mass themselves to make an easy buffet for any passing bear. The dog glided up the slope and over into the draw, we followed, and there they were, hundreds of gray ghosts quiet in the heat, contemplating us remorselessly as we rode up.

Adair anxiously asked, "Is it all of them?"

"I can't tell until I walk them. Make the dog stay here with you, Dair."

I went slowly on foot to the sheep, easing among them, moving ever so gradually back and forth through them, a drifting figure they did not really like to accept but did not find worth agitating themselves about. All the while I scanned for the band's marker sheep. Found Percy, with his bell. Found nine of the ten black ewes, but not the tenth. Found the brownheaded bum lamb with the lop ear, but did not find the distinctive pair of big twin lambs with the number brand 69 on their sides.

When I had accounted for the markers that were and weren't there, I went back down the slope to Adair.

"Most of them are here," I phrased it to her, "but not quite all."

It was noon of the next day before Rob appeared with a herder in tow, a snuff-filled Norwegian named Gustafson. "And I had to go all the way to Cut Bank even to come up with him," Rob gritted out. His eyes were on the sheep, back and forth across them, estimating. "Much loss?"

"At least a couple of hundred, maybe a few over."

"Lambs, do you mean? Or that many ewes and lambs together? Spit it out, man."

And so I did. "That many of each, is what I mean."

Rob looked as if my words had taken skin off him in a serious place. In a sense, they had. He knew as well as I did that such a loss would nick away our entire year's profit. But dwelling on it wasn't going to change it, was it. I asked him, "How's Davie?"

"Sick as a poisoned pup." Rob cast a wide gaze around, as if hoping to see sheep peeking at him from up in the treetops, out the cracks in rocks, anywhere. "Let's don't just stand here moving our mouths," he began, "we've got to get to looking—"

"Dair and I have done what looking we could," I informed him, "and now that you're here, the three of us can try some more. But there hasn't been a trace of the rest of the sheep. Wherever the hell those sheep are, they're seriously lost."

We never found them. From that day on, the only existence of those four hundred head of vanished sheep was in the arithmetic at shipping time; because of them, our sheep year of 1918 subtracted down into a break-even one. Not profit, not loss. Neither the one thing nor the other.

"Sweet suffering Christ," Rob let out bitterly as we stuffed the disappointing lamb checks into our shirt pockets. "What does it take, in this life? I put up with this goddamn partnership Adair keeps us in, and for no pay whatsoever?"

"Just think of all the exercise we get out of it, Rob," I answered him wearily.

By that September day when we shipped the lambs and turned toward the short weeks before winter, Davie had recuperated. His malady stayed on among us, however. Doc Murdoch could not account for how the illness had found Davie, as remote and alone on his mountainside as a person could ever be, but he was definite in his dire diagnosis: this was the influenza which had first bred in the army camps. Here in its earliest appearance in Scotch Heaven, it let Davie Erskine live, barely, while it killed his father.

From all we heard and read, the influenza was the strangest of epidemics, with different fathoms of death—sudden and selective in one instance, slow and widespread in another. Donald Erskine's fatality was in the shallows, making it all the more casual and awful. One morning while he and Jen were tending Davie, he came down with what he thought was the start of a cold, and by noon he was feeling a raging fever. For the first time since childhood, he went to bed during the day. Two days after that, the uneasy crowd of us at the Gros Ventre cemetery were burying that vague and generous man.

Man goeth to his long home, and the mourners go about the streets. Donald Erskine and Ninian Duff were the first who homesteaded in Scotch Heaven, and now there was just Ninian. I only half heard Ninian's grief-choked Bible words, there at graveside. I was remembering Adair and myself, our night together in Davie's sheepwagon, our slow wonderful writhe onto and into each other, there on his bedding. Davie had not been in that wagon, that bed, for some days before his illness, tepeeing behind the sheep as he grazed them on the northern reach of the mountain. Had he been, would one or both of us now be down with the influenza? Or be going into final earth as Donald was? *Ever the silver cord be loosed, or the golden bowl be broken* . . . My thoughts went all the way into the past, to my family's house of storm in Nethermuir. To Frank and Jack and Christie, my brothers and sister I never really knew, killed by the cholera when I was barely at a remembering age. To the husk that the McCaskill family was after that epidemic; my embittered and embattled parents, and the afterthought child who was me. Thin as spiderspin, the line of a family's fate can be. *Or the pitcher be broken at the fountain, or the wheel broken at the cistern* . . . And now another time of abrupt random deaths? What kind of a damn disease was this influenza, a cholera on modern wings? With everything medicine can do, how could all of life be at hazard in such a way? Maybe Ninian had an answer, somewhere in the growlings of John Knox that a fingersnap in heaven decided our doom as quick as we were born. I knew I didn't have one. *Then shall the dust return to the earth as it was* . . .

Adair and I were silent on our wagon ride home from Donald's funeral. I supposed her thoughts were where my own were, at

Camp Lewis. Winter was not far now, Varick's frail season. What chance did he have, there in one of the cesspools of this epidemic?

What chance did anyone have, the question suddenly began to be. You couldn't turn around without hearing of someone having lost an uncle in Chicago, a cousin in Butte, a sister on a homestead east of Conrad. Distant deaths were one thing. News of catastrophe almost next door was quite another. At a homestead on the prairie between Gros Ventre and Valier a Belgian family of six was found, the mother and four children dead in their beds, the father dead on the floor of the barn where he had tried to saddle a horse and go for help.

People were resorting to whatever they could think of against the epidemic. Out on the bare windy benchlands, 'steader families were sleeping in their dirt cellars, if they were lucky enough to have one, in hope of keeping warmer than they could in their drafty shacks. Mavis and George Frew became Bernarr Mcfadden believers, drinking hot water and forcing themselves into activity whenever they felt the least chill coming on. Others said onion syrup was the only influenza remedy. Mustard plasters, said others. Whiskey, said others. Asafetida sacks appeared at the necks of my schoolchildren that fall. When a newspaper story said masks must be worn to keep from breathing flu germs, the Gros Ventre mercantile sold out of gauze by noon of that day. The next newspaper story said masks were useless because a microbe could pass through gauze as easily as a mouse going through a barn door.

During all the precautions and debates, the flu kept on killing. Or if it didn't manage to do the job, the pneumonia that so often followed it did. Not more than ten days after our burial of Donald Erskine, it was being said that more were dying of the flu than of combat on the battlefields in Europe.

Odd, what a person will miss most. As the flu made people stay away from each other, Adair and I had our end of the North Fork valley to ourselves. Except for my daily ride to the schoolhouse, we were as isolated as if the homestead had become an island. An evening when Adair had fallen silent, but in what seemed a speculating way, I waited to see whether she would offer what was on her mind.

When Adair became aware I was watching her, she smiled a bit and asked: "Worth a halfpenny to you, is it?"

"At least," I answered, and waited again.

"Angus, I was thinking about our dances. And wondering when there will ever be one again."

Adair in the spell of the music, light and deft as she glided into a tune. Yes. A sharp absence to her, that the epidemic had made a casualty of the schoolroom dances. I missed them, too, for they meant Anna to me. Seeing her across the floor, gathering her anew each time in the quickest of looks between us, remembering, anticipating.

I looked across the room at Adair. If our senses of loss were different, at least they were shared. I got to my feet.

"We'd better not forget how, had we," I said to my wife. My best way to carry a tune is in a tub, but I hummed the approximate melody of *Dancing at the Rascal Fair* and put out my hands to Adair.

"Angus, are you serious?"

"I'm downright solemn," I said, and hummed another batch.

She gave me a gaze, the Adair gray-eyed glint that I had encountered in the depot at Browning all the years ago. Then she came up into my arms, her head lightly against my shoulder, the soft sound of her humming matching itself to mine, and we began the first of our transits around the room, quiet with each other except for the tune from our throats.

Less than two weeks after the beginning of school that autumn, every schoolhouse in the county had to close because of the influenza peril. It seemed that the last piece of my life that I could count on to be normal was gone now. At the homestead the next week or so, I went restlessly from chore to chore, rebuilding my damnable west fence that always needed it, patching the sheep shed roof, anything, everything, that could stand to have work done to it.

How Adair was managing to put up with me, I don't know. It must have been like living with a persistent cyclone, and one whose mood wasn't improved by how achy and stiff he felt from all his labors.

She persevered with me, though. "There's just one item on the place you haven't repaired lately," she told me one noon, "and that's you. Let me give you a haircut."

"What, in the middle of the day? Dair, I've got—"

"Right now," she inserted firmly, "while the light is best. It won't take time at all. Go get yourself sat, while I find the scissors."

I grumpily took my place by the south window. The mountains were gray in the thin first-of-October light. The year was waning down toward winter every day now. Toward another season of feeding hay with Rob, ample justification for gloom if I needed any further reason.

Over my head and then up under my chin came a quick cloud of fabric, Adair snugly knotting the dish towel at the back of my neck. "Stop squirming," she instructed, "or the lariat is next." From the edge of my eye I could see the dark-brown outline of the barn, and impatiently reminded myself I'd better go repair harness as soon as Adair had trimmed me to her satisfaction.

Her scissorwork and even the touch of her fingers as she handled my hair were an annoyance today. After I flinched a third or fourth time, Adair ruffled my hair with mock gruffness as she used to do to Varick when he was small and misbehaving, and said questioningly, "You're a touchy one today."

"It's not your barbering. I've got a bit of a headache, is all."

The scissors stopped on the back of my neck, the blades so cold against my skin I felt their chill travel all through me. "Angus, you never get headaches."

"I'm here to tell you, I've got a major one now," I stated with an amount of irritation that surprised me. But it genuinely did feel as if a clamp was squeezing the outer corner of each of my eyes, the halves of my head being made to press hard against each other.

"Dair, let's finish making me beautiful," I managed to say somewhat more civilly. "I need to get on with the afternoon work."

It wasn't an hour from then when she found me in the barn, sitting on a nail keg with my head down, trying to catch my breath.

When Adair asked if I was able to walk, I sounded ragged even to myself when I told her of course I could, any distance.

"The house, Angus," she answered that, her voice strangely brave and frightened at once. "Hold onto me, we're going to the house."

House, the distant echo of the woman's voice said. But we were in a wagon, weren't we, at the edge of a cliff. River below. *Those*

Blackfeet, Angus. The Two Medicine. Those Blackfeet put their medicine lodge near. Two times. Wait: the horses didn't answer to the reins. I yanked back but they were beginning to trot, running now. The cliff. *I fell through life . . .* The woman beside me clung to my arm. Bodies below. Bigger than sheep, darker. Cows, no, bigger. Buffalo. *The buffalo cliff, Angus. It was a good one.* The river was so far, so far down. Harness rattling. She clung to me. The cliff. I could see down over the edge, the buffalo were broken, heaped. *Fell through life.* She clung to me, crying something I couldn't hear. The horses were going to run forever. Our wagon wheels were inches from the cliff, I had to count the wheelspoke with the white knot of handkerchief *one* as it went around *two* count the wheelspin *three* as the ground flew . . . What. She was crying something. Hooves of the horses, wagon bumping. *Hang on,* I tell the woman, *we've got to . . .* Count the wheelspoke, start over. *One,* no, *two.* Tell the woman, *you count. While I . . .* what. Helpless. They don't answer the reins. Quiet now, horses run silently. But so close to the cliff. Two Medicine. *Those Blackfeet. Two times. Count,* I tell her. Too late. The spoke is coming loose. Rim breaking from the wheel. *Can't,* I tell her. *A wheel can't just . . .* Wheel breaking apart now, nearest the cliff. Iron circle of the rim peeling off, the spokes flying out of the hub. *Hold on,* tell the woman. Tipping, falling. I shout into her staring face: Anna! *Anna!* ANNA!

The bedroom was silent except for the heaviness of my breathing.

"You decided to wake up, did you."

Adair's voice. Her face followed it to the bed and me. The back of her small hand, cool and light, rested on my forehead a long moment, testing. "You're a bit fevery, but nothing to what you were a few days ago. And if you're finally well enough to wonder, the doctor says you don't have any pneumonia." Adair sat on the side of the bed and regarded me with mock severity. "He says you're recovering nicely now, but it'll be a while before you're up and dancing."

I felt weak as a snail. "Dair," I croaked out. "Did I . . . shout . . . something?"

A change flickered through her eyes. And then she was looking at me as steadily as before. "You do know how to make a commotion." She got up from the bedside and went out of the room.

My head felt big as a bucket, and as empty. It took an effort to lick my lips, an exertion to swallow.

In a minute or several, Adair was back, a bowl of whiteness in her hands.

"You need to eat," she insisted. "This is just milk toast. You can get it down if you try a bit."

The spoon looked too heavy to lift, the bowl as big as a pond. I shook my head an enormous inch. "I don't want—"

"Adair doesn't care," stated Adair, "what you don't want. It's what you're going to get." And began to spoonfeed me.

In a few days I was up from bed in brief stints, feeling as pale as I looked. My body of sticks and knobs was not the only thing vigor had gone out of. It was gravely noticeable how quiet Scotch Heaven seemed. No visiting back and forth, no sounds of neighbors sawing wood for winter.

As my head cleared, thoughts sharp as knives came. Donald Erskine being put into his grave, gone of the same illness I had just journeyed through. Those reports of the epidemic's efficient carnage in the army camps. Varick. No, Adair would have told me if— yet could she have, deeply ill as I was, wobbly as I still was? She had said nothing about our son, was saying nothing. That was just Adair. Or was it what I could not be told.

"Dair," I at last had to ask, "this influenza. Who else—?"

The gray eyes of my wife gave me a gauging look. "I've been keeping the newspaper for you. Maybe you're as ready to see it as you'll ever be. It has the list."

I pushed the prospect away with a wince. "If it's so bad they have to have a list, I don't want to see it."

Adair gauged me again. Then she went over to the sideboard, reached deep in a drawer and brought me the *Gleaner*.

VICTIMS OF THE EPIDEMIC

My eyes shot to the bottom of the page.

Munson, Theodore, homesteader. Age 51. Died at his homestead east of Gros Ventre, Oct. 11.

Not anyone I knew; but more *M* names were stacked above

that one. My scan of the list fled upward through them—*Morgan*
. . . *Mitulski* . . . *Mellisant*—toward the dreaded *Mc*s:

McWhirter . . .

McNee . . .

McCorkill . . .

McCallister . . .

And then *Kleinsasser* . . . *Jorgensen* . . . *Varick was safely absent
from this list, among the living. Mercy I sought, mercy I got.* I was as
thankful as any person had ever been. But while Adair and I still
had a son, a name known to me even longer than Varick's came out
of the list at me.

*Frew, Allan, soldier of the American Expeditionary Force. Age 45.
Died in a field hospital near Montfaucon, Sept. 26.*

Allan in the shearing contest I had let him win. Allan dancing
with Adair afterward, the two of them the melody of my hope that
she would find a husband and a Montana niche for herself, in that
far ago summer, while Anna and I—life isn't something you can
catechize into happening the way you intend, is it. I looked up now
at Adair, whose marriage could have been with Allan, for better or
for worse but surely for different than all she had been through with
me. "It's too bad about Allan," I offered to her, and she nodded a
slight nod which was agreement but also instruction for me to look
at the list again.

Erskine, Jennie, widow of Donald, mother of David . . . "Not Jen,"
I squeezed out of my constricted throat. "Not old Jen, too, after
poor Donald . . ."

"Yes. It's an awful time, Angus," Adair answered in a voice as
strained as mine.

My thoughts were blurred, numb, as my eyes climbed the rest of
the list. *Benson* . . . *Baker* . . . Between them would have been
Rob's slot, if Barclays were susceptible to the mere ills of the rest of
the world. What would I be feeling now, if his name stood in stark
print there? Or he, if mine was in rank back down there in the *Mc*s?
I did not know, you never can except in the circumstance, but I
could feel it all regathering, the old arguments, the three angry
years apart from Rob after the Two Medicine and the angry time
with him since then in this benighted damn sheep partnership—I
was too weary, done in, to go where that train of thought led. I fast

read the rest of its list to the first of its names, *Angutter, Hans, homesteader* . . . and put the *Gleaner* away from me.

"Angus." I heard Adair draw a breath. The newspaper was back in her hand, thrust to me.

"Dair, what?" I asked wearily. "I read the damn list once, I'm not going to again."

Then I saw. Beside Adair's thumb there on the page, was that name at the bottom of the list, *Munson, Theodore;* but there was also the small print beneath that. *List continues on p. 3.*

"Angus," my wife said with a catch in her voice, "you have to."

No.

No no no.

But I did have to. Did have to know. The newspaper shook in my hands as I opened it to the third page, as I dropped my eyes to the end of the remainder of the list and forced them, the tears already welling, back up to the *R*s.

Reese, Anna, wife of Isaac, mother of Lisabeth and Peter. Age 44. At the family ranch on Noon Creek, during the night of Oct. 12.

_Times are as thin in Montana as they can get. No
one needs telling that this has been a summer so
dry it takes a person three days to work up a whistle. But we urge our homesteading brethren to hold
themselves in place on their thirsty acres if they in
any way can, and not enlist in the exodus of those
who have given up heart and hope. As surely as
the weather will change from this driest of times,
so shall the business climate._

—GROS VENTRE WEEKLY GLEANER,
AUGUST 21, 1919

LET IT tell itself, that season of loss.

By first snowfall, as much of me as could mend was up and out
in the tasks of the homestead, of the sheep, of the oncoming
winter. Had I been able, I would have filled myself with work
twenty-four hours a day, to have something in me where the
Anna emptiness always waited. Yet even as I tried to occupy
myself with tasks of this, that, and the other, I knew I was con-
tending against the kind of time that has no hours nor minutes to
it. Memory's time. In its calendarless swirl the fact of Anna's
death did not recede, did not alter. Smallest things hurt. A glance
north to read the weather, and I was seeing the ridge that divided the North Fork from Noon Creek, the shoulder of geography between my life and hers. A chorus of bleats from the sheep
as they grazed the autumn slope of Breed Butte, choir of elegy
for the Blackfeet grass and the moment when I recognized Anna
at the reins of the arriving wagon. And each dawn when I went
out to the first of the chores, the slant of lantern light from the
kitchen window a wedge between night and day—each was the
dawn of Anna and myself and the colors of morning beginning to
come to the Two Medicine country. Each time, each memory, I

told myself with determination that it would be the last, that here was the logical point for the past to grow quiet. But no known logic works on that worst of facts, death of someone you loved, does it.

By Armistice Day, when the war pox in Europe finally ended, the influenza epidemic was concluding itself, too. In the Gros Ventre cemetery the mounded soil on the graves of Anna and its dozens of other victims was no longer fresh. When the schools reopened and Ninian came to ask if I was well enough to resume teaching, I told him no, he would need to make a new hire. Whether it was my health or not that lacked the strength, I could not face the South Fork schoolroom just then. Anna dancing in my arms there the first time ever, my voice asking, *And we'll be dancing next at Noon Creek, will we?* and hers answering, *I'll not object.* Before Ninian could go, I had to know: "What's being done about the Noon Creek school?" He reported, "Mrs. Reese's daughter is stepping in for them there." Lisabeth. In younger replica, the same beautiful face with an expression as frank as a clock, still in place at Noon Creek. But not.

By Christmas week, Rob and I were meeting wordlessly each day at a haystack to pitch a load onto the sled and feed the sheep. Maybe the man knew how to keep a decent silence in the face of a sorrow. Maybe he thought the hush between us added cruel weight to his indictment of me and my hopelessness about Anna. Who knew, and who cared. Whatever I was getting from Rob, cold kindness or mean censure, I at least had mercy from the weather. There was just enough snow to cover the ground, and only a chill in the air instead of deep cold. Day upon day the mountains stood their tallest, clear in every detail, cloud-free, as if storm had forgotten how to find them. Any number of times in those first days of feeding, I saw Rob cock his head up at this open winter and look satisfied.

On New Year's Day of 1919, Varick came home.

He was taller, thinner, and an eon older than the boy-man I had fearfully watched ride the Fort Benton steer. To say the truth, there was a half-moment when I first glanced down from the haystack at the Forest Service horse and the Stetsoned person atop it, that I thought he was Stanley Meixell.

"'Lo, Dad," he called up to me. His gaze shifted to Rob, and in another tone he simply uttered with a nod, "Unk."

"Varick, lad," Rob got out. I watched him glance at me, at Varick, confusion all over him. When no thunderbolt hit him from either of us, he decided conversation could be tried. "You're looking a bit gaunt. How bad was the army life?"

Varick gave him a flat look. "Bad enough." It was not until the weeks ahead that I heard his story of Camp Lewis. *Christamighty, Dad, the flu killed them like flies. Whole barracks of guys in quarantine. You'd see them one day, standing at the window looking out, not even especially sick, and the next day we'd be packing them out of there on stretchers to the base hospital. And a couple of days after that, we'd be burying them. A truckload of coffins at a time. I didn't figure you and Mother needed to know this, but I was doing the burying. They found out on the rifle range this eye of mine only squints when it takes a notion to, so they decided I wasn't worth shipping to France to get shot. Instead they put a bunch of us guys who knew which end of a shovel to take hold of onto the graveyard detail. The Doom Platoon, we were called. That was the war I had, Dad. Digging graves for the all the ones the flu got.* But now, in the first moments of his homecoming, Varick moved his gaze from Rob, not saying anything more to him but somehow making a dismissal known. My breath caught, as I waited for the version I would get from him.

Varick swung down from the borrowed horse. Reins at the ready to tie to the haystack fence, he called up to me: "Can you stand a hand with that hay?"

"Always," I said.

When the sheep were fed and Rob went off alone and silent to Breed Butte, Varick rode home with me on the hay sled, his horse tied behind, and we talked of the wonderful mild winter, of his train journey from Seattle to Browning with his discharge paper in his pocket, of much and of nothing, simply making the words bridge the air between us. I am well beyond the age to think all things are possible. I had been ever since Anna's name on the death list in the *Gleaner*. But going home, that first day of the year, my son beside me unexpected as a griffin, I would have told you there is as much possibility in life as not.

As the crunching sounds of our sled and the team's hooves halted at the barn, Varick cupped his hands to his mouth and shouted toward the house:

"MOTHER! YOUR COOKING IS BETTER THAN THE ARMY'S!"

Adair flew out and came through the snow of the yard as if it wasn't there. She hugged the tall figure, saying not a word, not crying, not laughing, simply holding and holding.

Ultimately Varick said down to the head of auburn ringlets, "You better get in out of the weather. We'll be right along, as soon as I help this geezer unharness the horses."

Amid that barn chore, Varick's voice came casual above the rattle and creak of the harnesses we were lifting off. "I hear we just about lost you."

"As near to it as I care to come." I hung my set of harness on its peg. When my throat would let me, I said the next painful words: "Others didn't have my luck."

"Dad, I heard about Mrs. Reese." Varick stood with his armful of harness, facing me. His eyes were steady into mine. They held no apology, no attempt at reparation for the years he had held himself away from me; but they conceded that those years were ended now. The Varick facing me here knew something of the storm countries of the mind, latitudes of life and loss. Now he said with simple sympathy: "It must be tough on you."

"It is," I answered my son. "Let's go in the house to your mother."

At long last now, Varick's life took its place within comfortable distance of mine and his mother's. Stanley Meixell provided him work and wage at the ranger station through the next few months of that shortest and mildest of winters, then in calving time the job of association rider for the Noon Creek cattlemen came to him.

"I don't remember raising a cow herder," I twitted Adair. "He must be yours."

"And I don't remember doing him by myself," she gave me back, with a lift of her chin and a sudden smile.

The other climate kept getting warmer, too. Spring came early and seemed to mean it. By lambing time the last of the snow was gone from even the deepest coulees. Rob and I shed our overshoes a good three weeks earlier than usual, and the nights of March and on into April stayed so mild that Adair did not even have to have lamb guests in her oven.

So if I was never far from the fact that Anna was gone, that fact which stood like a stone above all tides, at least now I had the

shelter of Varick and Adair. What I did not have, as spring hurried
its way toward the summer of 1919, was any lessening of Rob.

At first I figured it was simply a case of seasonal bachelorhood.
Now that their girls were grown and gone, Rob had installed Judith
and himself in a house in Gros Ventre—or quite possibly Judith in
her quiet way had done the installing—and so during the feeding
time of winter and the start of lambing, Rob had been staying by
himself at the Breed Butte place. With just one more year ahead of
us to the fulfillment of Lucas's will and the sale of the sheep, you'd
have thought he would have been gritting hard and putting all his
energy into enduring the next dozen months. You'd have been as
wrong in that expectation as I was. A day soon after lambing began
in mid-March, when I asked him something he at first didn't answer
at all, simply kept on casting glances out the shed door to the valley
and the ridges around. Eventually he rounded on me and declared
as if lodging a complaint: "There isn't enough green in this whole
goddamn valley this spring to cover a billiard table."

Despite his tone, I forbore from answering him that the wan
spring wasn't my fault, that I knew of. "It's early yet," I said instead. "There's still time for the moisture to catch up with the season."

But when the rest of March and all of April brought no moisture,
I became as uneasy as he was. It ought to have been no bad thing,
to have us joined in concern about the scantiness of the grass and
the grazing future of the sheep. The air around us could stand a rest
from our winter of silent antagonism. But Rob took that spring's
lackings as an affront to him personally.

"Sweet Jesus!" he burst out in early May when we were forced to
throw the sheep back onto a slope of Breed Butte they had already
eaten across once, "what's a man supposed to do, pack a lunch for
fifteen hundred sheep?"

Before thinking, I said to him the reassurance I had been trying
on myself day after day. "Maybe we'll get it yet."

It. A cold damp blanket of it, heavy as bread dough. It had happened before; more than a few times we had known mid-May snow-
falls to fill this valley above our shoe tops. Normally snow was not a
thing Scotch Heaven had to yearn for, but we wildly wanted it now,
one of May's fat wet snowstorms, a grass bringer. Let that soak the
ground for a week, then every so often bestow a slow easy rain, the

kind that truly does some good, and the Two country's summer could be salvaged.

Not even so much as a dour retort from Rob. He simply sicced the dog after a lagging bunch of ewes and their lambs and whooped the rest of the sheep along. I swung another look to the mountains, the clear sky above them. What was needed had to begin up there. No sign of it yet.

On through the moistureless remainder of May, I wanted not to believe the mounting evidence of drought. But the dry proof was everywhere around. Already the snowpack was gone from the mountains, the peaks bare. Hay meadows were thin and wan. The worst absence, among all that the drought weather was withholding from the usual course of spring, was of sound from the North Fork. The rippling runoff of high water from the mountains was not heard that May.

The creek's stillness foretold the kind of summer that arrived to us. With June the weather turned immediately hot and stayed that way.

The summer of 1918 had been dry. This one of 1919 was parched.

"Fellows, I hate like all hell to do it," Stanley Meixell delivered the edict to Rob and me when we trailed the sheep up onto our national forest allotment. "But in green years when the country could stand it I let you bend the grazing rules a little, and now that it's a lean year we got to go the other way. I like to think it all evens out in the end."

Rob looked as if he'd been poked in a private place. I did a moment of breath catching, myself. What the forest ranger was newly rigorous about was the policy of moving our band of sheep onto a new area of the scant grass every day. Definitely *moving* them, not letting them graze at all in the previous day's neighborhood.

"We can't fatten sheep by parading them all over the mountains every day!" Rob objected furiously. "What you're asking is damn near the same as not letting them touch the grass at all. So what in the goddamn hell are we supposed to do, have these sheep eat each other?"

"It's a thought," Stanley responded, looking at Rob as if in genial agreement. "Lamb chops ought to taste better to them than grass as poor as this."

"Just tell me a thing, Meixell," Rob demanded. "If we can't use this forest for full grazing now when we most need it, then what is it you're saving it for?"

"The idea is to keep the forest a forest. Insofar as I can let you run sheep on it—or Wampus Cat Williamson or the Noon Creek Association run cattle on it—I do. But I think I maybe told you somewhere before along the line, my job is to not let any of you wear it out."

"Wear it out?" burst from Rob. "A forest as far as a person can see?"

"It all depends," answered the ranger, "how far you're looking."

What do you do when the land itself falls ill with fever? Throughout that summer in Scotch Heaven and the rest of the Two country, each day and every day the heat would build all morning until by noon you could feel it inside your eyes—the wanting to squint, to save the eyeballs from drying as if they were pebbles. And the blaze of the sun on your cheekbones, too, as if you were standing too near a stove. Most disquieting of all, the feel of the heat in your lungs. Not even in the fire summer of 1910 had there been this, the day's angry hotness coming right into you with every breath.

Then after the worst of the heat each day, the sky brought the same disappointment. Clouds, but never rain. Evenings of July, as sundown neared, the entire sky over the mountains would fill with thick gray clouds. While the clouds came over us they swirled into vast wild whorls, as if slowly boiling. Then there would be frail rainlike fringes down from the distant edges of the cloud mass; if those ever reached the ground, it was not in the valley of the North Fork or anywhere else near. Ghost showers.

The first to be defeated by the hot brunt of the summer were the 'steaders. With no rain, their dry-land grain withered day by day. The high prices of the war were gone now, too; last year's $2-a-bushel wheat abruptly was $1-a-bushel or less. By the first of August, the wagons of the 'steaders and their belongings were beginning to come out of the south benchlands. The Thorkelsons were somehow managing to stay, and to my surprise, the Hebners;

but then there was so little evidence of how the Hebners made a living that hard times barely applied to them. The others, though, were evacuating. The Keevers, family and furniture. A wagonload of the Toskis. Billy Reinking rode down to return the copy of *Kidnapped* I had lent him and reported that his family was moving into Gros Ventre, his father was taking a job as printer at the *Gleaner* office.

I watched the wheel tracks of the 'steaders now undoing the wheel tracks from when I had marked off their homestead claims. And I watched Rob for any sign that he regretted the land locating we had done. I saw none in him, but by now I knew you do not glimpse so readily into a person.

It was midsummer when I rode up onto Roman Reef on a camp-tending trip and heard a dog giving something a working-over. The barking was not in the direction of our herder and sheep, but farther north; unless I missed my guess, somewhere in the allotment of the Noon Creek cattle. At the next trail branch in that direction, I left the pack horse tied to a pine tree and rode toward the commotion.

I met the red-brown file of Double W cattle first, lolloping down the mountainside. Then the dog who was giving close attention to their heels. Then the roan horse with Varick in its saddle.

My son grinned and lifted a hand when he saw me. "That's enough, Pooch," he called to the dog.

"That's not very charitable of you," I observed as I rode up and stopped next to Varick. "All Warren Williamson wants is your grass as well as his."

"We go through this about once a week, Dad," he told me with a laugh. "Wampus Cat sends somebody up to sneak as many cattle as he can here onto the Association's allotment. As soon as I find them, I dog them back down the countryside onto his allotment. Those cows are going to have a lot of miles on them before the summer's over."

Watching the last tail-switching rumps disappear into the forest, I was doubly pleased—at the thought of Wampus Cat Williamson having to contend with a new generation who pushed back as quick as he pushed, and at this impromptu chance to visit with Varick. "Other than having the Double W for a neighbor, how is cow life?"

"About as good as can be expected." Varick's tone was a good deal more cheerful than the words. In fact, he looked as if this was high summer in Eden instead of stone-dry Montana. He lost no time in letting me know why.

"Dad, there's something you better know about. I'm going to marry Beth Reese."

Everything in me went still, as if a great wind had stopped, gathering itself to hurl again. Across the plain of my mind the girl—almost woman—Lisabeth looking at me in that steady gauging way, the Two Medicine morning. Knowing there had been something between her mother and me, something, but having no way to know that from my direction it was deepest love. Maybe worse if she did know, if she had asked Anna, for Anna would have told her it all. That springtime pairing, Anna and I, that had come unclasped. And now the two resemblances of us, about to clasp?

I managed to say to Varick: "Are you. When's all this to happen?"

He grinned. "She doesn't quite know it yet."

I stared at this son of mine. Doesn't any generation ever learn the least scrap about life from the—

"Don't give me that look," Varick said. "Beth and I aren't you and—her mother. All this got started at a dance last spring when we kind of noticed each other. I didn't know what the hell else to do, so I just outright tried her on that. Told her that I hoped whatever she thought of me it was on my own account, not anything that had to do with our families. She told me right back she was born with a head with her own mind in it, so there was no reason why she couldn't make her own decisions. You know how she has that Sunday voice when she gets going." Like Anna. "Christamighty," Varick shook his head, "I even love that voice of hers."

Varick won where I had not. Beth said yes to his proposal, they were to be married that autumn after shipping time. Alongside my gladness for the two of them was my ache where Anna had been. Solve that, Solomon. How do you do away with a pang for what you have missed in life, even as you see it attained by your son?

If you are me you don't do away with it, you only shove it deeper into the satchel of that summer's hard thoughts. The latest worry was waiting for me in the hay meadows beside the trickle of the North Fork. I knew this was the thinnest hay crop I'd ever had, but until I began mowing it there was no knowing how utterly paltry it was. This was hay that was worth cutting only because it was better to have little than none. I could cover the width of each windrow with my hat.

I stood there with the sweat of that summer on me, dripping like a fish, and made myself look around at it all. The ridges rimming the valley, the longsail slopes of Breed Butte, the humped foothills beneath the mountains, anywhere that there should have been the tawny health of grass was instead simply faded, sickly-looking. The stone colonnades of the mountains stood out as dry as ancient bones. There was a pale shine around the horizon, more silvery than the deeper blue of the sky overhead. The silver of heat, today as every other day.

But the sight that counted was the one I was avoiding looking down at, until at last I had to again. The verdict was written in those thin skeins of dry stalks that were purportedly hay. Now the summer, the drought, had won. Now there was a *yes* I absolutely had to get.

When I came into the house for supper at the end of that first day of cutting hay, Adair looked drained. Cooking over a hot stove on such a day would boil the spirit out of anybody, I supposed. I took a first forkful of sidepork, then put it back down. I had to say what I had seen in the scantiness of the hayfield.

"Dair, Lucas's sheep. We've got to sell them this fall."

"The lambs, you mean. But we always—"

"I mean them all. The ewes too, the whole band."

She regarded me patiently. "You know I don't want us to."

"This isn't that. This time I don't mean because of Rob and me. I can go on with it for as long as he can and a minute longer, you know that. No, it's the sheep themselves. There's just not enough hay to carry them through the winter. We won't get half enough off our meadows. We can buy whatever we can find, but there isn't any hay to speak of, anywhere, this summer." She still looked at me that same patient way. "Dair, we dasn't go into winter this way. That band of sheep can't make it through on what little feed we're going to have, unless we teach them to eat air."

"Not even if it's an open winter?"

"If it's the most open winter there ever was and we only had to feed the least bit of hay, maybe, they might."

"Last winter was an open one, Angus."

"That was once, Dair. Do you really want to bet Lucas's sheep on it happening twice in a row?"

She studied her plate, and then gave me her grave gray-eyed look. "Those sheep will die?"

"Dair, they will. A whole hell of a bunch of them, if not all. They and the lambs in them. We've never had so poor a grass summer, the band isn't going to be as strong as it ought to be by fall. And you know what winter can be in this country. I realize this is sudden, but I figured if I pointed it out to you now we'd still have time to get out of this sheep situation with our skins on. All I ask is that you start thinking this over and—"

"I don't need to," she answered. "Sell the sheep, Angus."

"Sell the sheep now?" Rob repeated in disbelief. "Man, did you and Adair check your pillows this morning, to see whether your brains leaked out during the night?"

He may have been right. Certainly I felt airheaded at this reaction of his to my news of Adair's willingness to sell. This person in front of me, Robert Burns Barclay as far as the eye could attest, from the first minute in the lawyer's office had been the one for selling Lucas's sheep, and now—

"There's not money to be made by selling while prices are as low as they are," he was saying to me contemptuously. "A babe coming out of his mother could tell you that. No, we're not selling."

"Christ on a raft, Rob! You don't remember the years of '93? Four years in a row, and prices stayed sunk the whole while."

"That was then, this is now." When that didn't brush me away, he gave the next flourish. "I remember that we hung on without selling, and we came out of it with full pockets."

"We didn't start off with a summer like this."

"Will you make yourself look at the dollars of this situation?" he resorted to. "For once in your life, will you do that?" He cocked his head, then resumed: "The first year of these goddamn sheep of Lucas's, we made decent money. Last year, we only came out even. This year we're not making a penny on the wool or the lambs, either, and if we sell the ewes at these prices we're all but giving them away, too. It'd mean we've spent three years for no gain, man. And I want a hell of a lot better pay than that, for having to go through this goddamn partnership with you."

"You can want until you turn green with it and that still doesn't mean it'll happen. Rob, for Christ's sake, listen—"

"Listen yourself," he shot back. "Prices are bound to come back up. All we've got to do is wait until next year and sell the whole outfit, ewes and lambs and all."

"And what about this winter, with no more hay than we've got?"

"We've never seen a winter in this country we couldn't get through. I even got through one under the same roof with you, somehow. If we have to buy a dab of hay, all right, then we'll trot out and buy it. You'd worry us into the invalids' home if you had your way."

I shook my head and took us back around the circle to where this had begun. "Adair and I want to sell now."

"Want all you please. I'm telling you, I'm not selling. Which means you're not."

I had pummeled him down to gruel once, why not pound him again now? And again every day until he agreed to sell the sheep? I was more than half ready to. But the fist didn't exist that could bring an answer out of Rob that he didn't want to give. I withheld my urge to bash him and said: "Rob, you're not right about this. I hope to Christ you'll think it over before winter gets here."

"Try holding your breath until I do, why don't you." He looked both riled and contemptuous now. "In the meantime, I'm not hearing any more mewling from you about selling the sheep."

What walloped me next was Ninian Duff's decision to leave the North Fork.

"Ay, Angus, I would rather take a beating with a thick stick." For the first time in all the years I had known this man he seemed embarrassed, as if he was going against a belief. "But I know nothing else to do." Ninian stared past me at the puddled creek, the scant grass. "Had Samuel not been called by the Lord, I would go on with the sheep and say damn to this summer and the prices and all else. But I am not the man I was." Age. It is the ill of us all. "So, Flora and I will go to Helena, to be near Susan."

That early September day when I rode home from the Duffs' and the news of their leaving, the weather ahead of me was as heavy as my mood. Clouds lay in a long gray front, woolly, caught atop the peaks, while behind the mountains the sky was turning inky. All the way from the South Fork to Jericho Reef, a forming storm that was half a year overdue.

Despite the homestead houses and outbuildings I was passing as I rode, the valley of the North Fork seemed emptier to me just then than on the day I first looked down into it from the knob hill. Tom Mortensen and the Speddersons, gone those years ago. The Erskines taken by the epidemic. The year before last the Findlaters had bought a place on the main creek and moved down there. Allan Frew, gone in the war. And now the Duffs. Except for George Frew, Rob and I now suddenly were the last of Scotch Heaven's homesteaders; and George, too, was talking of buying on the main creek whenever a chance came.

A person could count on meeting wind at the side road up Breed Butte to Rob's place, and today it was stiff, snappy. In minutes it brought the first splatting drops of rain. The first real rain in months and months, now that the summer of 1919 had done us all the damage it could.

Beside me on the wagon seat Adair said, "I wish they had a better day for it."

I put an arm around her to help shelter her from the wind. Only the start of October, and already the wind was blowing through snow somewhere. Above the mountains the sky looked bruised, resentfully promising storm. It had rained almost daily ever since that first September gullywasher, and today didn't seem willing to be an exception. Below Adair and me now as our wagon climbed the shoulder of Breed Butte before descending the other slope to Noon Creek, we could see Rob's reservoir brimming as if it had never tasted drought; a glistening portal of water in the weary autumn land.

By the time we were down from the divide and about to cross Noon Creek, clouds like long rolls of damp cotton were blotting out the summits of the mountains. Weather directly contrary to Adair's wish. She'd had her original moment of staring startlement, too, about the daughter of Anna Reese being spliced into our family. But as quick as she could, she granted that if Lisabeth was Varick's choice in life, so be it. I tried to muster cheer for her against the sky's mood: "If you can remember so far back, the night of this counts for more than the day."

Her arm came inside my sheepskin coat and around my back, holding me. "Adair remembers," she declared.

How dreamlike it seemed, when we arrived at the old Ramsay place and stepped into the wedding festivities of Varick and Lisabeth. I had not put foot in that house since my time of courting Anna. In my memory I saw again the vinegar cruet that was Meg Ramsay. *So, Mr. McCaskill, you too are of Forfar. That surprises me.* Plump Peter Ramsay, silent as a stuffed duck. Not only were they gone now, but so was the one I saw everywhere here: Anna.

She came to the door now on the arm of Varick to greet Adair and me. She was in every line of Lisabeth, Anna was; the lovely round cheeks, the eyes as blue and frank as sky, the lush body, even the perfect white skin hinting down from her throat toward her breastbone. *Beauty bestowed upon her full receipt,/vouching her in every way complete.*

"Mother, Dad," Varick greeted us. "You came to see if Beth is going to come to her senses before the knot gets tied, I guess?"

"We came to gain Beth," Adair said simply and directly. Our daughter-in-law-to-be gave her a gracious enough look, but in an instant those steady blue eyes were gauging me. I got out some remark I hoped wasn't damaging, then Adair and I were moving on into the house out of the way of the other wedding-comers arriving behind us.

Glad as I was for Varick and Beth, this event of theirs was a gauntlet I had to make myself endure. Over there was Isaac. Despite the efforts of that concealing mustache and the unreadable crinkles around his eyes, the year since Anna's death was plainly there in the lines of his face. His son Peter was hovering near him, still too young to quite believe marriage was a necessity in life but enough of a man now to have to participate in this family day. Then over here was Rob, with Judith beside. For once he was not as brash as brass, whatever was on his mind. I saw him glance every so often toward Varick and Beth. I hoped he was seeing the past there, too, and I hoped his part of it was gnawing in him. Probably remorse would break its teeth if it even tried to gnaw him, though.

Then through the throng of the wedding crowd I saw with relief that Stanley Meixell had come in. While Adair was occupied accepting congratulations for the union of the McCaskills and the Reeses, I crossed the room to him.

Stanley was at the window that looked west to the mountains, a glass in his hand. Since the inanity called Prohibition, we were reduced to bootleg whiskey; I had to admit, whoever Isaac's source was, the stuff wasn't bad.

After we had greeted, I asked Stanley: "What's this I hear about you aiding and abetting matrimony here today?"

"Yeah, when Mac asked me to be best man I told him I would." He paused and resumed his window vigil. "Though it's closer to a preacher than I promised myself I'd ever get."

"Maybe it's not catching," I consoled him.

"I'm trying to ward it off with enough vaccine," Stanley remarked a bit absently with a lift of his glass. The major part of his attention was still gazing outside, away from the hubbub of the room. He said, "Angus, take a look at this, would you."

I stood beside Stanley at the window and saw what he was keeping vigil on. The mountains by now were entirely concealed under clouds, but along the ragged bottom of the curtain of weather occasional patches of the foothills showed through. Patches of startling white. First snow.

"It's christly early for that, seems to me," Stanley mused. "You ever know it to come already this time of year?"

"No," I had to admit. "Never."

Stanley watched the heavy veil of weather a long moment more, then shrugged. "Well, I guess if it wants to snow, it will." He started to lift his glass, then stopped. "Actually, we got something to drink to, don't we." He looked across the room toward Varick and Beth, and my eyes followed his. I heard the clink of his glass meeting mine, then Stanley's quiet toast: "To them and any they get."

I was returning around the room to Adair when the picture halted me. Just inside the open door into the bedroom, it hung on the wall in an oval frame the size of a face mirror. I had never seen it, yet I knew the scene instantly. The wedding photo of Anna and Isaac.

I stepped inside the bedroom to see her more closely. A last visit, in a way. She was standing, shoulders back and that lovely head as level as ever, gazing forthrightly into the camera. Into the wedded future, for that matter. I stood rooted in front of the photo, gazing now not only at Anna but at the pair there, Isaac seated beside and below her in the photographic studio's ornate chair and seeming entertained by the occasion, and I thought of the past that put him in the picture instead of me.

The presence behind me spoke at last. "It's a good likeness of them, isn't it," Beth said.

I faced around to her. My words were out before I knew they were coming.

"Beth, I'm glad about you and Varick."

She regarded me with direct blue eyes. Her mother's eyes. Then said: "So am I."

Operas could be made from all I could have told this young woman, of my helpless love for her mother, of what had and had not happened that morning above the Two Medicine when she registered her mother and then me. Of her mother's interest in me, of the verdict that was never quite final. But any of it worth telling, this about-to-be Beth McCaskill already knew and had framed her own judgment of. She was thoroughly Anna's daughter, after all.

By her presence in front of me now, was Beth forgiving me for having loved her mother? No, I think that cannot be said. She would relent toward me for Varick's sake, but forgive is too major. Probably more than anyone except Anna and myself, Beth knew the lure I was to her mother. The daybreak scene at the Two Medicine would always rule Beth's attitude toward me.

Hard, but fair enough. For twenty-one years I endured not having Anna as my wife. For however long is left to me, I can face Beth's opinion of me.

"Beth. I know we don't have much we can say to each other. But maybe you'll let me get this in. To have you and Varick in a life together makes up for a lot that I—I missed out on." I held her gaze with mine. "May you have the best marriage ever."

She watched me intently for another long moment, as if deciding. Then she gave me most of a familiar half-smile. "I intend to."

Beth and Varick said their vows as bride and groom ever do, as if they were the first to utter those words. The ritual round of congratulations then, and while those were still echoing, George Frew was tuning his fiddle, the dancing was about to begin. Adair here on my arm in a minute would be gliding with me, so near, so far, as the music took her into herself. Music and Adair inside the silken motion I would be dancing with, the wife-mask with auburn ringlets on the outside. Well, why not. There was music in me just now as well, the necessary song to be given our son and daughter-in-law, in the echoing hall of my mind.

> *Dancing at the rascal fair,*
> *Lisabeth Reese, she was there,*
> *the answer to Varick's prayer,*
> *dancing at the rascal fair.*
> *Varick's partnered with her there,*
> *giving Beth his life to share,*
> *dancing at the rascal fair.*
> *Devils and angels all were there,*
> *heel and toe, pair by pair,*
> *dancing at the rascal fair.*

Winter was with us now. The snow that whitened the foothills the day of Varick and Beth's wedding repeated within forty-eight hours, this time piling itself shin-deep all across the Two country. We did the last of autumn chores in December circumstances.

That first sizable snowstorm, and for that matter the three or four that followed it by the first week in November, proved to be just the thin edge of the wedge of the winter of 1919. On the fifteenth of November, thirty inches of snow fell on us. Lacelike flakes in a perfect silence dropped on Scotch Heaven that day as if the clouds suddenly were crumbling, every last shred of them tumbling down in a slow thick cascade. From the windows Adair and I watched everything outside change, become absurdly fattened in fresh white outline; our woodpile took on the smooth disguise of a snow-colored haystack. It was equally beautiful and dismaying, that floury tier on everything, for we knew it lay poised, simply waiting for wind the way a handful of dandelion seeds in a boy's hand awaits the first flying puff from him. That day I did something I had done only a few times in all my years in Scotch Heaven: I tied together lariats and strung them like a rope railing between the house and the barn, to grasp my way along so as not to get lost if a blizzard blinded the distance between while I was out at the chores.

The very next day I needed that rope. Blowing snow shrouded the world, or at least our polar corner of it. The sheep had to be fed, somehow, and so in all the clothes I could pile on I went out

to make my way along the line to the barn, harnessed the workhorses Sugar and Duke, and prayed for a lull.

When a lessening of the blizzard finally came, Rob came with
it, a plaster man on a plaster horse. He had followed fencelines
down from Breed Butte to the North Fork, then guided himself
up the creek by its wall of willows and trees. Even now I have to
hand it to him. Here he was, blue as a pigeon from the chill of
riding in that snow-throwing wind, yet as soon as he could make
his mouth operate he was demanding that we plunge out there
and provide hay to the sheep.

"Put some of Adair's coffee in you first," I stipulated, "then
we'll get at it."

"I don't need—" he began croakily.

"Coffee," I reiterated. "I'm not going to pack you around today like a block of ice." When Adair had thawed him, back out
we went into the white wind, steering the horses and hay sled
along the creek the way Rob had done, then we grimly managed
to half-fling half-sail a load of hay onto the sled rack, and next
battled our way to my sheep shed where the sheep were sheltering themselves. By the time we got there they were awful to
hear—a bleated chorus of hunger and fear rending the air. Not
until we pitched the hay off to them did they put those fifteen
hundred woolly throats to work on something besides telling us
their agony.

That alarming day was the sample, the tailor's swatch, of our
new season. The drought of that summer, the snow and wind of
that winter: the two great weathers of 1919. Through the rest of
November and December, days were either frigid or blowy and
too often both. By New Year's, Rob and I were meeting the
mark of that giant winter each day on our route to the sheep's
feedground. At a place where my meadow made a bit of a dip,
snow drifted and hardened and drifted some more and hardened
again and on and on until there was a mound eight or ten feet
deep and broad as a low hill there. "Big as the goddamn bridge
across the Firth of Forth," Rob called it with permissible exag-
geration in this case. This and other snow bridges built by the
furrowing blizzards we could go right over with the horses and
hay sled without breaking through, they were so thickly frozen.
Here winter plies his craft,/soldering the years with ice. Yes, and history can say the seam between 1919 and 1920 was triple thickness.

Thank heaven, or at least my winning cut of the cards, that we had bought twice as much hay as Rob wanted to, which still was not as much as I wanted to. Even so, every way I could calculate it now—and the worried look on Rob said his sums were coming out the same as mine—we were going to be scratching for hay in a few months if this harsh weather kept up.

It kept up.

As the chain of frozen days went on, our task of feeding the sheep seemed to grow heavier, grimmer. There were times now when I would have to stop from pitching hay for half a minute, to let my thudding heart slow a bit. The weariness seemed to be accumulating in me a little more each new time at a haystack; or maybe it was the sight of the hay dwindling and dwindling that fatigued me. In those catchbreath pauses I began to notice that Rob, too, was stopping from his pitchfork work for an occasional long instant, then making the hay fly again, then lapsing quiet for another instant. Behavior of that sort in him I at first couldn't figure. To look at, he was as healthy as a kettle of broth. No influenza had eroded anything of our Rob. But eventually it came to me what this was. Rob's pauses were for the sake of his ears. He was listening, in hope of hearing the first midair roar of a chinook.

From then on, my lulls were spent in listening, too. But the chinook, sudden sweet wind of thaw, refused to answer the ears of either of us.

Maybe I ought to have expected the next. But in all the snip and snap that went on between Rob and me, I never dreamt of this particular ambush from him.

Usually I drove the team and sled to whatever haystack we were feeding from and Rob simply met me there, neither of us wanting to spend any more time than necessary in the company of the other. But this day Rob had to bring me a larger horse collar—Sugar's was chafing a sore onto his neck, which we couldn't afford—before the team could be harnessed, and so he arrived into my barn just as I was feeding Scorpion.

No hellos passed between us these days, only dry glances of acknowledgment. I expected Rob to pass me by and step straight to the workhorses and their harness, but no, anything but.

He paused by Scorpion's stall. "This horse has seen his days, you know."

What I knew was the hateful implication in those words. To close off Rob from spouting any more of it, I just shook my head and gave Scorpion's brown velvet neck an affectionate rub as he munched into the hay.

Rob cocked a look at me and tried: "He's so old he'd be better off if you fed him your breakfast mush instead of that hay."

I turned away and went on with my feeding of Scorpion.

"The fact is," Rob's voice from close behind me now, "he ought to be done away with."

So he was willing to say it the worst he could. And more words of it yet: "I can understand that you're less than keen to have him done away with. It's never easy. The old rascals get to be like part of us." They do, Rob, my thought answered him, which is why I am keeping Scorpion alive this winter instead of putting the bullet you suggest into the brainplace behind his ear. "But," that voice behind me would not stop, "I can be the one to do away with the old fellow, if you'd rather."

"No. Neither of us is going to be the one, so long as Scorpion is up and healthy. Let's put a plug in this conversation and go feed the sheep."

But Rob blocked my way out of the stall. "Do you take telling?" he snapped. "We can't spare so much as a goddamn mouthful of hay this winter, and you're poking the stuff into a useless horse as if we've got worlds of it. Give yourself a looking-at, why don't you, man. This winter is no time for charity cases. Any spear of hay that goes into Scorpion doesn't go into one of those ewes half-starving, out there."

I knew that. I knew, too, that our hay situation was so wretched that Scorpion's daily allowance mattered little one way or the other. We needed tons of the stuff, not armfuls. We needed a chinook, we needed an early spring, we needed a quantity of miracles that the killing of one old horse would not provide. I instructed Rob as levelly as I could:

"I know the word doesn't fit in your ears, but I've told you no. He's my horse and you're not going to do away with him. Now let's go, we've got sheep waiting for us."

He didn't move. "I have to remind you, do I. He's the horse of us both."

Then I remembered, out of all the years ago. The two of us pointing ourselves down from Breed Butte toward Noon Creek on my horse-buying mission; that generous side of Rob suddenly declaring itself, clear and broad as the air. *Angus, you'll be using him on the band of sheep we own together, so it's only logical I put up half the price of him, am I right?*

And now the damn man demanded: "Get out the cards."

Those cold words of his sickened me. How could he live with himself, as sour as he had become? None of us are what we could be. But for Rob to invoke this, to ask the sacrifice of Scorpion and all the years this tall horse had given me, when it was his own blind gamble that delivered us into this hay-starved winter—right then I loathed this person I was yoked to, this brother of Adair's whom I had vowed to persist with because she wanted it so. Enduring him was like trying to carry fire in a basket.

I choked back the disgust that filled me to my throat. I turned so that Scorpion was not in my vision, so that I was seeing only this creature Rob Barclay. I slowly got out the deck of cards.

Rob studied the small packet they made in the palm of my hand. As if this was some teatime game of children, he proclaimed, "Cut them thin and win," and turned up the top card. The four of diamonds.

I handed the deck to him. He shuffled it twice, the rapid whir of the cards the only sound in the barn. Now the deck lay waiting for me in his hand.

I reached and took the entire deck between my thumb and first finger. Then I flipped it upside down, bringing the bottom card face-up to be my choice.

The two of us stood a moment, looking down at it. The deuce of hearts.

Rob only shook his head bitterly, as if my luck, Scorpion's luck, was an unfair triumph. As we turned from the old brown horse and began harnessing the workhorses, he stayed dangerously silent.

Near the end of January I made a provisioning trip into town. Every house, shed, barn I passed, along the North Fork and the main creek, was white-wigged with snow. Gros Ventre's main street was a rutted trench between snowpiles, and no one was out who didn't have dire reason to be. All the more unexpected, then, when

I stomped the white from my boots and went into the mercantile, and the person in a chair by the stove was Toussaint Rennie.

"What, is it springtime on the Two Medicine?" I husked out to him, my voice stiff from the cold of my ride. "Because if it is, send some down to us."

"Angus, were you out for air?" he asked in return, and gave a chuckle.

"I thought I was demented to come just a dozen miles in this weather. So what does that make you?"

"Do you know, Angus, this is that '86 winter back again." *No deer, no elk. No weather to hunt them in. West wind, all that winter. Everything drifted east. I went out, find a cow if I can. Look for a hump under the snow. Do you know, a lot of snowdrifts look like a cow carcass?* "That '86 winter went around a corner of the mountains and waited to circle back on us, Angus. Here it is."

"As good a theory as I've heard lately," I admitted ruefully. "Just how are your livestock faring, up there on the reservation?"

Toussaint's face altered. There was no chuckle behind what he said this time. "They are deadstock now."

The realization winced through me. Toussaint had not been merely making words about that worst-ever winter circling back. Again now, humps beneath the vast cowl of whiteness; carcasses that had been cattle, horses. The picture of the Two Medicine prairie that Toussaint's words brought was the scene ahead for Scotch Heaven sheep if this winter didn't break, soon.

I tried to put that away, out of mind until I had to face it tomorrow with a pitchfork, with another scanty feeding of hay by Rob and me. I asked the broad figure planted by the warm stove: "How is it you're here, Toussaint, instead of hunkered in at home?"

"You do not know a town man when you see him, Angus?"

I had to laugh. "A winter vacation in temperate Gros Ventre, is this. Where are you putting up?"

"That Blackfeet niece of Mary's." Nancy. And those words from Lucas, echoing across three decades: *Toussaint didn't know whether he was going to keep his own family alive up there on the Two Medicine River, let alone an extra. So he brought Nancy in here and gave her to the DeSalises.* "She has a lot of house now," Toussaint was saying. "That Blackfeet of mine"—Mary—"and kids and me, Nancy let us in her house for the winter." He chuckled. "It beats eating with the axe."

Before leaving town I swung by Judith's house for any mail she wanted to send out to Rob. She handed me the packet and we had a bit of standard conversation until I said I'd better get started on my ride home before the afternoon grew any colder. The question came out of Judith now as quietly as all her utterances, but it managed to ask everything: "How are you and Rob getting by together?"

To say the truth, the incident over Scorpion still burned like a coal in me. But I saw no reason to be more frank than necessary in answering her. "It's not good between us. But that's nothing new."

Judith had known Rob and me since our first winter in Scotch Heaven, when I still thought the world of him, so it was not unexpected when she said in an understanding voice, "Angus, I know this winter with him is hard for you." What did surprise me was when this loyalest of wives added: "It's even harder for Rob with himself."

February was identical to the frigid misery of January. At the very start of the last of its four white weeks, there came the day when Rob and I found fifteen fresh carcasses of ewes, dead of weakness and the constant cold. No, not right. Dead, most of all, of hunger.

Terrible as the winter had been, then, March was going to be worse. Scan the remaining hay twenty times and do its arithmetic every one of those times and the conclusion was ever the same. By the first of March, the hay would be gone. One week from today, the rest of the sheep would begin to starve.

A glance at Rob, as we drove the sled past the gray bumps of dead sheep, told me that his conclusion was the same as mine, with even more desperation added. He caught my gaze at him, and the day's words started.

"Don't work me over with your eyes, man. How in hell was I supposed to know that the biggest winter since snow got invented was on its way?"

"Tell it to the sheep, Rob. Then they'd have at least that to chew on."

"All it'd take is one good chinook. A couple of days of that, and enough of this snow would go so that the sheep could paw down and graze a bit. That'd let us stretch the hay and we'd come out of this winter as rosy as virgins. So just put away that gravedigger look of yours, for Christ's sake. We're not done for yet. A chinook will show up. It has to."

You're now going to guile the weather, are you, Rob? Cite Barclay logic to it and scratch its icy ears, and it'll bounce to attention like a fetching dog to go bring you your chinook? That would be like you, Rob, to think that life and its weather are your private pets. Despite the warning he had given me, I told him all this with my eyes, too.

The end of that feeding day, if it could be called so, I was barning the workhorses when a tall collection of coat, cap, scarf, mittens and the rest came into the yard atop a horse with the Long Cross brand. If I couldn't identify Varick in the bundle, I at least knew his saddlehorse. I gave a wave and he rode through the deep snow of the yard to join me inside the barn's shelter.

"How you doing?" asked my son when he had unwrapped sufficiently to let it out.

"A bit threadbare, to say the truth. Winter seems to be a whole hell of a lot longer than it ever used to be, not to mention deeper."

"I notice the sheep are looking a little lean." Lean didn't begin to say it, Varick. They were getting to resemble greyhounds. "You got enough hay to get through on, you think?"

"Rob and I were just discussing that." I scanned the white ridges, the white banks of the North Fork, the white roof of the sheep shed. Another week of this supreme snow sitting everywhere on us and we had might as well hire the coyotes to put the sheep out of their hungry misery. "Neither of us thinks we do have anywhere near enough, no."

Varick was plainly unsurprised. He said, part question and part not, "What about that Dakota spinach they've got at Valier?" Trainloads of what was being called hay, although it was merely slewgrass and other wiry trash, were being brought in from North Dakota to Valier and other rail points and sold at astounding prices.

"What about it?" I nodded to the east, across more than thirty miles. "It's in Valier and we're here."

"I could get loose for a couple days to help you haul," offered Varick. "Even bring my own hay sled. Can't beat that for a deal, now can you?"

I said nothing, while trying to think how to tell him his generosity was futile, Rob and I were so far beyond help.

Eyeing me carefully, Varick persisted: "If you and Unk and me each take a sled to Valier, we can haul back a hell of a bunch of hay, Dad."

"Varick, our workhorses can't stand that much journey. This winter has them about done in." *As it about has me, too,* I kept to myself.

"How about if I get you fresh horses?"

Well and good and fine but also impossible. Every horse in Scotch Heaven and anywhere around was a sack of bones by now. There wasn't a strong set of workhorses between here and—abruptly I realized where Varick intended to get fresh teams.

"Yeah, they'd be Isaac's," he confirmed.

Isaac. My nemesis who was never my enemy. In a better world, there would have been an Anna for each of us.

"Don't worry, Dad. He'll loan you the horses."

Why would he? Although I said it to Varick as: "What makes you so sure of that?"

"I already asked him. The old boy said, 'I hate for anyvun to get in a pince. Tell Annguz the horses is his.'"

A pinch definitely was what winter had us in, you were purely right about that, Isaac. I stared east again, to the white length of Scotch Heaven, the white miles beyond that to the railroad cars of hay in Valier. Why try, even. A sled journey of that sort, in a winter of this sort. *There is so much of this country, Angus.* That quiet mountaintop declaration of Adair's. *People keep having to stretch themselves out of shape trying to cope with so much. This Montana sets its own terms and tells you, do them or else.*

Or else. There in the snow of the valley where Rob and I had just pitched to them half the hay they ought to have had, the sheep were a single gray floe of wool in the universal whiteness. I remembered their bleating, the blizzard day we were late with the feeding; the awful hymn of their fear. Could I stand to hear that, day after day when the hay was gone?

Finally I gave Varick all the answer I had. "All right, I'm one vote for trying it. But we'll need to talk to Rob."

"He'll be for it. Dead sheep are lost dollars to him. He'll be for it, Dad."

In the winter-hazed sky, the dim sun itself seemed to be trying to find a clearer look at our puzzling procession. A square-ended craft with a figurehead of two straining horses was there in the white nowhere, plowing on a snow sea. Then an identical apparition behind it, and a third ghost boat in the wake of that.

Three long sleds with hay racks on them, Varick at the reins of the first, myself the next driver, Rob at the tail of this sled-runner voyage toward Valier, our convoy crept across the white land. But if slowly, we moved steadily. The big Reese horses walked through the snow as if they were polar creatures. Copenhagen and Woodrow, my pair was named. Even Isaac's horses had the mix of his two lands. Horse alloys, strong there in the dark harness in front of me.

We stopped at the Double W fenceline, half the way between Gros Ventre and Valier, to eat from the bundle of lunch Adair had fixed us. Rob and I stomped some warmth into ourselves while Varick cut the barbed wire strands so we could get the sleds through. Of the four-wire fence, only the top two strands were showing above the snow. While Varick was at that, I gazed around at the prairie. Cold and silence, stillness and snow. Once upon a time there were two young men, new to Montana, who thought they were seeing snow. *This is just a April skift,* was the freighter Herbert's croaking assessment. That April and its light white coverlet sounded like high summer to me now. That flurry that had taken the mountains and the wheel tracks from our long-ago trek toward Lucas and his nowhere town was a pinch of salt compared to this. And Rob and I of then, how did we compare with what we are now? The journeys we had made together, across thirty years. Steamship and railroad and horse and foot and every kind of wheel. And by ash sled runners, enmity accompanying us. What, were we different Rob and different Angus, all the time before? Else how did the enmity manage to come between us? In all likelihood I am not the best judge of myself. But I can tell you, from trudging through the days of this winter beside the unspeaking figure known as Rob Barclay, that this was not the Rob who would throw back his head and cockily call up to the hazed sun, *Can't you get the stove going up there?*

Onward from the fence, the marks of our sled runners falling away into the winter plain behind us. Silence and cold, snow and stillness. The murmurs within myself the only human sound. Adair asking, when Varick and I went into the house with his offer to make this hay trip: *Do both of you utterly have to go?* Reluctant *yeah* from her son, equally involuntary *yes* from her husband. From her:

370

Then I have to count on each of you to bring the other one back, don't I. Toussaint, when I arranged for him to feed the sheep while we were gone, saying only: *This winter. You have to watch out for it, Angus.* And myself, here on this first ground I ever went across on horseback, scouting for a homestead site. Did I choose rightly, Scotch Heaven over this prairie? That farmhouse there on the chalky horizon. If I had chosen that spot those years ago, I would right now be in there drinking hot coffee and watching hay-hungry sheepmen ply past on their skeleton ships. No, not that simple. In the past summer of drought and grasshoppers and deflated prices, that farm, too, was bitter acres. The year 1919 had shown that farming could be a desperate way of life, too. Maybe everything was, one time or another.

It was dusk when we came around the frozen length of Valier's lake and began to pass the stray houses of the outskirts. Valier did not have as much accumulation of winter as Scotch Heaven or Gros Ventre, but it still had about as much as a town can stand. The young trees planted along the residential streets looked like long sticks stuck in to measure the snowfall. The downtown streets had drifts graceful as sand dunes. Stores peeked over the snowbanks. Pathways had been shoveled like a chain of canals, and at the eastern edge of town we could see the highest white dike of all, where the railroad track had been plowed.

Along the cornices of the three-story hotel where we went for the night, thick icicles hung like winter's laundry. When we three numb things had managed to unharness the teams at the stable and at last could think of tending to ourselves, Varick gave his sum of our journey from Scotch Heaven: "That could've been a whole hell of a lot worse."

And Rob gave his. "Once we get those sleds heavy with hay, it will be."

At morning, the depot agent greeted us with: "I been keeping your hay cool for you out in the icebox."

When no hint of amusement showed on any of the three of us, he sobered radically and said: "I'll show you the boxcar. We can settle up after you're loaded."

We passed a dozen empty boxcars, huge husks without their cargo, and came to a final one with a stubbly barricade of hay behind its slatted side. The agent broke ice from its door with a blacksmith hammer, then used a pinch bar to pry the grudging door open. "All yours," he stated, and hustled back inside the warmth of the depot.

The railroad car was stacked full of large bales like shaggy crates. Rob thrust a mitten under his armpit, pulled out his hand and thrust it into a bale. The handful he pulled out was brown crackly swamp-grass, which only in a winter of this sort would qualify as hay at all. "Awful stuff," Rob proclaimed.

"The woollies won't think it's as awful as starving," I told him. "Let's load and go." The weather was ever over our shoulder, and this was a lead-colored day that showed no intention of brightening. First thing of morning, I had taken a look out the hotel window to the west for the mountains and they were there, white-toothed as if they had sawed up through the snow prairie. As long as the mountains stayed unclouded we had what we needed from the weather today, neutrality.

Our work was harsh, laboring the bales from their stacks in the boxcar to the sleds alongside, as if we were hauling hundreds of loaded trunks down out of an attic. Oftener and oftener, Rob and I had to stop for breath. The smoke of our breathing clouded between us, two aging engines of work. To say the truth, without Varick's limber young strength I do not know how we ever would have loaded those three hay sleds.

When the last bale was aboard, even Varick looked close to spent, but he said only, "I guess that's them." A marker in our journey, that final bale; with it, the easy half of our hay task was over. Now to haul these loads, and ourselves, all the miles to Gros Ventre before nightfall, and on to Scotch Heaven the next day. Rob and I headed for the depot with our checkbooks to pay an outlandish price for this god-awful hay that was the only hay there was, and then we would have to get ourselves gone, out onto the prairie of winter.

We had our own tracks of yesterday to follow on the white plain west of Valier, smooth grooves of the sled runners and twin rough channels chopped by the horses' hooves. The Reese horses strained steadily as they pulled our hay loads. With every step they were rescuing us a little more, drawing us nearer to Scotch Heaven and out of this width of winter.

All was silence except for the rhythm of the horses' labor, muscle against harness, hooves against snow. Existence crept no faster than our sleds, as if time had slowed to look gravely at itself, to ponder what way to go next, at what pace. I know I had thoughts—you can't not—but the lull we were traveling in held me. Keeping the team's leather reins wrapped in my mittened hands was the only occupation that counted in the world just then.

The change in the day began soon after we were beyond Valier's outlying farms and homesteads, where our tracks of yesterday went on into the prairie of the Double W range. At first the mountains only seemed oddly dimmed, as if dusk somehow had wandered into midday. I tried to believe it as a trick of light, all the while knowing the real likelihood.

In front of me I could see Varick letting only his hands and arms drive the team, the rest of him attentive to those dimming mountains. Behind me Rob undoubtedly was performing the same.

So the three of us simultaneously watched the mountains be taken by the murk. As if a gray stain was spreading down from the sky, the mountains gradually became more and more obscure, until they simply were absorbed out of sight. We had to hope that the weather covering the western horizon was only fog or fallow cloud and not true storm. We had to hope that mightily.

The wind, too, began faintly enough. Simply a sift along the top of the snow, soft little whiffs of white dust down there. I turtled deeper into the collar of my sheepskin coat in anticipation of the first gust to swoosh up onto the sled at me. But a windless minute passed, then another, although there were constant banners of snow weaving past the horses' hooves. I could see Varick and his sled clear as anything; but he and it seemed suspended in a landscape that was casually moving from under them. A ground blizzard. Gentle enough, so far. A breeze brooming whatever loose snow it could find, oddly tidy in its way. Another tease from the weather, but as long as the wind stayed down there at knee-high we were out of harm.

I believed we were nearly to our halfway mark, the Double W fence, yet it seemed an age before Varick's sled at last halted. I knew we were going to feed our teams, and for that matter ourselves, at this midpoint. But when Rob and I slogged up to Varick, we found he had more than replenishment on his mind.

"I don't know what you two think," he began, "but I figure we better just give up on the notion of going back the same route we came by."

Rob gave a grimace, which could have been either at Varick's words or at the sandwich frozen to the consistency of sawdust which he had just taken first bite of. "And do what instead?" he asked skeptically.

"Follow this fence," Varick proposed with a nod of his head toward it, "to where it hits the creek." Half a fence, really, in this deep winter; only the top portions of the fenceposts were above the snow, a midget line of march north and south from our cluster of hay sleds and horses. "Once we get to the creek," Varick was postulating, "we can follow that on into Gros Ventre easy enough."

"Man, that'd take twice as long," Rob objected. "And that's twice as much effort for these horses, not to mention us."

Varick gave me a moment's look, then a longer gaze at Rob. "Yeah, but at least this fence tells us where the hell we are," he answered. He inclined his head to the prairie the other side of the fence, where the wind's steady little sift had made our yesterday's tracks look softened. "It won't need a hell of a lot more of this to cover those tracks."

"Even if it does, Varick, we know that country," Rob persisted. "Christ, man, the hills are right out there in plain sight." The benchlands north of Noon Creek and the Double W were like distant surf above the flow of the blown snow.

"We won't know an inch of it in a genuine blizzard," Varick insisted. "If this starts really storming and we get to going in circles out there, we'll end up like the fillyloo bird."

Rob stared at him. "The which?"

"The fillyloo bird, Unk. That's the one that's got a wing shorter than the other, so that it keeps flying in littler and littler circles until it disappears up its own rear end."

Rob gave a short harsh laugh, but credit him, it was a laugh. I chortled as if I was filled with feathers. Were we all going giddy, the cold stiffening our brains? Would they find us here in the springtime, with ice grins on our faces?

"All right, all right," Rob was conceding, as much to the notion of the fillyloo bird as to Varick. If I had been the one to broach the fence route to him, Rob would have sniffed and snorted at it until we grew roots. But here he was, grudging but giving the words to Varick. "Lead on to your damn creek."

We began to follow the Double W fenceline south. The low stuttered pattern of the fenceposts could be seen ahead for maybe a quarter of a mile at a time, before fading into the ground blizzard. Occasionally there was a hump, or more often a series of them, next to the barbed wire—carcasses of Double W cattle that had drifted with the wind until the fence thwarted them. I wondered if Wampus Cat Williamson in his California money vault gave a damn.

A tiny cloud caught on my eyelash. I squinted to get rid of it and it melted coldly into my eye.

I blinked, and there were other snowflakes now, sliding across the air softly.

The stillness of their descent lasted only a few moments, before the first gust of wind hit and sent them spinning.

Quickly it was snowing so hard there seemed to be more white in the air than there was space between the flakes. In front of me Varick's sled was a squarish smudge.

The wind drove into us. No longer was it lazing along the ground. From the howl of it, this blizzard was blowing as high as the stars.

The Reese horses labored. Varick and I and Rob got off and walked on the lee side of our hay sleds, to lessen the load for the teams and to be down out of the wind and churning whatever warmth we could into ourselves. I had on socks and socks and socks, and even so my feet felt the cold. This was severe travel, and before long the ghostly sled in front of me halted, and Varick was emerging from the volleys of wind and snow to see how we were faring. Rob promptly materialized from behind. A gather seemed needed by all three of us.

The wind quibbled around our boots even in the shelter of my hay sled. There we huddled, with our flap caps tied down tight over our ears and scarves across our faces up to our eyes. Bedouins of the blizzard. One by one we pulled down our scarves and scrutinized each other for frostbite.

"We're doing about as good as we can, seems to me," Varick assessed after our inspection of each other. In the howl of the wind, each word had to be a sentence. "I can only see a fencepost or two at a time in this," Varick told us, "but that'll do. Unk, how's it going with you, back there?"

"Winterish," was all Rob replied.

"How about you, Dad—are you all right?"

That question of Varick's was many in one. I ached with cold, the rust of weariness was in every muscle I used, I knew how tiny we three dots of men, horses and hay were in the expanse of this winter-swollen land. But I took only the part of the question that Varick maybe had not even known he was asking: was I afraid? The answer, surprise to myself: I was not. Certainly not afraid for myself, for I could make myself outlast the cold and snow as long as Rob Barclay could. If one of us broke, then the other might begin to cave. But our stubbornnesses would carry each other far. We would not give one another the satisfaction of dying craven, would we, Rob.

"I'm good enough," I answered my son. "Let's go see more snow."

Trudge and try not to think about how much more trudging needed be done. Here was existence scoured down as far as it could go. Just the flecked sky, filled with fat snowflakes and spiteful wind; and us, six horse creatures and three human. Hoof-prints of our horses, sliced path of our sled runners, our boot-prints, wrote commotion into the snow. Yet a hundred yards behind Rob you would not be able to find a trace that we had ever been there. Maybe winter was trying to blow itself out in this one day. Maybe so, maybe no. It had been trying something since October. I felt pity for Woodrow, the horse of my team who was getting the wind full against his side. But being a Reese horse, he simply turned his head and persevered with his work.

I pounded my arm against my side and trudged. The wind whirled the air full of white flakes again. *Old mad winter/with snow hair flying.* This must be what mesmerism is, every particle of existence streaming to you and dreamily past. A white blanket for your mind. A storm such as this blew in all the way from legendary times, other winters great in their fury. The winter of '83. *The Starvation Winter, these Blackfeet call that, and by Jesus they did starve, poor bastards them, by the hundreds. Pure gruesome, what they went through.* Gruesome was the apt word for such winters, Lucas, yes. The winter of '86, Toussaint's telling of it. *That winter. That winter, we ate with the axe.* And Rob saying, *A once in a lifetime winter.* It depended on the size of the lifetime, didn't it.

The wind blowing, the snow flowing. Try to pound another arm's worth of warmth into myself and keep trudging. Every so often Varick, tall bundle of dimness ahead in the blowing snow, turned to look for me. I did the same for Rob. Rob. Rob who was all but vanished back there. Say he did vanish. Say he stumbled, sprawled in the miring snow, could not get up in time before I missed him, next time I glanced back. Say Rob did vanish into the blizzard, what would I feel? Truth now, Angus: what? As I tried to find honest reply in myself, a side of my mind said at least that would end it once and all, if Rob faltered back there in the snow and Varick and I could not find him, the poisoned time that had come between us—this entangled struggle between McCaskill and Barclay—would at last be ended. Or would it.

Whether it was decision or just habit, I kept watching behind me periodically to Rob. The team he had were big matched grays, and against the storm dusk they faded startlingly, so that at a glance there simply seemed to be harness standing in the air back there, blinders and collars and straps as if the wind had dressed itself in them. And ever, beside the floating sets of harness, the bulky figure of Rob.

We were stopped again. Varick came slogging to me like a man wading surf, and reported in a half shout that the fenceline had gone out of sight under a snowdrift that filled a coulee. We would need to veer down and around the pit of snow, then angle back up once we were past it to find the fenceline where it emerged from the coulee.

"If we've got to, we've got to," I assented to Varick, and while he returned to his sled I beckoned for Rob to come up and hear the situation. He looked as far from happy as a man could be, but he had to agree that the detour was all there was to do.

The horses must have wondered why they had to turn a corner here at the middle of nothingness, but they obediently veered left and floundered down the short slope.

Now the problem was up. The slope on the other side of the coulee was steep and angling, the top of it lost in the swirling snow, so that as the horses strained they seemed to be climbing a stormcloud. This was the cruelest work yet, the team plunging a few steps at a time and then gathering themselves for the next lunge, all the while the loaded sled dragging backward on them. It hurt even to watch such raw effort. I sang out every encouragement I could, but the task was entirely the horses'.

Up and up, in those awful surges, until at last the snow began to level out. The horses' sides still heaved from the exertions of getting us here, but I breathed easier now that we were atop the brow of the coulee and our way ahead to the fenceline would be less demanding.

Varick had halted us yet again. What this time?

One more time I waved Rob up to us as Varick trudged back from the lead sled.

"This don't feel right to me," Varick reported. He was squinting apprehensively. "I haven't found that fenceline yet and we ought've been back to it by now."

"We must not have come far enough to hit it yet, is all," Rob said impatiently, speaking what was in my mind, too.

Varick shook his head. "We've come pretty damn far. No, that fence ought to be here by now. But it isn't."

"Then where to Christ is it?" demanded Rob belligerently into the concealing storm. Our faces said that each of the three of us was morally certain we had come the right way after veering around the coulee. Hop with that first leg of logic and the second was inevitable: we ought to have come to the fence again. But no fence, logical or any other kind, was in evidence.

For a long moment we peered into the windblown snow, our breath smoking in front of our faces like separate small storms. Without that fence we were travelers with nowhere to go. Nowhere in life, that is. Bewilderment fought with reasoning, and I tried to clear my numb mind of everything except fence thoughts. Not even a blizzard could blow away a line of stoutly set posts and four lines of wire. Could it?

"There's just one other place I can think of for that fence to be," Varick suggested as if he hated to bring up the idea. "The sonofabitch might be under us."

With his overshoe he scuffed aside the day's powdery freshfall to show us the old hardened snow beneath. Rob and I stared down. Oh sweet Christ and every dimpled disciple. A snow bridge, was this? If it was, if we were huddled there on a giant drift where the snow had built and cemented itself onto the brow of the coulee all winter, fenceposts and barbed wire could be buried below us, right enough. Anything short of a steeple could be buried down there, if this truly was a snow bridge. And if we were overshooting the fenceline down there under the winter crust, we next were going to be on the blind plain, in danger of circling ourselves to death.

"Damn it," Rob seemed downright affronted by our predicament, "who ever saw snow like this?"

Varick had no time for that. Rapidly he said, "We can't just stand around here cussing the goddamn situation. What I'd better do is go out here a little way"—indicating to the left of us, what ought to be the southward slope of the long hump of drift we were on, if we were—"and take a look around for where the fence comes out of this."

His words scared my own into the air. "Not without a rope on you, you won't."

"Yeah, I'm afraid you're right about that," Varick agreed. The three of us peered to the route he proposed to take. Visibility came and went but it was never more than a few dozen strides' worth. I repeated that Varick was not moving one step into the blizzard without a rescue rope to follow back to us, even though we all knew the cumbersome minutes it would cost us to undo the ropes that were lashing the hay to the sled racks, knot them together, affix them around his waist—"It won't take time at all," I uttered unconvincingly.

Hateful as the task was, stiff-fingered and wind-harassed as we were, we got the ropes untied from each of our hay loads. Next, the reverse of that untying chore. "Rob, you're the one with the canny hands," I tried on him. He gave me a look, then with a grunt began knotting the several ropes together to make a single lifeline for Varick. One end of the line I tied firmly around Varick's waist while Rob was doing the splice knots, then we anchored the other end to Varick's hay rack.

"Let's try it," Varick said, and off he plunged into the blizzard. Rob and I, silent pillars side by side, lost sight of him before he had managed to take twenty effortful steps.

With my son out there in the oblivion of winter, each moment ached in me. But I could think of no other precaution we might have done. If Varick didn't come back within a reasonable time, Rob and I could follow the rope into the blizzard and fetch him. I would do it by myself if I had to. It might take every morsel of energy left in me, but I would get Varick back out of that swirling snow if I had to.

The rope went taut.

It stayed that way a long moment, as if Varick was dangling straight down from it instead of out across a plain of snow. Then the line alternately slackened and straightened, as Varick pulled himself back to us hand over hand.

His face, strained and wincing, told us before his words did. "I didn't make it to the fence. Ran out of rope."

Rob swore feelingly. I tried to think. We needed more rope, more line of life, to explore again into that snow world, and we did not have more rope. We just had ourselves, the three of us.

"Varick," I began. "Can you stand another try at it?"

"Floundering around out there isn't really anything I want to make a career of," he admitted, breathing as if he'd been in a race. "But yeah, I can do it again if I have to."

"Then this time I'll go out with you, for however far he can still see me." I jerked my head to indicate Rob. "You give us a yell when we're just about out of sight, Rob. Then you go out beyond me, Varick, while I hold the rope for you. What do you think? It would gain us that much distance"—I nodded to the edge of visibility out there—"for looking, at least."

"That sounds as good as any," Varick assented. Rob only bobbed his head once; we McCaskills could take it for yes if we wanted.

Varick and I set out, the wind sending scythes of snow at us. The cold sawed at us through every seam in our clothing. Quickly we were up to our knees in a fresh drift. Varick broke the way and I thrashed after him. A drift atop a drift, this latest dune of snow would be. And other layers beneath that as we slogged. October snow. November on top of that. And December atop that, and January, and February . . . How many tiers of this winter could there be. This wasn't a winter, it was geologic ages of snow. It was a storm planet building itself layer by layer. It was—

Abruptly I stopped, and reaching a hand ahead to Varick's shoulder brought him to a halt, too. When he turned, the apprehension in my manner made words unnecessary.

We looked back. Nothingness. The white void of snow, the blizzard erasing all difference between earth and sky. No glimpse of Rob. No sound in the air but the wind.

We stood like listening statues, our tracks already gone into the swirling snow we had come out of. Again, yet, no voice from the safety of there.

The bastard.

The utter betraying triple-slippery unforgiving bastard Rob had let us come too far. I ought to have killed him with my own hands, the day we fought there on Breed Butte, the day it all began. He was letting the blizzard eat us. Letting Varick and me vanish like two sparks into the whirl of this snow. Letting us—

Then sounds that were not quite the wind's.

. . . arrr . . .

. . . ough . . .

The blizzard swirled in a new way, and the wraith figure of Rob was there, waving both arms over his head.

"Far enough," his voice faintly carried to us. *"Far enough."*

Varick's heavy breathing was close to mine. "He always was one to press the luck, wasn't he," my son uttered. "Particularly when it's somebody else's."

We breathed together, marking the sight and sound of Rob into our senses, then turned ahead to squint for any sign of the fence-line. None.

"You ready to go fishing?" asked Varick, and away he plunged again, the rope around his waist and in my mittened hands.

Through my weariness I concentrated on the hemp in my hands. *To see a world in a grain of sand . . .* Would grains of snow do? By the dozens and hundreds they fell and fell, their whiteness coating my sleeves and mittens. *. . . Hold infinity in the palm of your hand . . .* Would mittened palms be deft enough, for that? I had to force my cold claw of a hand to keep making a fist around the moving line of rope. The rope paying out through my grip already had taken Varick from sight, into the snow cyclone. Thoughts swarmed to fill his absence. What if he stumbled out there, jerking the rope out of my stiff hands? Hold, Angus. Find a way to hold. I fumbled the end of the rope around my waist, clutching it tightly belted around me with my right hand while the left hand encircled the strand going out to Varick. If he fell I would fall, too, but nothing would make me let go of this rope. I would be Varick's anchor. Such as I was, I would be that much. A splice knot caught in my grip an instant before I let it belly out and away. The knots. Rob's knots. Lord of mercy, why hadn't I done them myself? What if he hadn't tied them firmly, what if just one began to slip loose? No. No, I could trust Rob's hands even if I couldn't trust him.

Only a few feet of rope left. If Varick did not find the fenceline now, we never would. My heart thundered in me, as if the enormity of clothing around it was making it echo. A quiver of chill went through me each time the wind clasped around my body. If we couldn't go on we would need to try to hide ourselves in caves of the hay, try to wait out the blizzard. But if this cold and wind went on through the night, our chances were slim. More likely they were none. If any one of us could live through, let it be Var—

Tugs on the rope, like something heavy quivering at the end of the hempen line. Or something floundering after it had fallen.

"VARICK!" I shouted as loud as I could. The wind took my words. I might as well have been yelling into a bale of that Dakota hay.

The tugs continued. I swallowed, held firm, clutching the jerking rope around me. I resisted a hundred impulses to plunge forward and help Varick in his struggle. I resisted another hundred to whirl around in search of Rob, to see whether he still was there as our guidemark. The distance back to him and the hay sleds was the same as it ever had been, I had to recite to my bolting instincts, only the snow was in motion, not the white distance stretching itself as it gave every appearance of. Motion of another wild sort at the invisible end of this rope, the tugs continuing in a ragged rhythm that I hoped had to be—

Varick suddenly coming hand over hand, materializing out of the whirl. A struggling upright slab of whiteness amid the coiling swirl of whiteness.

He saved his breath until he was back to me, my arms helping to hold him up.

"It's there!" he panted. "The fenceline. It comes out of the drift about there"—carefully pointing an angle to our left, although everything in me would have guessed it had to be to our right. "The sleds are actually on the other side of the sonofabitch. We about went too far, Dad."

Fixing ourselves on the figure whose waves and shouts came and went through the blowing flakes, we fought snow with our feet until we were back beside Rob. Varick saved him the burden of asking. "We got ourselves a fence again, Unk."

Laboriously we retied the ropes across the hay loads, as well as men in our condition could. Then Varick turned his team to the left—they were glad enough to, suffering in the wind as they had been—and I reined Woodrow and Copenhagen around to follow them, and Rob and his grays swung in behind us. Once our procession was down off the mound of snow, the tops of fenceposts appeared and then the topmost single strand of barbwire, the three strands beneath it in the accumulated white depth. This white iron winter, with a brutal web in it. That single top strand, though. That was our tether to the creek, to survival. I had never known until then that I could be joyously glad to see barbed bramble.

Now how far to the creek? We had to keep going, following the line of fence, no matter what distance it was. There was no knowing the hour of the day, either. The storm had made it all dusk. The complicated effort of trying to fumble out my pocket watch for a look, I couldn't even consider. Slog was all we needed to know, really. But how far?

Another laborious half-mile, mile. Who knew. This day's distances had nothing to do with numbers.

Then thin shadows stood in the snowy air.

Trees, willows of the creek. Dim frieze that hung on the white wall of weather. But as much guidance as if it was all the direction posts on earth, every one of them pointing us to Gros Ventre and safety.

A person is never too weary to feel victory. Blearily exultant, I stood and watched while Varick halted his sled and began to slog back to meet Rob and me. Now that we had the creek, consultation wasn't really needed any more. But maybe he simply had to share success with us, maybe—then as I squinted at the treeline of the creek, something moved in the bottom corner of my vision, there where the fence cornered into the creek.

I blinked and the something still moved, slowly, barely. A lower clot of forms beneath the willow shadows: Double W cattle, white with the snow coated onto them, caught there in the fence corner.

"The two of you go ahead and take your sleds across the creek, why not," my son said as nonchalantly as if our day of struggle was already years into the past. "I'll snip the fence for these cows and give them a shove out into the brush, then catch up with you."

"Man, why bother," Rob spoke bitterly. He still wore that bleak look, as if being prodded along by the point of an invisible bayonet. "They're goddamn Williamson's."

"That isn't their fault," Varick gave him back. "Head on across, you two. I won't be long."

I made my tired arms and tired legs climb atop the hay on the sled, then rattled the reins to start Copenhagen and Woodrow on their last few plodded miles to town, miles with the guarantee of the creek beside us. When we had crossed the narrow creek and made our turn toward Gros Ventre, Rob and his gray team copying behind us, I could hear faintly above the wind the grateful moans of the cattle Varick was freeing from the blizzard.

In the morning, our procession from Gros Ventre west toward home was a slow glide through white peace. New snow had freshened everything, and without the wind the country sat plump and calm.

As we passed the knob ridge at the mouth of the North Fork valley, branchloads in the tops of its pine trees were dislodging and falling onto the lower branches, sending up snow like white dust. The all-but-silent plummets of snow in the pines and the sounds of our teams and sleds were the only things to be heard in Scotch Heaven.

We went past the empty Duff homestead, and then the empty Erskine place, and what had been Archie Findlater's homestead, and the silent buildings of Allan Frew's. The lone soul anywhere here in the center of the valley was George Frew, feeding his sheep beside the creek. George's wave to us was slow and thoughtful, as if he was wondering whether he, too, would soon be making such a journey as we had.

And now we were around the final turn of the valley to my homestead, mine and Adair's, and there on their feedground beside the North Fork were the sheep in their gray gather, and the broad bundled figure of Toussaint distributing dabs of hay. For a long minute he watched our tiny fleet of bale-laden sleds, Varick in the lead, next me, Rob at the tail. Then Toussaint gripped his pitchfork in the middle of the handle, hoisted it above his head and solemnly held it there as if making sure we could see what it was, as if showing us it was not an axe.

We had hay now, but we still had the winter, too.

Each day was one more link in the chain of cold. For the first week after our Valier journey, Rob and I were men with smoke for breath as we fed the sheep in the frozen glistening weather.

Memory takes a fix from landmarks as any other traveler will. That week of bright silver winter after our hay journey was a time when Scotch Heaven never looked better. The mountains stood up as white majesties in the blue and the sun. The long ridgelines wore scarves of fresh snow that made them seem gentle, content. Every tree of the timbered top of Breed Butte stood out like a proud black sprig. Sunshaft and shadow wove bold wild patterns amid the willows along the North Fork. Only an eyeblink of time ago Montana was at its worst, and here it was at its best.

I would like to say that the clear weather and the Dakota hay and our survival of the blizzard made a poultice for the tension between Rob and me. That we put aside the winterlong wrangling—the yearslong enmity—and simply shouldered together toward spring. I would like to say that, but it would be farthest from the truth.

Maybe Rob would have been able to hold himself in if sheep had not continued to die. We found a few every day, in stiffened collapse; weak from the long winter and the short ration of hay, they no longer could withstand the cold and simply laid down into it and died. You could look on the hay journey as having saved the great majority of the sheep, as I did. Or you could look on the fact that in spite of that journey and its expensive hay, some of the sheep still insisted on dying, as Rob did.

It was about the third time he muttered something about "this Dakota hay of yours" that I rapped back, "What, you think we ought to have let the whole damn band just starve to death?"

"Goddamn it, you didn't hear me say that."

"If it wasn't that, it was the next thing to it."

"Up a rope, why don't you," he snapped back. It occurred to me we really ought not be arguing while we had pitchforks in our hands.

Wordlessly we shoveled the rest of the day's hay, and wordlessly I headed home to Adair and he to Breed Butte. By now I was not in my best mood. Overnight the clear weather had faded and gone, today's was a milky indecisive overcast, neither one thing nor another. The feedground wasn't far behind me when I heard the KAPOW of Rob's rifle as he blazed away, as he lately had begun doing, at some coyote attempting to dine on one of our dead sheep. The Winchester thunder rolled and rolled through the cold air, echoing around in the white day that had no horizon between earth and sky for it to escape through. Myself, I was not giving the coyotes any aggravation this winter. As long as they were eating the dead ones maybe they weren't eating the live ones, was my wishful theory. But apparently Rob had to take his frustration out on something, and as a second KAPOW billowed through the winter air, the coyotes were the ones getting it at the moment.

When I reached home with the hay sled, Varick's horse was in the barn. These visits of his through all the deep-drifted country between here and Noon Creek were more than outings, they were major pilgrimages. For Adair's sake, I was greatly glad that he came across the divide to us as often as he did. In full honesty, I was just as glad for my own sake.

Stiff and weary and chilly to the bottom sides of my bones, I clomped into the house. My wife and my son were at the table keeping coffee cups company. "Easy life for some people," I chattered out.

Greatly casual, Varick remarked: "There's news on Noon Creek. I been keeping this table warm for you until you could get here to hear it."

Hot coffee was all I wanted to hear of. Adair reached to the stove for the pot and poured me a cup as I thumped myself into a chair and began to unbuckle my overshoes. "If the news has winter in it," I expelled tiredly to Varick, "I can stand not to hear it."

"Yeah, well, maybe winter had a little something to do with it." Our son grinned all the grin a face could. "Beth's going to have a baby."

Adair stood up. Her face spoke *take care of her,* while her voice was saying: "Varick, that's fine!"

"You're ready to be grandma, are you?"

She hugged him from behind and declared: "It's bound to be easier than raising you ever was."

In her encircling arms our son turned his head to me. "If, ah, if he's a he"—Varick laughed at his word tangle—"Beth and I are going to give him that *Alexander* someplace in his name. Both of us figure maybe we can stand that much of the old country in any son of ours."

A bit dizzily I said, "Thank you both," which of course didn't come within a million miles of saying it enough. Then from Adair: "And if it's a girl?"

Varick paused. "Then we'd name her after Beth's mother."

There was nothing I could say. Not of Anna, not to this family of mine that had put itself through so much because of my love for her. It was Adair who moved us beyond the moment, put something major behind us. "That's an apt name, too," she said quietly to Varick. "You and Beth are honoring both families."

The second week in March, the chinook at last came. It arrived in the night, as if guilty about how tardy it had been, and when I realized from the changed feel of the air that this was a warm gush of wind instead of yet another icy one, I slid out of bed and went to the window.

Already there were trickles of melt, like running tears, down through the frost pattern on the glass. The warm wind outside was a steady swoosh. I looked back to the bed and my sleeping wife. In a few hours, at her end of our shared night, Adair would wake up into spring.

That morning at the feeding, I wished Rob was still in hibernation somewhere.

"Where the hell was this six weeks ago, when it would have saved our skins?" was his bitter welcome to the thaw.

His mood didn't sweeten in the next few days of warmth, either. Now that there was melt and slop everywhere, he grumbled against the thaw's mess as fervidly as he had against the snow it was dispelling. Maybe the chinook air itself was on his nerves—the change from winter coming so sudden that the atmosphere seemed charged, eerie. Or maybe this simply was the way Rob was anymore—resentful against the world.

Whatever his case was, it was not easy to be around. Not far from where we had stacked the Dakota hay there was a pile of dead sheep we had skinned throughout the winter and I had dragged off the meadow when the chinook came, and the boldest of the coyotes sometimes came to eat away at those corpses now that they were thawing. Rob took to bringing the rifle with him on the hay sled, to cut loose a shot if he saw a flash of coyote color there at the dead pile. The first time he yelled at me to hold the team while he aimed and fired, I had all I could do to keep the workhorses under control.

"Why don't you give the artillery a furlough until we're done feeding?" I tried on him. "The horses don't like it, the sheep don't like it, and I hereby make it unanimous."

He didn't even deign to answer, unless you can call a cold scowl an answer. He simply hung the rifle by its sling, back onto the upright of the hay rack where he kept it while we pitched hay, in a way designed to tell me that he would resume combat with the coyotes whenever he damn well felt like it.

Where had this Rob come from, out of the years? Watching him at this kind of behavior, I couldn't help but remember another Rob, of another spring, of another hard time. A lambing time, back in the years of '93. It had been one of those days to wonder why I didn't just walk away from the sheep business and join other certified lunatics in the asylum. The bunch herder we'd hired had lost thirty lambs in the past ten days, and another five had died on him that day. At that rate, by shipping time Rob and I were going to need to buy him a total new supply of lambs if we wanted to have any lambs to ship.

We've got to send this geezer down the road, I had said to Rob that remembered day.

I know, I know, he agreed glumly. *The man is a mortal enemy to sheep. I'll take the band while you trundle him to town, why not. Hire the nearest breathing body in the Medicine Lodge, McAngus. You can't do any worse than we did with this disgrace to the race.*

What if the nearest is Lucas? We both had to laugh.

Then the sheep would hear in a hurry what's expected of them, Rob vouched. *Lads and lasses,* his voice so very like Lucas's, *that's pure wonderful grass you're walking around on, so I want to see your noses down in it, ay? Do you know how much money you're costing me by your silly habit of dying? So let's have no more of that, you woollies, and we'll all get along together grand.*

As I had gone off, still laughing, I stopped to call back: *Rob, do you ever wonder if we're in the right line of work?*

His cocked head, his bright face. *There's an occasional minute when I don't, McAngus.*

In those times I would have walked into fire for Rob, and he for me. Yet that was the Rob who eventually cost me Varick, those years after the Two Medicine. Yet again, that was the Rob who had

gained me Adair, all but brought her with frosting and candles on.
Done that, and then put a boot through my family because of Anna.
Where was the set of weights to measure such things; where was
balance when you tried to align the different Robs. If they were
different ones.

Going home that day, I heard another clap of Rob's Winchester
thunder. He wasn't getting much done in life except trying to ambush coyotes. The man had me worried.

I had some downright dread the next morning. I knew this was
the day we were going to have to move the sheep to a new
and higher feedground, the chinook having made a soggy mess of
where we had been feeding them in my hay meadow. In other
times it would have been a task as automatic and easy as scratching
an ear, but I could already hear Rob in full bay about having to
work the sheep to a fresh site. Then, too, there was the small chore
of liberating Scorpion out onto the coming grass, and Rob had already made himself known on the topic of the old horse and his
menu.

And so I asked Adair. "What about coming with us today?"

"You want me to, do you?"

I smiled to the extent I could. "It can't hurt, and it might help."

"All right then," she agreed readily. "I'd better come see spring
while it's still here, hadn't I."

"Then why don't you ride Scorpion out and we'll turn him loose
to graze up there where the sheep are going to be—he and the
woollies will be some company for each other, that way. I'll saddle
him for you, all right?"

"No," she informed me. "I've known how to saddle a horse ever
since five minutes after I married you. You get your old workhorses
ready, Scorpion and I will take care of ourselves."

A good sight to see, Adair atop Scorpion as the pair of them accompanied alongside the hay sled and myself. If she pressed me to
the hilt, I would have had to say that the day's most enchanting
vision was the rivulets of melt running from beneath every snowdrift we passed. Glorious, the making of mud where winter had
stood. But definitely this wife of mine and the tall brown horse,
elderly and stiff as he was, made the second finest scene today.

Try tell that or anything else to Rob, though.

"What's this, a mounted escort for us on our way to the poorhouse?" he met us with at the haystack.

Degraded as that was, it seemed to be the top of his mood this day. I told him shortly that Scorpion was on his way out to pasture, which drew only Rob's scornful study of the elderly horse. At least he didn't start a recapitulation of how mawkish I was in keeping Scorpion among the living. But then as soon as I suggested that we needed to move the sheep from the muddy feedground in my meadow, the Rob response to that was hundred-proof sarcasm.

"So that hay can be grown to be fed to sheep that are worth less than the hay, do you mean? That definitely sounds like the Mc-Caskill high road to wealth, I can be the first to vouch."

"Rob, there's no sense in being owly about a little thing like this. Christ, man, we always put the sheep onto a fresh feedground after a chinook. You know that as well as I do." Or you would if you'd let your Barclay mind rule your Barclay mouth, for a change. "They can at least get a little grass into them if we move them onto the butte there," I went on, indicating with a nod the slope beside his reservoir, where broad swathes of ground showed themselves amid the melting patches of snow. The earthwork of the reservoir itself was already clear of snow, a chocolate pocket on the mottled slope of Breed Butte.

"Put the bastards up the backside of the moon, for all I care," Rob grumped next, and turned his back on me. He climbed onto the hay rack and hung his rifle by its sling onto the upright. "Let's get this damn feeding done," was his next impatient pronouncement.

Adair's gaze seemed to silence him after that, at least during our effort of loading the hay onto the sled rack. When we were done and standing there puffing, she announced she would drive the team for us now rather than ride Scorpion up the slope. "Adair needs the practice," she stated. Scorpion could follow, his reins tied to the back of the hay rack as they were; no problem to that. The problem anywhere in the vicinity went by the name of Rob, and I knew as well as Adair that the true need for her to be on the sled was to stay between her brother and me when he was this sulphurous.

The sheep were curious about the sled going up the slope instead of toward the meadow and them. *Prrrrr prrrrr*, I purled as loudly as

I could, and the bellwether Percy and the first few ewes began to get the idea and started toward the slope.

The siege of winter was withdrawing but not yet gone. Gray snowdrifts still clutched the treeline of Breed Butte and any swale of the broad slope. The entire country looked tattered and hungry. Up here above the still-white valley our sled runners were passing across as much muddy ground as they were snow, and in those bare damp patches the sickly grass from last year lay crushed, flattened by the burden of a hundred and fifty days of winter. Yet under the old clots of stems there was a faint almost-green blush, even today, after just this half-week of chinook and thaw, that said new grass was making its intentions known.

"Where to, gentlemen?" Adair called back to us from her position at the team's reins.

I asked Rob, "What do you think, maybe here?"

He said acidly, "It's the same muck everywhere, so this is as good as any."

He was going to be thoroughly that way today, was he. Then the thing to do was to get this hay flung off the sled and the sheep up here onto their new venue and be done with the man and his red mood. That curative for today—tomorrow would have to contrive its own Rob remedy as needed—could begin just as soon as Scorpion was turned loose out of the path of the hay, and so I climbed swiftly down to take his saddle and bridle off. I was untying Scorpion's reins from the back of the hay rack when Rob's voice slashed above me.

"*Angus.*"

The first time in years he had used my name. And now it snapped out quick and bitter, as if he wanted to be rid of it.

I swung around to see what this fusillade was going to be.

"Don't turn that geezer of a horse loose yet," Rob directed. "I just saw something I need to do with him."

"What's that, now?" I said up to him in surprise.

"My reservoir. This is a chance to tamp it." There atop the hay, he was gazing in a stony way along the slope to the long narrow mound of the dam and the ice-skinned impoundment behind it. Rob aiming his chin down at the valley and its creek, now and that first time I had watched him do it: *By damn, I didn't come all the miles from one River Street to live down there on another.* "The sheep have got to come up here anyway," he was saying, "the bastards might as well tromp across the dam and do me some good while they're at it. I'm going to ride old horsemeat here down and start shoving them to the reservoir."

"Why don't you wait with that until the next time we move the band," I tried. "The ground will be drier by then and the tamping will go better."

"Rob, yes," Adair interceded. "Angus is right about waiting for another day. Let's just get on with the feeding."

That brother of hers shook his head, his gaze still fixed across at the reservoir and its watery gray disc of ice. So far as I could see, winter and spring were knotted together there, ice and slush in the swale behind the dam versus mud on its sides and top; whatever moment of opportunity Rob Barclay thought he was viewing there made no sense whatsoever to me. But then we had made our separate decisions about water, about Breed Butte and the North Fork, a full thirty years ago, so when had we ever seen with the same eyes?

One thing I was determined to enforce: "Scorpion isn't the best horse for this, after all winter in the barn. You'd be as well off on foot. I'll walk down with you to the sheep, what about, and the two of us can—"

Rob came down off the hay sled. But I saw he hadn't come anywhere toward my line of thinking. His face was tight as a drumhide, and I suppose my own was taut enough. His tone was its most scornful yet, as he unloaded the words onto me:

"Pushing the sheep across that dam is a minute's work, is all. This goddamn horse has been gobbling up hay and doing not one thing to earn it all winter long. And you'd let it be that way." His helmeted look, his high-and-mighty mood when he wouldn't hear any words but his own. He gave me a last lash: "Your heart always has been as soft as your head."

Through it all, he still scanned with determination the reservoir, the sheep, the saddle horse. He would not so much as glance at me. Heart, mind, tongue, and now eyes, the last of Rob that was left to turn from me.

"Rob, Angus," Adair spoke up from the front of the hay sled where she had been waiting for this to abate. "You know how you're supposed to settle these things."

I hated to toss Scorpion to chance one more time. But if that's what it took . . .

"All right," I said with disgusted resignation, "we'll cut the cards for it, then," and reached into my coat pocket for the well-worn deck. "If I draw the low, Scorpion gets turned loose here and now. If you draw it—"

"No."

Before I knew it he had Scorpion's reins out of my hand, snatched into his.

"This horse has been living beyond his time ever since you won that other card cut." The face in front of me was cocked to one side, atilt with anger and the abrupt spill of declaring it. "He can do this one bit of work, and he's by Christ going to." With that, Rob shoved his overshoed foot into the stirrup and swung heavily up onto Scorpion, the horse grunting in surprise at the force of the rider clamping onto him.

I managed to grab hold of Scorpion's bridle and kept Rob from reining the brown head around as he was trying to do.

"Rob, I'm telling you, once," I delivered my own cold anger to this situation. "Behave yourself with this horse or I'll talk to you by hand."

There was a startled whinny from Scorpion as Rob jammed his heels into him and spun the horse out of my grasp, down the slope toward the approaching straggle of sheep.

"Go operate a pitchfork," Rob flung back at me without looking. "It's what you're good for."

So we had reached this, had we. Rob storming off, breaking the last of the terms I knew for enduring him. How in the name of anything were we going to survive lambing, shearing, summering the sheep in the national forest, all the steps that needed decision, if the damn man wouldn't hew to any way of deciding? We had come through the winter and now here was winter coming out of Rob as a white rage.

I climbed onto the back of the hay sled. His coyote rifle hung there on the upright from its sling.

I reached and unslung it, the grip of the wooden stock cold in my hand.

I could feel Adair's eyes on me.

I met her gaze as I jacked the shells out of the rifle one by one and pocketed them. When I had checked the breech to be thoroughly sure the weapon was empty, I hung the Winchester back where Rob had left it. "Just in case that temper of his doesn't know where to quit," I said to Adair.

"I'll talk to him, Angus," Adair said. "Let him get today out of his system, and I'll talk to him."

"I'm afraid his case is more than today, Dair."

"We'll just have to see. Why don't we get on with the feeding. It'll bring the sheep up here that much faster if they see the hay."

She was right. This day and Rob Barclay in it should be sped along, any way possible. I nodded to her to start the team, and began breaking the bales and pitching the dry brown Dakota hay off the sled. I cast glances along the slope as Rob commenced to work the sheep up to the embankment of the reservoir. They were not keen for the scheme. Recalcitrant sheep weren't going to help his mood at all. I would have to try every way in me to steel myself to let this behavior of Rob's pass until tomorrow, as Adair was asking of me. Because I knew, as if it was a memory in my fists, that I would pound Rob if I saw him mistreat Scorpion down there. With the rifle empty, he would be able to do nothing but take my beating, if it came to that. I would try not let it come to fists again, but given the mood the damn man was in, the trend wasn't promising.

I kept a watchful eye on Rob's doings while I kept at the feeding task. At last the sheep were skittishly filing across the top of the dam, a first few, then several, then many, the avalanche of behavior by which they went through life. Even now that the sheep were crossing the dam in maximum numbers, Rob kept reining Scorpion back and forth impatiently close behind the waiting remainder of the band. Scorpion was performing creakily but gamely, like an octogenarian going through remembered steps on a dance floor. The wind blew, the hay flew, and for a bit I had to take my attention from the escapade at the reservoir to feed some bales off the lee side of the sled.

When I looked again, the last of the sheep were halfway across the dam and Rob was right on top of them with Scorpion, shoving them relentlessly. Half that much commotion would gain him twice the results. *There are so goddamn many ways to be a fool a man can't expect to avoid them all,* and our Rob was determined to try them all out today, ay, Lucas? By Jesus, I missed Lucas. If he were alive,

Rob would not be down there in a major pout, furiously performing the unnecessary and making an overage horse labor like a—

I saw Scorpion make his stumble, then his hindquarters slip off the edge of the embankment toward the reservoir as he tried to find his footing there at the middle of the dam.

Rob did not even attempt to vault off him to safety. Instead he yanked the reins and stood back hard into the stirrups, seeming to want to stiffen the horse back into steadiness with the iron line of his own body. But Scorpion still was not able to scramble back securely onto the muddy rim of the dam. He tottered. There was an instant of waver, as if the horse's sense of balance was in a contest with his aged muscles. Then Scorpion began to flounder backwards down the brown bank, sliding, skidding.

It took a moment for the sound to travel to me—a crisp clatter, thin iceskin breaking as horse and man tumbled through. The sheep ran, heads up in alarm, never looking back.

"DAIR!" My shout startled her around to me. "Turn the team! Get us to the reservoir!"

She jerked the team and sled in a quick half-loop as I plunged through the hay to the front of the rack. There beside her I grabbed the rack frame with one arm and held Adair upright with my other as she whipped the team with the loose ends of the reins and the hay sled began to trundle and jolt. The sled seemed monumentally awkward, slow, although I knew it was going faster than I ever could on foot through the mud and snow.

Ahead of us there in the reservoir I kept expecting Rob to throw himself out of Scorpion's saddle and lunge or swim his way the eight or ten feet to the embankment. But he and the horse continued to be a single struggling mass amid the shattered ice. Scorpion was thrashing terrifically while Rob clung down onto his back and brown-maned neck. The stubborn fool, to be trying to maul Scorpion out of that water instead of getting himself to the shore.

The top of the reservoir was too narrow for the hay sled. Where the embankment began, Adair jerked the team to a halt and I leaped down from the sled, running as I alit. Adair's cry, "Angus, be careful!" followed me.

Rob and Scorpion were thrashing even worse now, Scorpion tipping far down onto one side with all of Rob except head and arms under him, struggling together like water beasts fighting. The goddamn man, why didn't he leave the horse and start toward—Rob's face, shining wet, appeared for an instant between Scorpion's jerking neck and the murky water. His expression was perplexed, as if the world had rolled over beneath him and left him hanging horizontal this way. Then I heard his hoarse gasped shout of the word.

"STIRRUP!"

Good Christ, he's caught in the stirrup, those overshoes of his. Rob was not stubbornly staying with Scorpion, he was trapped on the underside of the off-balance horse.

I ran and ran, slipping, sliding, at last slewing myself on one hip down the bank to where they had tumbled in.

The star-jagged circle of broken ice. Brown roily water. Scorpion's head and neck and side, crazily tilted as if he was trying to roll in a meadow and dark water had opened under him instead.

The water, waiting, welling in steady arcs toward me from the struggling pair. I had to force myself not to back away, up the bank away from the awful water of the reservoir. If Varick were here. If anyone who could swim, could face water without my blood-deep fear of it, were here. It all returned into me—the black steerage gut of the *Jemmy* where I lay in sick scared sweat, the ceaseless waiting sea, the trembling dread of having water over me. *You ask was I afraid,* the McCaskill family voice ever since the treacherous work on the Bell Rock lighthouse. *Every hour and most of the minutes, drowning was on my mind. I was afraid enough, yes.* Out in the water Scorpion floundered in fresh frenzy, Rob's arms clenching his wet-maned neck.

I swallowed as much fear as I could and made myself start to wade.

The reservoir embankment was ungodly steep. My first step and a half, I abruptly was in the cold filthy water up to my waist. Eight feet out from me, no, ten, the splashing fight raged on, Scorpion for all his effort unable to right himself with Rob's weight slung all on one side of him, Rob not able to pull free from the thrashing bulk of the horse angled above him.

"ROB! TRY PULL HIM THIS WAY! I CAN'T REACH—"

I was in the shocking cold of the water to my breastbone now. Down in the hole in the water. Chips of ice big as platters bumped my shoulders. Frantically I pushed them away. The horse and man still were six feet from me. If I could manage another step toward the struggle, if Rob would let go his death grip around Scorpion's neck and reach toward me—"ROB! THIS WAY! REACH TOWARD—"

More sudden than it can be said, they went over, Scorpion atop Rob.

The water-darkened brown of the horse's hip as it vanished. The *W* brand glistening wet there.

Now only the agitated water, the splintered ice.

The reservoir's surface burst again, Scorpion's head emerging, eyes white and wild, nostrils streaming muddy water, ears laid back. I could not see Rob, the horse was between us, I was reaching as far as I could but the water was at my collarbone. I arched my head as high out of the clutching water as I could, struggling to keep my feet planted on the reservoir bottom. If I slid, out there under under them, the water— Scorpion's splashes filled my eyes and mouth. Through that wet new fear I managed to splutter, "Reach around him to me, Rob, you've got to!" Scorpion still could not find footing, could not get upright to swim, could not—abruptly the horse went under again.

The hammering in my chest filled me as I waited desperately for Scorpion to come up.

Neck deep, I waited, waited. The water was not so agitated now. The ice shards bobbed gently.

For as long as I could, I refused the realization that Scorpion was not coming up. Then I made myself suck in breath, and thrust my head under the water.

Murk. Nothing but murk, the mud and roil of the struggle between trapped Rob and burdened Scorpion.

My head broke the surface of the reservoir again and I spewed the awful water. Adair's voice from the embankment was there in the air.

"Angus! You can't! They're gone, you can't—"

I lurched myself backward toward the sound of her, fighting the clawing panic of the water pulling down on me, the skid of my footing on the slant of the reservoir bottom.

Then somehow I was on my side, mud of the reservoir bank under me, the water only at my knees. Adair was holding me with her body, clutching me there to the safety of the embankment. Gasping, shuddering with cold, I still stared out at the broken place in the ice, the silent pool it made.

Seven days now, since Rob's drowning.

More thaw has come. I saw in my ride up to Breed Butte yesterday to check on the sheep that the reservoir has only a pale edge of ice here and there. Today will shrink those, too. From here in the kitchen I have been watching the first of morning arrive to the white-patterned mountains, young sunlight of spring that will be honestly warm by noon.

A week. Yet it seems not much more than moments ago. Stanley Meixell galloping off to summon men from the main creek and the South Fork and Noon Creek, while Adair and I headed on from the ranger station to town with the ugly news for Judith. Then while Adair stayed with her, I returned to the reservoir and the men gathering there. It was Varick who plunged and plunged until he managed, just before dusk, to secure the hook-and-cable around Scorpion's hind leg. Isaac Reese's biggest team of horses, struggling on the muddy footing of the dam to draw their hidden load out of the reservoir. At last the burden broke up through the water and onto the bank, Scorpion's body bringing the other with it. Rob's overshoed foot was jammed through the stirrup so tightly we had to cut the stirrup leather from the saddle. I was the one who put my hat over Rob's face, after closing his eyes forever, while we worked at freeing him.

A person has to sit perfectly still to hear it, but the sound of the North Fork's water rattling softly over stones is in the air these mornings. The creek's lid of ice has fallen through in sufficient places to let the sound out. After so much winter, the constant evidence of spring is a surprise. Grass creeps its green into the slopes and valley bottom of Scotch Heaven noticeably more each day. And the first lambs were born the night before last. The sheep we have left I can handle by myself this lambing time, with a bit of help now and then from Varick. Judith made her decision while still in widow black there at Rob's funeral, asking me to run the sheep until they have lambed and then sell them all for whatever we can get. It was there at the graveside, too, that Judith asked me to write the *Gleaner* remembrance about Rob.

So, here at dawn, the shining mountains up there are the high windows of memory. My night thoughts were a stopless procession, thirty years returning across their bridge of time, to here and now. I was told once I am a great one for yesterdays, and I said back that they have brought us to where we are. In a blue Irish harbor the bumboat women leap away like cats over the side of the steamship, and the rest of us bring our hopes to America. At a nowhere town with the name of Gros Ventre, a saloonkeeper with a remembered face and voice puts on the bar his arms with no hands. Below a stonecliff skyline, a rider with feedbag whiskers looms as the sentry of a calm green valley. A wedding band goes onto an unintended finger. On the trail to the Two Medicine River a thousand lambs go down on their knees to suckle from their thousand mothers, the prayerful noon of the sheep kingdom. A son stands baffled and resentful in a blazing day. Out of all the hiding places in the head, they return.

And so I have thought through the past and words ought to come now, oughtn't they. But which ones. *The word is never quite the deed./How can I write what you can read?* Whichever words will make all the truth, of course. But there is so much of that, starting so far back. The dock at Greenock, where one far figure turns to another with the words *Are we both for it?* and that other makes himself say *Both.* What began there has not ended yet. This autumn, luck willing, there will be Varick and Beth's child. Luck willing, maybe other McCaskills in other autumns. And there will be Adair and me, here where we are. This morning as I began to get up in the dim start of dawn, she reached across the bed and stopped me. I had not been the only one with night thoughts processioning through. Adair's grief for Rob was deep but quick; after all, she is a Barclay, and life hasn't yet found how to make them buckle. Now she has put this winter away. As Adair held me she told me she will stay in Scotch Heaven as long as I do—which I suppose is the same as saying as long as I have breath in me. It makes everything ahead less hard, hearing that decision from her. How long before the sheep business and the Two Medicine country and for that matter Montana recuperate from the drought and winter of 1919, there is just no telling. What is certain is that I will be buying another band of the woollies at the earliest chance. And the teaching job at the South Fork school this autumn is mine for the asking, Fritz Hahn of the school board has informed me. I will ask. It seems that the McCaskills will get by. We start at the next of life in another minute: "Adair will come right out and cook you her famous sidepork for breakfast, old Angus McCaskill," she has just advised me from the bedroom. I am glad she will find this crystal day, the mountains now glistening and near, when she comes.

Lad, at least Montana is the prettiest place in the world to work yourself to death, ay? You were right more often than not, Lucas, handless Lucas who touched my life time upon time.

Angus, you are one who wants to see how many ways life can rhyme. Anna. The divide between our lives, twenty years of divide. It is permanent at last, our being apart, but you were the rhythm in my life I could do nothing about. You still are.

See now, McAngus, it's time you had a talking-to. Rob. My friend who was my enemy. Equally ardent at both, weren't you, bless you, damn you. You I knew longest of any, Rob, and I barely fathomed you at all, did I.

Hard ever to know, whether time is truly letting us see from the pattern of ourselves into those next to us. Rob's is my remembrance that will appear in the clear ink of the *Gleaner* this coming week. But where are the boundaries, the exact threadlines in the weave, between his life and ours? Tell me, tell me that, whoever can.

Acknowledgments

This novel continues the blend I began in *English Creek*—a fictional population inhabiting the actual area along the Rocky Mountain Front near Dupuyer Creek, Montana, the cherished country of my growing-up years. In general I've retained nearby existing places such as Valier, Choteau, Conrad, Heart Butte and so on, but anything within what I've stretched geography to call "the Two Medicine country," I have felt free to change or invent.

For the Scottish background of this book, I'm much indebted to: the Watt Library in Greenock; the St. Andrews University Library and Robert N. Smart, Keeper of Manuscripts and University Muniments; the Mitchell Library in Glasgow; the National Library of Scotland; the General Register Office for Scotland; the Edinburgh Central Library; the Crail Museum; the Angus Folk Museum at Glamis; the Fife Folk Museum at Ceres; the Scottish Fisheries Museum at Anstruther; and the Signal Tower Museum at Arbroath. My particular thanks for their generous help go to Mrs. Couperwhite of the Watt Library, Morag M. Fowler of the St. Andrews University library, and D.L. McCallum of the Mitchell Library's Social Sciences Department.

My version of the Montana period of this novel, 1889–1919, was greatly aided by the historical troves at: the Great Falls Public Library; the Montana Historical Society at Helena; the Mansfield Library of the University of Montana at Missoula; and the Renne Library of Montana State University at Bozeman. I'm indebted to skilled members of all those staffs: Sister Marita Bartholome, Ellie Arguimbau, Dale Johnson, Ilah Shriver, Bob Clark, Richard Gercken, Dave Walter, Howard Morris, Laurie Mercier, Susan Storey, Marianne Keddington, Lory Morrow, Jane Smilie, Kathy Schaefer and Rick Newby.

Other institutions and their members were also vitally helpful: the University of Washington Library at Seattle; the Forest History Society; the Bancroft Library at the University of California, Berkeley; the Shoreline Community College Library at Seattle; and Glenda Pearson, Pat Kelley, Mary Beth Johnson, John Backes, Pete Steen, Carla Rickerson, Melvylei Johnson, Kathy and Ron Fahl, Susan Cunningham, John James, Bob Bjoring, and definitely not least, Jean Roden.

I'm deeply indebted to those who told me, in interview or letter, the everyday details of their lives as youngsters during the Montana homestead boom in the first decades of this century: Florence and Tom Friedt, Dene Reber, Irene Olson, Cecelia Waltman, Georgia Farrington, Eva Farrington, Mary Gwendolyn Dawson, Fern Moore Gregg, Howard Gribble, Margaret Saylor, and Fern Eggers.

It's been of immense benefit to me to be able to draw on the work, encouragement and friendship of Montana's corps of professional historians: Bill Farr, Paula Petrik, Harry Fritz, Duane Hampton, Bill Lang, Merrill Burlingame, Mike Malone, Rich Roeder—and the late Stan Davison, a fellow

Montana kid, who I'm sorry did not live to see this book of the era he was born into. Malone and Roeder's *Montana: A History of Two Centuries* has been my guide as I've tried to make the lives of my characters respond to what might be called the laws of historical gravity; and Rich Roeder deserves full due for his homestead research reflecting the fact that more land was homesteaded in Montana than any other state, and that the peak of the Montana homestead boom was remarkably late in "frontier" history, 1914–1918.

As usual in the long birth of a book, a considerable community of friends and acquaintances provided me encouragement, hospitality, information, advice, or other aid. My appreciation to John Roden, Tom Chadwick, Abigail Thomas, Kathy Malone, Orville Lanham, Howard Vogel, the Lang family of Clancy, blacksmith Richard Connolly, Marilyn Ridge, Richard Maxwell Brown, Gail Steen, Nancy Meiselas, Edith Brekke, the Arnst-Bonnet-Hallingstad-Payton clan of Great Falls, Clyde Milner, Burt Weston, Mick Hager, Kathlene Mirgon, Bob Roripaugh, Solomon Katz, George Engler, Rodney Chapple, Dick Nelson, Sue Mathews, Chris Partman, Marshall Nelson, Ted and Jean Schwinden, Merlyn Talbot, Patti Talmadge, Lois and Jim Welch, Annick Smith, Juliette Crump, Bill Bevis, Joy and Brad Hamlett, Walker Wyman, Mark Wyman, Art Watson, Eric Ford, Bill Kittredge, Caroline and Ron Manheimer, William W. Krippaehne Jr., Mary Farrington, Ken Weydert, Ann Nelson, and Rae-Ellen Hamilton.

My wife, Carol, and her camera captured the Two country and the town of Gros Ventre in the research for *English Creek*, and for this book she added the Scottish backdrop from the Bell Rock to Greenock. For her pictures of what I am trying to say, for her insights into this manuscript during my three years of work on it, and for all else, I can't thank her enough.

Once again, Liz Darhansoff, Tom Stewart, and Jon Rantala in their distinctive inspiriting ways have been entirely essential to bringing this book to life.

"The stillness, the dancing": this book and I have benefited immeasurably from the keen poetic eye of Linda Bierds.

Another sharp-sighted professional who made this a better book than it otherwise would have been: copy editor Elaine Robbins.

The dedication of this book speaks a general thanks to Vernon Carstensen for the past twenty years of knowing him; but I also owe him specific gratitude for so generously sharing his insights into the history of the American West, any time I've ever asked.

Patricia Armstrong, peerless researcher, not only aided me with material about the influenza epidemic but provided me a helpful reading of this novel's opening chapter. Similarly, Ann McCartney's reading of the first three chapters helped me see things I hadn't. For those and for the depth of their friendship with me, thanks one more time to Pat and Ann.

A few words about derivations and inspirations. Scholars of Robert Burns may be mystified by a number of the lines mentally quoted by Angus McCaskill herein. Some of Angus's remembered verse is indeed Burns; some is Burns and Doig; and some is, alas, merely Doig. In all instances, I've used words in their form more readily recognized on this side of the Atlantic—"you" instead of "ye," "old" instead of "auld," for instance. The quote in chapter three from the *"Choteau Quill,"* "You can fight armies or disease or trespass, but the settler never," the *Quill* and I owe to John Clay, *My Life on the Range*. Details of wheelwrighting came from George Sturt's fascinating memoir, *The Wheelwright's Shop*. Whenever I needed to know how the sheep business was doing in any particular year, I had only to resort to Alexander Campbell McGregor's meticulous account of his family's history in the business, *Counting Sheep*. The Crofuttian advice early in chapter one to emigrate "with no divided heart" I fashioned from a similar paragraph in *The Emigrants' Guide,* 1883 edition; the rest of *Crofutt* I made up.

Finally, I wish to thank the National Endowment for the Arts for its grant of a fiction fellowship, and the members of that 1985 selection panel: Alice Adams, David Bradley, Stanley Elkin, Ivy Goodman, Tim O'Brien, Walker Percy, Elizabeth Tallent, and Geoffrey Wolff.

St. Andrews-Glasgow-Edinburgh
Helena-Dupuyer-Seattle, 1983–86

ABOUT THE AUTHOR

IVAN DOIG grew up in northern Montana along the Rocky Mountain Front, where *Dancing at the Rascal Fair* takes place. He has worked as a ranch hand, newspaperman, and magazine editor and writer. His 1978 book, *This House of Sky*, was nominated for the National Book Award in contemporary thought. *Dancing at the Rascal Fair* is the second novel of a trilogy about his fictional McCaskill family and their Two Medicine country. *English Creek* (1984) was the first. Mr. Doig lives in Seattle.